Cyrus the Great

the

Cyrus
the
Great

Edited and Introduced by
Ian Macgregor Morris

General Editor: Jake Jackson

FLAME TREE
PUBLISHING

This is a FLAME TREE Book

FLAME TREE PUBLISHING
6 Melbray Mews
Fulham, London SW6 3NS
United Kingdom
www.flametreepublishing.com

First published 2022
Copyright © 2022 Flame Tree Publishing Ltd

22 24 26 25 23
1 3 5 7 9 8 6 4 2

ISBN: 978-1-83964-995-0

The text in this book is based on and updated from the following sources:
Cyrus the Great (1850) by Jacob Abbott, published by Harper & Brothers
Publishers, New York and London, 1904; *The Ancient History of the Egyptians,
Carthaginians, Assyrians, Babylonians, Medes and Persians, Macedonians, and
Grecians* (1730–38) by Charles Rollin, published by Knapton, London, 1733–38;
A New Cyropaedia; or The Travels of Cyrus (1729) by Andrew Michael Ramsey,
published by Pratt & Doubleday, Albany, 1814; *The Cyropædia; or, The institution
of Cyrus* (1728) by Maurice Ashley-Cooper, published by Noon & Knapton,
London 1728; and the *Rawẓat aṣ-ṣafāʾ* (c. 1490) by Muhammad ibn Khvandshah
ibn Mahmud, translated by David Shea in *The History of the Early Kings of Persia*
(1832), published by John Murray and Parbury, Allen, & Co., London, 1832.

Printed and bound in the UK by Clays Ltd, Elcograf S.p.A

Contents

Series Foreword

STRETCHING BACK to the oral traditions of thousands of years ago, tales of heroes and disaster, creation and conquest have been told by many different civilizations in many different ways. Their impact sits deep within our culture even though the detail in the tales themselves are a loose mix of historical record, transformed narrative and the distortions of hundreds of storytellers.

Today the language of mythology lives with us: our mood is jovial, our countenance is saturnine, we are narcissistic and our modern life is hermetically sealed from others. The nuances of myths and legends form part of our daily routines and help us navigate the world around us, with its half truths and biased reported facts.

The nature of a myth is that its story is already known by most of those who hear it, or read it. Every generation brings a new emphasis, but the fundamentals remain the same: a desire to understand and describe the events and relationships of the world. Many of the great stories are archetypes that help us find our own place, equipping us with tools for self-understanding, both individually and as part of a broader culture.

For Western societies it is Greek mythology that speaks to us most clearly. It greatly influenced the mythological heritage of the ancient Roman civilization and is the lens through which we still see the Celts, the Norse and many of the other great peoples and religions. The Greeks themselves learned much from their neighbours, the Egyptians, an older culture that became weak with age and incestuous leadership.

It is important to understand that what we perceive now as mythology had its own origins in perceptions of the divine and the rituals of the sacred. The earliest civilizations, in the crucible of the Middle East, in the Sumer of the third millennium BC, are the source to which many of the mythic archetypes can be traced. As humankind collected together in cities for the first time, developed writing and industrial scale agriculture, started to irrigate the rivers and attempted to control rather than be at the mercy of its environment, humanity began to write down its tentative explanations of natural events, of floods and plagues, of disease.

Early stories tell of Gods (or god-like animals in the case of tribal societies such as African, Native American or Aboriginal cultures) who are crafty and use their wits to survive, and it is reasonable to suggest that these were the first rulers of the gathering peoples of the earth, later elevated to god-like status with the distance of time. Such tales became more political as cities vied with each other for supremacy, creating new Gods, new hierarchies for their pantheons. The older Gods took on primordial roles and became the preserve of creation and destruction, leaving the new gods to deal with more current, everyday affairs. Empires rose and fell, with Babylon assuming the mantle from Sumeria in the 1800s BC, then in turn to be swept away by the Assyrians of the 1200s BC; then the Assyrians and the Egyptians were subjugated by the Greeks, the Greeks by the Romans and so on, leading to the spread and assimilation of common themes, ideas and stories throughout the world.

The survival of history is dependent on the telling of good tales, but each one must have the 'feeling' of truth, otherwise it will be ignored. Around the firesides, or embedded in a book or a computer, the myths and legends of the past are still the living materials of retold myth, not restricted to an exploration of origins. Now we have devices and global communications that give us unparalleled access to a diversity of traditions. We can find out about Indigenous American, Indian, Chinese and tribal African mythology in a way that was denied to our ancestors, we can find connections, match the archaeology, religion and the mythologies of the world to build a comprehensive image of the human adventure.

The great leaders of history and heroes of literature have also adopted the mantle of mythic experience, because the stories of historical figures – Cyrus the Great, Alexander, Genghis Khan – and mytho-poetic warriors such as Beowulf achieve a cultural significance that transcends their moment in the chronicles of humankind. Myth, history and literature have become powerful, intwined instruments of perception, with echoes of reported fact and symbolic truths that convey the sweep of human experience. In this series of books we are glad to share with you the wonderful traditions of the past.

Jake Jackson
General Editor

Introduction to Cyrus the Great

Between Myth and History

THE LEGACY OF CYRUS THE GREAT is a most unusual one in the annals of world history. Few historical characters have been remembered in such a positive way by such diverse, indeed violently opposed, national traditions. Yet Cyrus stands as a model of good kingship and moral excellence in Iranian, Jewish and Greek memory. Much of the reason for this lies in the simple fact that we know virtually nothing about the historical reality that lies behind the legends.

The texts in this volume were all written before the staggering archaeological discoveries of the late nineteenth century, which included the so-called *Cyrus Cylinder* and the *Chronicle of Nabonidus*, texts from the sixth to fifth centuries BCE that were written either on the orders of Cyrus himself or of his successors. These lines, preserved on clay buried in the sand, represent the official self-presentation of the Persian kings, the justification of their actions and the legitimization of their empire. They are quite brilliant spin, as we would say today, subtly realized in a poetical language that astounds even in translation. Their discovery, far from challenging the semi-mythical status of Cyrus, actually affirmed it. We have become so accustomed to imagining Cyrus in an idealized form that readers quickly accepted the claims of tolerance and magnanimity.

Any history of Cyrus inevitably becomes the history of the legends told about him. The inscriptions represent the way he wished to be seen; this image was quickly absorbed into the rhetoric of the later Persian kings: firstly, that of Darius, a usurper who styled himself as the saviour of Cyrus's realm; and then in turn his son Xerxes, who through his mother could claim direct descent from Cyrus. They moulded an image of Cyrus as the ideal founder-king, because this image was integral to *their* claim to rule. Thus, within a generation of his conquests, Cyrus had become more an *idea* than a real man.

The Greek and Jewish writers who provide the earliest surviving accounts of Cyrus record this idea, and provide the basis of the Western legend. Elements also persisted in Iranian folk traditions, emerging in medieval Persian literature that presents a rather different, although recognizable, image of an ideal king. Yet although this idea was first and foremost propaganda, it was by no means entirely false. For all the importance of the great inscriptions erected by the kings, ancient societies were primarily oral. Stories were told, and retold, by different groups of peoples, each reflecting their own perspectives of events. Even within the Persian Empire, webs of rumour and gossip circulated, some supportive, others critical. These stories overlapped and distorted one another, like the concentric ripples caused by pebbles thrown into a pond: a myriad of interweaving, shifting tales. The great kings of Persia could not simply ignore what had happened: their version of events had, at the very least, to reflect popular rumour in order to be convincing. Thus, in the main, they manipulated and exaggerated what was already being said; absolute fabrication, when necessary, was carefully framed in terms of precedent and religious belief.

So the legend that Cyrus became was based, however distantly, on the self-image he promoted as the legitimization of his right to rule. This is not, of course, the 'real' Cyrus, but the way he *wanted* to be seen. It is a flimsy foundation, perhaps, for an understanding of the historical figure; but it is all we have. And, indeed, it is the image he wished future generations to celebrate.

Seeking Cyrus

Little can be said with any certainty about the life of Cyrus. The Persians appear to have been quite marginal to the politics of the great powers until the middle of the sixth century BCE. At this point they emerge – and with remarkable speed – to achieve what none had before: uniting the peoples of Asia Minor and the Near East under one king. Beyond the mythologizing and eulogizing lie the simple facts of a phenomenal political-military achievement.

Cyrus appears to have been the leader of one of a number of the Iranian tribes that constituted the Medes and the Persians. These peoples had long been nomadic, but were becoming more settled as a series of leaders managed to unite the tribes, possibly into a loose confederation, and then expanded their power across much of Mesopotamia. At one point the Median king was allied with the Babylonians against the Assyrians, but this friendship soon became a rivalry. One of the earliest references to Cyrus sets him in this context of shifting alliances:

> *Cyrus, the king of Anšan … scattered the vast Median hordes with his small army. He captured Astyages, the king of the Medes, and took him to his country as captive.*

The text dates the battle to around 550 BCE, and clearly presents Cyrus as defeating an enemy of Babylon, possibly with the support of the Babylonian gods. We have little clue here as to who Cyrus was or the causes of his rift with the Mede king, but it does give an insight into the context. It was composed in Babylonia shortly before war broke out between Cyrus and Nabonidus, the last king of Babylon, who may have commissioned the text; and the positive tone suggests that the two kings were on friendly terms, if not allies. The Median Empire had grown into a major threat, and the Babylonian king no doubt delighted in his rival's downfall. That Cyrus appears as the tool of the Babylonian god, and that his victory directly benefits Nabonidus, raises the possibility that the two kings were in league with one another. Perhaps the Babylonian king encouraged the Persian. If so, it would prove to be a costly mistake.

The Greek sources claim Cyrus was related to the Mede king he overthrew, a distinct possibility considering the practices of alliance through marriage; however, the detailed tales of the relationship are imbued with standard folktale motifs. The story of a great leader, usually a founding figure, being abandoned to die as a baby appears in numerous cultures, from the Jewish (Moses) to the Greek (Perseus) and Roman (Romulus and Remus). It is a standard tale, in which a fearful monarch responds to omens or dreams of an unborn child that will take his throne. Cautious of incurring bloodguilt, the principle that such a murder would curse the monarch in question, he orders others to abandon the child somewhere it will perish. But in every case, the child somehow survives, and as he grows his 'inborn excellence' becomes apparent. Eventually he is recognized, in some cases reunited with his long-grieving parents, and often exacts a terrible revenge. These tales show that the will of the god, or gods, cannot be so easily averted; and, most importantly, that the child in question is indeed chosen by the gods.

Such formulaic legends were created after the event to legitimize what amounted to outright rebellion, retrospectively 'proving' both the capricious nature of the older king and the divine credentials of the hero. More plausibly, the rivalry between the leaders of various Iranian tribes was exacerbated by the conflict between the Mede Empire and the Babylonians; and Cyrus, perhaps encouraged by the latter, saw his chance to seize control of what was a vast, but unstable, swath of territories. The detail that many of the Mede king's men quickly accepted Cyrus need not be entirely fictional. Loyalties may shift with remarkable speed, and the various tribal leaders would have prioritized the interest of their own people over their service to a Mede overlord. The circumstances remain obscure, but a general pattern can be seen.

Cyrus as Legend

Once master of the Median Empire, Cyrus consolidated his position through further conquest. The accounts of his war against Croesus of Lydia, which brought him control of Asia Minor, are repeated by Greek writers with a wonderful array of poetic, but hardly historical, details. For the Greeks of the following centuries, these events carried huge significance. They involved the first encounters between Persia and the Greek city-states, many of which now found themselves under the rule of Cyrus; and these initial contacts formed the backdrop to the epic struggles of the Greeks against the later Persian kings, Darius and Xerxes. So they decked the story in legendary details that foreshadowed what was to come.

In contrast, we are relatively well informed about the capture of Babylon. A number of inscriptions on clay tablets and cylinders tell of the wicked mismanagement of Nabonidus, who supposedly neglected both the gods and the people; and the masterful campaign of Cyrus to right these wrongs. He defeats the Babylonian forces and is welcomed in the city as a liberator; he restores the temples and frees the people from the onerous impositions of Nabonidus. The accounts preserved on these objects tally rather well with many details in both the Greek and Jewish sources; however, this does not verify those details, but merely shows that the later writers drew upon such declarations. These texts were either commissioned by Cyrus to justify his campaign or were composed by pro-Persian individuals in Babylon, and are clearly propaganda. But in order to be convincing – that is, to be effective propaganda – they needed at the very least to correspond to what some people believed, or wished to believe, had happened. And more significantly, they stand as Cyrus's statements of intent: they outline the kind of king he wished to be, the principles upon which his rule was to be based. In this way, they might not tell us a great deal about the battle for Babylon, but they do reveal the ideology of the man who proved victorious.

The key to understanding the accounts of Cyrus is to consider how they developed over the reigns of the next three Persian kings: firstly his son Cambyses, who ruled from 530 to around 523/2; then Darius, a previously obscure aristocrat, whom, as we will see, came to the throne in somewhat dubious circumstances; and finally his son Xerxes, who, because Darius had married a daughter of Cyrus, was also the grandson of the founder-king. It was under these kings that the legend of Cyrus was retold and repurposed; and it is these later versions which, in various guises, formed the basis of the Greek and Jewish accounts.

Cyrus's Successors

Much of what we know of ancient Persian culture, religion and politics is based on the later Achaemenid dynasty, founded by Darius in 522 BCE. After Cyrus's death in around 530, the empire underwent a string of crises. Traditionally, these problems have been attributed to Cambyses. History has not been kind to the heir of Cyrus. His conquest of Egypt – a phenomenal military achievement in its own right – has been depicted as the unjustifiable aggression of a madman. Where Cyrus was mild and persistently pious, respecting and restoring indigenous religious practices, Cambyses was brutal and sacrilegious. His atrocities contravened the most fundamental norms of every culture. It is even claimed that he murdered his own brother, before succumbing himself to a tormented death, punished by the gods for his transgressions.

The vacant throne is then filled, so we are told, by a usurper posing as Cambyses' brother, whose death had been kept secret. The usurper is no better than Cambyses, but soon is discovered by a small group of heroic noblemen who overthrow the imposter and then choose a new king from amongst themselves. This new king, Darius, then faces a series of challenges from a number of dubious ne'er-do-wells, each claiming to be either a son of Cyrus or of another recently fallen monarch. But in every case, they are deceitful. These are the 'Liar Kings', desperate individuals who mislead and cajole the people into following them. In a lightning campaign, Darius defeats them one after another, saving the people and the empire from the tyranny that each of these figures represents. They are exposed in their falsehood: 'This is Phraortes,' declares Darius in his monumental inscription carved into the face of Mount Bisitun:

> *He lied…. Phraortes was taken and brought unto me. I cut off his nose, his ears, and his tongue, and I put out one eye, and he was kept in fetters at my palace entrance, and all the people beheld him. Then did I crucify him in Ecbatana.*

And so Darius restored order, instituted justice and brought peace.

We are remarkably well-informed about these events because Darius ensured the world knew. His inscription at Bisitun should be regarded as one of the wonders of the ancient world: some twenty-five metres across, a detailed account written in three languages, and at the centre the massive relief of Darius himself, holding the 'Liar Kings' in chains, while standing on the prone figure of the slain usurper. Copies of the text were circulated throughout the empire, and it was clearly well known. The account of Darius by the historian Herodotus – who was born in one of the many Greek cities under Persian rule – despite some significant differences, by and large tells the same story.

It is a masterpiece of propaganda. No ruler before or since has so absolutely controlled the narrative of his assent to the throne. Indeed, the king insisted all who read must both believe and spread his word:

> *Now let what has been done by me convince you. For the sake of the people, do not conceal it…. If you conceal this edict and do not publish it to the world, may [the god] Ahuramazda slay you and may your house cease.*

The only flaw to the entire tale, of course, is that it is Darius's word against no one's. The lack of alternatives is in itself suspicious, as is the insistence that he speaks the truth, a claim repeated so often that one suspects that not all at the time were convinced. While Herodotus tells much the same tale, he does allow a few glimpses into other versions, probably reflecting local variations to the account of Darius. For all the king's insistence on a transparent honesty, Herodotus often delights in retelling of moments in which the Persian is less than entirely truthful.

The circumstances of Darius's rise to power lie in the crises of Cambyses' reign, which in turn reflect the final legacy of Cyrus. The new king needed to justify his seizure of power, and chose to do this by presenting himself as the rightful successor of Cyrus, which in turn demanded a very specific representation of the previous king. Beyond this association lie the Mesopotamian practices of kingship that Cyrus and his successors tried to incorporate and develop in their own idea of kingship. Once we understand each of these, then it might be possible to draw some conclusions about the life and deeds of Cyrus.

Empire and Kingship

It appears that the vast territories Cyrus had conquered were in disarray soon after his death. This is by no means improbable: the history of the ancient Near East is replete with short-lived empires that disintegrated once the conquering king died. Issues of succession were often sharply contested, brothers bitterly battling for a power that none of them could wield, because that power was based primarily on the charisma of the founder-king and the network of allies he had made through the very act of conquest. Those states that did endure did so through the creation of a notion of kingship that was intertwined with the gods on the one hand and the people on the other. While such kings owed their legitimacy to the favour of a certain god, they exercised it through carefully contrived rituals that bound them to the people they ruled. Thus in Babylon, every year the king had to undergo a quite remarkable ceremony in which he briefly laid aside his power. The *akitu* festival was an annual celebration of religious and cultural life, and absolutely central to the king's right to rule. In one part, the king had to surrender his crown and sceptre, the very symbols of his kingship; he had to swear that he had not sinned against the god Bel-Marduk and had respected the rights of the people; and perhaps most astonishing of all, a priest would slap him across the face as he made his oath. It is said that this was no gentle action – the king was meant to have tears in his eyes. The importance of this performance is attested in the pro-Cyrus *Nabonidus Chronicle*: the fact that Nabonidus did not celebrate the *akitu* for several years is cited as a fundamental failure of kingship that rendered his entire reign illegitimate.

In Babylon, Cyrus presented himself as restoring the traditional rituals and rights of both gods and people. This was not in itself something new: Babylonian history was awash with conquerors styling themselves this way. Often, they claimed to have quite literally brought the gods home, returning sacred statues and other objects; and thus Cyrus consciously echoed the actions of previous invading kings. His actions become all the more clear through comparison with the imperial practices of Darius and Xerxes. These later kings appear to have built upon Cyrus's approach, although it is difficult to be certain which features were developed by Cyrus and which were later attributed to him. Nevertheless, taken together we can detect a general approach to empire and kingship that defines the legend, if not the historical reality, of Cyrus.

The *Cyrus Cylinder*, a proclamation now in the British Museum, is perhaps the most famous of the statements attributed to him. For a range of contemporary reasons, some have claimed it is the first 'declaration of human rights' – sparking often furious debates that have far more to do with modern politics than with ancient. It is certainly a quite astonishing document; but its genius lies in presenting wholesale change not as innovation, but as a return to ancient, traditional rights. It stands in a long tradition of Babylonian and Assyrian political rhetoric that define and defend the rights of the people in often quite sophisticated ways.

On the *Cylinder*, Cyrus claims to have relieved the citizens from a *corvée* – forced unpaid labour – that 'was not the gods' wish and not befitting them, [so] I relieved their weariness and freed them from their service.' The genius of the statement lies in its vagueness: it can be seen as a general principle ('I will not allow the exploitation of the people'), an insistence that he respects the status of certain subjects ('this labour was not suitable – befitting – for people of this class'), a statement of achievement ('I freed them'), and of piety ('this was not the will of the gods'). It could betoken the liberation of thousands from slavery, or of a handful of aristocrats from excessive taxation. Much depends on the perspective of the reader; and that, I suspect, was the entire point. A modern democrat will read this text quite differently from an aristocratic priest of Bel-Marduk.

The *Pax Persiana*

The fundamental problem that faced Cyrus and his successors was how to maintain control over a realm of unprecedented size and diversity. Many of the rituals which conferred the right to rule, such as the *akitu* festival, required the literal presence of the king; to be absent negated the entire meaning, and with it royal legitimacy. Yet across such a vast realm, that simply was not possible. Cyrus's condemnation of Nabonidus shows he knew what a king should, and should not, do. And so he tried to develop a form of kingship in which the image of a benevolent 'King of Kings' hovered above the many rulers and peoples of the empire. Once more, this idea had precedent, especially in the Assyrian rulers who perhaps first coined the phrase. But it needed to be expressed in a way that echoed both Mesopotamian and Iranian cultural values, without suffocating the identities of the subject peoples.

In the political proclamations of the later Persian kings, we can see these practices far more clearly. Perhaps initiated by Cyrus, they were given a much sharper ideological form by Darius and Xerxes, to create a notion of empire that was inclusive, diverse and, most importantly, *participatory*. On the great tomb facades of the later rulers are images of the king facing a winged figure that may represent the god Ahuramazda, or possibly the spirit, or 'essence' of the king himself. He stands on a platform supported by two layers of figures, who quite literally hold up the monarch. The figures represent the various peoples of the empire: most carry weapons, indicating that they are free men, not slaves forced to support the king against their will; and they are sharply differentiated by their clothing, hairstyles and weapons, implying that the traditional ways of each people persist, even thrive, under the peaceful watch of the king. The entire image is one of mutually beneficial co-operation. The rule of the king is only possible due to the willing participation of the people; he in turn creates a peaceful realm, the *Pax Persiana*, that ensures justice and an equilibrium between all. A number of other inscriptions and reliefs develop these ideas, placing the king at the centre of a network of relationships between the peoples of the empire on the one hand, and the gods on the other.

The roots of these ideas can be seen in the claims of the *Cyrus Cylinder*, which presents Cyrus as restoring and liberating, but nevertheless remaining very much in control.

> *All the people of Babylon, all the land of Sumer and Akkad, princes and governors, bowed to him and kissed his feet. They rejoiced at his kingship and their faces shone … Cyrus says: '…all the kings who sit upon thrones throughout the world, from the Upper Sea to the Lower Sea, who live in the districts far-off, the kings of the West, who dwell in tents, all of them, brought their heavy tribute before me and in Babylon they kissed my feet.'*

The peoples and kings of the empire submit joyfully, and find fulfilment in absolute submission. For Cyrus to maintain his royal legitimacy even while absent required an all-embracing, abstracting, presentation of his reign as beneficial to all. The references in the Hebrew Bible to Cyrus as the chosen one of Yahweh reveal how this was achieved: to each subject people he was presented in terms of their own belief systems, 'restoring' their temples and traditional rights.

These presentations may or may not reflect that actual deeds of Cyrus: the Greek writer Herodotus does include some alternative stories, rumours and counter-memories preserved by various subject peoples, implying that his rule may not have always been so benign. What we find in all the declarations of Cyrus and his successors is ideology and propaganda, not historical fact. This is not to say they are inherently false; rather that they are a very specific perspective, created for a very specific purpose.

The Image of Cyrus

Such an image of Cyrus was carefully curated by Darius and Xerxes, who were sharply aware of the crisis that followed the founder-king's death. Cyrus may have laid the foundations for the notion of empire they espoused; or they may have merely used his memory to legitimize principles they had developed themselves. The dates of the supposed proclamations of Cyrus are not secure enough for us to say with certainty that they were produced in his reign. And the desperate civil strife after his death suggests that the vision of a royal authority that could seamlessly be transferred – which does appear in the transition from Darius to Xerxes – was not part of his legacy.

Nevertheless, in order to ensure stability in their own reigns, they sought to perfect the image of Cyrus and to absolve him of responsibility for the disastrous reign of Cambyses. And so a semi-mythic portrait was recorded, embellished with details and anecdotes drawn from the many stories about him that circulated throughout the empire, some based on half-remembered events, others invoking legendary predecessors and folktale traditions.

These tales, in turn, were recorded by the Greek and Jewish writers who formed the basis of the Western tradition. The texts that comprise this volume are representative of that tradition: Cyrus as the ideal monarch, wise and just. But they also persisted in Iranian memory, to emerge in the literature of the Islamic Golden Age, as represented by the final chapter.

History is often not so much about what occurred, but more about how we remember. Each of the works reproduced here was written before the discovery and deciphering of the Persian and Babylonian documents that form our most reliable sources for Cyrus; but they represent traditions that ultimately derive from them. They retell and rework these stories for their own purposes, and in doing so they show how the story of Cyrus has been changed and reimagined, which, in turn, allows us to understand this distant figure from different perspectives.

Ian Macgregor Morris
Cairo Research Centre, Zamalek, April 2022

Ian Macgregor Morris (Introduction) is a Senior Lecturer at the University of Salzburg, and a Visiting Research Fellow at the Netherlands Institute for the Near East at the University of Leiden. He has published extensively on Achaemenid Persia, Sparta, early modern political culture and the classical tradition. He is currently working on a study of the Persian king Xerxes, and is editing Brill's *Companion to the Spartan Tradition*; and recently served as consultant and primary contributor on *Finding Sparta's 300* (*Unearthed*, Season 5, Ep. 06: Discovery Science Channel).

Cyrus the Great

JACOB ABBOTT (1803–79), the author of this text, was an American writer and educator. He published numerous books on a variety of subjects, with a particular focus on history and religion. Mainly aimed at the general reader, his work sought to inform and entertain at the same time, introducing topics in an accessible way to a wide audience. Thus, his books are not dry treatises but lively tales, meant to bring subjects to life and highlight their enduring relevance.

Abbott does not pretend to be a historian; he summarizes stories of the past rather than making conclusions about that past. In this his life of Cyrus, he freely admits that the sources are far from reliable, and that he is presenting the traditions and legends that have been told for hundreds of years. It is, as he stresses, the story of the legend, rather than of the man. On several occasions, he includes tales of dubious veracity, suggesting it is up to the reader to decide how truthful they are; and on others he repeats some rather fanciful anecdotes because they illustrate the tone and character of a certain person, place or text.

Much of the text is based upon the accounts of the two main Greek sources: Herodotus and Xenophon. Abbott approaches both with a critical judgment, comparing contrasting details and considering the relative value of the two writers. He also makes ample use of Biblical sources – a standard practice in this type of literature. While this certainly does colour his opinions, it also adds a further element of context and a perspective rather different from the Greek historians.

Abbott is also deeply aware of how little was known about the life of Cyrus, so he includes lengthy passages on individuals such as Croesus of Lydia and the Biblical prophet Jeremiah, whom either interact with Cyrus or illustrate some aspect of the context. Often Cyrus appears to lurk in the background, a frame for the stories of others; but this is a typical feature of the Cyrus tradition, both ancient and modern.

In general, Abbott seeks to tell a story of Cyrus's legend, and in that sense he offers a useful summary of how Cyrus has been perceived throughout the centuries. But Abbott does also make general observations on the nature of the historical Cyrus, and this means that his book is an important part of that Cyrus tradition. It reveals how nineteenth-century readers sought to understand and assess the ancient world in general, and Persia in particular; and it reveals the popular perceptions of Cyrus at the very moment of the archaeological discoveries that would so invigorate the tradition of the Persian founder-king.

Chapter I
Herodotus and Xenophon, BCE 550–401

The Persian Monarchy
Singular Principle of Human Nature

CYRUS WAS THE FOUNDER of the ancient Persian empire – a monarchy, perhaps, the most wealthy and magnificent which the world has ever seen. Of that strange and incomprehensible principle of human nature, under the influence of which vast masses of men, notwithstanding the universal instinct of aversion to control, combine, under certain circumstances, by millions and millions, to maintain, for many successive centuries, the representatives of some one great family in a condition of exalted, and absolute, and utterly irresponsible ascendency over themselves, while they toil for them, watch over them, submit to endless and most humiliating privations in their behalf, and commit, if commanded to do so, the most inexcusable and atrocious crimes to sustain the demigods they have thus made in their lofty estate, we have, in the case of this Persian monarchy, one of the most extraordinary exhibitions.

Grandeur of the Persian Monarchy – Its Origin

The Persian monarchy appears, in fact, even as we look back upon it from this remote distance both of space and of time, as a very vast wave of human power and grandeur. It swelled up among the populations of Asia, between the Persian Gulf and the Caspian Sea, about five hundred years before Christ, and rolled on in undiminished magnitude and glory for many centuries. It bore upon its crest the royal line of Astyages and his successors. Cyrus was, however, the first of the princes whom it held up conspicuously to the admiration of the world and he rode so gracefully and gallantly on the lofty crest that mankind have given him the credit of raising and sustaining the magnificent billow on which he was borne.

How far we are to consider him as founding the monarchy, or the monarchy as raising and illustrating him, will appear more fully in the course of this narrative.

The Republics of Greece – Written Characters Greek and Persian – Preservation of the Greek Language

Contemporaneous with this Persian monarchy in the East, there flourished in the West the small but very efficient and vigorous republics of Greece. The Greeks had a written character for their language which could be easily and rapidly executed, while the ordinary language of the Persians was scarcely written at all. There was, it is true, in this latter nation, a certain learned character, which was used by the priests for their mystic records, and also for certain sacred books which constituted the only national archives. It was, however, only slowly and with difficulty that this character could be penned, and, when penned, it was unintelligible to the great mass of the population. For this reason, among others, the Greeks wrote narratives of the great events which occurred in their day, which narratives they so embellished and adorned by the picturesque lights and shades in which their genius enabled them to present the scenes and characters described as to make them universally admired, while the surrounding nations produced nothing but formal governmental records, not worth to the community at large the toil and labour necessary to decipher them and make them intelligible. Thus the Greek writers became the historians, not only of their own republics, but also of all the nations around them; and with such admirable genius and power did they fulfil this function, that, while the records of all other nations contemporary with them have been almost entirely neglected and forgotten, the language of the Greeks has been preserved among mankind, with infinite labour and toil, by successive generations of scholars, in every civilized nation, for two thousand years, solely in order that men may continue to read these tales.

Herodotus and Xenophon

Two Greek historians have given us a narrative of the events connected with the life of Cyrus – Herodotus and Xenophon. These writers disagree very materially in the statements which they make, and modern readers are divided in opinion on the question which to believe. In order to present this question fairly to the minds of our readers, we must commence this volume with some account of these two authorities, whose guidance, conflicting as it is, furnishes all the light which we have to follow.

Herodotus was a philosopher and scholar. Xenophon was a great general. The one spent his life in solitary study, or in visiting various countries in the pursuit of knowledge; the other distinguished himself in the command of armies, and in distant military expeditions, which he conducted with great energy and skill. They were both, by birth, men of wealth and high station, so that they occupied, from the beginning, conspicuous positions in society; and as they were both energetic and enterprising in character, they were led, each, to a very romantic and adventurous career, the one in his travels, the other in his campaigns, so that their personal history and their exploits attracted great attention even while they lived.

Birth of Herodotus – Education of the Greeks – How Public Affairs Were Discussed – Literary Entertainments – Herodotus's Early Love of Knowledge

Herodotus was born in the year 484 before Christ, which was about fifty years after the death of the Cyrus whose history forms the subject of this volume. He was born in the Grecian state of Caria, in Asia Minor, and in the city of Halicarnassus. Caria, as may be seen from the map at the commencement of this volume, was in the southwestern part of Asia Minor, near the shores of the Aegean Sea. Herodotus became a student at a very early age. It was the custom in Greece, at that time, to give to young men of his rank a good intellectual education. In other nations, the training of the young men, in wealthy and powerful families, was confined almost exclusively to the use of arms, to horsemanship, to athletic feats, and other such accomplishments as would give them a manly and graceful personal bearing, and enable them to excel in the various friendly contests of the public games, as well as prepare them to maintain their ground against their enemies in personal combats on the field of battle. The Greeks, without neglecting these things, taught their young men also to read and to write, explained to them the structure and the philosophy of language, and trained them to the study of the poets, the orators, and the historians which their country had produced. Thus, a general taste for intellectual pursuits and pleasures was diffused throughout the community. Public affairs were discussed, before large audiences assembled for the purpose, by orators who felt a great pride and pleasure in the exercise of the power which they had acquired of persuading, convincing, or exciting the mighty masses that listened to them; and at the great public celebrations which were customary in those days, in addition to the wrestlings, the races, the games, and the military spectacles, there were certain literary entertainments provided, which constituted an essential part of the public pleasures. Tragedies were acted, poems recited, odes and lyrics sung, and narratives of martial enterprises and exploits, and geographical and historical descriptions of neighbouring nations, were read to vast throngs of listeners, who, having been accustomed from infancy to witness such performances, and to hear them applauded, had learned to appreciate and enjoy them. Of course, these literary exhibitions would make impressions, more or less strong, on different minds, as the mental temperaments and characters of individuals varied. They seem to have exerted a very powerful influence on the mind of Herodotus in his early years. He was inspired, when very young, with a great zeal and ardour for the attainment of knowledge; and as he advanced toward maturity, he began to be ambitious of making new discoveries, with a view of communicating to his countrymen, in these great public assemblies, what he should thus acquire. Accordingly, as soon as he arrived at a suitable age, he resolved to set out upon a tour into foreign countries, and to bring back a report of what he should see and hear.

Intercourse of Nations – Military Expeditions – Plan of Herodotus's Tour

The intercourse of nations was, in those days, mainly carried on over the waters of the Mediterranean Sea; and in times of peace, almost the only mode of communication was by the ships and the caravans of the merchants who traded from country to country, both by sea and on the land. In fact, the knowledge which one country possessed of the geography and the manners and customs of another, was almost wholly confined to the reports which these merchants circulated. When military expeditions invaded a territory, the commanders, or the writers who accompanied them, often wrote descriptions of the scenes which they witnessed in their campaigns, and described briefly the countries through which they passed. These cases were, however, comparatively rare; and yet, when they occurred, they furnished accounts better authenticated, and more to be relied upon, and expressed, moreover, in a more systematic and regular form, than the reports of the merchants, though the information which was derived from both these sources combined was very insufficient, and tended to excite more curiosity than it gratified. Herodotus, therefore, conceived that, in thoroughly exploring the countries on the shores of the Mediterranean and in the interior of Asia, examining their geographical position, inquiring into their history, their institutions, their manners, customs and laws, and writing the results for the entertainment and instruction of his countrymen, he had an ample field before him for the exercise of all his powers.

Herodotus visits Egypt

He went first to Egypt. Egypt had been until that time, closely shut up from the rest of mankind by the jealousy and watchfulness of the government. But now, on account of some recent political changes, which will be hereafter more particularly alluded to, the way was opened for travellers from other countries to come in. Herodotus was the first to avail himself of this opportunity. He spent some time in the country, and made himself minutely acquainted with its history, its antiquities, its political and social condition at the time of his visit, and with all the other points in respect to which he supposed that his countrymen would wish to be informed. He took copious notes of all that he saw. From Egypt he went westward into Libya, and thence he travelled slowly along the whole southern shore of the Mediterranean Sea as far as to the Straits of Gibraltar, noting, with great care, everything which presented itself to his own personal observation, and availing himself of every possible source of information in respect to all other points of importance for the object which he had in view.

Libya and the Straits of Gibraltar – Route of Herodotus in Asia – His Return to Greece

The Straits of Gibraltar were the ends of the earth toward the westward in those ancient days, and our traveller accordingly, after reaching them, returned again to the eastward. He visited Tyre, and the cities of Phoenicia, on the eastern coast of the Mediterranean Sea, and thence went still farther eastward to Assyria and Babylon. It was here that he obtained the materials for what he has written in respect to the Medes and Persians, and to the history of Cyrus. After spending some time in these countries, he went on by land still further to the eastward, into the heart of Asia. The country of Scythia was considered as at 'the end of the earth' in this direction. Herodotus penetrated for some distance into the almost trackless wilds of this remote land, until he found that he had gone as far from the great centre of light and power on the shores of the Aegean Sea as he could expect the curiosity of his countrymen to follow him. He passed thence round toward the north, and came down through the countries north of the Danube into Greece, by way of the Epirus and Macedon. To make such a journey as this was, in fact, in those days, almost to explore the whole known world.

Doubts as to the Extent of Herodotus's Tour – His History 'Adorned' – Herodotus's Credibility Questioned – Sources of Bias

It ought, however, here to be stated, that many modern scholars, who have examined, with great care, the accounts which Herodotus has given of what he saw and heard in his wanderings, doubt very seriously whether his journeys were really as extended as he pretends. As his object was to read what he was intending to write at great public assemblies in Greece, he was, of course, under every possible inducement to make his narrative as interesting as possible, and not to detract at all from whatever there might be extraordinary either in the extent of his wanderings or in the wonderfulness of the objects and scenes which he saw, or in the romantic nature of the adventures which he met with in his protracted tour. Cicero, in lauding him as a writer, says that he was the first who evinced the power to *adorn* a historical narrative. Between adorning and *embellishing*, the line is not to be very distinctly marked; and Herodotus has often been accused of having drawn more from his fancy than from any other source, in respect to a large portion of what he relates and describes. Some do not believe that he ever even entered half the countries which he professes to have thoroughly explored, while others find, in the minuteness of his specifications, something like conclusive proof that he related only what he actually saw. In a word, the question of his credibility has been discussed by successive generations of scholars ever since his day, and strong parties have been formed who have gone to extremes in the opinions they have taken; so that, while some confer upon him the title of the father of *history*, others say it would be more in accordance with his merits to call him the father of *lies*. In controversies like this, and, in fact, in all controversies, it is more agreeable to the mass of mankind to take sides strongly with one party or the other, and either to believe or disbelieve one or the other fully and cordially. There is a class of minds, however, more calm and better balanced than the rest, who can deny themselves this pleasure, and who see that often, in the most bitter and decided controversies, the truth lies between. By this class of minds it has been generally supposed that the narratives of Herodotus are substantially true, though in many cases highly coloured and embellished, or, as Cicero called it, adorned, as, in fact, they inevitably must have been under the circumstances in which they were written.

Samos – Patmos

We cannot follow minutely the circumstances of the subsequent life of Herodotus. He became involved in some political disturbances and difficulties in his native state after his return, in consequence of which he retired, partly a fugitive and partly an exile, to the island of Samos, which is at a little distance from Caria, and not far from the shore. Here he lived for some time in seclusion, occupied in writing out his history. He divided it into nine books, to which, respectively, the names of the nine Muses were afterward given, to designate them. The island of Samos, where this great literary work was performed, is very near to Patmos, where, a few hundred years later, the Evangelist John, in a similar retirement, and in the use of the same language and character, wrote the Book of Revelation.

The Olympiads

When a few of the first books of his history were completed, Herodotus went with the manuscript to Olympia, at the great celebration of the eighty-first Olympiad. The Olympiads were periods recurring at intervals of about four years. By means of them the Greeks reckoned their time. The Olympiads were celebrated as they occurred, with games, shows, spectacles and parades, which were conducted on so magnificent a scale that vast crowds were accustomed to assemble from every part of Greece to witness and join in them. They were held at Olympia, a city on the western side of Greece. Nothing now remains to mark the spot but some acres of confused and unintelligible ruins.

Herodotus at Olympia – History Received with Applause

The personal fame of Herodotus and of his travels had preceded him, and when he arrived at Olympia he found the curiosity and eagerness of the people to listen to his narratives extreme. He read copious extracts from his accounts, so far as he had written them, to the vast assemblies which convened to hear him, and they were received with unbounded applause; and inasmuch as these assemblies comprised nearly all the statesmen, the generals, the philosophers and the scholars of Greece, applause expressed by them became at once universal renown. Herodotus was greatly gratified at the interest which his countrymen took in his narratives, and he determined thenceforth to devote his time assiduously to the continuation and completion of his work.

Herodotus at Athens

It was twelve years, however, before his plan was finally accomplished. He then repaired to Athens, at the time of a grand festive celebration which was held in that city, and there he appeared in public again, and read extended portions of the additional books that he had written. The admiration and applause which his work now elicited was even greater than before. In deciding upon the passages to be read, Herodotus selected such as would be most likely to excite the interest of his Grecian hearers, and many of them were glowing accounts of Grecian exploits in former wars which had been waged in the countries which he had visited. To expect that, under such circumstances, Herodotus should have made his history wholly impartial, would be to suppose the historian not human.

His Literary Fame

The Athenians were greatly pleased with the narratives which Herodotus thus read to them of their own and of their ancestors' exploits. They considered him a national benefactor for having made such a record of their deeds, and, in addition to the unbounded applause which they bestowed upon him, they made him a public grant of a large sum of money. During the remainder of his life Herodotus continued to enjoy the high degree of literary renown which his writings had acquired for him – a renown which has since been extended and increased, rather than diminished, by the lapse of time.

Birth of Xenophon – Cyrus the Younger

As for Xenophon, the other great historian of Cyrus, it has already been said that he was a military commander, and his life was accordingly spent in a very different manner from that of his great competitor for historic fame. He was born at Athens, about thirty years after the birth of Herodotus, so that he was but a child while Herodotus was in the midst of his career. When he was about twenty-two years of age, he joined a celebrated military expedition which was formed in Greece, for the purpose of proceeding to Asia Minor to enter into the service of the governor of that country. The name of this governor was Cyrus; and to distinguish him from Cyrus the Great, whose history is to form the subject of this volume, and who lived about one hundred and fifty years before him, he is commonly called Cyrus the Younger.

Ambition of Cyrus – He Attempts to Assassinate His Brother – Rebellion of Cyrus

This expedition was headed by a Grecian general named Clearchus. The soldiers and the subordinate officers of the expedition did not know for what special service it was designed, as Cyrus had a treasonable and guilty object in view, and he kept it accordingly concealed, even from the agents who were to aid him in the execution of it. His plan was to make war upon and dethrone his brother Artaxerxes, then king of Persia, and consequently his sovereign. Cyrus was a very young man, but he was a man of a very energetic and accomplished character, and of unbounded ambition. When his father died, it was arranged that Artaxerxes, the older son, should succeed him. Cyrus was extremely unwilling to submit to this supremacy of his brother. His mother was an artful and unprincipled woman, and Cyrus, being the youngest of her children, was her favourite. She encouraged him in his ambitious designs; and so desperate was Cyrus himself in his determination to accomplish them, that it is said he attempted to assassinate his brother on the day of his coronation. His attempt was discovered, and it failed. His brother, however, instead of punishing him for the treason, had the generosity to pardon him, and sent him to his government in Asia Minor. Cyrus immediately turned all his thoughts to the plan of raising an army and making war upon his brother, in order to gain forcible possession of his throne. That he might have a plausible pretext for making the necessary military preparations, he pretended to have a quarrel with one of his neighbours, and wrote, hypocritically, many letters to the king, affecting solicitude for his safety, and asking aid. The king was thus deceived, and made no preparations to resist the force which Cyrus was assembling, not having the remotest suspicion that its destiny was Babylon.

The Greek Auxiliaries

The auxiliary army which came from Greece to enter into Cyrus's service under these circumstances, consisted of about thirteen thousand men. He had, it was said, a hundred thousand men besides; but so celebrated were the Greeks in those days for their courage, their discipline, their powers of endurance, and their indomitable tenacity and energy, that Cyrus very properly considered this corps as the flower of his army. Xenophon was one of the younger Grecian generals. The army crossed the Hellespont, and entered Asia Minor, and, passing across the country, reached at last the famous pass of Cilicia, in the southwestern part of the country – a narrow defile between the mountains and the sea, which opens the only passage in that quarter toward the Persian regions beyond. Here the suspicions which the Greeks had been for some time inclined to feel, that they were going to make war upon the Persian monarch himself, were confirmed, and they refused to proceed. Their unwillingness, however, did not arise from any compunctions of conscience about the guilt of treason, or the wickedness of helping an ungrateful and unprincipled wretch, whose forfeited life had once been given to him by his brother, in making war upon and destroying his benefactor. Soldiers have never, in any age of the world, anything to do with compunctions of conscience in respect to the work which their commanders give them to perform. The Greeks were perfectly willing to serve in this or in any other undertaking; but, since it was rebellion and treason that was asked of them, they considered it as especially hazardous, and so they concluded that they were entitled to extra pay. Cyrus made no objection to this demand; an arrangement was made accordingly, and the army went on. Artaxerxes assembles his army.

The Battle – Cyrus Slain

Artaxerxes assembled suddenly the whole force of his empire on the plains of Babylon – an immense army, consisting, it is said, of over a million of men. Such vast forces occupy, necessarily, a wide extent of country, even when drawn up in battle array. So great, in fact, was the extent occupied in this case, that the Greeks, who conquered all that part of the king's forces which was directly opposed to them, supposed, when night came, at the close of the day of battle, that Cyrus had been everywhere victorious; and they were only undeceived when, the next day, messengers came from the Persian camp to inform them that Cyrus's whole force, excepting themselves, was defeated and dispersed, and that Cyrus himself was slain, and to summon them to surrender at once and unconditionally to the conquerors.

Murder of the Greek Generals – Critical Situation of the Greeks

The Greeks refused to surrender. They formed themselves immediately into a compact and solid body, fortified themselves as well as they could in their position, and prepared for a desperate defence. There were about ten thousand of them left, and the Persians seem to have considered them too formidable to be attacked. The Persians entered into negotiations with them, offering them certain terms on which they would be allowed to return peaceably into Greece. These negotiations were protracted from day to day for two or three weeks, the Persians treacherously using toward them a friendly tone, and evincing a disposition to treat them in a liberal and generous manner. This threw the Greeks off their guard, and finally the Persians contrived to get Clearchus and the leading Greek generals into their power at a feast, and then they seized and murdered them, or, as they would perhaps term it, *executed* them as rebels and traitors. When this was reported in the Grecian camp, the whole army was thrown at first into the utmost consternation. They found themselves two thousand miles from home, in the heart of a hostile country, with an enemy nearly a hundred times their own number close upon them, while they themselves were without provisions, without horses, without money; and there were deep rivers, and rugged mountains, and every other possible physical obstacle to be surmounted, before they could reach their own frontiers. If they surrendered to their enemies, a hopeless and most miserable slavery was their inevitable doom.

Xenophon's Proposal – Retreat of the Ten Thousand

Under these circumstances, Xenophon, according to his own story, called together the surviving officers in the camp, urged them not to despair, and recommended that immediate measures should be taken for commencing a march toward Greece. He proposed that they should elect commanders to take the places of those who had been killed, and that, under their new organization, they should immediately set out on their return. These plans were adopted. He himself was chosen as the commanding general, and under his guidance the whole force was conducted safely through the countless difficulties and dangers which beset their way, though they had to defend themselves, at every step of their progress, from an enemy so vastly more numerous than they, and which was hanging on their flanks and on their rear, and making the most incessant efforts to surround and capture them. This retreat occupied two hundred and fifteen days. It has always been considered as one of the greatest military achievements that has ever been performed. It is called in history the Retreat of the Ten Thousand. Xenophon acquired by it a double immortality. He led the army, and thus attained to a military renown which will never fade; and he afterward wrote a narrative of the exploit, which has given him an equally extended and permanent literary fame.

Xenophon's Retirement and Writings

Sometime after this, Xenophon returned again to Asia as a military commander, and distinguished himself in other campaigns. He acquired a large fortune, too, in these wars, and at length retired to a villa, which he built and adorned magnificently, in the neighbourhood of Olympia, where Herodotus had acquired so extended a fame by reading his histories. It was probably, in some degree, through the influence of the success which had attended the labours of Herodotus in this field, that Xenophon was induced to enter it. He devoted the later years of his life to writing various historical memoirs, the two most important of which that have come down to modern times are, first, the narrative of his own expedition, under Cyrus the Younger, and, secondly, a sort of romance or tale founded on the history of Cyrus the Great. This last is called the *Cyropaedia*; and it is from this work, and from the history written by Herodotus, that nearly all our knowledge of the great Persian monarch is derived.

Credibility of Herodotus and Xenophon – Importance of the Story – Object of This Work

The question how far the stories which Herodotus and Xenophon have told us in relating the history of the great Persian king are true, is of less importance than one would at first imagine; for the case is one of those numerous instances in which the narrative itself, which genius has written, has had far greater influence on mankind than the events themselves exerted which the narrative professes to record. It is now far more important for us to know what the story is which has for eighteen hundred years been read and listened to by every generation of men, than what the actual events were in which the tale thus told had its origin. This consideration applies very extensively to history, and especially to ancient history. The events themselves have long since ceased to be of any great interest or importance to readers of the present day; but the *accounts*, whether they are fictitious or real, partial or impartial, honestly true or embellished and coloured, since they have been so widely circulated in every age and in every nation, and have impressed themselves so universally and so permanently in the mind and memory of the whole human race, and have penetrated into and coloured the literature of every civilized people, it becomes now necessary that every well-informed man should understand. In a word, the real Cyrus is now a far less important personage to mankind than the Cyrus of Herodotus and Xenophon, and it is, accordingly, their story which the author proposes to relate in this volume. The reader will understand, therefore, that the end and aim of the work is not to guarantee an exact and certain account of Cyrus as he actually lived and acted, but only to give a true and faithful summary of the story which for the last two thousand years has been in circulation respecting him among mankind.

Chapter II
The Birth of Cyrus, BCE 599–588

The Three Asiatic Empires – Marriage of Cambyses

THERE ARE RECORDS coming down to us from the very earliest times of three several kingdoms situated in the heart of Asia-Assyria, Media and Persia, the two latter of which, at the period when they first emerge indistinctly into view, were more or less connected with and dependent upon the former. Astyages was the King of Media; Cambyses was the name of the ruling prince or magistrate of Persia. Cambyses married Mandane, the daughter of Astyages, and Cyrus was their son. In recounting the circumstances of his birth, Herodotus relates, with all seriousness, the following very extraordinary story:

Story of Mandane – Dream of Astyages

While Mandane was a maiden, living at her father's palace and home in Media, Astyages awoke one morning terrified by a dream. He had dreamed of a great inundation, which overwhelmed and destroyed his capital, and submerged a large part of his kingdom. The great rivers of that country were liable to very destructive floods, and there would have been nothing extraordinary or alarming in the king's imagination being haunted, during his sleep, by the image of such a calamity, were it not that, in this case, the deluge of water which produced such disastrous results seemed to be, in some mysterious way, connected with his daughter, so that the dream appeared to portend some great calamity which was to originate in her. He thought it perhaps indicated that after her marriage she should have a son who would rebel against him and seize the supreme power, thus overwhelming his kingdom as the inundation had done which he had seen in his dream.

To guard against this imagined danger, Astyages determined that his daughter should not be married in Media, but that she should be provided with a husband in some foreign land, so as to be taken away from Media altogether. He finally selected Cambyses, the king of Persia, for her husband. Persia was at that time a comparatively small and circumscribed dominion, and Cambyses, though he seems to have been the supreme ruler of it, was very far beneath Astyages in rank and power. The distance between the two countries was considerable, and the institutions and customs of the people of Persia were simple and rude, little likely to awaken or encourage in the minds of their princes any treasonable or ambitious designs. Astyages thought, therefore, that in sending Mandane there to be the wife of the king, he had taken effectual precautions to guard against the danger portended by his dream.

Astyages' Second Dream – Its Interpretation

Mandane was accordingly married, and conducted by her husband to her new home. About a year afterward her father had another dream. He dreamed that a vine proceeded from his daughter, and, growing rapidly and luxuriantly while he was regarding it, extended itself over the whole land. Now the vine being a symbol of beneficence and plenty, Astyages might have considered this vision as an omen of good; still, as it was good which was to be derived in some way from his daughter, it naturally awakened his fears anew that he was doomed to find a rival and competitor for the possession of his kingdom in Mandane's son and heir. He called together his soothsayers, related his dream to them, and asked for their interpretation. They decided that it meant that Mandane would have a son who would one day become a king.

Astyages was now seriously alarmed, and he sent for Mandane to come home, ostensibly because he wished her to pay a visit to her father and to her native land, but really for the purpose of having her in his power, that he might destroy her child so soon as one should be born.

Birth of Cyrus

Mandane came to Media, and was established by her father in a residence near his palace, and such officers and domestics were put in charge of her household as Astyages could rely upon to do whatever he should command. Things being thus arranged, a few months passed away, and then Mandane's child was born.

Astyages Determines to Destroy Him

Immediately on hearing of the event, Astyages sent for a certain officer of his court, an unscrupulous and hardened man, who possessed, as he supposed, enough of depraved and reckless resolution for the commission of any crime, and addressed him as follows:

Harpagus – The King's Command to Him

'I have sent for you, Harpagus, to commit to your charge a business of very great importance. I confide fully in your principles of obedience and fidelity, and depend upon your doing, yourself, with your own hands, the work that I require. If you fail to do it, or if you attempt to evàde it by putting it off upon others, you will suffer severely. I wish you to take Mandane's child to your own house and put him to death. You may accomplish the object in any mode you please, and you may arrange the circumstances of the burial of the body, or the disposal of it in any other way, as you think best; the essential thing is, that you see to it, yourself, that the child is killed.'

Harpagus replied that whatever the king might command it was his duty to do, and that, as his master had never hitherto had occasion to censure his conduct, he should not find him wanting now. Harpagus then went to receive the infant. The attendants of Mandane had been ordered to deliver it to him. Not at all suspecting the object for which the child was thus taken away, but naturally supposing, on the other hand, that it was for the purpose of some visit, they arrayed their unconscious charge in the most highly wrought and costly of the robes which Mandane, his mother, had for many months been interested in preparing for him, and then gave him up to the custody of Harpagus, expecting, doubtless, that he would be very speedily returned to their care.

Distress of Harpagus – His Consultation with His Wife

Although Harpagus had expressed a ready willingness to obey the cruel behest of the king at the time of receiving it, he manifested, as soon as he received the child, an extreme degree of anxiety and distress. He immediately sent for a herdsman named Mitridates to come to him. In the meantime, he took the child home to his house, and in a very excited and agitated manner related to his wife what had passed. He laid the child down in the apartment, leaving it neglected and alone, while he conversed with his wife in a harried and anxious manner in respect to the dreadful situation in which he found himself placed. She asked him what he intended to do. He replied that he certainly should not, himself, destroy the child. 'It is the son of Mandane,' said he. 'She is the king's daughter. If the king should die, Mandane would succeed him, and then what terrible danger would impend over me if she should know me to have been the slayer of her son!' Harpagus said, moreover, that he did not dare absolutely to disobey the orders of the king so far as to save the child's life, and that he had sent for a herdsman, whose pastures extended to wild and desolate forests and mountains – the gloomy haunts of wild beasts and birds of prey – intending to give the child to him, with orders to carry it into those solitudes and abandon it there. His name was Mitridates.

The Herdsman

While they were speaking this herdsman came in. He found Harpagus and his wife talking thus together, with countenances expressive of anxiety and distress, while the child, uneasy under the confinement and inconveniences of its splendid dress, and terrified at the strangeness of the scene and the circumstances around it, and perhaps, moreover, experiencing some dawning and embryo emotions of resentment at being laid down in neglect, cried aloud and incessantly. Harpagus gave the astonished herdsman his charge. He, afraid, as Harpagus had been in the presence of Astyages, to evince any hesitation in respect to obeying the orders of his superior, whatever they might be, took up the child and bore it away.

He Conveys the Child to His Hut – The Herdsman's Wife

He carried it to his hut. It so happened that his wife, whose name was Spaco, had at that very time a newborn child, but it was dead. Her dead son had, in fact, been born during the absence of Mitridates. He had been extremely unwilling to leave his home at such a time, but the summons of Harpagus must, he knew, be obeyed. His wife, too, not knowing what could have occasioned so sudden and urgent a call, had to bear, all day, a burden of anxiety and solicitude in respect to her husband, in addition to her disappointment and grief at the loss of her child. Her anxiety and grief were changed for a little time into astonishment and curiosity at seeing the beautiful babe, so magnificently dressed, which her husband brought to her, and at hearing his extraordinary story.

Conversation in the Hut

He said that when he first entered the house of Harpagus and saw the child lying there, and heard the directions which Harpagus gave him to carry it into the mountains and leave it to die, he supposed that the babe belonged to some of the domestics of the household, and that Harpagus wished to have it destroyed in order to be relieved of a burden. The richness, however, of the infant's dress, and the deep anxiety and sorrow which was indicated by the countenances and by the conversation of Harpagus and his wife, and which seemed altogether too earnest to be excited by the concern which they would probably feel for any servant's offspring, appeared at the time, he said, inconsistent with that supposition, and perplexed and bewildered him. He said, moreover, that in the end, Harpagus had sent a man with him a part of the way when he left the house, and that this man had given him a full explanation of the case. The child was the son of Mandane, the daughter of the king, and he was to be destroyed by the orders of Astyages himself, for fear that at some future period he might attempt to usurp the throne.

Entreaties of the Herdsman's Wife to Save the Child's Life

They who know anything of the feelings of a mother under the circumstances in which Spaco was placed, can imagine with what emotions she received the little sufferer, now nearly exhausted by abstinence, fatigue and fear, from her husband's hands, and the heartfelt pleasure with which she drew him to her bosom, to comfort and relieve him. In an hour she was, as it were, herself his mother, and she began to plead hard with her husband for his life.

Mitridates said that the child could not possibly be saved. Harpagus had been most earnest and positive in his orders, and he was coming himself to see that they had been executed. He would demand, undoubtedly, to see the body of the child, to assure himself that it was actually dead. Spaco, instead of being convinced by her husband's reasoning, only became more and more earnest in her desires that the child might be saved. She rose from her couch and clasped her husband's knees, and begged him with the most earnest entreaties and with many tears to grant her request. Her husband was, however, inexorable. He said that if he were to yield, and attempt to save the child from its doom, Harpagus would most certainly know that his orders had been disobeyed, and then their own lives would be forfeited, and the child itself sacrificed after all, in the end.

Spaco Substitutes Her Dead Child for Cyrus

The thought then occurred to Spaco that her own dead child might be substituted for the living one, and be exposed in the mountains in its stead. She proposed this plan, and, after much anxious doubt and hesitation, the herdsman consented to adopt it. They took off the splendid robes which adorned the living child, and put them on the corpse, each equally unconscious of the change. The little limbs of the son of Mandane were then more simply clothed in the coarse and scanty covering which belonged to the new character which he was now to assume, and then the babe was restored to its place in

Spaco's bosom. Mitridates placed his own dead child, completely disguised as it was by the royal robes it wore, in the little basket or cradle in which the other had been brought, and, accompanied by an attendant, whom he was to leave in the forest to keep watch over the body, he went away to seek some wild and desolate solitude in which to leave it exposed.

The Artifice Successful – The Body Buried

Three days passed away, during which the attendant whom the herdsman had left in the forest watched near the body to prevent its being devoured by wild beasts or birds of prey, and at the end of that time he brought it home. The herdsman then went to Harpagus to inform him that the child was dead, and, in proof that it was really so, he said that if Harpagus would come to his hut he could see the body. Harpagus sent some messenger in whom he could confide to make the observation. The herdsman exhibited the dead child to him, and he was satisfied. He reported the result of his mission to Harpagus, and Harpagus then ordered the body to be buried. The child of Mandane, whom we may call Cyrus, since that was the name which he subsequently received, was brought up in the herdsman's hut, and passed everywhere for Spaco's child.

Remorse of Astyages

Harpagus, after receiving the report of his messenger, then informed Astyages that his orders had been executed, and that the child was dead. A trusty messenger, he said, whom he had sent for the purpose, had seen the body. Although the king had been so earnest to have the deed performed, he found that, after all, the knowledge that his orders had been obeyed gave him very little satisfaction. The fears, prompted by his selfishness and ambition, which had led him to commit the crime, gave place, when it had been perpetrated, to remorse for his unnatural cruelty. Mandane mourned incessantly the death of her innocent babe, and loaded her father with reproaches for having destroyed it, which he found it very hard to bear. In the end, he repented bitterly of what he had done.

The secret of the child's preservation remained concealed for about ten years. It was then discovered in the following manner:

Boyhood of Cyrus – Cyrus a King Among the Boys

Cyrus, like Alexander, Caesar, William the Conqueror, Napoleon and other commanding minds, who obtained a great ascendancy over masses of men in their more mature years, evinced his dawning superiority at a very early period of his boyhood. He took the lead of his playmates in their sports, and made them submit to his regulations and decisions. Not only did the peasants' boys in the little hamlet where his reputed father lived thus yield the precedence to him, but sometimes, when the sons of men of rank and station came out from the city to join them in their plays, even then Cyrus was the acknowledged head. One day the son of an officer of King Astyages's court – his father's name was Artembaris – came out, with other boys from the city, to join these village boys in their sports. They were playing *king*. Cyrus was the king. Herodotus says that the other boys *chose* him as such. It was, however, probably such a sort of choice as that by which kings and emperors are made among men, a yielding more or less voluntary on the part of the subjects to the resolute and determined energy with which the aspirant places himself upon the throne.

A Quarrel

During the progress of the play, a quarrel arose between Cyrus and the son of Artembaris. The latter would not obey, and Cyrus beat him. He went home and complained bitterly to his father. The father went to Astyages to protest against such an indignity offered to his son by a peasant boy, and demanded that the little tyrant should be punished. Probably far the larger portion of intelligent readers of history consider the whole story as a romance; but if we look upon it as in any respect true, we must conclude that the Median monarchy must have been, at that time, in a very rude and simple condition indeed, to allow of the submission of such a question as this to the personal adjudication of the reigning king.

However this may be, Herodotus states that Artembaris went to the palace of Astyages, taking his son with him, to offer proofs of the violence of which the herdsman's son had been guilty, by showing the contusions and bruises that had been produced by the blows. 'Is this the treatment,' he asked, indignantly, of the king, when he had completed his statement, 'that my boy is to receive from the son of one of your slaves?'

43

Cyrus Summoned into the Presence of Astyages

Astyages seemed to be convinced that Artembaris had just cause to complain, and he sent for Mitridates and his son to come to him in the city. When they arrived, Cyrus advanced into the presence of the king with that courageous and manly bearing which romance writers are so fond of ascribing to boys of noble birth, whatever may have been the circumstances of their early training. Astyages was much struck with his appearance and air. He, however, sternly laid to his charge the accusation which Artembaris had brought against him. Pointing to Artembaris's son, all bruised and swollen as he was, he asked, 'Is that the way that you, a mere herdsman's boy, dare to treat the son of one of my nobles?'

The little prince looked up into his stern judge's face with an undaunted expression of countenance, which, considering the circumstances of the case, and the smallness of the scale on which this embryo heroism was represented, was partly ludicrous and partly sublime.

Cyrus's Defence

'My lord,' said he, 'what I have done I am able to justify. I did punish this boy, and I had a right to do so. I was king, and he was my subject, and he would not obey me. If you think that for this I deserve punishment myself, here I am; I am ready to suffer it.'

Astonishment of Astyages

If Astyages had been struck with the appearance and manner of Cyrus at the commencement of the interview, his admiration was awakened far more strongly now, at hearing such words, uttered, too, in so exalted a tone, from such a child. He remained a long time silent. At last he told Artembaris and his son that they might retire. He would take the affair, he said, into his own hands, and dispose of it in a just and proper manner. Astyages then took the herdsman aside, and asked him, in an earnest tone, whose boy that was, and where he had obtained him.

The Discovery

Mitridates was terrified. He replied, however, that the boy was his own son, and that his mother was still living at home, in the hut where they all resided. There seems to have been something, however, in his appearance and manner, while making these assertions, which led Astyages not to believe what he said. He was convinced that there was some unexplained mystery in respect to the origin of the boy, which the herdsman was wilfully withholding. He assumed a displeased and threatening air, and ordered in his guards to take Mitridates into custody. The terrified herdsman then said that he would explain all, and he accordingly related honestly the whole story.

Mingled Feelings of Astyages – Inhuman Monsters

Astyages was greatly rejoiced to find that the child was alive. One would suppose it to be almost inconsistent with this feeling that he should be angry with Harpagus for not having destroyed it. It would seem, in fact, that Harpagus was not amenable to serious censure, in any view of the subject, for he had taken what he had a right to consider very effectual measures for carrying the orders of the king into faithful execution. But Astyages seems to have been one of those inhuman monsters which the possession and long-continued exercise of despotic power have so often made, who take a calm, quiet, and deliberate satisfaction in torturing to death any wretched victim whom they can have any pretext for destroying, especially if they can invent some new means of torment to give a fresh piquancy to their pleasure. These monsters do not act from passion. Men are sometimes inclined to palliate great cruelties and crimes which are perpetrated under the influence of sudden anger, or from the terrible impulse of those impetuous and uncontrollable emotions of the human soul which, when once excited, seem to make men insane; but the crimes of a tyrant are not of this kind. They are the calm, deliberate and sometimes carefully economized gratifications of a nature essentially malign.

Astyages Determines to Punish Harpagus

When, therefore, Astyages learned that Harpagus had failed of literally obeying his command to destroy, with his own hand, the infant which had been given him, although he was pleased with the consequences which had resulted from it, he immediately perceived that there was another pleasure besides that he was to derive from the transaction, namely, that of gratifying his own imperious and ungovernable will by taking vengeance on him who had failed, even in so slight a degree, of fulfilling its dictates. In a word, he was glad that the child was saved, but he did not consider that that was any reason why he should not have the pleasure of punishing the man who saved him.

Interview Between Artyages and Harpagus – Explanation of Harpagus

Thus, far from being transported by any sudden and violent feeling of resentment to an inconsiderate act of revenge, Astyages began, calmly and coolly, and with a deliberate malignity more worthy of a demon than of a man, to consider how he could best accomplish the purpose he had in view. When, at length, his plan was formed, he sent for Harpagus to come to him. Harpagus came. The king began the conversation by asking Harpagus what method he had employed for destroying the child of Mandane, which he, the king, had delivered to him some years before. Harpagus replied by stating the exact truth. He said that, as soon as he had received the infant, he began immediately to consider by what means he could affect its destruction without involving himself in the guilt of murder; that, finally, he had determined upon employing the herdsman Mitridates to expose it in the forest till it should perish of hunger and cold; and, in order to be sure that the king's behest was fully obeyed, he charged the herdsman, he said, to keep strict watch near the child till it was dead, and then to bring home the body. He had then sent a confidential messenger from his own household to see the body and provide for its interment. He solemnly assured the king, in conclusion, that this was the real truth, and that the child was actually destroyed in the manner he had described.

Dissimulation of Astyages – He Proposes an Entertainment

The king then, with an appearance of great satisfaction and pleasure, informed Harpagus that the child had not been destroyed after all, and he related to him the circumstances of its having been exchanged for the dead child of Spaco, and brought up in the herdsman's hut. He informed him, too, of the singular manner in which the fact that the infant had been preserved, and was still alive, had been discovered. He told Harpagus, moreover, that he was greatly rejoiced at this discovery. 'After he was dead, as I supposed,' said he, 'I bitterly repented of having given orders to destroy him. I could not bear my daughter's grief, or the reproaches which she incessantly uttered against me. But the child is alive, and all is well; and I am going to give a grand entertainment as a festival of rejoicing on the occasion.'

Astyages Invites Harpagus to a Grand Entertainment

Astyages then requested Harpagus to send his son, who was about thirteen years of age, to the palace, to be a companion to Cyrus, and, inviting him very specially to come to the entertainment, he dismissed him with many marks of attention and honour. Harpagus went home, trembling at the thought of the imminent danger which he had incurred, and of the narrow escape by which he had been saved from it. He called his son, directed him to prepare himself to go to the king, and dismissed him with many charges in respect to his behaviour, both toward the king and toward Cyrus. He related to his wife the conversation which had taken place between himself and Astyages, and she rejoiced with him in the apparently happy issue of an affair which might well have been expected to have been their ruin.

Horrible Revenge

The sequel of the story is too horrible to be told, and yet too essential to a right understanding of the influences and effects produced on human nature by the possession and exercise of despotic and irresponsible power to be omitted.

Harpagus came to the festival. It was a grand entertainment. Harpagus was placed in a conspicuous position at the table. A great variety of dishes were brought in and set before the different guests, and were eaten without question. Toward the close of the feast, Astyages asked Harpagus what he thought of his fare. Harpagus, half terrified with some mysterious presentiment of danger, expressed himself well pleased with it. Astyages then told him there was plenty more of the same kind, and ordered the attendants to bring the basket in. They came accordingly, and uncovered a basket before the wretched guest, which contained, as he saw when he looked into it, the head, hands and feet of his son. Astyages asked him to help himself to whatever part he liked!

Action of Harpagus

The most astonishing part of the story is yet to be told. It relates to the action of Harpagus in such an emergency. He looked as composed and placid as if nothing unusual had occurred. The king asked him if he knew what he had been eating. He said that he did; and that whatever was agreeable to the will of the king was always pleasing to him!

It is hard to say whether despotic power exerts its worst and most direful influences on those who wield it, or on those who have it to bear; on its masters, or on its slaves.

Astyages Becomes Uneasy

After the first feelings of pleasure which Astyages experienced in being relieved from the sense of guilt which oppressed his mind so long as he supposed that his orders for the murder of his infant grandchild had been obeyed, his former uneasiness lest the child should in future years become his rival and competitor for the possession of the Median throne, which had been the motive originally instigating him to the commission of the crime, returned in some measure again, and he began to consider whether it was not incumbent on him to take some measures to guard against such a result. The end of his deliberations was, that he concluded to send for the magi, or soothsayers, as he had done in the case of his dream, and obtain their judgment on the affair in the new aspect which it had now assumed.

The Magi Again Consulted – Advice of the Magi

When the magi had heard the king's narrative of the circumstances under which the discovery of the child's preservation had been made, through complaints which had been preferred against him on account of the manner in which he had exercised the prerogatives of a king among his playmates, they decided at once that Astyages had no cause for any further apprehensions in respect to the dreams which had disturbed him previous to his grandchild's birth. 'He has been a king,' they said, 'and the danger is over. It is true that he has been a monarch only in play, but that is enough to satisfy and fulfil the presages of the vision. Occurrences very slight and trifling in themselves are often found to accomplish what seemed of very serious magnitude and moment, as portended. Your grandchild has been a king, and he will never reign again. You have, therefore, no further cause to fear, and may send him to his parents in Persia with perfect safety.'

Astyages Adopts It

The king determined to adopt this advice. He ordered the soothsayers, however, not to remit their assiduity and vigilance, and if any signs or omens should appear to indicate approaching danger, he charged them to give him immediate warning. This they faithfully promised to do. They felt, they said, a personal interest in doing it; for Cyrus being a Persian prince, his accession to the Median throne would involve the subjection of the Medes to the Persian dominion, a result which they wished in every account to avoid. So, promising to watch vigilantly for every indication of danger, they left the presence of the king. The king then sent for Cyrus.

Cyrus Sets Out for Persia

It seems that Cyrus, though astonished at the great and mysterious changes which had taken place in his condition, was still ignorant of his true history. Astyages now told him that he was to go into Persia. 'You will rejoin there,' said he, 'your true parents, who, you will find, are of very different rank in life from the herdsman whom you have lived with thus far. You will make the journey under the charge and escort of persons that I have appointed for the purpose. They will explain to you, on the way, the mystery in which your parentage and birth seems to you at present enveloped. You will find that I was induced many years ago, by the influence of an untoward dream, to treat you injuriously. But all has ended well, and you can now go in peace to your proper home.'

His Parents' Joy

As soon as the preparations for the journey could be made, Cyrus set out, under the care of the party appointed to conduct him, and went to Persia. His parents were at first dumb with astonishment, and were then overwhelmed with gladness and joy at seeing their much-loved and long-lost babe reappear, as if from the dead, in the form of this tall and handsome boy, with health, intelligence and happiness beaming in his countenance. They overwhelmed him with caresses, and the heart of Mandane, especially, was filled with pride and pleasure.

As soon as Cyrus became somewhat settled in his new home, his parents began to make arrangements for giving him as complete an education as the means and opportunities of those days afforded.

Life at Cambyses's Court – Instruction of the Young Men

Xenophon, in his narrative of the early life of Cyrus, gives a minute, and, in some respects, quite an extraordinary account of the mode of life led in Cambyses's court. The sons of all the nobles and officers of the court were educated together, within the precincts of the royal palaces, or, rather, they spent their time together there, occupied in various pursuits and avocations, which were intended to train them for the duties of future life, though there was very little of what would be considered, in modern times, as education. They were not generally taught to read, nor could they, in fact, since there were no books, have used that art if they had acquired it. The only intellectual instruction which they seem to have received was what was called learning justice. The boys had certain teachers, who explained to them, more or less formally, the general principles of right and wrong, the injunctions and prohibitions of the laws, and the obligations resulting from them, and the rules by which controversies between man and man, arising in the various relations of life, should be settled. The boys were also trained to apply these principles and rules to the cases which occurred among themselves, each acting as judge in turn, to discuss and decide the questions that arose from time to time, either from real transactions as they occurred, or from hypothetical cases invented to put their powers to the test. To stimulate the exercise of their powers, they were rewarded when they decided right, and punished when they decided wrong. Cyrus himself was punished on one occasion for a wrong decision, under the following circumstances:

Cyrus a Judge – His Decision in That Capacity – Cyrus Punished

A bigger boy took away the coat of a smaller boy than himself, because it was larger than his own, and gave him his own smaller coat instead. The smaller boy complained of the wrong, and the case was referred to Cyrus for his adjudication. After hearing the case, Cyrus decided that each boy should keep the coat that fitted him. The teacher condemned this as a very unjust decision. 'When you are called upon,' said he, 'to consider a question of what fits best, then you should determine as you have done in this case; but when you are appointed to decide whose each coat is, and to adjudge it to the proper owner, then you are to consider what constitutes right possession, and whether he who takes a thing by force from one who is weaker than himself, should have it, or whether he who made it or purchased it should be protected in his property. You have decided against law, and in favour of violence and wrong.' Cyrus's sentence was thus condemned, and he was punished for not reasoning more soundly.

Manly Exercises – Hunting Excursions

The boys at this Persian court were trained to many manly exercises. They were taught to wrestle and to run. They were instructed in the use of such arms as were employed in those times, and rendered dexterous in the use of them by daily exercises. They were taught to put their skill in practice, too, in hunting excursions, which they took, by turns, with the king, in the neighbouring forest and mountains. On these occasions, they were armed with a bow, a quiver of arrows, a shield, a small sword or dagger which was worn at the side in a sort of scabbard and two javelins. One of these was intended to be thrown, the other to be retained in the hand, for use in close combat, in case the wild beast, in his desperation, should advance to a personal re-encounter. These hunting expeditions were considered extremely important as a part of the system of youthful training. They were often long and fatiguing. The young men became inured, by means of them, to toil, privation and exposure. They had to make long marches, to encounter great dangers, to engage in desperate conflicts and to submit sometimes to the inconveniences of hunger and thirst, as well as exposure to the extremes of heat and cold, and to the violence of storms. All this was considered as precisely the right sort of discipline to make them good soldiers in their future martial campaigns.

Personal Appearance of Cyrus – Disposition and Character of Cyrus – A Universal Favourite

Cyrus was not, himself, at this time, old enough to take a very active part in these severer services, as they belonged to a somewhat advanced stage of Persian education, and he was yet not quite twelve years old. He was a very beautiful boy, tall and graceful in form and his countenance was striking and expressive. He was very frank and open in his disposition and character, speaking honestly, and without fear, the sentiments of his heart, in any presence and on all occasions. He was extremely kind-hearted, and amiable, too, in his disposition, averse to saying or doing anything which could give pain to those around him. In fact, the openness and cordiality of his address and manners, and the unaffected ingenuousness and sincerity which characterized his disposition, made him a universal favourite. His frankness, his childish simplicity, his vivacity, his personal grace and beauty and his generous and self-sacrificing spirit, rendered him the object of general admiration throughout the court, and filled Mandane's heart with maternal gladness and pride.

Chapter III
The Visit to Media, BCE 587–584

⚜

Astyages Sends for Cyrus – Cyrus Goes to Media

WHEN CYRUS WAS about twelve years old, if the narrative which Xenophon gives of his history is true, he was invited by his grandfather Astyages to make a visit to Media. As he was about ten years of age, according to Herodotus, when he was restored to his parents, he could have been residing only two years in Persia when he received this invitation. During this period, Astyages had received, through Mandane and others, very glowing descriptions of the intelligence and vivacity of the young prince, and he naturally felt a desire to see him once more. In fact, Cyrus's personal attractiveness and beauty, joined to a certain frank and noble generosity of spirit which he seems to have manifested in his earliest years, made him a universal favourite at home, and the reports of these qualities, and of the various sayings and doings on Cyrus's part, by which his disposition and character were revealed, awakened strongly in the mind of Astyages that kind of interest which a grandfather is always very prone to feel in a handsome and precocious grandchild.

Cyrus's Reception – His Astonishment – Sympathy with Childhood – Pleasures of Old Age

As Cyrus had been sent to Persia as soon as his true rank had been discovered, he had had no opportunities of seeing the splendour of royal life in Media, and the manners and habits of the Persians were very plain and simple. Cyrus was accordingly very much impressed with the magnificence of the scenes to which he was introduced when he arrived in Media, and with the gayeties and luxuries, the pomp and display and the spectacles and parades in which the

Median court abounded. Astyages himself took great pleasure in witnessing and increasing his little grandson's admiration for these wonders. It is one of the most extraordinary and beautiful of the provisions which God has made for securing the continuance of human happiness to the very end of life, that we can renew, through sympathy with children, the pleasures which, for ourselves alone, had long since, through repetition and satiety, lost their charm. The rides, the walks, the flowers gathered by the roadside, the rambles among pebbles on the beach, the songs, the games and even the little picture book of childish tales which have utterly and entirely lost their power to affect the mind even of middle life, directly and alone, regain their magic influence, and call up vividly all the old emotions, even to the heart of decrepit age, when it seeks these enjoyments in companionship and sympathy with children or grandchildren beloved. By giving to us this capacity for renewing our own sensitiveness to the impressions of pleasure through sympathy with childhood, God has provided a true and effectual remedy for the satiety and insensibility of age. Let anyone who is in the decline of years, whose time passes but heavily away, and who supposes that nothing can awaken interest in his mind or give him pleasure, make the experiment of taking children to a ride or to a concert, or to see a menagerie or a museum, and he will find that there is a way by which he can again enjoy very highly the pleasures which he had supposed were for him forever exhausted and gone.

Character of Cyrus

This was the result, at all events, in the case of Astyages and Cyrus. The monarch took a new pleasure in the luxuries and splendours which had long since lost their charm for him, in observing their influence and effect upon the mind of his little grandson. Cyrus, as we have already said, was very frank and open in his disposition, and spoke with the utmost freedom of everything that he saw. He was, of course, a privileged person, and could always say what the feeling of the moment and his own childish conceptions prompted, without danger. He had, however, according to the account which Xenophon gives, a great deal of good sense, as well as of sprightliness and brilliancy; so that, while his remarks, through their originality and point, attracted everyone's attention, there was a native politeness and sense of propriety which restrained him from saying anything to give pain. Even when he disapproved of and condemned what he saw in the arrangements of his grandfather's court or household, he did it in such a manner – so ingenuous, good-natured and unassuming, that it amused all and offended none.

First Interview with His Grandfather – Dress of the King

In fact, on the very first interview which Astyages had with Cyrus, an instance of the boy's readiness and tact occurred, which impressed his grandfather very much in his favour. The Persians, as has been already remarked, were accustomed to dress very plainly, while, on the other hand, at the Median court the superior officers, and especially the king, were always very splendidly adorned. Accordingly, when Cyrus was introduced into his grandfather's presence, he was quite dazzled with the display. The king wore a purple robe, very richly adorned, with a belt and collars, which were embroidered highly, and set with precious stones. He had bracelets, too, upon his wrists, of the most costly character. He wore flowing locks of artificial hair, and his face was painted, after the Median manner. Cyrus gazed upon this gay spectacle for a few moments in silence, and then exclaimed, 'Why, mother! what a handsome man my grandfather is!'

Cyrus's Considerate Reply

Such an exclamation, of course, made great amusement both for the king himself and for the others who were present; and at length Mandane, somewhat indiscreetly, it must be confessed, asked Cyrus which of the two he thought the handsomest, his father or his grandfather. Cyrus escaped from the danger of deciding such a formidable question by saying that his father was the handsomest man in Persia, but his grandfather was the handsomest of all the Medes he had ever seen. Astyages was even more pleased by this proof of his grandson's adroitness and good sense than he had been with the compliment which the boy had paid to him; and thenceforward Cyrus became an established favourite, and did and said, in his grandfather's presence, almost whatever he pleased.

Habits of Cyrus – Horsemanship Among
the Persians – Cyrus Learns to Ride
His Delights – Amusements with the Boys

When the first childish feelings of excitement and curiosity had subsided, Cyrus seemed to attach very little value to the fine clothes and gay trappings with which his grandfather was disposed to adorn him, and to all the other external marks of parade and display, which were generally so much prized among the Medes. He was much more inclined to continue in his former habits of plain dress and frugal means than to imitate Median ostentation and luxury. There was one pleasure, however, to be found in Media, which in Persia he had never enjoyed, that he prized very highly. That was the pleasure of learning to ride on horseback. The Persians, it seems, either because their country was a rough and mountainous region, or for some other cause, were very little accustomed to ride. They had very few horses, and there were no bodies of cavalry in their armies. The young men, therefore, were not trained to the art of horsemanship. Even in their hunting excursions they went always on foot, and were accustomed to make long marches through the forests and among the mountains in this manner, loaded heavily, too, all the time, with the burden of arms and provisions which they were obliged to carry. It was, therefore, a new pleasure to Cyrus to mount a horse. Horsemanship was a great art among the Medes. Their horses were beautiful and fleet, and splendidly caparisoned. Astyages provided for Cyrus the best animals which could be procured, and the boy was very proud and happy in exercising himself in the new accomplishment which he thus had the opportunity to acquire. To ride is always a great source of pleasure to boys; but in that period of the world, when physical strength was so much more important and more highly valued than at present, horsemanship was a vastly greater source of gratification than it is now. Cyrus felt that he had, at a single leap, quadrupled his power, and thus risen at once to a far higher rank in the scale of being than he had occupied before; for, as soon as he had once learned to be at home in the saddle, and to subject the spirit and the power of his horse to his own will, the courage, the strength, and the speed of the animal became, in fact, almost personal acquisitions of his own. He felt, accordingly, when he was galloping over the plains, or pursuing deer in the park or running over the racecourse with his companions, as if it was some newly acquired strength and speed of his own that he was exercising, and which, by some magic power, was attended by no toilsome exertion, and followed by no fatigue.

The Cupbearer

The various officers and servants in Astyages's household, as well as Astyages himself, soon began to feel a strong interest in the young prince. Each took a pleasure in explaining to him what pertained to their several departments, and in teaching him whatever he desired to learn. The attendant highest in rank in such a household was the cupbearer. He had the charge of the tables and the wine, and all the general arrangements of the palace seem to have been under his direction. The cupbearer in Astyages's court was a Sacian. He was, however, less a friend to Cyrus than the rest. There was nothing within the range of his official duties that he could teach the boy; and Cyrus did not like his wine. Besides, when Astyages was engaged, it was the cupbearer's duty to guard him from interruption, and at such times he often had occasion to restrain the young prince from the liberty of entering his grandfather's apartments as often as he pleased.

The Entertainment – Cyrus's Conversation

At one of the entertainments which Astyages gave in his palace, Cyrus and Mandane were invited; and Astyages, in order to gratify the young prince as highly as possible, set before him a great variety of dishes – meats, sauces and delicacies of every kind – all served in costly vessels, and with great parade and ceremony. He supposed that Cyrus would have been enraptured with the luxury and splendour of the entertainment. He did not, however, seem much pleased. Astyages asked him the reason, and whether the feast which he saw before him was not a much finer one than he had been accustomed to see in Persia. Cyrus said, in reply, that it seemed to him to be very troublesome to have to eat a little of so many separate things. In Persia they managed, he thought, a great deal better. 'And how do you manage in Persia?' asked Astyages. 'Why, in Persia,' replied Cyrus, 'we have plain bread and meat, and eat it when we are hungry; so we get health and strength, and have very little trouble.' Astyages laughed at this simplicity, and told Cyrus that he might, if he preferred it, live on plain bread and meat while he remained in Media, and then he would return to Persia in as good health as he came.

Cyrus and the Sacian Cupbearer –
Cyrus Slights Him

Cyrus was satisfied; he, however, asked his grandfather if he would give him all those things which had been set before him, to dispose of as he thought proper; and on his grandfather's assenting, he began to call the various attendants up to the table, and to distribute the costly dishes to them, in return, as he said, for their various kindnesses to him. 'This,' said he to one, 'is for you, because you take pains to teach me to ride; this,' to another, 'for you, because you gave me a javelin; this to you, because you serve my grandfather well and faithfully; and this to you, because you honour my mother.' Thus he went on until he had distributed all that he had received, though he omitted, as it seemed designedly, to give anything to the Sacian cupbearer. This Sacian being an officer of high rank, of tall and handsome figure and beautifully dressed, was the most conspicuous attendant at the feast, and could not, therefore, have been accidentally passed by. Astyages accordingly asked Cyrus why he had not given anything to the Sacian – the servant whom, as he said, he liked better than all the others.

'And what is the reason,' asked Cyrus, in reply, 'that this Sacian is such a favourite with you?'

'Have you not observed,' replied Astyages, 'how gracefully and elegantly he pours out the wine for me, and then hands me the cup?'

Accomplishments of the Cupbearer – Cyrus
Mimics Him – Cyrus Declines to Taste the Wine

The Sacian was, in fact, uncommonly accomplished in respect to the personal grace and dexterity for which cupbearers in those days were most highly valued, and which constitute, in fact, so essential a part of the qualifications of a master of ceremonies at a royal court in every age. Cyrus, however, instead of yielding to this argument, said, in reply, that he could come into the room and pour out the wine as well as the Sacian could do it, and he asked his grandfather to allow him to try. Astyages consented. Cyrus then took the goblet of wine, and went out. In a moment he came in again, stepping grandly, as he entered, in mimicry of the Sacian, and with a countenance of assumed gravity and self-importance, which imitated so well the air and manner of the cupbearer as greatly to amuse the whole company assembled. Cyrus advanced thus toward the king and presented him with the cup, imitating, with the grace and dexterity natural to childhood, all the ceremonies which he had seen the cupbearer himself perform, except that of tasting the wine. The king and Mandane laughed heartily. Cyrus then, throwing off his assumed character, jumped up into his grandfather's lap and kissed him, and turning to the cupbearer, he said, 'Now, Sacian, you are ruined. I shall get my grandfather to appoint me in your place. I can hand the wine as well as you, and without tasting it myself at all.'

'But why did you not taste it?' asked Astyages; 'you should have performed that part of the duty as well as the rest.'

Duties of a Cupbearer

It was, in fact, a very essential part of the duty of a cupbearer to taste the wine that he offered before presenting it to the king. He did this, however, not by putting the cup to his lips, but by pouring out a little of it into the palm of his hand. This custom was adopted by these ancient despots to guard against the danger of being poisoned; for such a danger would of course be very much diminished by requiring the officer who had the custody of the wine, and without whose knowledge no foreign substance could well be introduced into it, always to drink a portion of it himself immediately before tendering it to the king.

Cyrus's Reason for Not Tasting the Wine – His Description of a Feast

To Astyages's question why he had not tasted the wine, Cyrus replied that he was afraid it was poisoned. 'What led you to imagine that it was poisoned?' asked his grandfather. 'Because,' said Cyrus, 'it was poisoned the other day, when you made a feast for your friends, on your birthday. I knew by the effects. It made you all crazy. The things that you do not allow us boys to do, you did yourselves, for you were very rude and noisy; you all bawled together, so that nobody could hear or understand what any other person said. Presently you went to singing in a very ridiculous manner, and when a singer ended his song, you applauded him, and declared that he had sung admirably, though nobody had paid attention. You went to telling stories, too, each one of his own accord, without succeeding in making any body listen to him. Finally, you got up and began to dance, but it was out of all rule and measure; you could not even stand erect and steadily. Then, you all seemed to forget who and what you were. The guests paid no regard to you as their king, but treated you in a very familiar and disrespectful manner, and you treated them in the same way; so I thought that the wine that produced these effects must have been poisoned.'

Of course, Cyrus did not seriously mean that he thought the wine had been actually poisoned. He was old enough to understand its nature and effects. He undoubtedly intended his reply as a playful satire upon the intemperate excesses of his grandfather's court.

'But have not you ever seen such things before?' asked Astyages. 'Does not your father ever drink wine until it makes him merry?'

Cyrus's Dislike of the Cupbearer

'No,' replied Cyrus, 'indeed he does not. He drinks only when he is thirsty, and then only enough for his thirst, and so he is not harmed.' He then added, in a contemptuous tone, 'He has no Sacian cupbearer, you may depend, about *him*.'

'What is the reason, my son,' here asked Mandane, 'why you dislike this Sacian so much?'

His Reason for It

'Why, every time that I want to come and see my grandfather,' replied Cyrus, 'this teasing man always stops me, and will not let me come in. I wish, grandfather, you would let me have the rule over him just for three days.'

'Why, what would you do to him?' asked Astyages.

'I would treat him as he treats me now,' replied Cyrus. 'I would stand at the door, as he does when I want to come in, and when he was coming for his dinner, I would stop him and say, 'You cannot come in now; he is busy with some men.''

In saying this, Cyrus imitated, in a very ludicrous manner, the gravity and dignity of the Sacian's air and manner.

'Then,' he continued, 'when he came to supper, I would say, 'He is bathing now; you must come some other time;' or else, 'He is going to sleep, and you will disturb him.' So I would torment him all the time, as he now torments me, in keeping me out when I want to come and see you.'

Amusement of the Guests – Cyrus Becomes a Greater Favourite Than Ever

Such conversation as this, half playful, half earnest, of course amused Astyages and Mandane very much, as well as all the other listeners. There is a certain charm in the simplicity and confiding frankness of childhood, when it is honest and sincere, which in Cyrus's case was heightened by his personal grace and beauty. He became, in fact, more and more a favourite the longer he remained. At length, the indulgence and the attentions which he received began to produce, in some degree, their usual injurious effects. Cyrus became too talkative, and sometimes he appeared a little vain. Still, there was so much true kindness of heart, such consideration for the feelings of others, and so respectful a regard for his grandfather, his mother and his uncle, that his faults were overlooked, and he was the life and soul of the company in all the social gatherings which took place in the palaces of the king.

Mandane Proposes to Return to Persia

At length the time arrived for Mandane to return to Persia. Astyages proposed that she should leave Cyrus in Media, to be educated there under his grandfather's charge. Mandane replied that she was willing to gratify her father in everything, but she thought it would be very hard to leave Cyrus behind, unless he was willing, of his own accord, to stay. Astyages then proposed the subject to Cyrus himself. 'If you will stay,' said he, 'the Sacian shall no longer have power to keep you from coming in to see me; you shall come whenever you choose. Then, besides, you shall have the use of all my horses, and of as many more as you please, and when you go home at last you shall take as many as you wish with you. Then you may have all the animals in the park to hunt. You can pursue them on horseback, and shoot them with bows and arrows, or kill them with javelins, as men do with wild beasts in the woods. I will provide boys of your own age to play with you, and to ride and hunt with you, and will have all sorts of arms made of suitable size for you to use; and if there is anything else that you should want at any time, you will only have to ask me for it, and I will immediately provide it.'

Cyrus Consents to Remain – Fears of Mandane

The pleasure of riding and of hunting in the park was very captivating to Cyrus's mind, and he consented to stay. He represented to his mother that it would be of great advantage to him, on his final return to Persia, to be a skilful and powerful horseman, as that would at once give him the superiority over all the Persian youths, for they were very little accustomed to ride. His mother had some fears lest, by too long a residence in the Median court, her son should acquire the luxurious habits, and proud and haughty manners, which would be constantly before him in his grandfather's example; but Cyrus said that his grandfather, being imperious himself, required all around him to be submissive, and that Mandane need not fear but that he would return at last as dutiful and docile as ever. It was decided, therefore, that Cyrus should stay, while his mother, bidding her child and her father farewell, went back to Persia.

Departure of Mandane – Rapid Progress of Cyrus

After his mother was gone, Cyrus endeared himself very strongly to all persons at his grandfather's court by the nobleness and generosity of character which he evinced, more and more, as his mind was gradually developed. He applied himself with great diligence to acquiring the various accomplishments and arts then most highly prized, such as leaping, vaulting, racing, riding, throwing the javelin and drawing the bow. In the friendly contests which took place among the boys, to test their comparative excellence in these exercises, Cyrus would challenge those whom he knew to be superior to himself, and allow them to enjoy the pleasure of victory, while he was satisfied, himself, with the superior stimulus to exertion which he derived from coming thus into comparison with attainments higher than his own. He pressed forward boldly and ardently, undertaking everything which promised to be, by any possibility, within his power; and, far from being disconcerted and discouraged at his mistakes and failures, he always joined merrily in the laugh which they occasioned, and renewed his attempts with as much ardour and alacrity as before. Thus, he made great and rapid progress, and learned first to equal and then to surpass one after another of his companions, and all without exciting any jealousy or envy.

Hunting in the Park – Game Becomes Scarce

It was a great amusement both to him and to the other boys, his playmates, to hunt the animals in the park, especially the deer. The park was a somewhat extensive domain, but the animals were soon very much diminished by the slaughter which the boys made among them. Astyages endeavoured to supply their places by procuring more. At length, however, all the sources of supply that were conveniently at hand were exhausted; and Cyrus, then finding that his grandfather was put to no little trouble to obtain tame animals for his park, proposed, one day, that he should be allowed to go out into the forests, to hunt the wild beasts with the men. 'There are animals enough there, grandfather,' said Cyrus, 'and I shall consider them all just as if you had procured them expressly for me.'

Development of Cyrus's Powers, Both of Body and Mind

In fact, by this time Cyrus had grown up to be a tall and handsome young man, with strength and vigour sufficient, under favourable circumstances, to endure the fatigues and exposures of real hunting. As his person had become developed, his mind and manners, too, had undergone a change. The gayety, the thoughtfulness, the self-confidence and talkative vivacity of his childhood had disappeared, and he was fast becoming reserved, sedate, deliberate and cautious. He no longer entertained his grandfather's company by his mimicry, his repartees and his childish wit. He was silent; he observed, he listened, he shrank from publicity and spoke, when he spoke at all, in subdued and gentle tones. Instead of crowding forward eagerly into his grandfather's presence on all occasions, seasonable and unseasonable, as he had done before, he now became, of his own accord, very much afraid of occasioning trouble or interruption. He did not any longer need a Sacian to restrain him, but became, as Xenophon expresses it, a Sacian to himself, taking great care not to go into his grandfather's apartments without previously ascertaining that the king was disengaged; so that he and the Sacian now became very great friends.

Hunting Wild Beasts – Cyrus's Conversation with His Attendants

This being the state of the case, Astyages consented that Cyrus should go out with his son Cyaxares into the forests to hunt at the next opportunity. The party set out, when the time arrived, on horseback, the hearts of Cyrus and his companions bounding, when they mounted their steeds, with feelings of elation and pride. There were certain attendants and guards appointed to keep near to Cyrus, and to help him in the rough and rocky parts of the country, and to protect him from the dangers to which, if left alone, he would doubtless have been exposed. Cyrus talked with these attendants, as they rode along, of the mode of hunting, of the difficulties of hunting, the characters and the habits of the various wild beasts and of the dangers to be shunned. His attendants told him that the dangerous beasts were bears, lions, tigers, boars and leopards; that such animals as these often attacked and killed men, and that he must avoid them; but that stags, wild goats, wild sheep and wild asses were harmless, and that he could hunt such animals as they as much as he pleased. They told him, moreover, that steep, rocky and broken ground was more dangerous to the huntsman than any beasts, however ferocious; for riders, off their guard, driving impetuously over such ways, were often thrown from their horses, or fell with them over precipices or into chasms, and were killed.

Pursuit of a Stag – Cyrus's Danger and Recklessness

Cyrus listened very attentively to these instructions, with every disposition to give heed to them; but when he came to the trial, he found that the ardour and impetuosity of the chase drove all considerations of prudence wholly from his mind. When the men got into the forest, those that were with Cyrus roused a stag, and all set off eagerly in pursuit, Cyrus at the head. Away went the stag over rough and dangerous ground. The rest of the party turned aside, or followed cautiously, while Cyrus urged his horse forward in the wildest excitement, thinking of nothing, and seeing nothing but the stag bounding before him. The horse came to a chasm which he was obliged to leap. But the distance was too great; he came down upon his knees, threw Cyrus violently forward almost over his head, and then, with a bound and a scramble, recovered his feet and went on. Cyrus clung tenaciously to the horse's mane, and at length succeeded in getting back to the saddle, though, for a moment his life was in the most imminent danger. His attendants were extremely terrified, though he himself seemed to experience no feeling but the pleasurable excitement of the chase; for, as soon as the obstacle was cleared, he pressed on with new impetuosity after the stag, overtook him and killed him with his javelin. Then, alighting from his horse, he stood by the side of his victim, to wait the coming up of the party, his countenance beaming with an expression of triumph and delight.

He is Reproved by His Companions – Cyrus Kills a Wild Boar

His attendants, however, on their arrival, instead of applauding his exploit, or seeming to share his pleasure, sharply reproved him for his recklessness and daring. He had entirely disregarded their instructions, and they threatened to report him to his grandfather. Cyrus looked perplexed and uneasy. The excitement and the pleasure of victory and success were struggling in his mind against his dread of his grandfather's displeasure. Just at this instant he heard a new halloo. Another party in the neighbourhood had roused fresh game. All Cyrus's returning sense of duty was blown at once to the winds. He sprang to his horse with a shout of wild enthusiasm, and rode off toward the scene of action. The game which had been started, a furious wild boar, just then issued from a thicket directly before him. Cyrus, instead of shunning the danger, as he ought to have done, in obedience to the orders of those to whom his grandfather had intrusted him, dashed on to meet the boar at full speed, and aimed so true a thrust with his javelin against the beast as to transfix him in the forehead. The boar fell, and lay upon the ground in dying struggles, while Cyrus's heart was filled with joy and triumph even greater than before.

He is Again Reproved

When Cyaxares came up, he reproved Cyrus anew for running such risks. Cyrus received the reproaches meekly, and then asked Cyaxares to give him the two animals that he had killed; he wanted to carry them home to his grandfather.

'By no means,' said Cyaxares, 'your grandfather would be very much displeased to know what you had done. He would not only condemn you for acting thus, but he would reprove us too, severely, for allowing you to do so.'

'Let him punish me,' said Cyrus, 'if he wishes, after I have shown him the stag and the boar, and you may punish me too, if you think best; but do let me show them to him.'

Cyrus Carries His Game Home

Cyaxares consented, and Cyrus made arrangements to have the bodies of the beasts and the bloody javelins carried home. Cyrus then presented the carcasses to his grandfather, saying that it was some game which he had taken for him. The javelins he did not exhibit directly, but he laid them down in a place where his grandfather would see them. Astyages thanked him for his presents, but he said he had no such need of presents of game as to wish his grandson to expose himself to such imminent dangers to take it.

Distributes it Among His Companions

'Well, grandfather,' said Cyrus, 'if you do not want the meat, give it to me, and I will divide it among my friends.' Astyages agreed to this, and Cyrus divided his booty among his companions, the boys, who had before hunted with him in the park. They, of course, took their several portions home, each one carrying with his share of the gift a glowing account of the valour and prowess of the giver. It was not generosity which led Cyrus thus to give away the fruits of his toil, but a desire to widen and extend his fame.

Another Hunting Party

When Cyrus was about fifteen or sixteen years old, his uncle Cyaxares was married, and in celebrating his nuptials, he formed a great hunting party, to go to the frontiers between Media and Assyria to hunt there, where it was said that game of all kinds was very plentiful, as it usually was, in fact, in those days, in the neighbourhood of disturbed and unsettled frontiers. The very causes which made such a region as this a safe and frequented haunt for wild beasts, made it unsafe for men, and Cyaxares did not consider it prudent to venture on his excursion without a considerable force to attend him. His hunting party formed, therefore, quite a little army. They set out from home with great pomp and ceremony, and proceeded to the frontiers in regular organization and order, like a body of troops on a march. There was a squadron of horsemen, who were to hunt the beasts in the open parts of the forest, and a considerable detachment of light-armed footmen also, who were to rouse the game, and drive them out of their lurking places in the glens and thickets. Cyrus accompanied this expedition.

A Plundering Party

When Cyaxares reached the frontiers, he concluded, instead of contenting himself and his party with hunting wild beasts, to make an incursion for plunder into the Assyrian territory, that being, as Xenophon expresses it, a more noble enterprise than the other. The nobleness, it seems, consisted in the greater imminence of the danger, in having to contend with armed men instead of ferocious brutes, and in the higher value of the prizes which they would obtain in case of success. The idea of there being any injustice or wrong in this wanton and unprovoked aggression upon the territories of a neighbouring nation seems not to have entered the mind either of the royal robber himself or of his historian.

Cyrus distinguished himself very conspicuously in this expedition, as he had done in the hunting excursion before; and when, at length, this nuptial party returned home, loaded with booty, the tidings of Cyrus's exploits went to Persia. Cambyses thought that if his son was beginning to take part, as a soldier, in military campaigns, it was time for him to be recalled. He accordingly sent for him, and Cyrus began to make preparations for his return.

Cyrus Departs for Media – Parting Presents

The day of his departure was a day of great sadness and sorrow among all his companions in Media, and, in fact, among all the members of his grandfather's household. They accompanied him for some distance on his way, and took leave of him, at last, with much regret and many tears. Cyrus distributed among them, as they left him, the various articles of value which he possessed, such as his arms, ornaments of various kinds and costly articles of dress. He gave his Median robe, at last, to a certain youth whom he said he loved the best of all. The name of this special favourite was Araspes. As these his friends parted from him, Cyrus took his leave of them, one by one, as they returned, with many proofs of his affection for them, and with a very sad and heavy heart.

The Presents Returned – Cyrus Sends Them Back Again

The boys and young men who had received these presents took them home, but they were so valuable, that they or their parents, supposing that they were given under a momentary impulse of feeling, and that they ought to be returned, sent them all to Astyages. Astyages sent them to Persia, to be restored to Cyrus. Cyrus sent them all back again to his grandfather, with a request that he would distribute them again to those to whom Cyrus had originally given them, 'which,' said he, 'grandfather, you must do, if you wish me ever to come to Media again with pleasure and not with shame.'

Character of Xenophon's Narrative – Its Trustworthiness – Character of Cyrus as Given by Xenophon

Such is the story which Xenophon gives of Cyrus's visit to Media, and in its romantic and incredible details it is a specimen of the whole narrative which this author has given of his hero's life. It is not, at the present day, supposed that these, and the many similar stories with which Xenophon's books are filled, are true history. It is not even thought that Xenophon really intended to offer his narrative as history, but rather as an historical romance – a fiction founded on fact, written to amuse the warriors of his times, and to serve as a vehicle for inculcating such principles of philosophy, of morals and of military science as seemed to him worthy of the attention of his countrymen. The story has no air of reality about it from beginning to end, but only a sort of poetical fitness of one part to another, much more like the contrived coincidences of a romance writer than like the real events and transactions of actual life. A very large portion of the work consists of long discourses on military, moral and often metaphysical philosophy, made by generals in council, or commanders in conversation with each other when going into battle. The occurrences and incidents out of which these conversations arise always take place just as they are wanted and arrange themselves in a manner to produce the highest dramatic effect; like the stag, the broken ground and the wild boar in Cyrus's hunting, which came, one after another, to furnish the hero with poetical occasions for displaying his juvenile bravery, and to produce the most picturesque and poetical grouping of incidents and events. Xenophon too, like other writers of romances, makes his hero a model of military virtue and magnanimity, according to the ideas of the times. He displays superhuman sagacity in circumventing his foes, he performs prodigies of valour, he forms the most sentimental attachments, and receives with a romantic confidence the adhesions of men who come over to his side from the enemy, and who, being traitors to old friends, would seem to be only worthy of suspicion and distrust in being received by new ones. Everything, however, results well; all whom he confides in prove worthy; all whom he distrusts prove base. All his friends are generous and noble, and all his enemies treacherous and cruel. Every prediction which he makes is verified, and all his enterprises succeed; or if, in any respect, there occurs a partial failure, the incident is always of such a character as to heighten the impression which is made by the final and triumphant success.

Herodotus More Trustworthy than Xenophon

Such being the character of Xenophon's tale, or rather drama, we shall content ourselves, after giving this specimen of it, with adding, in some subsequent chapters, a few other scenes and incidents drawn from his narrative. In the meantime, in relating the great leading events of Cyrus's life, we shall take Herodotus for our guide, by following his more sober, and, probably, more trustworthy record.

Chapter IV
Croesus, BCE 718–545

The Wealth of Croesus

THE SCENE OF OUR NARRATIVE must now be changed, for a time, from Persia and Media, in the East, to Asia Minor, in the West, where the great Croesus, originally King of Lydia, was at this time gradually extending his empire along the shores of the Aegean Sea. The name of Croesus is associated in the minds of men with the idea of boundless wealth, the phrase 'as rich as Croesus' having been a common proverb in all the modern languages of Europe for many centuries. It was to this Croesus, king of Lydia, whose story we are about to relate, that the proverb alludes.

The Mermnadae – Origin of the Mermnadean Dynasty

The country of Lydia, over which this famous sovereign originally ruled, was in the western part of Asia Minor, bordering on the Aegean Sea. Croesus himself belonged to a dynasty called the Mermnadae. The founder of this line was Gyges, who displaced the dynasty which preceded him and established his own by a revolution effected in a very remarkable manner. The circumstances were as follows:

Candaules and Gyges – Infamous Proposal of Candaules Remonstrance of Gyges

The name of the last monarch of the old dynasty – the one, namely, whom Gyges displaced – was Candaules. Gyges was a household servant in Candaules's family – a sort of slave, in fact, and yet, as such slaves often were in those rude days, a personal favourite and boon companion of his master. Candaules was a dissolute and unprincipled tyrant. He had, however, a very beautiful and modest wife, whose name was Nyssia. Candaules was very proud of the beauty of his queen, and was always extolling it, though, as the event proved, he could not have felt for her any true and honest affection. In some of his revels with Gyges, when he was boasting of Nyssia's charms, he said that the beauty of her form and figure, when unrobed, was even more exquisite than that of her features; and, finally, the monster, growing more and more excited, and having rendered himself still more of a brute than he was by nature by the influence of wine, declared that Gyges should see for himself. He would conceal him, he said, in the queen's bedchamber, while she was undressing for the night. Gyges remonstrated very earnestly against this proposal. It would be doing the innocent queen, he said, a great wrong. He assured the king, too, that he believed fully all that he said about Nyssia's beauty, without applying such a test, and he begged him not to insist upon a proposal with which it would be criminal to comply.

Nyssia's Suppressed Indignation

The king, however, did insist upon it, and Gyges was compelled to yield. Whatever is offered as a favour by a half-intoxicated despot to a humble inferior, it would be death to refuse. Gyges allowed himself to be placed behind a half-opened door of the king's apartment, when the king retired to it for the night. There he was to remain while the queen began to unrobe herself for retiring, with a strict injunction to withdraw at a certain time which the king designated, and with the utmost caution, so as to prevent being observed by the queen. Gyges did as he was ordered. The beautiful queen laid aside her garments and made her toilet for the night with all the quiet composure and confidence which a woman might be expected to feel while in so sacred and inviolable a sanctuary, and in the presence and under the guardianship of her husband. Just as she was about to retire to rest, some movement alarmed her. It was Gyges going away. She saw him. She instantly understood the case. She was overwhelmed with indignation and shame. She, however, suppressed and concealed her emotions; she spoke to Candaules in her usual tone of voice, and he, on his part, secretly rejoiced in the adroit and successful manner in which his little contrivance had been carried into execution.

71

She Sends for Gyges

The next morning Nyssia sent, by some of her confidential messengers, for Gyges to come to her. He came, with some forebodings, perhaps, but without any direct reason for believing that what he had done had been discovered. Nyssia, however, informed him that she knew all, and that either he or her husband must die. Gyges earnestly remonstrated against this decision, and supplicated forgiveness. He explained the circumstances under which the act had been performed, which seemed, at least so far as he was concerned, to palliate the deed. The queen was, however, fixed and decided. It was wholly inconsistent with her ideas of womanly delicacy that there should be two living men who had both been admitted to her bedchamber. 'The king,' she said, 'by what he has done, has forfeited his claims to me and resigned me to you. If you will kill him, seize his kingdom, and make me your wife, all shall be well; otherwise you must prepare to die.'

From this hard alternative, Gyges chose to assassinate the king, and to make the lovely object before him his own. The excitement of indignation and resentment which glowed upon her cheek, and with which her bosom was heaving, made her more beautiful than ever.

'How shall our purpose be accomplished?' asked Gyges. 'The deed,' she replied, 'shall be perpetrated in the very place which was the scene of the dishonour done to me. I will admit you into our bedchamber in my turn, and you shall kill Candaules in his bed.'

Candaules is Assassinated – Gyges Succeeds

When night came, Nyssia stationed Gyges again behind the same door where the king had placed him. He had a dagger in his hand. He waited there till Candaules was asleep. Then at a signal given him by the queen, he entered, and stabbed the husband in his bed. He married Nyssia, and possessed himself of the kingdom. After this, he and his successors reigned for many years over the kingdom of Lydia, constituting the dynasty of the Mermnadae, from which, in process of time, King Croesus descended.

The Lydian Power Extended – The Wars of Alyattes – Destruction of Minerva's Temple

The successive sovereigns of this dynasty gradually extended the Lydian power over the countries around them. The name of Croesus's father, who was the monarch that immediately preceded him, was Alyattes. Alyattes waged war toward the southward, into the territories of the city of Miletus. He made annual incursions into the country of the Milesians for plunder, always taking care, however, while he seized all the movable property that he could find, to leave the villages and towns, and all the hamlets of the labourers without injury. The reason for this was, that he did not wish to drive away the population, but to encourage them to remain and cultivate their lands, so that there might be new flocks and herds, and new stores of corn, fruit and wine, for him to plunder from in succeeding years. At last, on one of these marauding excursions, some fires which were accidentally set in a field spread into a neighbouring town, and destroyed, among other buildings, a temple consecrated to the goddess Minerva. After this, Alyattes found himself quite unsuccessful in all his expeditions and campaigns. He sent to a famous oracle to ask the reason.

'You can expect no more success,' replied the oracle, 'until you rebuild the temple that you have destroyed.'

But how could he rebuild the temple? The site was in the enemy's country. His men could not build an edifice and defend themselves, at the same time, from the attacks of their foes. He concluded to demand a truce of the Milesians until the reconstruction should be completed, and he sent ambassadors to Miletus, accordingly, to make the proposal.

Stratagem of Thrasybulus – Success of the Stratagem – A Treaty of Peace Concluded

The proposition for a truce resulted in a permanent peace, by means of a very singular stratagem which Thrasybulus, the king of Miletus, practiced upon Alyattes. It seems that Alyattes supposed that Thrasybulus had been reduced to great distress by the loss and destruction of provisions and stores in various parts of the country, and that he would soon be forced to yield up his kingdom. This was, in fact, the case; but Thrasybulus determined to disguise his real condition, and to destroy, by an artifice, all the hopes which Alyattes had formed from the supposed scarcity in the city. When the herald whom Alyattes sent to Miletus was about to arrive, Thrasybulus collected all the corn, grain and other provisions which he could command, and had them heaped up in a public part of the city, where the herald was to be received, so as to present indications of the most ample abundance of food. He collected a large body of his soldiers, too, and gave them leave to feast themselves without restriction on what he had thus gathered. Accordingly, when the herald came in to deliver his message, he found the whole city given up to feasting and revelry, and he saw stores of provisions at hand, which were in process of being distributed and consumed with the most prodigal profusion. The herald reported this state of things to Alyattes. Alyattes then gave up all hopes of reducing Miletus by famine, and made a permanent peace, binding himself to its stipulations by a very solemn treaty. To celebrate the event, too, he built two temples to Minerva instead of one.

Story of Arion and the Dolphin

A story is related by Herodotus of a remarkable escape made by Arion at sea, which occurred during the reign of Alyattes, the father of Croesus. We will give the story as Herodotus relates it, leaving the reader to judge for himself whether such tales were probably true, or were only introduced by Herodotus into his narrative to make his histories more entertaining to the Grecian assemblies to whom he read them. Arion was a celebrated singer. He had been making a tour in Sicily and in the southern part of Italy, where he had acquired considerable wealth, and he was now returning to Corinth. He embarked at Tarentum, which is a city in the southern part of Italy, in a Corinthian vessel, and put to sea. When the sailors found that they had him in their power, they determined to rob and murder him. They accordingly seized his gold and silver, and then told him that he might either kill himself or jump overboard into the sea. One or the other he must do. If he would kill himself on board the vessel, they would give him decent burial when they reached the shore.

The Alternative – Arion Leaps into the Sea – He is Preserved by a Dolphin

Arion seemed at first at a loss how to decide in so hard an alternative. At length he told the sailors that he would throw himself into the sea, but he asked permission to sing them one of his songs before he took the fatal plunge. They consented. He accordingly went into the cabin, and spent some time in dressing himself magnificently in the splendid and richly ornamented robes in which he had been accustomed to appear upon the stage. At length he reappeared, and took his position on the side of the ship, with his harp in his hand. He sang his song, accompanying himself upon the harp, and then, when he had finished his performance, he leaped into the sea. The seamen divided their plunder and pursued their voyage. Arion, however, instead of being drowned, was taken up by a dolphin that had been charmed by his song, and was borne by him to Taenarus, which is the promontory formed by the southern extremity of the Peloponnesus. There Arion landed in safety. From Taenarus he proceeded to Corinth, wearing the same dress in which he had plunged into the sea. On his arrival, he complained to the king of the crime which the sailors had committed, and narrated his wonderful escape. The king did not believe him, but put him in prison to wait until the ship should arrive. When at last the vessel came, the king summoned the sailors into his presence, and asked them if they knew anything of Arion. Arion himself had been previously placed in an adjoining room, ready to be called in as soon as his presence was required. The mariners answered to the question which the king put to them, that they had seen Arion in Tarentum, and that they had left him there. Arion was then himself called in. His sudden appearance, clothed as he was in the same dress in which the mariners had seen him leap into the sea, so terrified the conscience-stricken criminals, that they confessed their guilt, and were all punished by the king. A marble statue, representing a man seated upon a dolphin, was erected at Taenarus to commemorate this event, where it remained for centuries afterward, a monument of the wonder which Arion had achieved.

Death of Alyattes – Succession of Croesus

At length Alyattes died and Croesus succeeded him. Croesus extended still further the power and fame of the Lydian empire, and was for a time very successful in all his military schemes. By looking upon the map, the reader will see that the Aegean Sea, along the coasts of Asia Minor, is studded with islands. These islands were in those days very fertile and beautiful, and were densely inhabited by a commercial and maritime people, who possessed a multitude of ships, and were very powerful in all the adjacent seas. Of course, their land forces were very few, whether of horse or of foot, as the habits and manners of such a seagoing people were all foreign to modes of warfare required in land campaigns. On the sea, however, these islanders were supreme.

Plans of Croesus for Subjugating the Islands

Croesus formed a scheme for attacking these islands and bringing them under his sway, and he began to make preparations for building and equipping a fleet for this purpose, though, of course, his subjects were as unused to the sea as the nautical islanders were to military operations on the land. While he was making these preparations, a certain philosopher was visiting at his court: he was one of the seven wise men of Greece, who had recently come from the Peloponnesus. Croesus asked him if there was any news from that country. 'I heard,' said the philosopher, 'that the inhabitants of the islands were preparing to invade your dominions with a squadron of ten thousand horse.' Croesus, who supposed that the philosopher was serious, appeared greatly pleased and elated at the prospect of his seafaring enemies attempting to meet him as a body of cavalry. 'No doubt,' said the philosopher, after a little pause, 'you would be pleased to have those sailors attempt to contend with you on horseback; but do you not suppose that they will be equally pleased at the prospect of encountering Lydian landsmen on the ocean?'

Croesus perceived the absurdity of his plan, and abandoned the attempt to execute it.

The Golden Sands of the Pactolus – The Story of Midas

Croesus acquired the enormous wealth for which he was so celebrated from the golden sands of the River Pactolus, which flowed through his kingdom. The river brought the particles of gold, in grains, globules and flakes, from the mountains above, and the servants and slaves of Croesus washed the sands, and thus separated the heavier deposit of the metal. In respect to the origin of the gold, however, the people who lived upon the banks of the river had a different explanation from the simple one that the waters brought down the treasure from the mountain ravines. They had a story that, ages before, a certain king, named Midas, rendered some service to a god, who, in his turn, offered to grant him any favour that he might ask. Midas asked that the power might be granted him to turn whatever he touched into gold. The power was bestowed, and Midas, after changing various objects around him into gold until he was satisfied, began to find his new acquisition a source of great inconvenience and danger. His clothes, his food, and even his drink, were changed to gold when he touched them. He found that he was about to starve in the midst of a world of treasure, and he implored the god to take back the fatal gift. The god directed him to go and bathe in the Pactolus, and he should be restored to his former condition. Midas did so, and was saved, but not without transforming a great portion of the sands of the stream into gold during the process of his restoration.

Wealth and Renown of Croesus – Visit of Solon – Croesus and Solon

Croesus thus attained quite speedily to a very high degree of wealth, prosperity and renown. His dominions were widely extended; his palaces were full of treasures; his court was a scene of unexampled magnificence and splendour. While in the enjoyment of all this grandeur, he was visited by Solon, the celebrated Grecian lawgiver, who was travelling in that part of the world to observe the institutions and customs of different states. Croesus received Solon with great distinction, and showed him all his treasures. At last, he one day said to him, 'You have travelled, Solon, over many countries, and have studied, with a great deal of attention and care, all that you have seen. I have heard great commendations of your wisdom, and I should like very much to know who, of all the persons you have ever known, has seemed to you most fortunate and happy.'

The king had no doubt that the answer would be that he himself was the one.

'I think,' replied Solon, after a pause, 'that Tellus, an Athenian citizen, was the most fortunate and happy man I have ever known.'

'Tellus, an Athenian!' repeated Croesus, surprised. 'What was there in his case which you consider so remarkable?'

What Constitutes Happiness

'He was a peaceful and quiet citizen of Athens,' said Solon. 'He lived happily with his family, under a most excellent government, enjoying for many years all the pleasures of domestic life. He had several amiable and virtuous children, who all grew up to maturity, and loved and honoured their parents as long as they lived. At length, when his life was drawing toward its natural termination, a war broke out with a neighbouring nation, and Tellus went with the army to defend his country. He aided very essentially in the defeat of the enemy, but fell, at last, on the field of battle. His countrymen greatly lamented his death. They buried him publicly where he fell, with every circumstance of honour.'

Solon was proceeding to recount the domestic and social virtues of Tellus, and the peaceful happiness which he enjoyed as the result of them, when Croesus interrupted him to ask who, next to Tellus, he considered the most fortunate and happy man.

Cleobis and Bito

Solon, after a little farther reflection, mentioned two brothers, Cleobis and Bito, private persons among the Greeks, who were celebrated for their great personal strength, and also for their devoted attachment to their mother. He related to Croesus a story of a feat they performed on one occasion, when their mother, at the celebration of some public festival, was going some miles to a temple, in a car to be drawn by oxen. There happened to be some delay in bringing the oxen, while the mother was waiting in the car. As the oxen did not come, the young men took hold of the pole of the car themselves, and walked off at their ease with the load, amid the acclamations of the spectators, while their mother's heart was filled with exultation and pride.

Croesus Displeased with Solon

Croesus here interrupted the philosopher again, and expressed his surprise that he should place private men, like those whom he had named, who possessed no wealth, prominence or power, before a monarch like him, occupying a station of such high authority and renown, and possessing such boundless treasures.

'Croesus,' replied Solon, 'I see you now, indeed, at the height of human power and grandeur. You reign supreme over many nations, and you are in the enjoyment of unbounded affluence, and every species of luxury and splendour. I cannot, however, decide whether I am to consider you a fortunate and happy man, until I know how all this is to end. If we consider seventy years as the allotted period of life, you have a large portion of your existence yet to come, and we cannot with certainty pronounce any man happy till his life is ended.'

Solon Treated with Neglect

This conversation with Solon made a deep impression upon Croesus's mind, as was afterward proved in a remarkable manner; but the impression was not a pleasant or a salutary one. The king, however, suppressed for the time the resentment which the presentation of these unwelcome truths awakened within him, though he treated Solon afterward with indifference and neglect, so that the philosopher soon found it best to withdraw.

The Two Sons of Croesus – The King's Dream

Croesus had two sons. One was deaf and dumb. The other was a young man of uncommon promise, and, of course, as he only could succeed his father in the government of the kingdom, he was naturally an object of the king's particular attention and care. His name was Atys. He was unmarried. He was, however, old enough to have the command of a considerable body of troops, and he had often distinguished himself in the Lydian campaigns. One night the king had a dream about Atys which greatly alarmed him. He dreamed that his son was destined to die of a wound received from the point of an iron spear. The king was made very uneasy by this ominous dream. He determined at once to take every precaution in his power to avert the threatened danger. He immediately detached Atys from his command in the army, and made provision for his marriage. He then very carefully collected all the darts, javelins and every other iron-pointed weapon that he could find about the palace, and caused them to be deposited carefully in a secure place, where there could be no danger even of an accidental injury from them.

Arrival of Adrastus

About that time there appeared at the court of Croesus a stranger from Phrygia, a neighbouring state, who presented himself at the palace and asked for protection. He was a prince of the royal family of Phrygia, and his name was Adrastus. He had had the misfortune, by some unhappy accident, to kill his brother; his father, in consequence of it, had banished him from his native land, and he was now homeless, friendless and destitute.

Croesus received him kindly. 'Your family have always been my friends,' said he, 'and I am glad of the opportunity to make some return by extending my protection to any member of it suffering misfortune. You shall reside in my palace, and all your wants shall be supplied. Come in, and forget the calamity which has befallen you, instead of distressing yourself with it as if it had been a crime.'

The Wild Boar – Precautions of Croesus

Thus, Croesus received the unfortunate Adrastus into his household. After the prince had been domiciliated in his new home for some time, messengers came from Mysia, a neighbouring state, saying that a wild boar of enormous size and unusual ferocity had come down from the mountains, and was lurking in the cultivated country, in thickets and glens, from which, at night, he made great havoc among the flocks and herds, and asking that Croesus would send his son, with a band of hunters and a pack of dogs, to help them destroy the common enemy. Croesus consented immediately to send the dogs and the men, but he said that he could not send his son. 'My son,' he added, 'has been lately married, and his time and attention are employed about other things.'

Remonstrance of Atys

When, however, Atys himself heard of this reply, he remonstrated very earnestly against it, and begged his father to allow him to go. 'What will the world think of me,' said he 'if I shut myself up to these luxurious pursuits and enjoyments, and shun those dangers and toils which other men consider it their highest honour to share? What will my fellow citizens think of me, and how shall I appear in the eyes of my wife? She will despise me.'

Explanation of Croesus

Croesus then explained to his son the reason why he had been so careful to avoid exposing him to danger. He related to him the dream which had alarmed him. 'It is on that account,' said he, 'that I am so anxious about you. You are, in fact, my only son, for your speechless brother can never be my heir.'

Atys said, in reply, that he was not surprised, under those circumstances, at his father's anxiety; but he maintained that this was a case to which his caution could not properly apply.

'You dreamed,' he said, 'that I should be killed by a weapon pointed with iron; but a boar has no such weapon. If the dream had portended that I was to perish by a tusk or a tooth, you might reasonably have restrained me from going to hunt a wild beast; but iron-pointed instruments are the weapons of men, and we are not going, in this expedition, to contend with men.'

Atys Joins the Expedition

The king, partly convinced, perhaps, by the arguments which Atys offered, and partly overborne by the urgency of his request, finally consented to his request and allowed him to go. He consigned him, however, to the special care of Adrastus, who was likewise to accompany the expedition, charging Adrastus to keep constantly by his side, and to watch over him with the utmost vigilance and fidelity.

He is Killed by Adrastus

The band of huntsmen was organized, the dogs prepared and the train departed. Very soon afterward, a messenger came back from the hunting ground, breathless, and with a countenance of extreme concern and terror, bringing the dreadful tidings that Atys was dead. Adrastus himself had killed him. In the ardour of the chase, while the huntsmen had surrounded the boar, and were each intent on his own personal danger while in close combat with such a monster, and all were hurling darts and javelins at their ferocious foe, the spear of Adrastus missed its aim, and entered the body of the unhappy prince. He bled to death on the spot.

Anguish of Adrastus

Soon after the messenger had made known these terrible tidings, the hunting train, transformed now into a funeral procession, appeared, bearing the dead body of the king's son, and followed by the wretched Adrastus himself, who was wringing his hands, and crying out incessantly in accents and exclamations of despair. He begged the king to kill him at once, over the body of his son, and thus put an end to the unutterable agony that he endured. This second calamity was more, he said, than he could bear. He had killed before his own brother, and now he had murdered the son of his greatest benefactor and friend.

Burial of Atys – Adrastus Kills Himself

Croesus, though overwhelmed with anguish, was disarmed of all resentment at witnessing Adrastus's suffering. He endeavoured to soothe and quiet the agitation which the unhappy man endured, but it was in vain. Adrastus could not be calmed. Croesus then ordered the body of his son to be buried with proper honours. The funeral services were performed with great and solemn ceremonies, and when the body was interred, the household of Croesus returned to the palace, which was now, in spite of all its splendour, shrouded in gloom. That night – at midnight – Adrastus, finding his mental anguish insupportable retired from his apartment to the place where Atys had been buried, and killed himself over the grave.

Grief of Croesus

Solon was wise in saying that he could not tell whether wealth and grandeur were to be accounted as happiness till he saw how they would end. Croesus was plunged into inconsolable grief, and into extreme dejection and misery for a period of two years, in consequence of this calamity, and yet this calamity was only the beginning of the end.

Chapter V
Accession of Cyrus to the Throne, BCE 560

Change in the Character of Cyrus – His Ambition

WHILE CROESUS HAD THUS, on his side of the River Halys – which was the stream that marked the boundary between the Lydian empire on the west and the Persian and Assyrian dominions on the east – been employed in building up his grand structure of outward magnificence and splendour, and in contending, within, against an overwhelming tide of domestic misery and woe, great changes had taken place in the situation and prospects of Cyrus. From being an artless and generous-minded child, he had become a calculating, ambitious and aspiring man, and he was preparing to take his part in the great public contests and struggles of the day, with the same eagerness for self-aggrandizement, and the same unconcern for the welfare and happiness of others, which always characterizes the spirit of ambition and love of power.

Capriciousness of Astyages

Although it is by no means certain that what Xenophon relates of his visit to his grandfather Astyages is meant for a true narrative of facts, it is not at all improbable that such a visit might have been made, and that occurrences, somewhat similar, at least, to those which his narrative records, may have taken place. It may seem strange to the reader that a man who should, at one time, wish to put his grandchild to death, should, at another, be disposed to treat him with such a profusion of kindness and attention. There is nothing, however, really extraordinary in this. Nothing is more fluctuating than the caprice of a despot. Man, accustomed from infancy to govern those around him by his own impetuous will, never learns self-control. He gives himself up to the dominion of the passing animal emotions of the hour. It may be jealousy, it may be revenge, it may be parental fondness, it may be hate, it may be love – whatever the feeling is that the various incidents of life, as they occur, or the influences, irritating or exhilarating, which are produced by food or wine, awaken in his mind, he follows its impulse blindly and without reserve. He loads a favourite with kindness and caresses at one hour, and directs his assassination the next. He imagines that his infant grandchild is to become his rival, and he deliberately orders him to be left in a gloomy forest alone, to die of cold and hunger. When the imaginary danger has passed away, he seeks amusement in making the same grandchild his plaything, and overwhelms him with favours bestowed solely for the gratification of the giver, under the influence of an affection almost as purely animal as that of a lioness for her young.

Favours of such a sort can awaken no permanent gratitude in any heart, and thus it is quite possible that Cyrus might have evinced, during the simple and guileless days of his childhood, a deep veneration and affection for his grandfather, and yet, in subsequent years, when he had arrived at full maturity, have learned to regard him simply in the light of a great political potentate, as likely as any other potentate around him to become his rival or his enemy.

Cyrus Makes Great Progress in Mental and Personal Accomplishments

This was, at all events, the result. Cyrus, on his return to Persia, grew rapidly in strength and stature, and soon became highly distinguished for his personal grace, his winning manners and for the various martial accomplishments which he had acquired in Media, and in which he excelled almost all his companions. He gained, as such princes always do, a vast ascendency over the minds of all around him. As he advanced toward maturity, his mind passed from its interest in games, hunting and athletic sports, to plans of war, of conquest and of extended dominion.

Harpagus's Plans for Revenge – Suspicions of Astyages

In the meantime, Harpagus, though he had, at the time when he endured the horrid punishment which Astyages inflicted upon him, expressed no resentment, still he had secretly felt an extreme indignation and anger, and he had now, for fifteen years, been nourishing covert schemes and plans for revenge. He remained all this time in the court of Astyages, and was apparently his friend. He was, however, in heart a most bitter and implacable enemy. He was looking continually for a plan or prospect which should promise some hope of affording him his long-desired revenge. His eyes were naturally turned toward Cyrus. He kept up a communication with him so far as it was possible, for Astyages watched very closely what passed between the two countries, being always suspicious of plots against his government and crown. Harpagus, however, contrived to evade this vigilance in some degree. He made continual reports to Cyrus of the tyranny and misgovernment of Astyages, and of the defencelessness of the realm of Media, and he endeavoured to stimulate his rising ambition to the desire of one day possessing for himself both the Median and Persian throne.

Condition of Persia

In fact, Persia was not then independent of Media. It was more or less connected with the government of Astyages, so that Cambyses, the chief ruler of Persia, Cyrus's father, is called sometimes a king and sometimes a *satrap*, which last title is equivalent to that of viceroy or governor general. Whatever his true and proper title may have been, Persia was a Median dependency, and Cyrus, therefore, in forming plans for gaining possession of the Median throne, would consider himself as rather endeavouring to rise to the supreme command in his own native country, than as projecting any scheme for foreign conquest.

Discontent in Media – Proceedings of Harpagus

Harpagus, too, looked upon the subject in the same light. Accordingly, in pushing forward his plots toward their execution, he operated in Media as well as Persia, He ascertained, by diligent and sagacious, but by very covert inquiries, who were discontented and ill at ease under the dominion of Astyages, and by sympathizing with and encouraging them, he increased their discontent and restlessness. Whenever Astyages, in the exercise of his tyranny inflicted an injury upon a powerful subject, Harpagus espoused the cause of the injured man, condemned, with him, the intolerable oppression of the king, and thus fixed and perpetuated his enmity. At the same time, he took pains to collect and to disseminate among the Medes all the information which he could obtain favourable to Cyrus, in respect to his talents, his character and his just and generous spirit, so that, at length, the ascendency of Astyages, through the instrumentality of these measures, was very extensively undermined, and the way was rapidly becoming prepared for Cyrus's accession to power.

His Deportment Toward Astyages

During all this time, moreover, Harpagus was personally very deferential and obsequious to Astyages, and professed an unbounded devotedness to his interests. He maintained a high rank at court and in the army, and Astyages relied upon him as one of the most obedient and submissive of his servants, without entertaining any suspicion whatever of his true designs.

Cooperation in Media

At length a favourable occasion arose, as Harpagus thought, for the execution of his plans. It was at a time when Astyages had been guilty of some unusual acts of tyranny and oppression, by which he had produced extensive dissatisfaction among his people. Harpagus communicated, very cautiously, to the principal men around him, the designs that he had long been forming for deposing Astyages and elevating Cyrus in his place. He found them favourably inclined to the plan. The way being thus prepared, the next thing was to contrive some secret way of communicating with Cyrus. As the proposal which he was going to make was that Cyrus should come into Media with as great a force as he could command, and head an insurrection against the government of Astyages, it would, of course, be death to him to have it discovered. He did not dare to trust the message to any living messenger, for fear of betrayal; nor was it safe to send a letter by any ordinary mode of transmission, lest the letter should be intercepted by some of Astyages's spies, and thus the whole plot be discovered. He finally adopted the following very extraordinary plan:

Harpagus Writes to Cyrus – Harpagus's Singular Method of Conveying His Letter to Cyrus

He wrote a letter to Cyrus, and then taking a hare, which some of his huntsmen had caught for him, he opened the body and concealed the letter within. He then sewed up the skin again in the most careful manner, so that no signs of the incision should remain. He delivered this hare, together with some nets and other hunting apparatus, to certain trustworthy servants, on whom he thought he could rely, charging them to deliver the hare into Cyrus's own hands, and to say that it came from Harpagus, and that it was the request of Harpagus that Cyrus should open it himself and alone. Harpagus concluded that this mode of making the communication was safe; for, in case the persons to whom the hare was entrusted were to be seen by any of the spies or other persons employed by Astyages on the frontiers, they would consider them as hunters returning from the chase with their game, and would never think of examining the body of a hare, in the hands of such a party, in search after a clandestine correspondence.

The plan was perfectly successful. The men passed into Persia without any suspicion. They delivered the hare to Cyrus, with their message. He opened the hare, and found the letter. It was in substance as follows:

Contents of Harpagus's Letter

'It is plain, Cyrus, that you are a favourite of Heaven, and that you are destined to a great and glorious career. You could not otherwise have escaped, in so miraculous a manner, the snares set for you in your infancy. Astyages meditated your death, and he took such measures to effect it as would seem to have made your destruction sure. You were saved by the special interposition of Heaven. You are aware by what extraordinary incidents you were preserved and discovered, and what great and unusual prosperity has since attended you. You know, too, what cruel punishments Astyages inflicted upon me, for my humanity in saving you. The time has now come for retribution. From this time the authority and the dominions of Astyages may be yours. Persuade the Persians to revolt. Put yourself at the head of an army, and march into Media. I shall probably myself be appointed to command the army sent out to oppose you. If so, we will join our forces when we meet, and I will enter your service. I have conferred with the leading nobles in Media, and they are all ready to espouse your cause. You may rely upon finding everything thus prepared for you here; come, therefore, without any delay.'

Excitement of Cyrus – Cyrus Accedes to Harpagus's Plan

Cyrus was thrown into a fever of excitement and agitation on reading this letter. He determined to accede to Harpagus's proposal. He revolved in his mind for some time the measures by which he could raise the necessary force. Of course, he could not openly announce his plan and enlist an army to effect it, for any avowed and public movement of that kind would be immediately made known to Astyages, who, by being thus forewarned of his enemies' designs, might take effectual measures to circumvent them. He determined to resort to deceit, or, as he called it, stratagem; nor did he probably have any distinct perception of the wrongfulness of such a mode of proceeding. The demon of war upholds and justifies falsehood and treachery, in all its forms, on the part of his votaries. He always applauds a forgery, a false pretence or a lie: he calls it a stratagem.

How to Raise an Army – The Day of Toil

Cyrus had a letter prepared, in the form of a commission from Astyages, appointing him commander of a body of Persian forces to be raised for the service of the king. Cyrus read the fabricated document in the public assembly of the Persians, and called upon all the warriors to join him. When they were organized, he ordered them to assemble on a certain day, at a place that he named, each one provided with a woodman's axe. When they were thus mustered, he marched them into a forest, and set them at work to clear a piece of ground. The army toiled all day, felling the trees, and piling them up to be burned. They cleared in this way, as Herodotus states, a piece of ground eighteen or twenty furlongs in extent. Cyrus kept them thus engaged in severe and incessant toil all day, giving them, too, only coarse food and little rest. At night he dismissed them, commanding them to assemble again the second day.

The Day of Festivity

On the second day, when they came together, they found a great banquet prepared for them, and Cyrus directed them to devote the day to feasting and making merry. There was an abundance of meats of all kinds, and rich wines in great profusion. The soldiers gave themselves up for the whole day to merriment and revelry. The toils and the hard fare of the day before had prepared them very effectually to enjoy the rest and the luxuries of this festival. They spent the hours in feasting about their campfires and reclining on the grass, where they amused themselves and one another by relating tales, or joining in merry songs and dances. At last, in the evening, Cyrus called them together, and asked them which day they had liked the best. They replied that there was nothing at all to like in the one, and nothing to be disliked in the other. They had had, on the first day, hard work and bad fare, and on the second, uninterrupted ease and the most luxurious pleasures.

Speech of Cyrus

'It is indeed so,' said Cyrus, 'and you have your destiny in your own hands to make your lives pass like either of these days, just as you choose. If you will follow me, you will enjoy ease, abundance and luxury. If you refuse, you must remain as you are, and toil on as you do now, and endure your present privations and hardships to the end of your days.' He then explained to them his designs. He told them that although Media was a great and powerful kingdom, still that they were as good soldiers as the Medes, and with the arrangements and preparations which he had made, they were sure of victory.

Ardour of the Soldiers

The soldiers received this proposal with great enthusiasm and joy. They declared themselves ready to follow Cyrus wherever he should lead them, and the whole body immediately commenced making preparations for the expedition. Astyages was, of course, soon informed of these proceedings. He sent an order to Cyrus, summoning him immediately into his presence. Cyrus sent back word, in reply, that Astyages would probably see him sooner than he wished, and went on vigorously with his preparations. When all was ready, the army marched, and, crossing the frontiers, they entered into Media.

Defection of Harpagus

In the meantime, Astyages had collected a large force, and, as had been anticipated by the conspirators, he put it under the command of Harpagus. Harpagus made known his design of going over to Cyrus as soon as he should meet him, to as large a portion of the army as he thought it prudent to admit to his confidence; the rest knew nothing of the plan; and thus the Median army advanced to meet the invaders, a part of the troops with minds intent on resolutely meeting and repelling their enemies, while the rest were secretly preparing to go over at once to their side.

The Battle

When the battle was joined, the honest part of the Median army fought valiantly at first, but soon, thunderstruck and utterly confounded at seeing themselves abandoned and betrayed by a large body of their comrades, they were easily overpowered by the triumphant Persians. Some were taken prisoners; some fled back to Astyages; and others, following the example of the deserters, went over to Cyrus's camp and swelled the numbers of his train. Cyrus, thus re-enforced by the accessions he had received, and encouraged by the flight or dispersion of all who still wished to oppose him, began to advance toward the capital.

Rage of Astyages – His Vengeance on the Magi

Astyages, when he heard of the defection of Harpagus and of the discomfiture of his army, was thrown into a perfect frensy of rage and hate. The long-dreaded prediction of his dream seemed now about to be fulfilled, and the magi, who had taught him that when Cyrus had once been made king of the boys in sport, there was no longer any danger of his aspiring to regal power, had proved themselves false. They had either intentionally deceived him, or they were ignorant themselves, and in that case they were worthless impostors. Although the danger from Cyrus's approach was imminent in the extreme, Astyages could not take any measures for guarding against it until he had first gratified the despotic cruelty of his nature by taking vengeance on these false pretenders. He directed to have them all seized and brought before him, and then, having upbraided them with bitter reproaches for their false predictions, he ordered them all to be crucified.

Defeat and Capture of Astyages

He then adopted the most decisive measures for raising an army. He ordered every man capable of bearing arms to come forward, and then, putting himself at the head of the immense force which he had thus raised, he advanced to meet his enemy. He supposed, no doubt, that he was sure of victory; but he underrated the power which the discipline, the resolution, the concentration and the terrible energy of Cyrus's troops gave to their formidable array. He was defeated. His army was totally cut to pieces, and he himself was taken prisoner.

Interview with Harpagus

Harpagus was present when he was taken, and he exulted in revengeful triumph over the fallen tyrant's ruin. Astyages was filled with rage and despair. Harpagus asked him what he thought now of the supper in which he had compelled a father to feed on the flesh of his child. Astyages, in reply, asked Harpagus whether he thought that the success of Cyrus was owing to what he had done. Harpagus replied that it was, and exultingly explained to Astyages the plots he had formed, and the preparations which he had made for Cyrus's invasion, so that Astyages might see that his destruction had been effected by Harpagus alone, in terrible retribution for the atrocious crime which he had committed so many years before, and for which the vengeance of the sufferer had slumbered, during the long interval, only to be more complete and overwhelming at last.

Astyages told Harpagus that he was a miserable wretch, the most foolish and most wicked of mankind. He was the most foolish, for having plotted to put power into another's hands which it would have been just as easy for him to have secured and retained in his own; and he was the most wicked, for having betrayed his country, and delivered it over to a foreign power, merely to gratify his own private revenge.

Cyrus King of Media and Persia – Confinement of Astyages – Acquiescence of the Medes

The result of this battle was the complete overthrow of the power and kingdom of Astyages, and the establishment of Cyrus on the throne of the united kingdom of Media and Persia. Cyrus treated his grandfather with kindness after his victory over him. He kept him confined, it is true, but it was probably that indirect and qualified sort of confinement which is all that is usually enforced in the case of princes and kings. In such cases, some extensive and often sumptuous residence is assigned to the illustrious prisoner, with grounds sufficiently extensive to afford every necessary range for recreation and exercise, and with bodies of troops for keepers, which have much more the form and appearance of military guards of honour attending on a prince, than of jailers confining a prisoner. It was probably in such an imprisonment as this that Astyages passed the remainder of his days. The people, having been wearied with his despotic tyranny, rejoiced in his downfall, and acquiesced very readily in the milder and more equitable government of Cyrus.

Death of Astyages

Astyages came to his death many years afterward, in a somewhat remarkable manner. Cyrus sent for him to come into Persia, where he was himself then residing. The officer who had Astyages in charge, conducted him, on the way, into a desolate wilderness, where he perished of fatigue, exposure and hunger. It was supposed that this was done in obedience to secret orders from Cyrus, who perhaps found the charge of such a prisoner a burden. The officer, however, was cruelly punished for the act; but even this may have been only for appearances, to divert the minds of men from all suspicion that Cyrus could himself have been an accomplice in such a crime.

Suddenness of Cyrus's Elevation

The whole revolution which has been described in this chapter, from its first inception to its final accomplishment, was affected in a very short period of time, and Cyrus thus found himself very unexpectedly and suddenly elevated to a throne.

Harpagus

Harpagus continued in his service, and became subsequently one of his most celebrated generals.

Chapter VI
The Oracles, BCE 547

Plans of Croesus

AS SOON AS CYRUS had become established on his throne as King of the Medes and Persians, his influence and power began to extend westward toward the confines of the empire of Croesus, king of Lydia. Croesus was aroused from the dejection and stupor into which the death of his son had plunged him, as related in a former chapter, by this threatening danger. He began to consider very earnestly what he could do to avert it.

The River Halys

The River Halys, a great river of Asia Minor, which flows northward into the Black Sea, was the eastern boundary of the Lydian empire. Croesus began to entertain the design of raising an army and crossing the Halys, to invade the empire of Cyrus, thinking that that would perhaps be safer policy than to wait for Cyrus to cross the Halys, and bring the war upon him. Still, the enterprise of invading Persia was a vast undertaking, and the responsibility great of being the aggressor in the contest. After carefully considering the subject in all its aspects, Croesus found himself still perplexed and undecided.

Nature of the Oracles

The Greeks had a method of looking into futurity, and of ascertaining, as they imagined, by supernatural means, the course of future events, which was peculiar to that people; at least no other nation seems ever to have practiced it in the precise form which prevailed among them. It was by means of the oracles. There were four or five localities in the Grecian countries which possessed, as the people thought, the property of inspiring persons who visited them, or of giving to some natural object certain supernatural powers by which future events could be foretold. The three most important of these oracles were situated respectively at Delphi, at Dodona and at the Oasis of Jupiter Ammon.

Situation of Delphi – The Gaseous Vapour – The Priestess – The Sacred Tripod

Delphi was a small town built in a sort of valley, shaped like an amphitheatre, on the southern side of Mount Parnassus. Mount Parnassus is north of the Peloponnesus, not very far from the shores of the Gulf of Corinth. Delphi was in a picturesque and romantic situation, with the mountain behind it, and steep, precipitous rocks descending to the level country before. These precipices answered instead of walls to defend the temple and the town. In very early times a cavern or fissure in the rocks was discovered at Delphi, from which there issued a stream of gaseous vapour, which produced strange effects on those who inhaled it. It was supposed to inspire them. People resorted to the place to obtain the benefit of these inspirations, and of the knowledge which they imagined they could obtain by means of them. Finally, a temple was built, and a priestess resided constantly in it, to inhale the vapour and give the responses. When she gave her answers to those who came to consult the oracle, she sat upon a sort of three-legged stool, which was called the sacred tripod. These stools were greatly celebrated as a very important part of the sacred apparatus of the place. This oracle became at last so renowned, that the greatest potentates, and even kings, came from great distances to consult it, and they made very rich and costly presents at the shrine when they came. These presents, it was supposed, tended to induce the god who presided over the oracle to give to those who made them favourable and auspicious replies. The deity that dictated the predictions of this oracle was Apollo.

There was another circumstance, besides the existence of the cave, which signalized the locality where this oracle was situated. The people believed that this spot was the exact centre of the earth, which of course they considered as one vast plain. There was an ancient story that Jupiter, in order to determine the central point of creation, liberated two eagles at the same time, in opposite quarters of the heavens, that they might fly toward one another, and so mark the middle point by the place of their meeting.

They Met at Delphi – The Oracle of Dodona – The Two Black Doves

Another of the most celebrated oracles was at Dodona. Dodona was northwest of Delphi, in the Epirus, which was a country in the western part of what is now Albania, and on the shores of the Adriatic Sea. The origin of the oracle at Dodona was, as the priestesses there told Herodotus, as follows: In very ancient times, two black doves were set at liberty in Thebes, which was a very venerable and sacred city of Egypt. One flew toward the north and the other toward the west. The former crossed the Mediterranean, and then continued its flight over the Peloponnesus, and over all the southern provinces of Greece, until it reached Dodona. There it alighted on a beech tree, and said, in a human voice, that that spot was divinely appointed for the seat of a sacred oracle. The other dove flew to the Oasis of Jupiter Ammon.

The Priestesses of Dodona – Manner of Obtaining Responses

There were three priestesses at Dodona in the days of Herodotus. Their names were Promenea, Timarete and Nicandre. The answers of the oracle were, for a time, obtained by the priestesses from some appearances which they observed in the sacred beech on which the dove alighted, when the tree was agitated by the wind. In later times, however, the responses were obtained in a still more singular manner. Then was a brazen statue of a man, holding a whip in his hand. The whip had three lashes, which were formed of brazen chains. At the end of each chain was an *astragalus*, as it was called, which was a row of little knots or knobs, such as were commonly appended to the lashes of whips used in those days for scourging criminals.

The Great Brazen Caldron

These heavy lashes hung suspended in the hand of the statue over a great brazen caldron, in such a manner that the wind would impel them, from time to time, against its sides, causing the caldron to ring and resound like a gong. There was, however, something in this resonance supernatural and divine; for, though it was not loud, it was very long continued, when once the margin of the caldron was touched, however gently, by the lashes. In fact, it was commonly said that if touched in the morning, it would be night before the reverberations would have died entirely away. Such a belief could be very easily sustained among the common people; for a large, open-mouthed vessel like the Dodona caldron, with thin sides formed of sonorous metal, might be kept in a state of continual vibration by the wind alone.

They who wished to consult this oracle came with rich presents both for the priestesses and for the shrine, and when they had made the offerings, and performed the preliminary ceremonies required, they propounded their questions to the priestesses, who obtained the replies by interpreting, according to certain rules which they had formed, the sounds emitted by the mysterious gong.

The Oasis of Jupiter Ammon – Discovery of the Oasis of Jupiter Ammon

The second black dove which took its flight from Thebes alighted, as we have already said, in the Oasis of Jupiter Ammon. This oasis was a small fertile spot in the midst of the deserts of Africa, west of Egypt, about a hundred miles from the Nile, and somewhat nearer than that to the Mediterranean Sea. It was first discovered in the following manner: A certain king was marching across the deserts, and his army, having exhausted their supplies of water, were on the point of perishing with thirst, when a ram mysteriously appeared, and took a position before them as their guide. They followed him, and at length came suddenly upon a green and fertile valley, many miles in length. The ram conducted them into this valley, and then suddenly vanished, and a copious fountain of water sprung up in the place where he had stood. The king, in gratitude for this divine interposition, consecrated the spot and built a temple upon it, which was called the temple of Jupiter Ammon. The dove alighted here, and ever afterward the oracles delivered by the priests of this temple were considered as divinely inspired.

Other Oracles – Mode of Consulting the Oracle

These three were the most important oracles. There were, however, many others of subordinate consequence, each of which had its own peculiar ceremonies, all senseless and absurd. At one there was a sort of oven-shaped cave in the rocks, the spot being enclosed by an artificial wall. The cave was about six feet wide and eight feet deep. The descent into it was by a ladder. Previously to consulting this oracle certain ceremonies were necessary, which it required several days to perform. The applicant was to offer sacrifices to many different deities, and to purify himself in various ways. He was then conducted to a stream in the neighbourhood of the oracle, where he was to be anointed and washed. Then he drank a certain magical water, called the water of forgetfulness, which made him forget all previous sorrows and cares. Afterward he drank of another enchanted cup, which contained the water of remembrance; this was to make him remember all that should be communicated to him in the cave. He then descended the ladder, and received within the cave the responses of the oracle.

Mystic Ceremonies

At another of these oracles, which was situated in Attica, the magic virtue was supposed to reside in a certain marble statue, carved in honour of an ancient and celebrated prophet, and placed in a temple. Whoever wished to consult this oracle must abstain from wine for three days, and from food of every kind for twenty-four hours preceding the application. He was then to offer a ram as a sacrifice; and afterward, taking the skin of the ram from the carcass, he was to spread it out before the statue and lie down upon it to sleep. The answers of the oracle came to him in his dreams.

Croesus Puts the Oracle to the Test

But to return to Croesus. He wished to ascertain, by consulting some of these oracles, what the result of his proposed invasion of the dominions of Cyrus would be, in case he should undertake it; and in order to determine which of the various oracles were most worthy of reliance, he conceived the plan of putting them all to a preliminary test. He effected this object in the following manner:

Manner of Doing It

He dispatched a number of messengers from Sardis, his capital, sending one to each of the various oracles. He directed these messengers to make their several journeys with all convenient dispatch; but, in order to provide for any cases of accidental detention or delay, he allowed them all one hundred days to reach their several places of destination. On the hundredth day from the time of their leaving Sardis, they were all to make applications to the oracles, and inquire what Croesus, king of Lydia, was doing at that time. Of course, he did not tell them what he should be doing; and as the oracles themselves could not possibly know how he was employed by any human powers, their answers would seem to test the validity of their claims to powers divine.

Return of the Messengers – The Replies

Croesus kept the reckoning of the days himself with great care, and at the hour appointed on the hundredth day, he employed himself in boiling the flesh of a turtle and of a lamb together in a brazen vessel. The vessel was covered with a lid, which was also of brass. He then awaited the return of the messengers. They came in due time, one after another, bringing the replies which they had severally obtained. The replies were all unsatisfactory, except that of the oracle at Delphi. This answer was in verse, as, in fact, the responses of that oracle always were. The priestess who sat upon the tripod was accustomed to give the replies in an incoherent and half-intelligible manner, as impostors are very apt to do in uttering prophecies, and then the attendant priests and secretaries wrote them out in verse.

The verse which the messenger brought back from the Delphic tripod was in Greek; but some idea of its style, and the import of it, is conveyed by the following imitation:

> *I number the sands, I measure the sea,*
> *What's hidden to others is known to me.*
> *The lamb and the turtle are simmering slow*
> *With brass above them and brass below.*

Croesus Decides in Favour of Delphi – His Costly Gifts

Of course, Croesus decided that the Delphic oracle was the one that he must rely upon for guidance in respect to his projected campaign. And he now began to prepare to consult it in a manner corresponding with the vast importance of the subject, and with his own boundless wealth. He provided the most extraordinary and sumptuous presents. Some of these treasures were to be deposited in the temple, as sacred gifts, for permanent preservation there. Others were to be offered as a burnt sacrifice in honour of the god. Among the latter, besides an incredible number of living victims, he caused to be prepared a great number of couches, magnificently decorated with silver and gold, and goblets and other vessels of gold, and dresses of various kinds richly embroidered and numerous other articles, all intended to be used in the ceremonies preliminary to his application to the oracle. When the time arrived, a vast concourse of people assembled to witness the spectacle. The animals were sacrificed, and the people feasted on the flesh; and when these ceremonies were concluded, the couches, the goblets, the utensils of every kind, the dresses – everything, in short, which had been used on the occasion, were heaped up into one great sacrificial pile, and set on fire. Everything that was combustible was consumed, while the gold was melted, and ran into plates of great size, which were afterward taken out from the ashes. Thus, it was the workmanship only of these articles which was destroyed and lost by the fire. The gold, in which the chief value consisted, was saved. It was gold from the River Pactolus.

The Silver Tank – The Golden Lion

Besides these articles, there were others made, far more magnificent and costly, for the temple itself. There was a silver cistern or tank, large enough to hold three thousand gallons of wine. This tank was to be used by the inhabitants of Delphi in their great festivals. There was also a smaller cistern, or immense goblet, as it might, perhaps, more properly be called, which was made of gold. There were also many other smaller presents, such as basins, vases and statues, all of silver and gold, and of the most costly workmanship. The gold, too, which had been taken from the fire, was cast again, a part of it being formed into the image of a lion, and the rest into large plates of metal for the lion to stand upon. The image was then set up upon the plates, within the precincts of the temple.

The Bread Maker – Her History

There was one piece of statuary which Croesus presented to the oracle at Delphi, which was, in some respects, more extraordinary than any of the rest. It was called the bread maker. It was an image representing a woman, a servant in the household of Croesus, whose business it was to bake the bread. The reason that induced Croesus to honour this bread-maker with a statue of gold was, that on one occasion during his childhood she had saved his life. The mother of Croesus died when he was young, and his father married a second time. The second wife wished to have some one of her children, instead of Croesus, succeed to her husband's throne. In order, therefore, to remove Croesus out of the way, she prepared some poison and gave it to the bread maker, instructing her to put it into the bread which Croesus was to eat. The bread maker received the poison and promised to obey. But, instead of doing so, she revealed the intended murder to Croesus, and gave the poison to the queen's own children. In gratitude for this fidelity to him, Croesus, when he came to the throne, caused this statue to be made, and now he placed it at Delphi, where he supposed it would forever remain. The memory of his faithful servant was indeed immortalized by the measure, though the statue itself, as well as all these other treasures, in process of time disappeared. In fact, statues of brass or of marble generally make far more durable monuments than statues of gold; and no structure or object of art is likely to be very permanent among mankind unless the workmanship is worth more than the material.

Croesus did not proceed himself to Delphi with these presents, but sent them by the hands of trusty messengers, who were instructed to perform the ceremonies required, to offer the gifts, and then to make inquiries of the oracle in the following terms.

The Oracle Questioned

'Croesus, the sovereign of Lydia and of various other kingdoms, in return for the wisdom which has marked your former declarations, has sent you these gifts. He now furthermore desires to know whether it is safe for him to proceed against the Persians, and if so, whether it is best for him to seek the assistance of any allies.' The answer was as follows:

The Response

'If Croesus crosses the Halys, and prosecutes a war with Persia, a mighty empire will be overthrown. It will be best for him to form an alliance with the most powerful states of Greece.'

Delight of Croesus

Croesus was extremely pleased with this response. He immediately resolved on undertaking the expedition against Cyrus; and to express his gratitude for so favourable an answer to his questions, he sent to Delphi to inquire what was the number of inhabitants in the city, and, when the answer was reported to him, he sent a present of a sum of money to everyone. The Delphians, in their turn, conferred special privileges and honours upon the Lydians and upon Croesus in respect to their oracle, giving them the precedence in all future consultations, and conferring upon them other marks of distinction and honour.

Supplementary Inquiry

At the time when Croesus sent his present to the inhabitants of Delphi, he took the opportunity to address another inquiry to the oracle, which was, whether his power would ever decline. The oracle replied in a couplet of Greek verse, similar in its style to the one recorded on the previous occasion. It was as follows:

> Whene'er a mule shall mount upon the Median throne,
> Then, and not till then, shall great Croesus fear to lose his own.'

Croesus's Feeling of Security

This answer pleased the king quite as much as the former one had done. The allusion to the contingency of a mule's reigning in Media he very naturally regarded as only a rhetorical and mystical mode of expressing an utter impossibility. Croesus considered himself and the continuance of his power as perfectly secure. He was fully confirmed in his determination to organize his expedition without any delay, and to proceed immediately to the proper measures for obtaining the Grecian alliance and aid which the oracle had recommended. The plans which he formed, and the events which resulted, will be described in subsequent chapters.

Nature of the Oracles – Means by Which the Credit of the Oracles Was Sustained

In respect to these Grecian oracles, it is proper here to state, that there has been much discussion among scholars on the question how they were enabled to maintain, for so long a period, so extended a credit among a people as intellectual and well-informed as the Greeks. It was doubtless by means of a variety of contrivances and influences that this end was attained. There is a natural love of the marvellous among the humbler classes in all countries, which leads them to be very ready to believe in what is mystic and supernatural; and they accordingly exaggerate and colour such real incidents as occur under any strange or remarkable circumstances, and invest any unusual phenomena which they witness with a miraculous or supernatural interest. The cave at Delphi might really have emitted gases which would produce quite striking effects upon those who inhaled them; and how easy it would be for those who witnessed these effects to imagine that some divine and miraculous powers must exist in the aerial current which produced them. The priests and priestesses, who inhabited the temples in which these oracles were contained, had, of course, a strong interest in keeping up the belief of their reality in the minds of the community; so were, in fact, all the inhabitants of the cities which sprung up around them. They derived their support from the visitors who frequented these places, and they contrived various ways for drawing contributions, both of money and gifts, from all who came. In one case there was a sacred stream near an oracle, where persons, on permission from the priests, were allowed to bathe. After the bathing, they were expected to throw pieces of money into the stream. What afterward, in such cases, became of the money, it is not difficult to imagine.

Whether the Priests Were Impostors

Nor is it necessary to suppose that all these priests and priestesses were impostors. Having been trained up from infancy to believe that the inspirations were real, they would continue to look upon them as such all their lives. Even at the present day we shall all, if we closely scrutinize our mental habits, find ourselves continuing to take for granted, in our maturer years, what we inconsiderately imbibed or were erroneously taught in infancy, and that, often, in cases where the most obvious dictates of reason, or even the plain testimony of our senses, might show us that our notions are false. The priests and priestesses, therefore, who imposed on the rest of mankind, may have been as honestly and as deep in the delusion themselves as any of their dupes.

Answers of the Oracles

The answers of the oracles were generally vague and indefinite, and susceptible of almost any interpretation, according to the result. Whenever the event corresponded with the prediction, or could be made to correspond with it by the ingenuity of the commentators, the story of the coincidence would, of course, be everywhere spread abroad, becoming more striking and more exact at each repetition. Where there was a failure, it would not be direct and absolute, on account of the vagueness and indefiniteness of the response, and there would therefore be no interest felt in hearing or in circulating the story. The cases, thus, which would tend to establish the truth of the oracle, would be universally known and remembered, while those of a contrary bearing would be speedily forgotten.

Collusion Between the Priests and Those Who Consulted the Oracle

There is no doubt, however, that in many cases the responses were given in collusion with the one who consulted the oracle, for the purpose of deceiving others. For example, let us suppose that Croesus wished to establish strongly the credibility of the Delphic oracle in the minds of his countrymen, in order to encourage them to enlist in his armies, and to engage in the enterprise which he was contemplating against Cyrus with resolution and confidence; it would have been easy for him to have let the priestess at Delphi know what he was doing on the day when he sent to inquire, and thus himself to have directed her answer. Then, when his messengers returned, he would appeal to the answer as proof of the reality of the inspiration which seemed to furnish it. Alexander the Great certainly did, in this way, act in collusion with the priests at the temple of Jupiter Ammon.

Chapter VII
The Conquest of Lydia, BCE 546

§

Reasons which induced Croesus to invade Media

THERE WERE, IN FACT, three inducements which combined their influence on the mind of Croesus, in leading him to cross the Halys, and invade the dominions of the Medes and Persians: first, he was ambitious to extend his own empire; secondly, he feared that if he did not attack Cyrus, Cyrus would himself cross the Halys and attack him; and, thirdly, he felt under some obligation to consider himself the ally of Astyages, and thus bound to espouse his cause, and to aid him in putting down, if possible, the usurpation of Cyrus, and in recovering his throne. He felt under this obligation because Astyages was his brother-in-law; for the latter had married, many years before, a daughter of Alyattes, who was the father of Croesus. This, as Croesus thought, gave him a just title to interfere between the dethroned king and the rebel who had dethroned him. Under the influence of all these reasons combined, and encouraged by the responses of the oracle, he determined on attempting the invasion.

The Lacedaemonians

The first measure which he adopted was to form an alliance with the most powerful of the states of Greece, as he had been directed to do by the oracle. After much inquiry and consideration, he concluded that the Lacedaemonian state was the most powerful. Their chief city was Sparta, in the Peloponnesus. They were a warlike, stern and indomitable race of men, capable of bearing every possible hardship, and of enduring every degree of fatigue and toil, and they desired nothing but military glory for their reward. This was a species of wages which it was very easy to pay; much more easy to furnish than coin, even for Croesus, notwithstanding the abundant supplies of gold which he was accustomed to obtain from the sands of the Pactolus.

Ambassadors to Sparta

Croesus sent ambassadors to Sparta to inform the people of the plans which he contemplated, and to ask their aid. He had been instructed, he said, by the oracle at Delphi, to seek the alliance of the most powerful of the states of Greece, and he accordingly made application to them. They were gratified with the compliment implied in selecting them, and acceded readily to his proposal. Besides, they were already on very friendly terms with Croesus; for, some years before, they had sent to him to procure some gold for a statue which they had occasion to erect, offering to give an equivalent for the value of it in such productions as their country afforded. Croesus supplied them with the gold that they needed, but generously refused to receive any return.

Preparations of Croesus – The Counsel of Sardaris

In the meantime, Croesus went on, energetically, at Sardis, making the preparations for his campaign. One of his counsellors, whose name was Sardaris, ventured, one day, strongly to dissuade him from undertaking the expedition. 'You have nothing to gain by it,' said he, 'if you succeed, and everything to lose if you fail. Consider what sort of people these Persians are whom you are going to combat. They live in the most rude and simple manner, without luxuries, without pleasures, without wealth. If you conquer their country, you will find nothing in it worth bringing away. On the other hand, if they conquer you, they will come like a vast band of plunderers into Lydia, where there is everything to tempt and reward them. I counsel you to leave them alone, and to remain on this side the Halys, thankful if Cyrus will be contented to remain on the other.'

But Croesus was not in a mood of mind to be persuaded by such reasoning.

The Army Begins to March – Thales the Milesian

When all things were ready, the army commenced its march and moved eastward, through one province of Asia Minor after another, until they reached the Halys. This river is a considerable stream, which rises in the interior of the country, and flows northward into the Black Sea. The army encamped on the banks of it, and some plan was to be formed for crossing the stream. In accomplishing this object, Croesus was aided by a very celebrated engineer who accompanied his army, named Thales. Thales was a native of Miletus, and is generally called in history, Thales the Milesian. He was a very able mathematician and calculator, and many accounts remain of the discoveries and performances by which he acquired his renown.

Mathematical Skill of Thales

For example, in the course of his travels, he at one time visited Egypt, and while there, he contrived a very simple way of measuring the height of the pyramids.

He set up a pole on the plain in an upright position, and then measured the pole and also its shadow. He also measured the length of the shadow of the pyramid. He then calculated the height of the pyramid by this proportion: as the length of shadow of the pole is to that of the pole itself, so is the length of the shadow of the pyramid to its height.

Thales was an astronomer as well as a philosopher and engineer. He learned more exactly the true length of the year than it had been known before; and he also made some calculations of eclipses, at least so far as to predict the year in which they would happen. One eclipse which he predicted happened to occur on the day of a great battle between two contending armies. It was cloudy, so that the combatants could not see the sun. This circumstance, however, which concealed the eclipse itself, only made the darkness which was caused by it the more intense. The armies were much terrified at this sudden cessation of the light of day, and supposed it to be a warning from heaven that they should desist from the combat.

His Theorems

Thales the Milesian was the author of several of the geometrical theorems and demonstrations now included in the Elements of Euclid. The celebrated fifth proposition of the first book, so famous among all the modern nations of Europe as the great stumbling block in the way of beginners in the study of geometry, was his. The discovery of the truth expressed in this proposition, and of the complicated demonstration which establishes it, was certainly a much greater mathematical performance than the measuring of the altitude of the pyramids by their shadow.

Ingenious Plan of Thales for Crossing the Halys

But to return to Croesus. Thales undertook the work of transporting the army across the river. He examined the banks, and found, at length, a spot where the land was low and level for some distance from the stream. He caused the army to be brought up to the river at this point, and to be encamped there, as near to the bank as possible, and in as compact a form. He then employed a vast number of labourers to cut a new channel for the waters, behind the army, leading out from the river above, and re-joining it again at a little distance below. When this channel was finished, he turned the river into its new course, and then the army passed without difficulty over the former bed of the stream.

Advance of Cyrus

The Halys being thus passed, Croesus moved on in the direction of Media. But he soon found that he had not far to go to find his enemy. Cyrus had heard of his plans through deserters and spies, and he had for some time been advancing to meet him. One after the other of the nations through whose dominions he had passed, he had subjected to his sway, or, at least, brought under his influence by treaties and alliances, and had received from them all re-enforcements to swell the numbers of his army. One nation only remained – the Babylonians. They were on the side of Croesus. They were jealous of the growing power of the Medes and Persians, and had made a league with Croesus, promising to aid him in the war. The other nations of the East were in alliance with Cyrus, and he was slowly moving on, at the head of an immense combined force, toward the Halys, at the very time when Croesus was crossing the stream.

Preparations for Battle

The scouts, therefore, that preceded the army of Croesus on its march, soon began to fall back into the camp, with intelligence that there was a large armed force coming on to meet them, the advancing columns filling all the roads, and threatening to overwhelm them. The scouts from the army of Cyrus carried back similar intelligence to him. The two armies accordingly halted and began to prepare for battle. The place of their meeting was called Pteria. It was in the province of Cappadocia, and toward the eastern part of Asia Minor.

Great Battle at Pteria – Undecisive Result

A great battle was fought at Pteria. It was continued all day, and remained undecided when the sun went down. The combatants separated when it became dark, and each withdrew from the field. Each king found, it seems, that his antagonist was more formidable than he had imagined, and on the morning after the battle they both seemed inclined to remain in their respective encampments, without evincing any disposition to renew the contest.

Croesus Returns to Sardis

Croesus, in fact, seems to have considered that he was fortunate in having so far repulsed the formidable invasion which Cyrus had been intending for him. He considered Cyrus's army as repulsed, since they had withdrawn from the field, and showed no disposition to return to it. He had no doubt that Cyrus would now go back to Media again, having found how well-prepared Croesus had been to receive him. For himself, he concluded that he ought to be satisfied with the advantage which he had already gained, as the result of one campaign, and return again to Sardis to recruit his army, the force of which had been considerably impaired by the battle, and so postpone the grand invasion till the next season. He accordingly set out on his return. He dispatched messengers, at the same time, to Babylon, to Sparta, to Egypt and to other countries with which he was in alliance, informing these various nations of the great battle of Pteria and its results, and asking them to send him, early in the following spring, all the re-enforcements that they could command, to join him in the grand campaign which he was going to make the next season.

He continued his march homeward without any interruption, sending off, from time to time, as he was moving through his own dominions, such portions of his troops as desired to return to their homes, enjoining upon them to come back to him in the spring. By this temporary disbanding of a portion of his army, he saved the expense of maintaining them through the winter.

Cyrus Follows Him

Very soon after Croesus arrived at Sardis, the whole country in the neighbourhood of the capital was thrown into a state of universal alarm by the news that Cyrus was close at hand. It seems that Cyrus had remained in the vicinity of Pteria long enough to allow Croesus to return, and to give him time to dismiss his troops and establish himself securely in the city. He then suddenly resumed his march, and came on toward Sardis with the utmost possible dispatch. Croesus, in fact, had no announcement of his approach until he heard of his arrival.

Confusion and Alarm at Sardis

All was now confusion and alarm, both within and without the city. Croesus hastily collected all the forces that he could command. He sent immediately to the neighbouring cities, summoning all the troops in them to hasten to the capital. He enrolled all the inhabitants of the city that were capable of bearing arms. By these means he collected, in a very short time, quite a formidable force, which he drew up, in battle array, on a great plain not far from the city, and there waited, with much anxiety and solicitude, for Cyrus to come on.

The Lydian Cavalry – Nature of Cavalry – Manner of Receiving a Cavalry Charge

The Lydian army was superior to that of Cyrus in cavalry, and as the place where the battle was to be fought was a plain, which was the kind of ground most favourable for the operations of that species of force, Cyrus felt some solicitude in respect to the impression which might be made by it on his army. Nothing is more terrible than the onset of a squadron of horse when charging an enemy upon the field of battle. They come in vast bodies, sometimes consisting of many thousands, with the speed of the wind, the men flourishing their sabres and rending the air with the most unearthly cries, those in advance being driven irresistibly on by the weight and impetus of the masses behind. The dreadful torrent bears down and overwhelms everything that attempts to resist its way. They trample one another and their enemies together promiscuously in the dust; the foremost of the column press on with the utmost fury, afraid quite as much of the headlong torrent of friends coming on behind them, as of the line of fixed and motionless enemies who stand ready to receive them before. These enemies, stationed to withstand the charge, arrange themselves in triple or quadruple rows, with the shafts of their spears planted against the ground, and the points directed forward and upward to receive the advancing horsemen. These spears transfix and kill the foremost horses; but those that come on behind, leaping and plunging over their fallen companions, soon break through the lines and put their enemies to flight, in a scene of indescribable havoc and confusion.

The Camels – Cyrus Opposes Them to the Cavalry

Croesus had large bodies of horse, while Cyrus had no efficient troops to oppose them. He had a great number of camels in the rear of his army, which had been employed as beasts of burden to transport the baggage and stores of the army on their march. Cyrus concluded to make the experiment of opposing these camels to the cavalry. It is frequently said by the ancient historians that the horse has a natural antipathy to the camel, and cannot bear either the smell or the sight of one, though this is not found to be the case at the present day. However, the fact might have been in this respect, Cyrus determined to arrange the camels in his front as he advanced into battle. He accordingly ordered the baggage to be removed, and, releasing their ordinary drivers from the charge of them, he assigned each one to the care of a soldier, who was to mount him, armed with a spear. Even if the supposed antipathy of the horse for the camel did not take effect, Cyrus thought that their large and heavy bodies, defended by the spears of their riders, would afford the most effectual means of resistance against the shock of the Lydian squadrons that he was now able to command.

The Battle Fought – Cyrus Victorious – Situation of Sardis

The battle commenced, and the squadrons of horse came on. But, as soon as they came near the camels, it happened that, either from the influence of the antipathy above referred to, or from alarm at the novelty of the spectacle of such huge and misshapen beasts, or else because of the substantial resistance which the camels and the spears of their riders made to the shock of their charge, the horses were soon thrown into confusion and put to flight. In fact, a general panic seized them, and they became totally unmanageable. Some threw their riders; others, seized with a sort of frenzy, became entirely independent of control. They turned, and trampled the foot soldiers of their own army under foot, and threw the whole body into disorder. The consequence was, that the army of Croesus was wholly defeated; they fled in confusion, and crowded in vast throngs through the gates into the city, and fortified themselves there.

Cyrus advanced to the city, invested it closely on all sides, and commenced a siege. But the appearances were not very encouraging. The walls were lofty, thick and strong, and the numbers within the city were amply sufficient to guard them. Nor was the prospect much more promising of being soon able to reduce the city by famine. The wealth of Croesus had enabled him to lay up almost inexhaustible stores of food and clothing, as well as treasures of silver and gold. He hoped, therefore, to be able to hold out against the besiegers until help should come from some of his allies. He had sent messengers to them, asking them to come to his rescue without any delay, before he was shut up in the city.

Its Walls – An Ancient Legend

The city of Sardis was built in a position naturally strong, and one part of the wall passed over rocky precipices which were considered entirely impassable. There was a sort of glen or rocky gorge in this quarter, outside of the walls, down which dead bodies were thrown on one occasion subsequently, at a time when the city was besieged, and beasts and birds of prey fed upon them there undisturbed, so lonely was the place and so desolate. In fact, the walls that crowned these precipices were considered absolutely inaccessible, and were very slightly built and very feebly guarded. There was an ancient legend that, a long time before, when a certain Males was king of Lydia, one of his wives had a son in the form of a lion, whom they called Leon, and an oracle declared that if this Leon were carried around the walls of the city, it would be rendered impregnable, and should never be taken. They carried Leon, therefore, around, so far as the regular walls extended. When they came to this precipice of rocks, they returned, considering that this part of the city was impregnable without any such ceremony. A spur or eminence from the mountain of Tmolus, which was behind the city, projected into it at this point, and there was a strong citadel built upon its summit.

Cyrus Besieges the City – The Reconnaissance – The Walls Scaled

Cyrus continued the siege fourteen days, and then he determined that he must, in some way or other, find the means of carrying it by assault, and to do this he must find some place to scale the walls. He accordingly sent a party of horsemen around to explore every part, offering them a large reward if they would find any place where an entrance could be affected. The horsemen made the circuit, and reported that their search had been in vain. At length a certain soldier, named Hyraeades, after studying for some time the precipices on the side which had been deemed inaccessible, saw a sentinel, who was stationed on the walls above, leave his post and come climbing down the rocks for some distance to get his helmet, which had accidentally dropped down. Hyraeades watched him both as he descended and as he returned. He reflected on this discovery, communicated it to others, and the practicability of scaling the rock and the walls at that point was discussed. In the end, the attempt was made and was successful. Hyraeades went up first, followed by a few daring spirits who were ambitious of the glory of the exploit. They were not at first observed from above. The way being thus shown, great numbers followed on, and so large a force succeeded in thus gaining an entrance that the city was taken.

Storming of the City – Croesus Made Prisoner

In the dreadful confusion and din of the storming of the city, Croesus himself had a very narrow escape from death. He was saved by the miraculous speaking of his deaf and dumb son – at least such is the story. Cyrus had given positive orders to his soldiers, both before the great battle on the plain and during the siege, that, though they might slay whomever else they pleased, they must not harm Croesus, but must take him alive. During the time of the storming of the town, when the streets were filled with infuriated soldiers, those on the one side wild with the excitement of triumph, and those on the other maddened with rage and despair, a party, rushing along, overtook Croesus and his helpless son, whom the unhappy father, it seems, was making a desperate effort to save. The Persian soldiers were about to transfix Croesus with their spears, when the son, who had never spoken before, called out, 'It is Croesus; do not kill him.' The soldiers were arrested by the words, and saved the monarch's life. They made him prisoner, and bore him away to Cyrus.

Croesus had sent, a long time before, to inquire of the Delphic oracle by what means the power of speech could be restored to his son. The answer was, that

that was a boon which he had better not ask; for the day on which he should hear his son speak for the first time, would be the darkest and most unhappy day of his life.

The Funeral Pile – Anguish and Despair of Crœsus

Cyrus had not ordered his soldiers to spare the life of Croesus in battle from any sentiment of humanity toward him, but because he wished to have his case reserved for his own decision. When Croesus was brought to him a captive, he ordered him to be put in chains, and carefully guarded. As soon as some degree of order was restored in the city, a large funeral pile was erected, by his directions, in a public square, and Croesus was brought to the spot. Fourteen Lydian young men, the sons, probably, of the most prominent men in the state, were with him. The pile was large enough for them all, and they were placed upon it. They were all laid upon the wood. Croesus raised himself and looked around, surveying with extreme consternation and horror the preparations which were making for lighting the pile. His heart sank within him as he thought of the dreadful fate that was before him. The spectators stood by in solemn silence, awaiting the end. Croesus broke this awful pause by crying out, in a tone of anguish and despair, 'Oh Solon! Solon! Solon!'

The Saying of Solon – Croesus is Saved

The officers who had charge of the execution asked him what he meant. Cyrus, too, who was himself personally superintending the scene, asked for an explanation. Croesus was, for a time, too much agitated and distracted to reply. There were difficulties in respect to language, too, which embarrassed the conversation, as the two kings could speak to each other only through an interpreter. At length Croesus gave an account of his interview with Solon, and of the sentiment which the philosopher had expressed, that no one could decide whether a man was truly prosperous and happy till it was determined how his life was to end. Cyrus was greatly interested in this narrative; but, in the meantime, the interpreting of the conversation had been slow, a considerable period had elapsed, and the officers had lighted the fire. The pile had been made extremely combustible, and the fire was rapidly making its way through the whole mass. Cyrus eagerly ordered it to be extinguished. The efforts which the soldiers made for this purpose seemed, at first, likely to be fruitless; but they were aided very soon by a sudden shower of rain, which, coming down from the mountains, began, just at this time, to fall; and thus the flames were extinguished, and Croesus and the captives saved.

He Becomes Cyrus's Friend

Cyrus immediately, with a fickleness very common among great monarchs in the treatment of both enemies and favourites, began to consider Croesus as his friend. He ordered him to be unbound, brought him near his person and treated him with great consideration and honour.

Croesus Sends His Fetters to the Oracle at Delphi

Croesus remained after this for a long time with Cyrus, and accompanied him in his subsequent campaigns. He was very much incensed at the oracle at Delphi for having deceived him by its false responses and predictions, and thus led him into the terrible snare into which he had fallen. He procured the fetters with which he had been chained when placed upon the pile, and sent them to Delphi with orders that they should be thrown down upon the threshold of the temple – the visible symbol of his captivity and ruin – as a reproach to the oracle for having deluded him and caused his destruction. In doing this, the messengers were to ask the oracle whether imposition like that which had been practiced on Croesus was the kind of gratitude it evinced to one who had enriched it by such a profusion of offerings and gifts.

Explanations of the Priests

To this the priests of the oracle said in reply, that the destruction of the Lydian dynasty had long been decreed by the Fates, in retribution for the guilt of Gyges, the founder of the line. He had murdered his master, and usurped the throne, without any title to it whatever. The judgments of Heaven had been denounced upon Gyges for this crime, to fall on himself or on some of his descendants. The Pythian Apollo at Delphi had done all in his power to postpone the falling of the blow until after the death of Croesus, on account of the munificent benefactions which he had made to the oracle; but he had been unable to effect it: the decrees of Fate were inexorable. All that the oracle could do was to postpone – as it had done, it said, for three years – the execution of the sentence, and to give Croesus warning of the evil that was impending. This had been done by announcing to him that his crossing the Halys would cause the destruction of a mighty empire, meaning that of Lydia, and also by informing him that when he should find a mule upon the throne of Media he must expect to lose his own. Cyrus, who was descended, on the father's side, from the Persian stock, and on the mother's from that of Media, was the hybrid sovereign represented by the mule.

Their Adroitness and Dexterity

When this answer was reported to Croesus, it is said that he was satisfied with the explanations, and admitted that the oracle was right, and that he himself had been unreasonable and wrong. However this may be, it is certain that, among mankind at large, since Croesus's day, there has been a great disposition to overlook whatever of criminality there may have been in the falsehood and imposture of the oracle, through admiration of the adroitness and dexterity which its ministers evinced in saving themselves from exposure.

Chapter VIII
The Conquest of Babylon, BCE 544–538

Babylon

IN HIS ADVANCE toward the dominions of Croesus in Asia Minor, Cyrus had passed to the northward of the great and celebrated city of Babylon. Babylon was on the Euphrates, toward the southern part of Asia. It was the capital of a large and very fertile region, which extended on both sides of the Euphrates toward the Persian Gulf. The limits of the country, however, which was subject to Babylon, varied very much at different times, as they were extended or contracted by revolutions and wars.

The River Euphrates – Canals

The River Euphrates was the great source of fertility for the whole region through which it flowed. The country watered by this river was very densely populated, and the inhabitants were industrious and peaceable, cultivating their land, and living quietly and happily on its fruits. The surface was intersected with canals, which the people had made for conveying the water of the river over the land for the purpose of irrigating it. Some of these canals were navigable. There was one great trunk which passed from the Euphrates to the Tigris, supplying many minor canals by the way, that was navigable for vessels of considerable burden.

Curious Boats – Their Mode of Construction – Primitive Navigation

The traffic of the country was, however, mainly conducted by means of boats of moderate size, the construction of which seemed to Herodotus very curious and remarkable. The city was enormously large, and required immense supplies of food, which were brought down in these boats from the agricultural country above. The boats were made in the following manner: first a frame was built, of the shape of the intended boat, broad and shallow, and with the stem and stern of the same form. This frame was made of willows, like a basket, and, when finished, was covered with a sheathing of skins. A layer of reeds was then spread over the bottom of the boat to protect the frame, and to distribute evenly the pressure of the cargo. The boat, thus finished, was laden with the produce of the country, and was then floated down the river to Babylon. In this navigation the boatmen were careful to protect the leather sheathing from injury by avoiding all contact with rocks, or even with the gravel of the shores. They kept their craft in the middle of the stream by means of two oars, or, rather, an oar and a paddle, which were worked, the first at the bows, and the second at the stern. The advance of the boat was in some measure accelerated by these boatmen, though their main function was to steer their vessel by keeping it out of eddies and away from projecting points of land, and directing its course to those parts of the stream where the current was swiftest, and where it would consequently be borne forward most rapidly to its destination.

Return of the Boatmen

These boats were generally of very considerable size, and they carried, in addition to their cargo and crew, one or more beasts of burden – generally asses or mules. These animals were allowed the pleasure, if any pleasure it was to them, of sailing thus idly down the stream, for the sake of having them at hand at the end of the voyage, to carry back again, up the country, the skins, which constituted the most valuable portion of the craft they sailed in. It was found that these skins, if carefully preserved, could be easily transported up the river, and would answer the purpose of a second voyage. Accordingly, when the boats arrived at Babylon, the cargo was sold, the boats were broken up, the skins were folded into packs, and in this form the mules carried them up the river again, the boatmen driving the mules as they walked by their side.

Extent of Babylon – Parks, Gardens, Palaces, etc.

Babylon was a city of immense extent and magnitude. In fact, the accounts given of the space which it covered have often been considered incredible. A great deal of this space was, however, occupied by parks and gardens connected with the royal palaces, and by open squares. Then, besides, the houses occupied by the common people in the ancient cities were of fewer stories in height, and consequently more extended on the ground, than those built in modern times. In fact, it is probable that, in many instances, they were mere ranges of huts and hovels, as is the case, indeed, to a considerable extent, in poorer countries, at the present day, so that it is not at all impossible that even so large an area as four or five times the size of London may have been included within the fortifications of the city.

The Walls of Babylon – Marvellous Accounts

In respect to the walls of the city, very extraordinary and apparently contradictory accounts are given by the various ancient authors who described them. Some make them seventy-five and others two or three hundred feet high. There have been many discussions in respect to the comparative credibility of these several statements, and some ingenious attempts have been made to reconcile them. It is not, however, at all surprising that there should be such a diversity in the dimensions given, for the walling of an ancient city was seldom of the same height in all places. The structure necessarily varied according to the nature of the ground, being high wherever the ground without was such as to give the enemy an advantage in an attack, and lower in other situations, where the conformation of the surface was such as to afford, of itself, a partial protection. It is not, perhaps, impossible that, at some particular points – as, for example, across glens and ravines, or along steep declivities – the walls of Babylon may have been raised even to the very extraordinary height which Herodotus ascribes to them.

The walls were made of bricks, and the bricks were formed of clay and earth, which was dug from a trench made outside of the lines. This trench served the purpose of a ditch, to strengthen the fortification when the wall was completed. The water from the river, and from streams flowing toward the river, was admitted to these ditches on every side, and kept them always full.

The Ditches

The sides of these ditches were lined with bricks too, which were made, like those of the walls, from the earth obtained from the excavations. They used for all this masonry a cement made from a species of bitumen, which was found in great quantities floating down one of the rivers which flowed into the Euphrates, in the neighbourhood of Babylon.

Streets and Gates

The River Euphrates itself flowed through the city. There was a breastwork or low wall along the banks of it on either side, with openings at the terminations of the streets leading to the water, and flights of steps to go down. These openings were secured by gates of brass, which, when closed, would prevent an enemy from gaining access to the city from the river. The great streets, which terminated thus at the river on one side, extended to the walls of the city on the other, and they were crossed by other streets at right angles to them. In the outer walls of the city, at the extremities of all these streets, were massive gates of brass, with hinges and frames of the same metal. There were a hundred of these gates in all. They were guarded by watchtowers on the walls above. The watchtowers were built on both the inner and outer faces of the wall, and the wall itself was so broad that there was room between these watchtowers for a chariot and four to drive and turn.

Palace of the King – Temple of Belus

The river, of course, divided the city into two parts. The king's palace was in the centre of one of these divisions, within a vast circular enclosure, which contained the palace buildings, together with the spacious courts, parks and gardens pertaining to them. In the centre of the other division was a corresponding enclosure, which contained the great temple of Belus. Here there was a very lofty tower, divided into eight separate towers, one above another, with a winding staircase to ascend to the summit. In the upper story was a sort of chapel, with a couch, a table and other furniture for use in the sacred ceremonies, all of gold. Above this, on the highest platform of all, was a grand observatory, where the Babylonian astrologers made their celestial observations.

The Bridge – Sculptures

There was a bridge across the river, connecting one section of the city with the other, and it is said that there was a subterranean passage under the river also, which was used as a private communication between two public edifices – palaces or citadels – which were situated near the extremities of the bridge. All these constructions were of the most grand and imposing character. In addition to the architectural magnificence of the buildings, the gates and walls were embellished with a great variety of sculptures: images of animals, of every form and in every attitude; and men, single and in groups, models of great sovereigns, and representations of hunting scenes, battle scenes and great events in the Babylonian history.

The Hanging Gardens – Construction
of the Gardens

The most remarkable, however, of all the wonders of Babylon – though perhaps not built till after Cyrus's time – were what were called the hanging gardens. Although called the hanging gardens, they were not suspended in any manner, as the name might denote, but were supported upon arches and walls. The arches and walls sustained a succession of terraces, rising one above another, with broad flights of steps for ascending to them, and on these terraces the gardens were made. The upper terrace, or platform, was several hundred feet from the ground; so high, that it was necessary to build arches upon arches within, in order to attain the requisite elevation. The lateral thrust of these arches was sustained by a wall twenty-five feet in thickness, which surrounded the garden on all sides, and rose as high as the lowermost tier of arches, upon which would, of course, be concentrated the pressure and weight of all the pile. The whole structure thus formed a sort of artificial hill, square in form, and rising, in a succession of terraces, to a broad and level area upon the top. The extent of this grand square upon the summit was four hundred feet upon each side.

The Platform and Terraces – Engine for
Raising Water

The surface which served as the foundation for the gardens that adorned these successive terraces and the area above was formed in the following manner: Over the masonry of the arches there was laid a pavement of broad flat stones, sixteen feet long and four feet wide. Over these there was placed a stratum of reeds, laid in bitumen, and above them another flooring of bricks, cemented closely together, so as to be impervious to water. To make the security complete in this respect, the upper surface of this brick flooring was covered with sheets of lead, overlapping each other in such a manner as to convey all the water which might percolate through the mould away to the sides of the garden. The earth and mould were placed upon this surface, thus prepared, and the stratum was so deep as to allow large trees to take root and grow in it. There was an engine constructed in the middle of the upper terrace, by which water could be drawn up from the river, and distributed over every part of the vast pile.

Floral Beauties

The gardens, thus completed, were filled to profusion with every species of tree, plant and vine, which could produce fruit or flowers to enrich or adorn such a scene. Every country in communication with Babylon was made to contribute something to increase the endless variety of floral beauty which was here literally enthroned. Gardeners of great experience and skill were constantly employed in cultivating the parterres, pruning the fruit trees and the vines, preserving the walks and introducing new varieties of vegetation. In a word, the hanging gardens of Babylon became one of the wonders of the world.

The Works of Nitocris – Her Canals and Levees

The country in the neighbourhood of Babylon, extending from the river on either hand was in general level and low, and subject to inundations. One of the sovereigns of the country, a queen named Nitocris, had formed the grand design of constructing an immense lake, to take off the superfluous water in case of a flood, and thus prevent an overflow. She also opened a great number of lateral and winding channels for the river, wherever the natural disposition of the surface afforded facilities for doing so, and the earth which was taken out in the course of these excavations was employed in raising the banks by artificial terraces, such as are made to confine the Mississippi at New Orleans, and are there called *levees*. The object of Nitocris in these measures was two-fold. She wished, in the first place, to open all practicable channels for the flow of the water, and then to confine the current within the channels thus made. She also wished to make the navigation of the stream as intricate and complicated as possible, so that, while the natives of the country might easily find their way, in boats, to the capital, a foreign enemy, if he should make the attempt, might be confused and lost. These were the rivers of Babylon on the banks of which the captive Jews sat down and wept when they remembered Zion.

The Bridge Over the Euphrates

This queen Nitocris seems to have been quite distinguished for her engineering and architectural plans. It was she that built the bridge across the Euphrates, within the city; and as there was a feeling of jealousy and ill will, as usual in such a case, between the two divisions of the town which the river formed, she caused the bridge to be constructed with a movable platform or draw, by means of which the communication might be cut off at pleasure. This draw was generally up at night and down by day.

The Tomb of the Queen

Herodotus relates a curious anecdote of this queen, which, if true, evinces in another way the peculiar originality of mind and the ingenuity which characterized all her operations. She caused her tomb to be built, before her death, over one of the principal gates of the city. Upon the façade of this monument was a very conspicuous inscription to this effect: 'If any one of the sovereigns, my successors, shall be in extreme want of money, let him open my tomb and take what he may think proper; but let him not resort to this resource unless the urgency is extreme.'

The tomb remained for some time after the queen's death quite undisturbed. In fact, the people of the city avoided this gate altogether, on account of the dead body deposited above it, and the spot became well-nigh deserted. At length, in process of time, a subsequent sovereign, being in want of money, ventured to open the tomb. He found, however, no money within. The gloomy vault contained nothing but the dead body of the queen, and a label with this inscription: 'If your avarice were not as insatiable as it is base, you would not have intruded on the repose of the dead.'

Cyrus Plans an Attack Upon Babylon –
Government of Lydia

It was not surprising that Cyrus, having been so successful in his enterprises thus far, should now begin to turn his thoughts toward this great Babylonian empire, and to feel a desire to bring it under his sway. The first thing, however, was to confirm and secure his Lydian conquests. He spent some time, therefore, in organizing and arranging, at Sardis, the affairs of the new government which he was to substitute for that of Croesus there. He designated certain portions of his army to be left for garrisons in the conquered cities. He appointed Persian officers, of course, to command these forces; but, as he wished to conciliate the Lydians, he appointed many of the municipal and civil officers of the country from among them. There would appear to be no danger in doing this, as, by giving the command of the army to Persians, he retained all the real power directly in his own hands.

Cyrus Returns Eastward

One of these civil officers, the most important, in fact, of all, was the grand treasurer. To him Cyrus committed the charge of the stores of gold and silver which came into his possession at Sardis, and of the revenues which were afterward to accrue. Cyrus appointed a Lydian named Pactyas to this trust, hoping by such measures to conciliate the people of the country, and to make them more ready to submit to his sway. Things being thus arranged, Cyrus, taking Croesus with him, set out with the main army to return toward the East.

Revolt of the Lydians

As soon as he had left Lydia, Pactyas excited the Lydians to revolt. The name of the commander-in-chief of the military forces which Cyrus had left was Tabalus. Pactyas abandoned the city and retired toward the coast where he contrived to raise a large army, formed partly of Lydians and partly of bodies of foreign troops, which he was enabled to hire by means of the treasures which Cyrus had put under his charge. He then advanced to Sardis, took possession of the town and shut up Tabalus, with his Persian troops, in the citadel.

When the tidings of these events came to Cyrus, he was very much incensed, and determined to destroy the city. Croesus, however, interceded very earnestly in its behalf. He recommended that Cyrus, instead of burning Sardis, should send a sufficient force to disarm the population, and that he should then enact such laws and make such arrangements as should turn the minds of the people to habits of luxury and pleasure. 'By doing this,' said Croesus, 'the people will, in a short time, become so enervated and so effeminate that you will have nothing to fear from them.'

Detachment of Mazares

Cyrus decided on adopting this plan. He dispatched a Median named Mazares, an officer of his army, at the head of a strong force, with orders to go back to Sardis, to deliver Tabalus from his danger, to seize and put to death all the leaders in the Lydian rebellion excepting Pactyas. Pactyas was to be saved alive, and sent a prisoner to Cyrus in Persia.

Flight of Pactyas – Pactyas at Cyme

Pactyas did not wait for the arrival of Mazares. As soon as he heard of his approach, he abandoned the ground, and fled northwardly to the city of Cyme, and sought refuge there. When Mazares had reached Sardis and re-established the government of Cyrus there, he sent messengers to Cyme, demanding the surrender of the fugitive.

The People Consult the Oracle – Reply of the Oracle

The people of Cyme were uncertain whether they ought to comply. They said that they must first consult an oracle. There was a very ancient and celebrated oracle near Miletus. They sent messengers to this oracle, demanding to know whether it was according to the will of the gods or not that the fugitive should be surrendered. The answer brought back was, that they might surrender him.

They were accordingly making arrangements for doing this, when one of the citizens, a very prominent and influential man, named Aristodicus, expressed himself not satisfied with the reply. He did not think it possible, he said, that the oracle could really counsel them to deliver up a helpless fugitive to his enemies. The messengers must have misunderstood or misreported the answer which they had received. He finally persuaded his countrymen to send a second embassy: he himself was placed at the head of it. On their arrival, Aristodicus addressed the oracle as follows:

'To avoid a cruel death from the Persians, Pactyas, a Lydian, fled to us for refuge. The Persians demanded that we should surrender him. Much as we are afraid of their power, we are still more afraid to deliver up a helpless suppliant for protection without clear and decided directions from you.'

The Embassy Received to This Demand the Same Reply as Before – Aristodicus and the Birds' Nests

Still Aristodicus was not satisfied; and, as if by way of bringing home to the oracle somewhat more forcibly a sense of the true character of such an action as it seemed to recommend, he began to make a circuit in the grove which was around the temple in which the oracle resided, and to rob and destroy the nests which the birds had built there, allured, apparently, by the sacred repose and quietude of the scene. This had the desired effect. A solemn voice was heard from the interior of the temple, saying, in a warning tone,

'Impious man! how dost thou dare to molest those who have placed themselves under my protection?'

To this Aristodicus replied by asking the oracle how it was that it watched over and guarded those who sought its own protection, while it directed the people of Cyme to abandon and betray suppliants for theirs. To this the oracle answered,

'I direct them to do it, in order that such impious men may the sooner bring down upon their heads the judgments of heaven for having dared to entertain even the thought of delivering up a helpless fugitive.'

Capture of Pactyas

When this answer was reported to the people of Cyme, they did not dare to give Pactyas up, nor, on the other hand, did they dare to incur the enmity of the Persians by retaining and protecting him. They accordingly sent him secretly away. The emissaries of Mazares, however, followed him. They kept constantly on his track, demanding him successively of every city where the hapless fugitive sought refuge, until, at length, partly by threats and partly by a reward, they induced a certain city to surrender him. Mazares sent him, a prisoner, to Cyrus. Soon after this Mazares himself died, and Harpagus was appointed governor of Lydia in his stead.

Situation of Belshazzar – Belshazzar's Feeling of Security

In the meantime, Cyrus went on with his conquests in the heart of Asia, and at length, in the course of a few years, he had completed his arrangements and preparations for the attack on Babylon. He advanced at the head of a large force to the vicinity of the city. The King of Babylon, whose name was Belshazzar, withdrew within the walls, shut the gates, and felt perfectly secure. A simple wall was in those days a very effectual protection against any armed force whatever, if it was only high enough not to be scaled, and thick enough to resist the blows of a battering ram. The artillery of modern times would have speedily made a fatal breach in such structures; but there was nothing but the simple force of man, applied through brazen-headed beams of wood, in those days, and Belshazzar knew well that his walls would bid all such modes of demolition a complete defiance. He stationed his soldiers, therefore, on the walls, and his sentinels in the watch towers, while he himself, and all the nobles of his court, feeling perfectly secure in their impregnable condition, and being abundantly supplied with all the means that the whole empire could furnish, both for sustenance and enjoyment, gave themselves up, in their spacious palaces and gardens, to gayety, festivity and pleasure.

Approach of Cyrus – Cyrus Draws Off the Water from the River – The City Captured

Cyrus advanced to the city. He stationed one large detachment of his troops at the opening in the main walls where the river entered into the city, and another one below, where it issued from it. These detachments were ordered to march into the city by the bed of the river, as soon as they should observe the water subsiding. He then employed a vast force of labourers to open new channels, and to widen and deepen those which had existed before, for the purpose of drawing off the waters from their usual bed. When these passages were thus prepared, the water was let into them one night, at a time previously designated, and it soon ceased to flow through the city. The detachments of soldiers marched in over the bed of the stream, carrying with them vast numbers of ladders. With these they easily scaled the low walls which lined the banks of the river, and Belshazzar was thunderstruck with the announcement made to him in the midst of one of his feasts that the Persians were in complete and full possession of the city.

Chapter IX
The Restoration of the Jews, BCE 608

§

The Jewish Captivity

THE PERIOD OF THE INVASION of Babylonia by Cyrus, and the taking of the city, was during the time while the Jews were in captivity there. Cyrus was their deliverer. It results from this circumstance that the name of Cyrus is connected with sacred history more than that of any other great conqueror of ancient times.

It was a common custom in the early ages of the world for powerful sovereigns to take the people of a conquered country captive, and make them slaves. They employed them, to some extent, as personal household servants, but more generally as agricultural labourers, to till the lands.

Jeremiah and the Book of Chronicles – Incursions of Nebuchadnezzar

An account of the captivity of the Jews in Babylon is given briefly in the closing chapters of the second book of Chronicles, though many of the attendant circumstances are more fully detailed in the book of Jeremiah. Jeremiah was a prophet who lived in the time of the captivity. Nebuchadnezzar, the king of Babylon, made repeated incursions into the land of Judea, sometimes carrying away the reigning monarch, sometimes deposing him and appointing another sovereign in his stead, sometimes assessing a tax or tribute upon the land, and sometimes plundering the city, and carrying away all the gold and silver that he could find. Thus, the kings and the people were kept in a continual state of anxiety and terror for many years, exposed incessantly to the inroads of this nation of robbers and plunderers, that had, so unfortunately for them, found their way across their frontiers. King Zedekiah was the last of this oppressed and unhappy line of Jewish kings.

Denunciations of Jeremiah – Predictions of Jeremiah

The prophet Jeremiah was accustomed to denounce the sins of the Jewish nation, by which these terrible calamities had been brought upon them, with great courage, and with an eloquence solemn and sublime. He declared that the miseries which the people suffered were the special judgments of Heaven, and he proclaimed repeatedly and openly, and in the most public places of the city, still heavier calamities which he said were impending. The people were troubled and distressed at these prophetic warnings, and some of them were deeply incensed against Jeremiah for uttering them. Finally, on one occasion, he took his stand in one of the public courts of the Temple, and, addressing the concourse of priests and people that were there, he declared that, unless the nation repented of their sins and turned to God, the whole city should be overwhelmed. Even the Temple itself, the sacred house of God, should be destroyed, and the very site abandoned.

Exasperation of the Priests and People

The priests and the people who heard this denunciation were greatly exasperated. They seized Jeremiah, and brought him before a great judicial assembly for trial. The judges asked him why he uttered such predictions, declaring that by doing so he acted like an enemy to his country and a traitor, and that he deserved to die. The excitement was very great against him, and the populace could hardly be restrained from open violence. In the midst of this scene Jeremiah was calm and unmoved, and replied to their accusations as follows:

Defence of Jeremiah

'Everything which I have said against this city and this house, I have said by the direction of the Lord Jehovah. Instead of resenting it, and being angry with me for delivering my message, it becomes you to look at your sins, and repent of them, and forsake them. It may be that by so doing God will have mercy upon you, and will avert the calamities which otherwise will most certainly come. As for myself, here I am in your hands. Yon can deal with me just as you think best. Yon can kill me if you will, but you may be assured that if you do so, you will bring the guilt and the consequences of shedding innocent blood upon yourselves and upon this city. I have said nothing and foretold nothing but by commandment of the Lord.'

He is Liberated

The speech produced, as might have been expected, a great division among the hearers. Some were more angry than ever, and were eager to put the prophet to death. Others defended him, and insisted that he should not die. The latter, for the time, prevailed. Jeremiah was set at liberty, and continued his earnest expostulations with the people on account of their sins, and his terrible annunciations of the impending ruin of the city just as before.

Symbolic Method of Teaching – The Wooden Yoke and the Iron Yoke

These unwelcome truths being so painful for the people to hear, other prophets soon began to appear to utter contrary predictions, for the sake, doubtless, of the popularity which they should themselves acquire by their promises of returning peace and prosperity. The name of one of these false prophets was Hananiah. On one occasion, Jeremiah, in order to present and enforce what he had to say more effectually on the minds of the people by means of a visible symbol, made a small wooden yoke, by divine direction, and placed it upon his neck, as a token of the bondage which his predictions were threatening. Hananiah took this yoke from his neck and broke it, saying that, as he had thus broken Jeremiah's wooden yoke, so God would break the yoke of Nebuchadnezzar from all nations within two years; and then, even those of the Jews who had already been taken captive to Babylon should return again in peace. Jeremiah replied that Hananiah's predictions were false, and that, though the wooden yoke was broken, God would make for Nebuchadnezzar a yoke of iron, with which he should bend the Jewish nation in a bondage more cruel than ever. Still, Jeremiah himself predicted that after seventy years from the time when the last great captivity should come, the Jews should all be restored again to their native land.

The Title Deeds of Jeremiah's Estate – The Deeds Deposited

He expressed this certain restoration of the Jews, on one occasion, by a sort of symbol, by means of which he made a much stronger impression on the minds of the people than could have been done by simple words. There was a piece of land in the country of Benjamin, one of the provinces of Judea, which belonged to the family of Jeremiah, and it was held in such a way that, by paying a certain sum of money, Jeremiah himself might possess it, the right of redemption being in him. Jeremiah was in prison at this time. His uncle's son came into the court of the prison, and proposed to him to purchase the land. Jeremiah did so in the most public and formal manner. The title deeds were drawn up and subscribed, witnesses were summoned, the money weighed and paid over, the whole transaction being regularly completed according to the forms and usages then common for the exchange of landed property. When all was finished, Jeremiah gave the papers into the hands of his scribe, directing him to put them safely away and preserve them with care, for after a certain period the country of Judea would again be restored to the peaceable possession of the Jews, and such titles to land would possess once more their full and original value.

Baruch writes Jeremiah's Prophecies – He Reads Them to the People – Baruch Summoned Before the Council

On one occasion, when Jeremiah's personal liberty was restricted so that he could not utter publicly his prophetical warnings, he employed Baruch, his scribe, to write them from his dictation, with a view of reading them to the people from some public and frequented part of the city. The prophecy thus dictated was inscribed upon a roll of parchment. Baruch waited, when he had completed the writing, until a favourable opportunity occurred for reading it, which was on the occasion of a great festival that was held at Jerusalem, and which brought the inhabitants of the land together from all parts of Judea. On the day of the festival, Baruch took the roll in his hand, and stationed himself at a very public place, at the entrance of one of the great courts of the Temple; there, calling upon the people to hear him, he began to read. A great concourse gathered around him, and all listened to him with profound attention. One of the bystanders, however, went down immediately into the city, to the king's palace, and reported to the king's council, that Baruch was there reading to them a discourse or prophecy which had been written by Jeremiah. The members of the council sent a summons to Baruch to come immediately to them, and to bring his writing with him.

When Baruch arrived, they directed him to read what he had written. Baruch accordingly read it. They asked him when and how that discourse was written. Baruch replied that he had written it, word by word, from the dictation of Jeremiah. The officers informed him that they should be obliged to report the circumstances to the king, and they counselled Baruch to go to Jeremiah and recommend to him to conceal himself, lest the king, in his anger, should do him some sudden and violent injury.

The Roll Sent to the King – The Roll Destroyed

The officers then, leaving the roll in one of their own apartments, went to the king, and reported the facts to him. He sent one of his attendants, named Jehudi, to bring the roll. When it came, the king directed Jehudi to read it. Jehudi did so, standing by a fire which had been made in the apartment, for it was bitter cold.

After Jehudi had read a few pages from the roll, finding that it contained a repetition of the same denunciations and warnings by which the king had often been displeased before, he took a knife and began to cut the parchment into pieces, and to throw it on the fire. Some other persons who were standing by interfered, and earnestly begged the king not to allow the roll to be burned. But the king did not interfere. He permitted Jehudi to destroy the parchment altogether, and then sent officers to take Jeremiah and Baruch, and bring them to him but they were nowhere to be found.

Jeremiah Attempts to Leave the City

The prophet, on one occasion, was reduced to extreme distress by the persecutions which his faithfulness, and the incessant urgency of his warnings and expostulations had brought upon him. It was at a time when the Chaldean armies had been driven away from Jerusalem for a short period by the Egyptians, as one vulture drives away another from its prey. Jeremiah determined to avail himself of the opportunity to go to the province of Benjamin, to visit his friends and family there. He was intercepted, however, at one of the gates, and accused of a design to make his escape from the city, and go over to the Chaldeans. The prophet earnestly denied this charge. They paid no regard to his declarations, but sent him back to Jerusalem, to the officers of the king's government, who confined him in a house which they used as a prison.

The King Sends for Jeremiah – He is Imprisoned

After he had remained in this place of confinement for several days, the king sent for him and he was brought to the palace. The king inquired whether he had any prophecy to utter from the Lord. Jeremiah replied that the word of the Lord was, that the Chaldeans should certainly return again, and that Zedekiah himself should fall into their hands, and be carried captive to Babylon. While he thus persisted so strenuously in the declarations which he had made so often before, he demanded of the king that he should not be sent back again to the house of imprisonment from which he had been rescued. The king said he would not send him back, and he accordingly directed, instead, that he should be taken to the court of the public prison, where his confinement would be less rigorous, and there he was to be supplied daily with food, so long, as the king expressed it, as there should be any food remaining in the city.

But Jeremiah's enemies were not at rest. They came again, after a time, to the king, and represented to him that the prophet, by his gloomy and terrible predictions, discouraged and depressed the hearts of the people, and weakened their hands; that he ought, accordingly, to be regarded as a public enemy; and they begged the king to proceed decidedly against him. The king replied that he would give him into their hands, and they might do with him what they pleased.

Jeremiah Cast into a Dungeon – The King Orders Him to be Taken Up

There was a dungeon in the prison, the only access to which was from above. Prisoners were let down into it with ropes, and left there to die of hunger. The bottom of it was wet and miry, and the prophet, when let down into its gloomy depths, sank into the deep mire. Here he would soon have died of hunger and misery; but the king, feeling some misgivings in regard to what he had done, lest it might really be a true prophet of God that he had thus delivered into the hands of his enemies, inquired what the people had done with their prisoner; and when he learned that he had been thus, as it were, buried alive, he immediately sent officers with orders to take him out of the dungeon. The officers went to the dungeon. They opened the mouth of it. They had brought ropes with them, to be used for drawing the unhappy prisoner up, and cloths, also, which he was to fold together and place under his arms, where the ropes were to pass. These ropes and cloths they let down into the dungeon, and called upon Jeremiah to place them properly around his body. Thus, they drew him safely up out of the dismal den.

Jerusalem Besieged by the Babylonians – Capture of the King

These cruel persecutions of the faithful prophet were all unavailing either to silence his voice or to avert the calamities which his warnings portended. At the appointed time, the judgments which had been so long predicted came in all their terrible reality. The Babylonians invaded the land in great force, and encamped about the city. The siege continued for two years. At the end of that time the famine became insupportable. Zedekiah, the king, determined to make a sortie, with as strong a force as he could command, secretly, at night, in hopes to escape with his own life, and intending to leave the city to its fate. He succeeded in passing out through the city gates with his band of followers, and in actually passing the Babylonian lines; but he had not gone far before his escape was discovered. He was pursued and taken. The city was then stormed, and, as usual in such cases, it was given up to plunder and destruction. Vast numbers of the inhabitants were killed; many more were taken captive; the principal buildings, both public and private, were burned; the walls were broken down, and all the public treasures of the Jews, the gold and silver vessels of the Temple, and a vast quantity of private plunder, were carried away to Babylon by the conquerors. All this was seventy years before the conquest of Babylon by Cyrus.

Captivity of the Jews – The Prophet Daniel

Of course, during the time of this captivity, a very considerable portion of the inhabitants of Judea remained in their native land. The deportation of a whole people to a foreign land is impossible. A vast number, however, of the inhabitants of the country were carried away, and they remained, for two generations, in a miserable bondage. Some of them were employed as agricultural labourers in the rural districts of Babylon; others remained in the city, and were engaged in servile labours there. The prophet Daniel lived in the palaces of the king. He was summoned, as the reader will recollect, to Belshazzar's feast, on the night when Cyrus forced his way into the city, to interpret the mysterious writing on the wall, by which the fall of the Babylonian monarchy was announced in so terrible a manner.

Cyrus Takes Possession of Babylon, and Allows the Jews to Return

One year after Cyrus had conquered Babylon, he issued an edict authorizing the Jews to return to Jerusalem, and to rebuild the city and the Temple. This event had been long before predicted by the prophets, as the result which God had determined upon for purposes of his own. We should not naturally have expected that such a conqueror as Cyrus would feel any real and honest interest in promoting the designs of God; but still, in the proclamation which he issued authorizing the Jews to return, he acknowledged the supreme divinity of Jehovah, and says that he was charged by him with the work of rebuilding his Temple, and restoring his worship at its ancient seat on Mount Zion. It has, however, been supposed by some scholars, who have examined attentively all the circumstances connected with these transactions, that so far as Cyrus was influenced by political considerations in ordering the return of the Jews, his design was to re-establish that nation as a barrier between his dominions and those of the Egyptians. The Egyptians and the Chaldeans had long been deadly enemies, and now that Cyrus had become master of the Chaldean realms, he would, of course, in assuming their territories and their power, be obliged to defend himself against their foes.

Assembling of the Jews – The Number That Returned

Whatever may have been the motives of Cyrus, he decided to allow the Hebrew captives to return, and he issued a proclamation to that effect. As seventy years had elapsed since the captivity commenced, about two generations had passed away, and there could have been very few then living who had ever seen the land of their fathers. The Jews were, however, all eager to return. They collected in a vast assembly, with all the treasures which they were allowed to take, and the stores of provisions and baggage, and with horses, and mules, and other beasts of burden to transport them. When assembled for the march, it was found that the number, of which a very exact census was taken, was forty-nine thousand six hundred and ninety-seven.

They had also with them seven or eight hundred horses, about two hundred and fifty mules, and about five hundred camels. The chief part, however, of their baggage and stores was borne by asses, of which there were nearly seven thousand in the train. The march of this peaceful multitude of families – men, women, and children together – burdened as they went, not with arms and ammunition for conquest and destruction, but with tools and implements for honest industry, and stores of provisions and utensils for the peaceful purposes of social life, as it was, in its bearings and results, one of the grandest events of history, so it must have presented, in its progress, one of the most extraordinary spectacles that the world has ever seen.

Arrival of the Caravan at Jerusalem – Building the Temple – Emotions of the Old Men – Rejoicings of the Young Men

The grand caravan pursued its long and toilsome march from Babylon to Jerusalem without molestation. All arrived safely, and the people immediately commenced the work of repairing the walls of the city and rebuilding the Temple. When, at length, the foundations of the Temple were laid, a great celebration was held to commemorate the event. This celebration exhibited a remarkable scene of mingled rejoicing and mourning. The younger part of the population, who had never seen Jerusalem in its former grandeur, felt only exhilaration and joy at their re-establishment in the city of their fathers. The work of raising the edifice, whose foundations they had laid, was to them simply a new enterprise, and they looked forward to the work of carrying it on with pride and pleasure. The old men, however, who remembered the former Temple, were filled with mournful recollections of days of prosperity and peace in their childhood and of the magnificence of the former Temple, which they could now never hope to see realized again. It was customary in those days, to express sorrow and grief by exclamations and outcries, as gladness and joy are expressed audibly now. Accordingly, on this occasion, the cries of grief and of bitter regret at the thought of losses which could now never be retrieved, were mingled with the shouts of rejoicing and triumph raised by the ardent and young, who knew nothing of the past, but looked forward with hope and happiness to the future.

The Jews encountered various hindrances, and met with much opposition in their attempts to reconstruct their ancient city, and to re-establish the Mosaic ritual there. We must, however, now return to the history of Cyrus, referring the reader for a narrative of the circumstances connected with the rebuilding of Jerusalem to the very minute account given in the sacred books of Ezra and Nehemiah.

Chapter X
The Story of Panthea

Xenophon's Romantic Tales

IN THE PRECEDING CHAPTERS of this work, we have followed mainly the authority of Herodotus, except, indeed, in the account of the visit of Cyrus to his grandfather in his childhood, which is taken from Xenophon. We shall, in this chapter, relate the story of Panthea, which is also one of Xenophon's tales. We give it as a specimen of the romantic narratives in which Xenophon's history abounds, and on account of the many illustrations of an ancient manners and customs which it contains, leaving it for each reader to decide for himself what weight he will attach to its claims to be regarded as veritable history. We relate the story here in our own language, but as to the facts, we follow faithfully the course of Xenophon's narration.

Panthea a Susian Captive – Valuable Spoil – Its Division

Panthea was a Susian captive. She was taken, together with a great many other captives and much plunder, after one of the great battles which Cyrus fought with the Assyrians. Her husband was an Assyrian general, though he himself was not captured at this time with his wife. The spoil which came into possession of the army on the occasion of the battle in which Panthea was taken was of great value. There were beautiful and costly suits of arms, rich tents made of splendid materials and highly ornamented, large sums of money, vessels of silver and gold and slaves – some prized for their beauty, and others for certain accomplishments which were highly valued in those days. Cyrus appointed a sort of commission to divide this spoil. He pursued always a very generous policy on all these occasions, showing no desire to secure such treasures to himself, but distributing them with profuse liberality among his officers and soldiers.

Share of Cyrus – Panthea Given to Cyrus

The commissioners whom he appointed in this case divided the spoil among the various generals of the army, and among the different bodies of soldiery, with great impartiality. Among the prizes assigned to Cyrus were two singing women of great fame, and this Susian lady. Cyrus thanked the distributors for the share of booty which they had thus assigned to him, but said that if any of his friends wished for either of these captives, they could have them. An officer asked for one of the singers. Cyrus gave her to him immediately, saying, 'I consider myself more obliged to you for asking her, than you are to me for giving her to you.' As for the Susian lady, Cyrus had not yet seen her, but he called one of his most intimate and confidential friends to him, and requested him to take her under his charge.

Araspes

The name of this officer was Araspes. He was a Mede, and he had been Cyrus's particular friend and playmate when he was a boy, visiting his grandfather in Media. The reader will perhaps recollect that he is mentioned toward the close of our account of that visit, as the special favourite to whom Cyrus presented his robe or mantle when he took leave of his friends in returning to his native land.

Abradates

Araspes, when he received this charge, asked Cyrus whether he had himself seen the lady. Cyrus replied that he had not. Araspes then proceeded to give an account of her. The name of her husband was Abradates, and he was the king of Susa, as they termed him. The reason why he was not taken prisoner at the same time with his wife was, that when the battle was fought and the Assyrian camp captured, he was absent, having gone away on an embassage to another nation. This circumstance shows that Abradates, though called a king, could hardly have been a sovereign and independent prince, but rather a governor or viceroy – those words expressing to our minds more truly the station of such a sort of king as could be sent on an embassy.

Account of Panthea's Capture – Her Great Loveliness

Araspes went on to say that, at the time of their making the capture, he, with some others, went into Panthea's tent, where they found her and her attendant ladies sitting on the ground, with veils over their faces, patiently awaiting their doom. Notwithstanding the concealment produced by the attitudes and dress of these ladies, there was something about the air and figure of Panthea which showed at once that she was the queen. The leader of Araspes's party asked them all to rise. They did so, and then the superiority of Panthea was still more apparent than before. There was an extraordinary grace and beauty in her attitude and in all her motions. She stood in a dejected posture, and her countenance was sad, though inexpressibly lovely. She endeavoured to appear calm and composed, though the tears had evidently been falling from her eyes.

Attempts at Consolation

The soldiers pitied her in her distress, and the leader of the party attempted to console her, as Araspes said, by telling her that she had nothing to fear; that they were aware that her husband was a most worthy and excellent man; and although, by this capture, she was lost to him, she would have no cause to regret the event, for she would be reserved for a new husband not at all inferior to her former one either in person, in understanding, in rank or in power.

Panthea's Renewed Grief

These well-meant attempts at consolation did not appear to have the good effect desired. They only awakened Panthea's grief and suffering anew. The tears began to fall again faster than before. Her grief soon became more and more uncontrollable. She sobbed and cried aloud, and began to wring her hands and tear her mantle – the customary Oriental expression of inconsolable sorrow and despair. Araspes said that in these gesticulations her neck, and hands, and a part of her face appeared, and that she was the most beautiful woman that he had ever beheld. He wished Cyrus to see her.

Cyrus Declines to See Panthea – His Reasons

Cyrus said, 'No; he would not see her by any means.' Araspes asked him why. He said that there would be danger that he should forget his duty to the army, and lose his interest in the great military enterprise in which he was engaged, if he should allow himself to become captivated by the charms of such a lady, as he very probably would be if he were now to visit her. Araspes said in reply that Cyrus might at least see her; as to becoming captivated with her, and devoting himself to her to such a degree as to neglect his other duties, he could certainly control himself in respect to that danger. Cyrus said that it was not certain that he could so control himself; and then there followed a long discussion between Cyrus and Araspes, in which Araspes maintained that every man had the command of his own heart and affections, and that, with proper determination and energy, he could direct the channels in which they should run, and confine them within such limits and bounds as he pleased. Cyrus, on the other hand, maintained that human passions were stronger than the human will; that no one could rely on the strength of his resolutions to control the impulses of the heart once strongly excited, and that a man's only safety was in controlling the circumstances which tended to excite them. This was especially true, he said, in respect to the passion of love. The experience of mankind, he said, had shown that no strength of moral principle, no firmness of purpose, no fixedness of resolution, no degree of suffering, no fear of shame, was sufficient to control, in the hearts of men, the impetuosity of the passion of love, when it was once fairly awakened. In a word, Araspes advocated, on the subject of love, a sort of new school philosophy, while that of Cyrus leaned very seriously toward the old.

Araspes's Self-Confidence

In conclusion, Cyrus jocosely counselled Araspes to beware lest he should prove that love was stronger than the will by becoming himself enamoured of the beautiful Susian queen. Araspes said that Cyrus need not fear; there was no danger. He must be a miserable wretch indeed, he said, who could not summon within him sufficient resolution and energy to control his own passions and desires. As for himself, he was sure that he was safe.

Panthea's Patience and Gentleness – Araspes's Kindness to Panthea – His Emotions Master Him – Araspes in Love

As usual with those who are self-confident and boastful, Araspes failed when the time of trial came. He took charge of the royal captive whom Cyrus committed to him with a very firm resolution to be faithful to his trust. He pitied the unhappy queen's misfortunes, and admired the heroic patience and gentleness of spirit with which she bore them. The beauty of her countenance, and her thousand personal charms, which were all heightened by the expression of sadness and sorrow which they bore, touched his heart. It gave him pleasure to grant her every indulgence consistent with her condition of captivity, and to do everything in his power to promote her welfare. She was very grateful for these favours, and the few brief words and looks of kindness with which she returned them repaid him for his efforts to please her a thousand-fold. He saw her, too, in her tent, in the presence of her maidens, at all times; and as she looked upon him as only her custodian and guard, and as, too, her mind was wholly occupied by the thoughts of her absent husband and her hopeless grief, her actions were entirely free and unconstrained in his presence. This made her only the more attractive; every attitude and movement seemed to possess, in Araspes's mind, an inexpressible charm. In a word, the result was what Cyrus had predicted. Araspes became wholly absorbed in the interest which was awakened in him by the charms of the beautiful captive. He made many resolutions, but they were of no avail. While he was away from her, he felt strong in his determination to yield to these feelings no more; but as soon as he came into her presence, all these resolutions melted wholly away, and he yielded his heart entirely to the control of emotions which, however vincible they might appear at a distance, were found, when the time of trial came, to possess a certain mysterious and magic power, which made it most delightful for the heart to yield before them in the contest, and utterly impossible to stand firm and resist. In a word, when seen at a distance, love appeared to him an enemy which he was ready to brave, and was sure that he could overcome; but when near, it transformed itself into the guise of a friend, and he accordingly threw down the arms with which he had intended to combat it, and gave himself up to it in a delirium of pleasure.

Progress of the Army

Things continued in this state for some time. The army advanced from post to post, and from encampment to encampment, taking the captives in their train. New cities were taken, new provinces overrun and new plans for future conquests were formed. At last, a case occurred in which Cyrus wished to send someone as a spy into a distant enemy's country. The circumstances were such that it was necessary that a person of considerable intelligence and rank should go, as Cyrus wished the messenger whom he should send to make his way to the court of the sovereign, and become personally acquainted with the leading men of the state, and to examine the general resources of the kingdom. It was a very different case from that of an ordinary spy, who was to go into a neighbouring camp merely to report the numbers and disposition of an organized army. Cyrus was uncertain whom he should send on such an embassy.

Araspes Confesses His Love – Panthea Offended – Panthea Appeals to Cyrus

In the meantime, Araspes had ventured to express to Panthea his love for her. She was offended. In the first place, she was faithful to her husband, and did not wish to receive such addresses from any person. Then, besides, she considered Araspes, having been placed in charge of her by Cyrus, his master, only for the purpose of keeping her safely, as guilty of a betrayal of his trust in having dared to cherish and express sentiments of affection for her himself. She, however, forbore to reproach him, or to complain of him to Cyrus. She simply repelled the advances that he made, supposing that, if she did this with firmness and decision, Araspes would feel rebuked and would say no more. It did not, however, produce this effect. Araspes continued to importune her with declarations of love, and at length she felt compelled to appeal to Cyrus.

Cyrus Reproves Araspes

Cyrus, instead of being incensed at what might have been considered a betrayal of trust on the part of Araspes, only laughed at the failure and fall in which all his favourite's promises and boastings had ended. He sent a messenger to Araspes to caution him in regard to his conduct, telling him that he ought to respect the feelings of such a woman as Panthea had proved herself to be. The messenger whom Cyrus sent was not content with delivering his message as Cyrus had dictated it. He made it much more stern and severe. In fact, he reproached the lover, in a very harsh and bitter manner, for indulging such a passion. He told him that he had betrayed a sacred trust reposed in him, and acted in a manner at once impious and unjust. Araspes was overwhelmed with remorse and anguish, and with fear of the consequences which might ensue, as men are when the time arrives for being called to account for transgressions which, while they were committing them, gave them little concern.

Cyrus's Generosity – Araspes's Continued Distress

When Cyrus heard how much Araspes had been distressed by the message of reproof which he had received, and by his fears of punishment, he sent for him.

Araspes came. Cyrus told him that he had no occasion to be alarmed. 'I do not wonder,' said he, 'at the result which has happened. We all know how difficult it is to resist the influence which is exerted upon our minds by the charms of a beautiful woman, when we are thrown into circumstances of familiar intercourse with her. Whatever of wrong there has been ought to be considered as more my fault than yours. I was wrong in placing you in such circumstances of temptation, by giving you so beautiful a woman in charge.'

Araspes was very much struck with the generosity of Cyrus, in thus endeavouring to soothe his anxiety and remorse, and taking upon himself the responsibility and the blame. He thanked Cyrus very earnestly for his kindness; but he said that, notwithstanding his sovereign's willingness to forgive him, he felt still oppressed with grief and concern, for the knowledge of his fault had been spread abroad in the army; his enemies were rejoicing over him, and were predicting his disgrace and ruin; and some persons had even advised him to make his escape, by absconding before any worse calamity should befall him.

Plan of Cyrus

'If this is so,' said Cyrus, 'it puts it in your power to render me a very essential service.' Cyrus then explained to Araspes the necessity that he was under of finding some confidential agent to go on a secret mission into the enemy's country, and the importance that the messenger should go under such circumstances as not to be suspected of being Cyrus's friend in disguise. 'You can pretend to abscond,' said he; 'it will be immediately said that you fled for fear of my displeasure. I will pretend to send in pursuit of you. The news of your evasion will spread rapidly, and will be carried, doubtless, into the enemy's country; so that, when you arrive there, they will be prepared to welcome you as a deserter from my cause, and a refugee.'

Araspes Pretends to Desert

This plan was agreed upon, and Araspes prepared for his departure. Cyrus gave him his instructions, and they concerted together the information – fictitious, of course – which he was to communicate to the enemy in respect to Cyrus's situation and designs. When all was ready for his departure, Cyrus asked him how it was that he was so willing to separate himself thus from the beautiful Panthea. He said in reply, that when he was absent from Panthea, he was capable of easily forming any determination, and of pursuing any line of conduct that his duty required, while yet, in her presence, he found his love for her, and the impetuous feelings to which it gave rise, wholly and absolutely uncontrollable.

Panthea Proposes to Send for Her Husband

As soon as Araspes was gone, Panthea, who supposed that he had really fled for fear of the indignation of the king, sent to Cyrus a message, expressing her regret at the unworthy conduct and the flight of Araspes, and saying that she could, and gladly would, if he consented, repair the loss which the desertion of Araspes occasioned by sending for her own husband. He was, she said, dissatisfied with the government under which he lived, having been cruelly and tyrannically treated by the prince. 'If you will allow me to send for him,' she added, 'I am sure he will come and join your army; and I assure you that you will find him a much more faithful and devoted servant than Araspes has been.'

Cyrus Consents – Joyful Meeting of Panthea and Her Husband

Cyrus consented to this proposal, and Panthea sent for Abradates. Abradates came at the head of two thousand horse, which formed a very important addition to the forces under Cyrus's command. The meeting between Panthea and her husband was joyful in the extreme. When Abradates learned from his wife how honourable and kind had been the treatment which Cyrus had rendered to her, he was overwhelmed with a sense of gratitude, and he declared that he would do the utmost in his power to requite the obligations he was under.

The Armed Chariots

Abradates entered at once, with great ardour and zeal, into plans for making the force which he had brought as efficient as possible in the service of Cyrus.

He observed that Cyrus was interested, at that time, in attempting to build and equip a corps of armed chariots, such as were often used in fields of battle in those days. This was a very expensive sort of force, corresponding, in that respect, with the artillery used in modern times. The carriages were heavy and strong, and were drawn generally by two horses. They had short, scythe-like blades of steel projecting from the axletrees on each side, by which the ranks of the enemy were mowed down when the carriages were driven among them. The chariots were made to contain, besides the driver of the horses, one or more warriors, each armed in the completest manner. These warriors stood on the floor of the vehicle, and fought with javelins and spears. The great plains which abound in the interior countries of Asia were very favourable for this species of warfare.

Abradates's Eight-Horse Chariot – Panthea's Presents for Her Husband – Imposing Spectacle

Abradates immediately fitted up for Cyrus a hundred such chariots at his own expense, and provided horses to draw them from his own troop. He made one chariot much larger than the rest, for himself, as he intended to take command of this corps of chariots in person. His own chariot was to be drawn by eight horses. His wife Panthea was very much interested in these preparations. She wished to do something herself toward the outfit. She accordingly furnished, from her own private treasures, a helmet, a corslet and arm-pieces of gold. These articles formed a suit of armour sufficient to cover all that part of the body which would be exposed in standing in the chariot. She also provided breast-pieces and sidepieces of brass for the horses. The whole chariot, thus equipped, with its eight horses in their gay trappings and resplendent armour, and with Abradates standing within it, clothed in his panoply of gold, presented, in the sight of the whole army, around the plain of the encampment, a most imposing spectacle. It was a worthy leader, as the spectators thought, to head the formidable column of a hundred similar engines which were to follow in its train. If we imagine the havoc which a hundred scythe-armed carriages would produce when driven, with headlong fury, into dense masses of men, on a vast open plain, we shall have some idea of one item of the horrors of ancient war.

Panthea's Preparations – Panthea Offers Her Presents

The full splendour of Abradates's equipments were not, however, displayed at first, for Panthea kept what she had done a secret for a time, intending to reserve her contribution for a parting present to her husband when the period should arrive for going into battle. She had accordingly taken the measure for her work by stealth, from the armour which Abradates was accustomed to wear, and had caused the artificers to make the golden pieces with the utmost secrecy. Besides the substantial defences of gold which she provided, she added various other articles for ornament and decoration. There was a purple robe, a crest for the helmet, which was of a violet colour, plumes, and likewise bracelets for the wrists. Panthea kept all these things herself until the day arrived when her husband was going into battle for the first time with his train, and then, when he went into his tent to prepare himself to ascend his chariot, she brought them to him.

Abradates's Pleasure

Abradates was astonished when he saw them. He soon understood how they had been provided, and he exclaimed, with a heart full of surprise and pleasure, 'And so, to provide me with this splendid armour and dress, you have been depriving yourself of all your finest and most beautiful ornaments!'
'No,' said Panthea, 'you are yourself my finest ornament, if you appear in other people's eyes as you do in mine, and I have not deprived myself of you.'

The appearance which Abradates made in other people's eyes was certainly very splendid on this occasion. There were many spectators present to see him mount his chariot and drive away; but so great was their admiration of Panthea's affection and regard for her husband, and so much impressed were they with her beauty, that the great chariot, the resplendent horses and the grand warrior with his armour of gold, which the magnificent equipage was intended to convey, were, all together, scarcely able to draw away the eyes of the spectators from her. She stood, for a while, by the side of the chariot, addressing her husband in an under tone, reminding him of the obligations which they were under to Cyrus for his generous and noble treatment of her, and urging him, now that he was going to be put to the test, to redeem the promise which she had made in his name, that Cyrus would find him faithful, brave and true.

Abradates Departs for the Field – The Farewell

The driver then closed the door by which Abradates had mounted, so that Panthea was separated from her husband, though she could still see him as he stood in his place. She gazed upon him with a countenance full of affection and solicitude. She kissed the margin of the chariot as it began to move away. She walked along after it as it went, as if, after all, she could not bear the separation. Abradates turned, and when he saw her coming on after the carriage, he said, waving his hand for a parting salutation, 'Farewell, Panthea; go back now to your tent, and do not be anxious about me. Farewell.' Panthea turned – her attendants came and took her away – the spectators all turned, too, to follow her with their eyes, and no one paid any regard to the chariot or to Abradates until she was gone.

The Order of Battle – Appearance of Abradates

On the field of battle, before the engagement commenced, Cyrus, in passing along the lines, paused, when he came to the chariots of Abradates, to examine the arrangements which had been made for them, and to converse a moment with the chief. He saw that the chariots were drawn up in a part of the field where there was opposed to them a very formidable array of Egyptian soldiers. The Egyptians in this war were allies of the enemy. Abradates, leaving his chariot in the charge of his driver, descended and came to Cyrus, and remained in conversation with him for a few moments, to receive his last orders. Cyrus directed him to remain where he was, and not to attack the enemy until he received a certain signal. At length the two chieftains separated; Abradates returned to his chariot, and Cyrus moved on. Abradates then moved slowly along his lines, to encourage and animate his men, and to give them the last directions in respect to the charge which they were about to make on the enemy when the signal should be given. All eyes were turned to the magnificent spectacle which his equipage presented as it advanced toward them; the chariot, moving slowly along the line, the tall and highly decorated form of its commander rising in the centre of it, while the eight horses, animated by the sound of the trumpets, and by the various excitements of the scene, stepped proudly, their brazen armour clanking as they came.

The Charge – Terrible Havoc Made by the Chariots

When, at length, the signal was given, Abradates, calling on the other chariots to follow, put his horses to their speed, and the whole line rushed impetuously on to the attack of the Egyptians. War horses, properly trained to their work, will fight with their hoofs with almost as much reckless determination as men will with spears. They rush madly on to encounter whatever opposition there may be before them, and strike down and leap over whatever comes in their way, as if they fully understood the nature of the work that their riders or drivers were wishing them to do. Cyrus, as he passed along from one part of the battlefield to another, saw the horses of Abradates's line dashing thus impetuously into the thickest ranks of the enemy. The men, on every side, were beaten down by the horses' hoofs, or overturned by the wheels, or cut down by the scythes; and they who here and there escaped these dangers, became the aim of the soldiers who stood in the chariots, and were transfixed with their spears. The heavy wheels rolled and jolted mercilessly over the bodies of the wounded and the fallen, while the scythes caught hold of and cut through everything that came in their way – whether the shafts of javelins and spears, or the limbs and bodies of men – and tore everything to pieces in their terrible career. As Cyrus rode rapidly by, he saw Abradates in the midst of this scene, driving on in his chariot, and shouting to his men in a frensy of excitement and triumph.

The Great Victory – The Council of War – Abradates Slain

The battle in which these events occurred was one of the greatest and most important which Cyrus fought. He gained the victory. His enemies were everywhere routed and driven from the field. When the contest was at length decided, the army desisted from the slaughter and encamped for the night. On the following day, the generals assembled at the tent of Cyrus to discuss the arrangements which were to be made in respect to the disposition of the captives and of the spoil, and to the future movements of the army. Abradates was not there. For a time, Cyrus, in the excitement and confusion of the scene did not observe his absence. At length he inquired for him. A soldier present told him that he had been killed from his chariot in the midst of the Egyptians, and that his wife was at that moment attending to the interment of the body, on the banks of a river which flowed near the field of battle. Cyrus, on hearing this, uttered a loud exclamation of astonishment and sorrow. He dropped the business in which he had been engaged with his council, mounted his horse, commanded attendants to follow him with everything that could be necessary on such an occasion, and then, asking those who knew to lead the way, he drove off to find Panthea.

Panthea's Grief

When he arrived at the spot, the dead body of Abradates was lying upon the ground, while Panthea sat by its side, holding the head in her lap, overwhelmed herself with unutterable sorrow. Cyrus leaped from his horse, knelt down by the side of the corpse, saying, at the same time, 'Alas! thou brave and faithful soul, and art thou gone?'

At the same time, he took hold of the hand of Abradates; but, as he attempted to raise it, the arm came away from the body. It had been cut off by an Egyptian sword. Cyrus was himself shocked at the spectacle, and Panthea's grief broke forth anew. She cried out with bitter anguish, replaced the arm in the position in which she had arranged it before, and told Cyrus that the rest of the body was in the same condition. Whenever she attempted to speak, her sobs and tears almost prevented her utterance. She bitterly reproached herself for having been, perhaps, the cause of her husband's death, by urging him, as she had done, to fidelity and courage when he went into battle. 'And now,' she said, 'he is dead, while I, who urged him forward into the danger, am still alive.'

Cyrus's Kindness to Panthea – She is Inconsolable

Cyrus said what he could to console Panthea's grief; but he found it utterly inconsolable. He gave directions for furnishing her with everything which she could need, and promised her that he would make ample arrangements for providing for her in future. 'You shall be treated,' he said, 'while you remain with me, in the most honourable manner; or if you have any friends whom you wish to join, you shall be sent to them safely whenever you please.'

Panthea Kills Herself on the Dead Body of Her Husband

Panthea thanked him for his kindness. She had a friend, she said, whom she wished to join, and she would let him know in due time who it was. In the meantime, she wished that Cyrus would leave her alone, for a while, with her servants, her waiting-maid and the dead body of her husband. Cyrus accordingly withdrew. As soon as he had gone, Panthea sent away the servants also, retaining the waiting-maid alone. The waiting-maid began to be anxious and concerned at witnessing these mysterious arrangements, as if they portended some new calamity. She wondered what her mistress was going to do. Her doubts were dispelled by seeing Panthea produce a sword, which she had kept concealed hitherto beneath her robe. Her maid begged her, with much earnestness and many tears, not to destroy herself; but Panthea was immovable. She said she could not live any longer. She directed the maid to envelop her body, as soon as she was dead, in the same mantle with her husband, and to have them both deposited together in the same grave; and before her stupefied attendant could do anything to save her, she sat down by the side of her husband's body, laid her head upon his breast, and in that position gave herself the fatal wound. In a few minutes she ceased to breathe.

* * *

Cyrus expressed his respect for the memory of Abradates and Panthea by erecting a lofty monument over their common grave.

Chapter XI
Conversations

General Character of Xenophon's History

WE HAVE GIVEN THE STORY of Panthea, as contained in the preceding chapter, in our own language, it is true, but without any intentional addition or embellishment whatever. Each reader will judge for himself whether such a narrative, written for the entertainment of vast assemblies at public games and celebrations, is most properly to be regarded as an invention of romance, or as a simple record of veritable history.

Dialogues and Conversations – Ancient Mode of Discussion

A great many extraordinary and dramatic incidents and adventures, similar in general character to the story of Panthea, are interwoven with the narrative in Xenophon's history. There are also, besides these, many long and minute details of dialogues and conversations, which, if they had really occurred, would have required a very high degree of skill in stenography to produce such reports of them as Xenophon has given. The incidents, too, out of which these conversations grew, are worthy of attention, as we can often judge, by the nature and character of an incident described, whether it is one which it is probable might actually occur in real life, or only an invention intended to furnish an opportunity and a pretext for the inculcation of the sentiments, or the expression of the views of the different speakers. It was the custom in ancient days, much more than it is now, to attempt to add to the point and spirit of a discussion, by presenting the various views which the subject naturally elicited in the form of a conversation arising out of circumstances invented to sustain it. The incident in such cases was, of course, a fiction, contrived to furnish points of attachment for the dialogue – a sort of trellis, constructed artificially to support the vine.

We shall present in this chapter some specimens of these conversations, which will give the reader a much more distinct idea of the nature of them than any general description can convey.

Cyrus's Games – Grand Procession – The Races

At one time in the course of Cyrus's career, just after he had obtained some great victory, and was celebrating his triumphs, in the midst of his armies, with spectacles and games, he instituted a series of races, in which the various nations that were represented in his army furnished their several champions as competitors The army marched out from the city which Cyrus had captured, and where he was then residing, in a procession of the most imposing magnificence. Animals intended to be offered in sacrifice, caparisoned in trappings of gold, horsemen most sumptuously equipped, chariots of war splendidly built and adorned and banners and trophies of every kind, were conspicuous in the train. When the vast procession reached the race ground, the immense concourse was formed in ranks around it, and the racing went on.

The Sacian – His Success

When it came to the turn of the Sacian nation to enter the course, a private man, of no apparent importance in respect to his rank or standing, came forward as the champion; though the man appeared insignificant, his horse was as fleet as the wind. He flew around the arena with astonishing speed, and came in at the finish while his competitor was still midway of the course. Everybody was astonished at this performance. Cyrus asked the Sacian whether he would be willing to sell that horse, if he could receive a kingdom in exchange for it – kingdoms being the coin with which such sovereigns as Cyrus made their purchases. The Sacian replied that he would not sell his horse for any kingdom, but that he would readily give him away to oblige a worthy man.

'Come with me,' said Cyrus, 'and I will show you where you may throw blindfold, and not miss a worthy man.'

Mode of Finding a Worthy Man

So saying, Cyrus conducted the Sacian to a part of the field where a number of his officers and attendants were moving to and fro, mounted upon their horses, or seated in their chariots of war. The Sacian took up a hard clod of earth from a bank as he walked along. At length they were in the midst of the group.

'Throw!' said Cyrus.

The Sacian shut his eyes and threw.

Pheraulas Wounded – Pheraulas Pursues His Course

It happened that, just at that instant, an officer named Pheraulas was riding by. He was conveying some orders which Cyrus had given him to another part of the field. Pheraulas had been originally a man of humble life, but he had been advanced by Cyrus to a high position on account of the great fidelity and zeal which he had evinced in the performance of his duty. The clod which the Sacian threw struck Pheraulas in the mouth, and wounded him severely. Now it is the part of a good soldier to stand at his post or to press on, in obedience to his orders, as long as any physical capacity remains; and Pheraulas, true to his military obligation, rode on without even turning to see whence and from what cause so unexpected and violent an assault had proceeded.

The Sacian opened his eyes, looked around, and coolly asked who it was that he had hit. Cyrus pointed to the horseman who was riding rapidly away, saying, 'That is the man, who is riding so fast past those chariots yonder. You hit *him*.'

'Why did he not turn back, then?' asked the Sacian.

'It is strange that he did not,' said Cyrus; 'he must be some madman.'

He Receives the Sacian's Horse

The Sacian went in pursuit of him. He found Pheraulas with his face covered with blood and dirt, and asked him if he had received a blow. 'I have,' said Pheraulas, 'as you see.' 'Then,' said the Sacian, 'I make you a present of my horse.' Pheraulas asked an explanation. The Sacian accordingly gave him an account of what had taken place between himself and Cyrus, and said, in the end, that he gladly gave him his horse, as he, Pheraulas, had so decisively proved himself to be a most worthy man.

Pheraulas accepted the present, with many thanks, and he and the Sacian became thereafter very strong friends.

Sumptuous Entertainment – Pheraulas and the Sacian

Sometime after this, Pheraulas invited the Sacian to an entertainment, and when the hour arrived, he set before his friend and the other guests a most sumptuous feast, which was served in vessels of gold and silver, and in an apartment furnished with carpets, canopies and couches of the most gorgeous and splendid description. The Sacian was much impressed with this magnificence, and he asked Pheraulas whether he had been a rich man at home, that is, before he had joined Cyrus's army. Pheraulas replied that he was not then rich. His father, he said, was a farmer, and he himself had been accustomed in early life to till the ground with the other labourers on his father's farm. All the wealth and luxury which he now enjoyed had been bestowed upon him, he said, by Cyrus.

'How fortunate you are!' said the Sacian; 'and it must be that you enjoy your present riches all the more highly on account of having experienced in early life the inconveniences and ills of poverty. The pleasure must be more intense in having desires which have long been felt gratified at last than if the objects which they rested upon had been always in one's possession.'

Riches a Source of Disquiet and Care – Argument of Pheraulas

'You imagine, I suppose,' replied Pheraulas, 'that I am a great deal happier in consequence of all this wealth and splendour; but it is not so. As to the real enjoyments of which our natures are capable, I cannot receive more now than I could before. I cannot eat any more, drink any more, or sleep any more, or do any of these things with any more pleasure than when I was poor. All that I gain by this abundance is, that I have more to watch, more to guard, more to take care of. I have many servants, for whose wants I have to provide, and who are a constant source of solicitude to me. One calls for food, another for clothes, and a third is sick, and I must see that he has a physician. My other possessions, too, are a constant care. A man comes in, one day, and brings me sheep that have been torn by the wolves; and, on another day, tells me of oxen that have fallen from a precipice, or of a distemper which has broken out among the flocks or herds. My wealth, therefore, brings me only an increase of anxiety and trouble, without any addition to my joys.'

Remark of the Sacian

'But those things,' said the Sacian, 'which you name, must be unusual and extraordinary occurrences. When all things are going on prosperously and well with you, and you can look around on all your possessions and feel that they are yours, then certainly you must be happier than I am.'

Reply of Pheraulas

'It is true,' said Pheraulas, 'that there is a pleasure in the possession of wealth, but that pleasure is not great enough to balance the suffering which the calamities and losses inevitably connected with it occasion. That the suffering occasioned by losing our possessions is greater than the pleasure of retaining them, is proved by the fact that the pain of a loss is so exciting to the mind that it often deprives men of sleep, while they enjoy the most calm and quiet repose so long as their possessions are retained, which proves that the pleasure does not move them so deeply. They are kept awake by the vexation and chagrin on the one hand, but they are never kept awake by the satisfaction on the other.'

'That is true,' replied the Sacian. 'Men are not kept awake by the mere continuing to possess their wealth, but they very often are by the original acquisition of it.'

'Yes, indeed,' replied Pheraulas; 'and if the enjoyment of *being* rich could always continue as great as that of first becoming so, the rich would, I admit, be very happy men; but it is not, and cannot be so. They who possess much, must lose, and expend, and give much; and this necessity brings more of pain than the possessions themselves can give of pleasure.'

Singular Proposal of Pheraulas

The Sacian was not convinced. The giving and expending, he maintained, would be to him, in itself, a source of pleasure. He should like to have much, for the very purpose of being able to expend much. Finally, Pheraulas proposed to the Sacian, since he seemed to think that riches would afford him so much pleasure, and as he himself, Pheraulas, found the possession of them only a source of trouble and care, that he would convey all his wealth to the Sacian, he himself to receive only an ordinary maintenance from it.

'You are in jest,' said the Sacian.

'No,' said Pheraulas, 'I am in earnest.' And he renewed his proposition, and pressed the Sacian urgently to accept of it.

The Sacian Accepts It

The Sacian then said that nothing could give him greater pleasure than such an arrangement. He expressed great gratitude for so generous an offer, and promised that, if he received the property, he would furnish Pheraulas with most ample and abundant supplies for all his wants, and would relieve him entirely of all responsibility and care. He promised, moreover, to obtain from Cyrus permission that Pheraulas should thereafter be excused from the duties of military service, and from all the toils, privations and hardships of war, so that he might thenceforth lead a life of quiet, luxury and ease, and thus live in the enjoyment of all the benefits which wealth could procure, without its anxieties and cares.

The Plan Carried into Effect – The Happy Result

The plan, thus arranged, was carried into effect. Pheraulas divested himself of his possessions, conveying them all to the Sacian. Both parties were extremely pleased with the operation of the scheme, and they lived thus together for a long time. Whatever Pheraulas acquired in any way, he always brought to the Sacian, and the Sacian, by accepting it, relieved Pheraulas of all responsibility and care. The Sacian loved Pheraulas, as Xenophon says, in closing this narrative, because he was thus continually bringing him gifts; and Pheraulas loved the Sacian, because he was always willing to take the gifts which were thus brought to him.

Cyrus's Dinner Party

Among the other conversations, whether real or imaginary, which Xenophon records, he gives some specimens of those which took place at festive entertainments in Cyrus's tent, on occasions when he invited his officers to dine with him. He commenced the conversation, on one of these occasions, by inquiring of some of the officers present whether they did not think that the common soldiers were equal to the officers themselves in intelligence, courage and military skill, and in all the other substantial qualities of a good soldier.

Conversation About Soldiers –
The Discontented Soldier

'I know not how that may be,' replied one of the officers. 'How they will prove when they come into action with the enemy, I cannot tell; but a more perverse and churlish set of fellows in camp, than these I have got in my regiment, I never knew. The other day, for example, when there had been a sacrifice, the meat of the victims was sent around to be distributed to the soldiers. In our regiment, when the steward came in with the first distribution, he began by me, and so went round, as far as what he had brought would go. The next time he came, he began at the other end. The supply failed before he had got to the place where he had left off before, so that there was a man in the middle that did not get anything. This man immediately broke out in loud and angry complaints, and declared that there was no equality or fairness whatever in such a mode of division, unless they began sometimes in the centre of the line.

His Repeated Misfortunes

'Upon this,' continued the officer, 'I called to the discontented man, and invited him to come and sit by me, where he would have a better chance for a good share. He did so. It happened that, at the next distribution that was made, we were the last, and he fancied that only the smallest pieces were left, so he began to complain more than before. 'Oh, misery!' said he, 'that I should have to sit here!' 'Be patient,' said I; 'pretty soon they will begin the distribution with us, and then you will have the best chance of all.' And so it proved for, at the next distribution, they began at us, and the man took his share first; but when the second and third men took theirs, he fancied that their pieces looked larger than his, and he reached forward and put his piece back into the basket, intending to change it; but the steward moved rapidly on, and he did not get another, so that he lost his distribution altogether. He was then quite furious with rage and vexation.'

Amusement of the Party – The Awkward Squad

Cyrus and all the company laughed very heartily at these mischances of greediness and discontent; and then other stories, of a somewhat similar character, were told by other guests. One officer said that a few days previous he was drilling a part of his troops, and he had before him on the plain what is called, in military language, a *squad* of men, whom he was teaching to march. When he gave the order to advance, one, who was at the head of the file, marched forward with great alacrity, but all the rest stood still. 'I asked him,' continued the officer, 'what he was doing. "Marching," said he, "as you ordered me to do." 'It was not you alone that I ordered to march,' said I, 'but all.' So I sent him back to his place, and then gave the command again. Upon this they all advanced promiscuously and in disorder toward me, each one acting for himself, without regard to the others, and leaving the file leader, who ought to have been at the head, altogether behind. The file leader said, 'Keep back! keep back!' Upon this the men were offended, and asked what they were to do about such contradictory orders. 'One commands us to advance, and another to keep back!' said they; 'how are we to know which to obey?'

Merriment of the Company

Cyrus and his guests were so much amused at the awkwardness of these recruits, and the ridiculous predicament in which the officer was placed by it, that the narrative of the speaker was here interrupted by universal and long-continued laughter.

'Finally,' continued the officer, 'I sent the men all back to their places, and explained to them that, when a command was given, they were not to obey it in confusion and unseemly haste, but regularly and in order, each one following the man who stood before him. "You must regulate your proceeding," said I, "by the action of the file leader; when he advances, you must advance, following him in a line, and governing your movements in all respects by his."

The File Leader and the Letters

'Just at this moment,' continued the officer, 'a man came to me for a letter which was to go to Persia, and which I had left in my tent. I directed the file leader to run to my tent and bring the letter to me. He immediately set off, and the rest, obeying literally the directions which I had just been giving them, all followed, running behind him in a line like a troop of savages, so that I had the whole squad of twenty men running in a body off the field to fetch a letter!'

Remark of Cyrus

When the general hilarity which these recitals occasioned had a little subsided, Cyrus said he thought that they could not complain of the character of the soldiers whom they had to command, for they were certainly, according to these accounts, sufficiently ready to obey the orders they received. Upon this, a certain one of the guests who was present, named Aglaitadas, a gloomy and austere-looking man, who had not joined at all in the merriment which the conversation had caused, asked Cyrus if he believed those stories to be true.

'Why?' asked Cyrus; 'what do *you* think of them?'

Animadversion Version of Aglaitadas

'*I* think,' said Aglaitadas, 'that these officers invented them to make the company laugh. It is evident that they were not telling the truth, since they related the stories in such a vain and arrogant way.'

'Arrogant!' said Cyrus; 'you ought not to call them arrogant; for, even if they invented their narrations, it was not to gain any selfish ends of their own, but only to amuse us and promote our enjoyment. Such persons should be called polite and agreeable rather than arrogant.'

'If, Aglaitadas,' said one of the officers who had related the anecdotes, 'we had told you melancholy stories to make you gloomy and wretched, you might have been justly displeased; but you certainly ought not to complain of us for making you merry.'

Aglaitadas's Argument for Melancholy

'Yes,' said Aglaitadas, 'I think I may. To make a man laugh is a very insignificant and useless thing. It is far better to make him weep. Such thoughts and such conversation as makes us serious, thoughtful and sad, and even moves us to tears, are the most salutary and the best.'

Defence of the Officers

'Well,' replied the officer, 'if you will take my advice, you will lay out all your powers of inspiring gloom, and melancholy, and of bringing tears, upon our enemies, and bestow the mirth and laughter upon us. There must be a prodigious deal of laughter in you, for none ever comes out. You neither use nor expend it yourself, nor do you afford it to your friends.'

'Then,' said Aglaitadas, 'why do you attempt to draw it from me?'

'It is preposterous!' said another of the company; 'for one could more easily strike fire out of Aglaitadas than get a laugh from him!'

Aglaitadas could not help smiling at this comparison; upon which Cyrus, with an air of counterfeited gravity, reproved the person who had spoken, saying that he had corrupted the most sober man in the company by making him smile, and that to disturb such gravity as that of Aglaitadas was carrying the spirit of mirth and merriment altogether too far.

General Character of Xenophon's *Cyropaedia*

These specimens will suffice. They serve to give a more distinct idea of the *Cyropaedia* of Xenophon than any general description could afford. The book is a drama, of which the principal elements are such narratives as the story of Panthea, and such conversations as those contained in this chapter, intermingled with long discussions on the principles of government, and on the discipline and management of armies. The principles and the sentiments which the work inculcates and explains are now of little value, being no longer applicable to the affairs of mankind in the altered circumstances of the present day. The book, however, retains its rank among men on account of a certain beautiful and simple magnificence characterizing the style and language in which it is written, which, however, cannot be appreciated except by those who read the narrative in the original tongue.

Chapter XII
The Death of Cyrus, BCE 530

Progress of Cyrus's Conquests

AFTER HAVING MADE THE CONQUEST of the Babylonian empire, Cyrus found himself the sovereign of nearly all of Asia, so far as it was then known. Beyond his dominions there lay, on every side, according to the opinions which then prevailed, vast tracts of uninhabitable territory, desolate and impassable. These wildernesses were rendered unfit for man, sometimes by excessive heat, sometimes by excessive cold, sometimes from being parched by perpetual drought, which produced bare and desolate deserts, and sometimes by incessant rains, which drenched the country and filled it with morasses and fens. On the north was the great Caspian Sea, then almost wholly unexplored, and extending, as the ancients believed, to the Polar Ocean.

The Northern Countries – The Scythians – Their Warlike Character

On the west side of the Caspian Sea were the Caucasian Mountains, which were supposed, in those days, to be the highest on the globe. In the neighbourhood of these mountains there was a country, inhabited by a wild and half-savage people, who were called Scythians. This was, in fact, a sort of generic term, which was applied, in those days, to almost all the aboriginal tribes beyond the confines of civilization. The Scythians, however, if such they can properly be called, who lived on the borders of the Caspian Sea, were not wholly uncivilized. They possessed many of those mechanical arts which are the first to be matured among warlike nations. They had no iron or steel, but they were accustomed to work other metals, particularly gold and brass. They tipped their spears and javelins with brass, and made brazen plates for defensive armour, both for themselves and for their horses. They made, also, many ornaments and decorations of gold. These they attached to their helmets, their belts and their banners. They were very formidable in war, being, like all other northern nations, perfectly desperate and reckless in battle. They were excellent horsemen, and had an abundance of horses with which to exercise their skill; so that their armies consisted, like those of the Cossacks of modern times, of great bodies of cavalry.

The various campaigns and conquests by which Cyrus obtained possession of his extended dominions occupied an interval of about thirty years. It was near the close of this interval, when he was, in fact, advancing toward a late period of life, that he formed the plan of penetrating into these northern regions, with a view of adding them also to his domains.

Cyrus's Sons – His Queen

He had two sons, Cambyses and Smerdis. His wife is said to have been a daughter of Astyages, and that he married her soon after his conquest of the kingdom of Media, in order to reconcile the Medians more easily to his sway, by making a Median princess their queen. Among the western nations of Europe such a marriage would be abhorred, Astyages having been Cyrus's grandfather; but among the Ancients, in those days, alliances of this nature were not uncommon. It would seem that this queen was not living at the time that the events occurred which are to be related in this chapter. Her sons had grown up to maturity, and were now princes of great distinction.

The Massagetae – Queen Tomyris – Spargapizes

One of the Scythian or northern nations to which we have referred were called the Massagetae. They formed a very extensive and powerful realm. They were governed, at this time, by a queen named Tomyris. She was a widow, past middle life. She had a son named Spargapizes, who had, like the sons of Cyrus, attained maturity, and was the heir to the throne. Spargapizes was, moreover, the commander-in-chief of the armies of the queen.

Selfish Views of Cyrus

The first plan which Cyrus formed for the annexation of the realm of the Massagetae to his own dominions was by a matrimonial alliance. He accordingly raised an army and commenced a movement toward the north, sending, at the same time, ambassadors before him into the country of the Massagetae, with offers of marriage to the queen. The queen knew very well that it was her dominions, and not herself, that constituted the great attraction for Cyrus, and, besides, she was of an age when ambition is a stronger passion than love. She refused the offers, and sent back word to Cyrus forbidding his approach.

Customs of the Savages

Cyrus, however, continued to move on. The boundary between his dominions and those of the queen was at the River Araxes, a stream flowing from west to east, through the central parts of Asia, toward the Caspian Sea. As Cyrus advanced, he found the country growing more and more wild and desolate. It was inhabited by savage tribes, who lived on roots and herbs, and who were elevated very little, in any respect, above the wild beasts that roamed in the forests around them. They had one very singular custom, according to Herodotus. It seems that there was a plant which grew among them, that bore a fruit, whose fumes, when it was roasting on a fire, had an exhilarating effect, like that produced by wine. These savages, therefore, Herodotus says, were accustomed to assemble around a fire, in their convivial festivities, and to throw some of this fruit in the midst of it. The fumes emitted by the fruit would soon begin to intoxicate the whole circle, when they would throw on more fruit, and become more and more excited, until, at length, they would jump up, dance about and sing, in a state of complete inebriation.

Cyrus Arrives at the Araxes – Difficulties of Crossing the River

Among such savages as these, and through the forests and wildernesses in which they lived, Cyrus advanced till he reached the Araxes. Here, after considering, for some time, by what means he could best pass the river, he determined to build a floating bridge, by means of boats and rafts obtained from the natives on the banks, or built for the purpose. It would be obviously much easier to transport the army by using these boats and rafts to *float* the men across, instead of constructing a bridge with them; but this would not have been safe, for the transportation of the army by such a means would be gradual and slow; and if the enemy were lurking in the neighbourhood, and should make an attack upon them in the midst of the operation, while a part of the army were upon one bank and a part upon the other, and another portion still, perhaps, in boats upon the stream, the defeat and destruction of the whole would be almost inevitable. Cyrus planned the formation of the bridge, therefore, as a means of transporting his army in a body, and of landing them on the opposite bank in solid columns, which could be formed into order of battle without any delay.

Embassy from Tomyris – Warning of Tomyris

While Cyrus was engaged in the work of constructing the bridge, ambassadors appeared, who said that they had been sent from Tomyris. She had commissioned them, they said, to warn Cyrus to desist entirely from his designs upon her kingdom, and to return to his own. This would be the wisest course, too, Tomyris said, for himself, and she counselled him, for his own welfare, to follow it. He could not foresee the result, if he should invade her dominions and encounter her armies. Fortune had favoured him thus far, it was true, but fortune might change, and he might find himself, before he was aware, at the end of his victories. Still, she said, she had no expectation that he would be disposed to listen to this warning and advice, and, on her part, she had no objection to his persevering in his invasion. She did not fear him. He need not put himself to the expense and trouble of building a bridge across the Araxes. She would agree to withdraw all her forces three days' march into her own country, so that he might cross the river safely and at his leisure, and she would await him at the place where she should have encamped; or, if he preferred it, she would cross the river and meet him on his own side. In that case, he must retire three days' march from the river, so as to afford her the same opportunity to make the passage undisturbed which she had offered him. She would then come over and march on to attack him. She gave Cyrus his option which branch of this alternative to choose.

Cyrus Calls a Council of War – Opinion of the Officers

Cyrus called a council of war to consider the question. He laid the case before his officers and generals, and asked for their opinion. They were unanimously agreed that it would be best for him to accede to the last of the two proposals made to him, viz., to draw back three days' journey toward his own dominions, and wait for Tomyris to come and attack him there.

Dissent of Croesus

There was, however, one person present at this consultation, though not regularly a member of the council, who gave Cyrus different advice. This was Croesus, the fallen king of Lydia. Ever since the time of his captivity, he had been retained in the camp and in the household of Cyrus, and had often accompanied him in his expeditions and campaigns. Though a captive, he seems to have been a friend; at least, the most friendly relations appeared to subsist between him and his conqueror; and he often figures in history as a wise and honest counsellor to Cyrus, in the various emergencies in which he was placed. He was present on this occasion, and he dissented from the opinion which was expressed by the officers of the army.

Speech of Croesus

'I ought to apologize, perhaps,' said he, 'for presuming to offer any counsel, captive as I am; but I have derived, in the school of calamity and misfortune in which I have been taught, some advantages for learning wisdom which you have never enjoyed. It seems to me that it will be much better for you not to fall back, but to advance and attack Tomyris in her own dominions; for, if you retire in this manner, in the first place, the act itself is discreditable to you: it is a retreat. Then, if, in the battle that follows, Tomyris conquers you, she is already advanced three days' march into your dominions, and she may go on, and, before you can take measures for raising another army, make herself mistress of your empire. On the other hand, if, in the battle, you conquer her, you will be then six days' march back of the position which you would occupy if you were to advance now.

His Advice to Cyrus

'I will propose,' continued Croesus, 'the following plan: Cross the river according to Tomyris's offer, and advance the three days' journey into her country. Leave a small part of your force there, with a great abundance of your most valuable baggage and supplies – luxuries of all kinds, and rich wines, and such articles as the enemy will most value as plunder. Then fall back with the main body of your army toward the river again, in a secret manner, and encamp in an ambuscade. The enemy will attack your advanced detachment. They will conquer them. They will seize the stores and supplies, and will suppose that your whole army is vanquished. They will fall upon the plunder in disorder, and the discipline of their army will be overthrown. They will go to feasting upon the provisions and to drinking the wines, and then, when they are in the midst of their festivities and revelry, you can come back suddenly with the real strength of your army, and wholly overwhelm them.'

Cyrus Adopts the Plan of Croesus – His Reply to Tomyris

Cyrus determined to adopt the plan which Croesus thus recommended. He accordingly gave answer to the ambassadors of Tomyris that he would accede to the first of her proposals. If she would draw back from the river three days' march, he would cross it with his army as soon as practicable, and then come forward and attack her. The ambassadors received this message, and departed to deliver it to their queen. She was faithful to her agreement, and drew her forces back to the place proposed, and left them there, encamped under the command of her son.

Forebodings of Cyrus

Cyrus seems to have felt some forebodings in respect to the manner in which this expedition was to end. He was advanced in life, and not now as well able as he once was to endure the privations and hardships of such campaigns. Then, the incursion which he was to make was into a remote, wild and dangerous country and he could not but be aware that he might never return. Perhaps he may have had some compunctions of conscience, too, at thus wantonly disturbing the peace and invading the territories of an innocent neighbour, and his mind may have been the less at ease on that account. At any rate, he resolved to settle the affairs of his government before he set out, in order to secure both the tranquillity of the country while he should be absent, and the regular transmission of his power to his descendants in case he should never return.

He Appoints Cambyses Regent

Accordingly, in a very formal manner, and in the presence of all his army, he delegated his power to Cambyses, his son, constituting him regent of the realm during his absence. He committed Croesus to his son's special care, charging him to pay him every attention and honour. It was arranged that these persons, as well as a considerable portion of the army, and a large number of attendants that had followed the camp thus far, were not to accompany the expedition across the river, but were to remain behind and return to the capital. These arrangements being all thus finally made, Cyrus took leave of his son and of Croesus, crossed the river with that part of the army which was to proceed, and commenced his march.

Hystaspes – His Son Darius – Cyrus's Dream

The uneasiness and anxiety which Cyrus seems to have felt in respect to his future fate on this memorable march affected even his dreams. It seems that there was among the officers of his army a certain general named Hystaspes. He had a son named Darius, then a youth of about twenty years of age, who had been left at home, in Persia, when the army marched, not being old enough to accompany them. Cyrus dreamed, one night, immediately after crossing the river, that he saw this young Darius with wings on his shoulders, that extended, the one over Asia and the other over Europe, thus overshadowing the world. When Cyrus awoke and reflected upon his dream, it seemed to him to portend that Darius might be aspiring to the government of his empire. He considered it a warning intended to put him on his guard.

Hystaspes's Commission

When he awoke in the morning, he sent for Hystaspes, and related to him his dream. 'I am satisfied,' said he, 'that it denotes that your son is forming ambitious and treasonable designs. Do you, therefore, return home, and arrest him in this fatal course. Secure him, and let him be ready to give me an account of his conduct when I shall return.'

Hystaspes, having received this commission, left the army and returned. The name of this Hystaspes acquired a historical immortality in a very singular way, that is, by being always used as a part of the appellation by which to designate his distinguished son. In after years Darius did attain to a very extended power. He became Darius the Great. As, however, there were several other Persian monarchs called Darius, some of whom were nearly as great as this the first of the name, the usage was gradually established of calling him Darius Hystaspes; and thus the name of the father has become familiar to all mankind, simply as a consequence and pendant to the celebrity of the son.

Cyrus Marches into the Queen's Country

After sending off Hystaspes, Cyrus went on. He followed, in all respects, the plan of Croesus. He marched his army into the country of Tomyris, and advanced until he reached the point agreed upon. Here he stationed a feeble portion of his army, with great stores of provisions and wines, and abundance of such articles as would be prized by the barbarians as booty. He then drew back with the main body of his army toward the Araxes, and concealed his forces in a hidden encampment. The result was as Croesus had anticipated. The body which he had left was attacked by the troops of Tomyris, and effectually routed. The provisions and stores fell into the hands of the victors. They gave themselves up to the most unbounded joy, and their whole camp was soon a universal scene of rioting and excess. Even the commander, Spargapizes, Tomyris's son, became intoxicated with the wine.

Success of the Stratagem – Spargapizes Taken Prisoner

While things were in this state, the main body of the army of Cyrus returned suddenly and unexpectedly, and fell upon their now helpless enemies with a force which entirely overwhelmed them. The booty was recovered, large numbers of the enemy were slain, and others were taken prisoners. Spargapizes himself was captured; his hands were bound; he was taken into Cyrus's camp, and closely guarded.

Tomyris's Concern for Her Son's Safety

The result of this stratagem, triumphantly successful as it was, would have settled the contest, and made Cyrus master of the whole realm, if as he, at the time, supposed was the case, the main body of Tomyris's forces had been engaged in this battle; but it seems that Tomyris had learned, by reconnoitrers and spies, how large a force there was in Cyrus's camp, and had only sent a detachment of her own troops to attack them, not judging it necessary to call out the whole. Two-thirds of her army remained still uninjured. With this large force she would undoubtedly have advanced without any delay to attack Cyrus again, were it not for her maternal concern for the safety of her son. He was in Cyrus's power, a helpless captive, and she did not know to what cruelties he would be exposed if Cyrus were to be exasperated against her. While her heart, therefore, was burning with resentment and anger, and with an almost uncontrollable thirst for revenge, her hand was restrained. She kept back her army, and sent to Cyrus a conciliatory message.

Her Conciliatory Message

She said to Cyrus that he had no cause to be specially elated at his victory; that it was only one-third of her forces that had been engaged, and that with the remainder she held him completely in her power. She urged him, therefore, to be satisfied with the injury which he had already inflicted upon her by destroying one third of her army, and to liberate her son, retire from her dominions and leave her in peace. If he would do so, she would not molest him in his departure; but if he would not, she swore by the sun, the great god which she and her countrymen adored, that, insatiable as he was for blood, she would give it to him till he had his fill.

Of course, Cyrus was not to be frightened by such threats as these. He refused to deliver up the captive prince, or to withdraw from the country, and both parties began to prepare again for war.

Mortification of Spargapizes

Spargapizes was intoxicated when he was taken, and was unconscious of the calamity which had befallen him. When at length he awoke from his stupor, and learned the full extent of his misfortune, and of the indelible disgrace which he had incurred, he was overwhelmed with astonishment, disappointment and shame. The more he reflected upon his condition, the more hopeless it seemed. Even if his life were to be spared, and if he were to recover his liberty, he never could recover his honour. The ignominy of such a defeat and such a captivity, he knew well, must be indelible.

Cyrus Gives Him Liberty Within the Camp – Death of Spargapizes

He begged Cyrus to loosen his bonds and allow him personal liberty within the camp. Cyrus, pitying, perhaps, his misfortunes, and the deep dejection and distress which they occasioned, acceded to this request. Spargapizes watched an opportunity to seize a weapon when he was not observed by his guards, and killed himself.

Grief and Rage of Tomyris

His mother Tomyris, when she heard of his fate, was frantic with grief and rage. She considered Cyrus as the wanton destroyer of the peace of her kingdom and the murderer of her son, and she had now no longer any reason for restraining her thirst for revenge. She immediately began to concentrate her forces, and to summon all the additional troops that she could obtain from every part of her kingdom. Cyrus, too, began in earnest to strengthen his lines, and to prepare for the great final struggle.

The Great Battle – Cyrus is Defeated and Slain

At length the armies approached each other, and the battle began. The attack was commenced by the archers on either side, who shot showers of arrows at their opponents as they were advancing. When the arrows were spent, the men fought hand to hand, with spears, javelins and swords. The Persians fought desperately, for they fought for their lives. They were in the heart of an enemy's country, with a broad river behind them to cut off their retreat, and they were contending with a wild and savage foe, whose natural barbarity was rendered still more ferocious and terrible than ever by the exasperation which they felt, in sympathy with their injured queen. For a long time, it was wholly uncertain which side would win the day. The advantage, here and there along the lines, was in some places on one side, and in some places on the other; but, though overpowered and beaten, the several bands, whether of Persians or Scythians, would neither retreat nor surrender, but the survivors, when their comrades had fallen, continued to fight on till they were all slain. It was evident, at last, that the Scythians were gaining the day. When night came on, the Persian army was found to be almost wholly destroyed; the remnant dispersed. When all was over, the Scythians, in exploring the field, found the dead body of Cyrus among the other ghastly and mutilated remains which covered the ground. They took it up with a ferocious and exulting joy, and carried it to Tomyris.

Tomyris's Treatment of Cyrus's Body

Tomyris treated it with every possible indignity. She cut and mutilated the lifeless form; as if it could still feel the injuries inflicted by her insane revenge. 'Miserable wretch!' said she; 'though I am in the end your conqueror, you have ruined my peace and happiness forever. You have murdered my son. But I promised you your fill of blood, and you shall have it.' So saying, she filled a can with Persian blood, obtained, probably, by the execution of her captives, and, cutting off the head of her victim from the body, she plunged it in, exclaiming, 'Drink there, insatiable monster, till your murderous thirst is satisfied.'

This was the end of Cyrus. Cambyses, his son, whom he had appointed regent during his absence, succeeded quietly to the government of his vast dominions.

Reflections – Hardheartedness, Selfishness and Cruelty Characterize the Ambitious

In reflecting on this melancholy termination of this great conqueror's history, our minds naturally revert to the scenes of his childhood, and we wonder that so amiable, and gentle, and generous a boy should become so selfish, unfeeling and overbearing as a man. But such are the natural and inevitable effects of ambition and an inordinate love of power. The history of a conqueror is always a tragical and melancholy tale. He begins life with an exhibition of great and noble qualities, which awaken in us, who read his history, the same admiration that was felt for him, personally, by his friends and countrymen while he lived, and on which the vast ascendency which he acquired over the minds of his fellow men, and which led to his power and fame, was, in a great measure, founded. On the other hand, he ends life neglected, hated and abhorred. His ambition has been gratified, but the gratification has brought with it no substantial peace or happiness; on the contrary, it has filled his soul with uneasiness, discontent, suspiciousness and misery. The histories of heroes would be far less painful in the perusal if we could reverse this moral change of character, so as to have the cruelty, the selfishness and the oppression exhaust themselves in the comparatively unimportant transactions of early life, and the spirit of kindness, generosity and beneficence blessing and beautifying its close. To be generous, disinterested and noble, seems to be necessary as the precursor of great military success; and to be hard-hearted, selfish and cruel is the almost inevitable consequence of it. The exceptions to this rule, though some of them are very splendid, are yet very few.

The Ancient History

CHARLES ROLLIN (1661–1741) was a French scholar, writer and dissident religious thinker: a member of the Jansenist movement that sought to bring radical ideas into Catholic belief. Although he encountered considerable opposition due to his religious convictions, he still managed to build a formidable reputation as a scholar and teacher. His multi-volume *The Ancient History* (1730–38), from which we here present 'The Character and Eulogy of Cyrus', surveyed the civilizations of the ancient world, and was quickly translated into many European languages. It became the standard reference for the next century, the principle modern history of the ancient world for students, philosophers and artists; and would later play a key role in the thought of the founding Fathers of the American Republic, and the leaders of the French Revolution.

Throughout his work, Rollin seeks to present a Christian perspective on a pagan world; but he often wavers between fervent admiration and moral disdain. The ancient world was a dangerous source of ideas that threatened the two certainties of early modern Europe: the power of kings and the moral authority of the Church. The period we call the Enlightenment – the philosophical, political and cultural revolution of the late seventeenth and eighteenth centuries – was first and foremost a challenge to these two institutions and their absolute control over modern life. In antiquity there lay alternatives, a veritable 'philosophical arsenal' in the words of one scholar, that were pre-Christian and often fervently anti-monarchic.

The ancient world was both inspiring and dangerous, and Rollin tried to balance the two. In his preface he warns his readers: 'Students ought to take care, and especially we, who by the duties of our profession are obliged to be perpetually conversant with heathen authors, not to enter too far into the spirit of them; not to imbibe, unperceived, their sentiments, by lavishing too great applauses on their heroes; nor to give into excesses which the heathens indeed did not consider as such, because they were not acquainted with virtues of a purer kind.' Thus, he seeks to view the pagan past through a lens of Christian morality; although all too often his lens slips, to reveal an ancient world that is fascinatingly seductive. In the case of Cyrus, a figure so vaunted in the Biblical tradition, Rollin perhaps felt he was on safer ground. His eulogy coalesced the praise of the ancients with the values of the philosophers, presenting an idealized portrait of the perfect king.

The Character and Eulogy of Cyrus
(From *The Ancient History of the Egyptians, Carthaginians, Assyrians, Babylonians, Medes and Persians, Macedonians, and Grecians*, 1730-38)

CYRUS MAY JUSTLY BE CONSIDERED as the wisest conqueror, and the most accomplished prince, to be found in profane history. He was possessed of all the qualities requisite to form a great man; wisdom, moderation, courage, magnanimity, noble sentiments, a wonderful ability in managing men's tempers and gaining their affections, a thorough knowledge of every branch of the military art as far as that age had carried it, a vast extent of genius and capacity for forming and an equal steadiness and prudence for executing the greatest designs.

It is very common for those heroes who shine in the field, and make a great figure in the time of action, to make but a very poor one upon other occasions, and in matters of a different nature. We are astonished, when we see them alone and without their armies, to find what a difference there is between a general and a great man; to see what low sentiments and mean actions they are capable of in private life; how they are influenced by jealousy, and governed by interest; how disagreeable and even odious they render themselves by their haughty deportment and arrogance, which they think necessary to preserve their authority, and which only serve to make them hated and despised

Cyrus had none of these defects. He appeared always the same, that is, always great, even in the most indifferent matters. Being assured of his greatness, of which real merit was the foundation and support, he thought of nothing more than to lender himself affable, and easy of access: and whatever he seemed to lose by this condescending, humble demeanour, was abundantly compensated by the cordial affection and sincere respect it procured him from his people.

Never was any prince a greater master of the art of insinuation, so necessary for those that govern, and yet so little understood or practised. He knew perfectly what advantages may result from a single word rightly timed, from an obliging carriage, from a command tempered with reason, from a little praise in granting a favour, and from softening a refusal with expressions of concern and good-will. His history abounds with beauties of this kind

He was rich in a sort of wealth which most sovereigns want, who are possessed of everything but faithful friends, and whose indigence in that particular is concealed by the splendour and affluence with which they are surrounded. Cyrus was beloved, because he himself had a love for others; for, has a man any friends, or does he deserve to have any when he himself is void of friendship? Nothing affects us more, than to see in Xenophon, the manner in which Cyrus lived and conversed with his friends, always preserving as much dignity as was requisite to keep up a due decorum, and yet infinitely removed from that ill-judged haughtiness, which deprives the great of the most innocent and agreeable pleasure in life, that of conversing freely and sociably with persons of merit, though of an inferior station.

The use he made of his friends may serve as a perfect model to all persons in authority. His friends had received from him not only the liberty, but an express command, to tell him whatever they thought. And though he was much superior to all his officers in understanding, yet he never undertook anything without asking their advice: and whatever was to be done, whether it was to reform anything in the government, to make changes in the army, or to form a new enterprise, he would always have every man speak his sentiments, and would often make use of them to correct his own.

Cicero observes, that, during the whole time of Cyrus's government, he was never heard to speak one rough or angry word (Cicero's Letters to Quintus 2.7), What a high encomium for a prince is comprehended in that short sentence! Cyrus must have had a very great command of himself, to be able, in the midst of so much agitation, and in spite of all the intoxicating effects of sovereign power, always to preserve his mind in such a state of calmness and composure, that no crosses, disappointments or unforeseen accidents, should ever ruffle its tranquillity, or provoke him to utter any harsh or offensive expression.

But, what was still greater in him, and more truly royal than all this, was his steadfast persuasion, that all his labours and endeavours ought to tend to the happiness of his people; and that it was not by the splendour of riches, by pompous equipages, luxurious living, or a magnificent table, that a king ought to distinguish himself from his subjects, but by a superiority of merit in every kind, and particularly by a constant indefatigable care and vigilance to promote their interests, and to secure the public welfare and tranquillity. He said himself one day, as he was discoursing with his courtiers upon the duties of a king, that a prince ought to consider himself as a shepherd (the image under which both sacred and profane antiquity represented good kings), and that he ought to exercise the same vigilance, care, and goodness.

'It is his duty,' says he, 'to watch, that his people may live in safety and quiet; to charge himself with anxieties, and cares, that they may be exempt from them: to choose whatever is salutary for them, and remove what is hurtful and prejudicial; to place his delight in seeing them increase and multiply, and valiantly expose his own person in their defence and protection.'

'This,' says he, 'is the natural idea, and the just image of a good king. It is reasonable, at the same time, that his subjects should render him all the service he stands in need of; but it is still more reasonable, that he should labour to make them happy; because it is for that very end that he is their king, as much as it is the end and office of a shepherd to take care of his flock.'

Indeed, to be the guardian of the commonwealth, and to be king; to be for the people, and to be their sovereign, is but one and the same thing. A man is born for others, when he is born to govern, because the reason and end of governing others is only to be useful and serviceable to them. The very basis and foundation of the condition of princes is, not to be for themselves; the very characteristic of their greatness is, that they are consecrated to the public good. They may properly be considered as a light, which is placed on high, only to diffuse and shed its beams on everything below. Are such sentiments as these any disparagement to the dignity of the regal state?

It was by the concurrence of all these virtues that Cyrus founded such an extensive empire in so short a time; that he peaceably enjoyed the fruits of his conquests for many years; that he made himself so much esteemed and beloved, not only by his own natural subjects, but by all the nations he had conquered; that after his death he was universally regretted as the common father of all the people. We ought not, indeed, to be surprised that Cyrus was so accomplished in every virtue (it will be readily understood, that I speak only of pagan virtues) because we know it was God himself, who had formed him to be the instrument and agent of his gracious designs towards his peculiar people.

When I say that God himself had formed this prince, I do not mean that he did it by any sensible miracle, nor that he immediately made him such as we admire in the accounts we have of him in history. God gave him a happy genius, and implanted in his mind the seeds of all the noblest qualities, disposing his heart at the same time to aspire after the most excellent and sublime virtues. But above all, he took care that this happy genius should be cultivated by a good education, and by that means be prepared for the great designs for which he intended him. We may venture to say, without fear of being mistaken, that the greatest excellencies in Cyrus were owing to his education, where the confounding of him, in some sort, with his subjects, and the keeping him under the same subjection to the authority of his teachers, served to eradicate that pride which is so natural to princes; taught him to hearken to advice, and to obey before he came to command; inured him to hardship and toil; accustomed him to temperance and sobriety; and, in a word, rendered him such as we have seen him throughout his whole conduct, gentle, modest, affable, obliging, compassionate; an enemy to all luxury and pride, and still more so to flattery.

It must be confessed, that such a prince is one of the most precious and valuable gifts that Heaven can make to mortal men. The infidels themselves have acknowledged this; nor has the darkness of their false religion been able to hide these two remarkable truths from their observation: that all good kings are the gift of God, and that, such a gift includes many others; for nothing can be so excellent as that which bears the most perfect resemblance to the Deity. And the noblest image of the Deity is a just, moderate, chaste and virtuous prince, who rules with no other view than to establish the reign of justice and virtue. This is the portraiture which Pliny has left us of Trajan, and which has a great resemblance to that of Cyrus: 'There is no better and more beautiful gift of God for mortals than the chaste, holy, and god-like prince.'

When I narrowly examine this hero's life, there seems to have been one circumstance advancing to his glory which would have enhanced it exceedingly; I mean that of having struggled under some grievous calamity for some time, and of having his virtue tried by some sudden reverse of fortune. I know, indeed, that the Roman emperor Galba, when he adopted Piso, told him that the stings of prosperity were infinitely sharper than those of adversity; and that the former put the soul to a much severer trial than the latter. And the reason he gives is, that when misfortunes come with their whole weight upon a man's soul, he exerts himself, and summons all his strength to bear the burden; whereas prosperity attacking the mind secretly or insensibly leaves it all its weakness, and insinuates a poison into it, by so much the more dangerous, as it is the more subtle.

However, it must be owned that adversity, when supported with nobleness and dignity, and surmounted by an invincible patience, adds a great lustre to a prince's glory, and gives him occasion to display many fine qualities and virtues, which would have been concealed in the bosom of prosperity; as a greatness of mind, independent of everything without; an unshaken constancy, proof against the severest strokes of fortune; an intrepidity of soul animated at the sight of danger; a fruitfulness in expedients, improving even from crosses and disappointments; a presence of mind, which views, and provides against everything; and lastly, a firmness of soul, that not only suffices to support itself, but is capable of supporting others.

Cyrus wanted this kind of glory. He himself informs us, that during the whole course of his life, which was pretty long, the happiness of it was never interrupted by any unfortunate accident; and that in all his designs the success had answered his utmost expectation. But he acquaints us, at the same time, with another thing almost incredible, and which was the source of all that moderation and evenness of temper so conspicuous in him, and for which he can never be sufficiently admired; namely, that in the midst of his uninterrupted prosperity he still preserved in his heart a secret fear, proceeding from the changes and misfortunes that might happen: and this prudent fear was not only a preservative against insolence, but even against intemperate joy.

There remains one point more to be examined, with regard to this prince's reputation and character; I mean the nature of his victories and conquests, upon which I shall touch but lightly. If these were founded only upon ambition, injustice and violence, Cyrus would be so far from meriting the praises bestowed upon him, that he would deserve to be ranked among those famous robbers of the universe, those public enemies to mankind, who acknowledged no right but that of force; who looked upon the common rules of justice, as laws which only private persons were obliged to observe, and derogatory to the majesty of kings; who set no other bounds to their designs and pretensions, than their incapacity of carrying them any farther;

who sacrificed the lives of millions to their particular ambition; who made their glory consist in spreading desolation and destruction, like fires and torrents; and who reigned as bears and lions would if they were masters.

This is indeed the true character of the greatest part of those pretended heroes whom the world admires; and by such ideas as these, we ought to correct the impressions made upon our minds by the undue praises of some historians, and the sentiments of many, deceived by his false images of greatness.

I do not know whether I am not biased in favour of Cyrus: it he seems to me to have been of a very different character from those conquerors, whom I have just now described. Not that I would justify Cyrus in every respect, or represent him as exempt from ambition, which undoubtedly was the route of all his undertakings; but he certainly reverenced the laws, and knew that there are unjust wars, which render him who wantonly provokes them accountable for all the blood that is shed. Now, every war is of this sort, to which the prince is induced by no other motive than that of enlarging his conquests, of acquiring a vain reputation, or rendering himself terrible to his neighbours.

Cyrus, as we have seen, at the beginning of the war, founded all his hopes of success on the justice of his cause, and represented to his soldiers, in order to inspire them with the greater courage and confidence, that they were not the aggressors; that it was the enemy that attacked them; and that therefore they were entitled to the protection of the gods, who seemed themselves to have put their arms into their hands, that they might fight in defence of their friends and allies, unjustly oppressed. If we carefully examine Cyrus's conquests, we shall find that they were all consequences of the victories he obtained over Croesus, king of Lydia, who was master of the greatest part of Lesser Asia; with over the king of Babylon, who was master of all upper Asia, and many other countries; both which princes were the aggressors.

With good reason, therefore, is Cyrus represented as one of the greatest princes recorded in history; and his reign justly proposed as the model of a perfect government, which it could not be, unless justice had been the basis and foundation of it.

A New Cyropaedia; or The Travels of Cyrus

A NDREW RAMSEY (1686–1743) was born in Scotland and as a young man emigrated to France and joined the Jacobite Court, the supporters of the exiled Stuart claimants to the thrones of England and Scotland. The last Stuart king, James II, had been driven from Britain in 1688 during the so-called 'Glorious Revolution', an event greatly celebrated in English history, but which, as the historian Simon Schama remarked, was neither a revolution nor glorious.

Ramsey soon gained prominence among the exiles, and was appointed tutor to the young Prince Charles Edward, the 'Bonnie Prince Charlie' of legend, whose fateful expedition to reclaim the throne would be the last hurrah of the exiles – and the last stand of the Highlanders – before the family would sink into a drunken irrelevance. Although he only held the post briefly – the Prince was barely four years old at the time – Ramsey remained focused on the question of royal education, leading to his epic novel, *The Travels of Cyrus* (1729), which quickly became a bestseller across Europe. His book imagines a young Cyrus crossing the ancient world, encountering many of the most famous figures from history, learning from each of them and partaking in their adventures: from the Iranian prophet Zoroaster, to the philosopher Solon and the Spartan Leonidas. The text is entirely fictional, as Ramsey admits at the very outset; and indeed, the historical figures included barely overlapped. However, each part involves a careful reconstruction of the context and the characters involved, albeit in a highly idealized manner. The novel becomes a journey through the civilizations of antiquity, each delineated and discussed by the Persian prince, so that the reader travels with him, seeing these cultures from a foreign – indeed a non-European – perspective. Ramsey's Cyrus continually learns from others even as he enriches *their* understanding.

The extracts give a brief taste of Ramsey's approach. The education of Cyrus in Persia is related in terms of their traditional practices. The wisdom of Zoroaster is used to expand on notions of science and religion, but also expressed as a result of the prophet's own tragic life story. Cyrus's visit to Sparta represents a quite unusual portrait of a city-state that was usually idealized in eighteenth-century writing: here Spartan virtues are apparent, but severely limited, and Cyrus makes a number of pertinent criticisms even as he learns from – and fights alongside – the Spartans. In each case Ramsey is drawing on contemporary knowledge of these places and peoples; but there are also inferences to the ongoing debates of Enlightenment thought. Moreover, he also weaves uncertainty in the reader's mind: for example, the Spartan Leonidas is clearly meant to evoke the hero of Thermopylae, but appears to be a different character altogether.

From the Preface

§

Conquerors have generally no other view in extending their dominions, than to satisfy their unbounded ambition: Cyrus on the contrary made use of his victories to procure the happiness of the conquered nations. The author's intention in making choice of such a Prince was to show, that courage, great exploits and military talents may indeed excite our admiration, but do not form the character of a true hero, without the addition of wisdom, virtue and noble sentiments. In order to form such a hero, it was thought allowable to make him travel; and the silence of Xenophon, who says nothing in his *Cyropaedia* of what happened to Cyrus from his sixteenth to his fortieth, year, leaves the author at liberty to imagine this fiction.

The relation of the Prince's travels furnishes an occasion to describe the religion, manners and politics of the several countries through which he passes. These travels cannot surely appear unnatural; a prudent Prince like Cambyses, a father who is supposed to be informed of the oracles concerning the future greatness of his son, a tributary King who knows the danger of sending the young Prince a second time to the court of Ecbatana, ought to be sensible that Cyrus at twenty-five years of age could not better employ his time during the interval of a profound peace, than by travelling into Egypt and Greece. It was necessary to prepare a Prince who was to be one day the founder and lawgiver of a mighty empire, to accomplish his high destiny by acquiring in each country some knowledge worthy of his great genius. Is there anything strained in all this? No other hero could answer the author's intention; had he made any other Prince travel, he would have lost all the advantages he has drawn from the choice of Cyrus, as the deliverer of the people of God, as contemporary with the great men with whom he consults, and as living in an age, the learning, manners and events of which, could alone be suitable to the design of this work.

All the author's episodes tend to instruction, and the instructions are, as he apprehends, proportioned to the age of Cyrus: in his youth he is in danger of being corrupted by vanity, love and irreligion; Mandana, Hystaspes and Zoroaster preserve him from these snares. The history of Apries lays open to him all the artifices of a perfidious courtier; that of the Kings of Sparta, the dangers of an excessive confidence in favourites, or of an unjust diffidence of ministers; that of Periander, the fatal mischiefs which attend despotic power and the dispensing with ancient laws; that of Pisistratus, the punishment of a base and crafty policy, and that of Nabuchodonosor, the dreadful consequences of relapsing into impiety, after due light and admonition. The Prince is at first instructed by fables, to preserve him from the passions of youth; he afterwards instructs himself by his own reflections, by the examples he sees, and by all the adventures he meets with in his travels; he goes from country to country, collecting all the treasures, conversing with the great men he finds there, and performing heroic exploits as occasion presents.

From the First Book: The Education of Cyrus

CYRUS WAS EDUCATED from his tender years after the manner of ancient Persia, where the youth were inured to hardship and fatigue; hunting and war were their only exercises; out confiding too much in their natural courage, they neglected military discipline. The Persians were hitherto rough, but virtuous; they were not versed in those arts and sciences which polish the mind and manners; but they were great masters of the sublime science of being content with simple nature, despising death for the love of their country, and flying all pleasures which emasculate the mind, and enervate the body. Being persuaded that sobriety and exercise prevent almost every disease, they habituated themselves to a rigorous abstinence and perpetual labour: the lightest indispositions proceeding from intemperance were thought shameful.

The youth were educated in public schools, where they were early instructed in the knowledge of the laws, and accustomed to hear causes, pass sentence and mutually to do one another the most exact justice; and hereby they discovered their dispositions, penetration and capacity for employments in a riper age. The virtues, which their masters were principally careful to inspire into them, were the love of truth, humanity, sobriety and obedience: the two former make us resemble the Gods; the two latter are necessary to the preservation of order. The chief aim of the laws in ancient Persia was to prevent the corruption of the heart: and for this reason the Persians punished ingratitude; a vice against which there is no provision made by the laws of other nations: whoever was capable of forgetting a benefit was looked upon as an enemy to society.

Cyrus had been educated according to these wise maxims; and though it was impossible to conceal from him his rank and birth, yet he was treated with the same severity as if he had not been heir to a throne; he was taught to practise an exact obedience, that he might afterwards know how to command. When he arrived at the age of fourteen, Astyages desired to see him: Mandana could not avoid complying with her father's orders, but the thought of carrying her son to the court of Ecbatana exceedingly grieved her.

For the space of three hundred years the kings of Media had by their bravery extended their conquests; and conquests had begot luxury, which is always the forerunner of the fall of empires. VALOR – CONQUEST – LUXURY – ANARCHY, this is the fatal circle, and these are the different periods of the politic life, in almost all states. The court of Ecbatana was then in its splendour; but this splendour had nothing in it of solidity. The days were spent in luxury, or in flattery; the love of glory, strict probity, severe honour, were no longer in esteem; the pursuit of solid knowledge was thought to argue a want of taste; agreeable trifling, fine spun thoughts and lively sallies of imagination, were the only kinds of wit admired there. No sort of writings pleased, but amusing fictions where there was a perpetual success of events, which surprised by their variety, without improving the understanding or ennobling the heart. Love was without delicacy; blind pleasure was its only attractive charm: the women thought themselves despised, when no attempts were made to ensnare them. That which contributed to increase this corruption of mind, manners and sentiments, was the new doctrine spread ever whereby the ancient Magi, that pleasure is the only moving spring of man's heart: for as each man placed his pleasure in what he liked best, this maxim authorised virtue or vice according to every one's taste, humour or complexion. This depravity, however, was not then so universal as it became afterwards. Corruption takes its rise in courts, and extends itself gradually through all the parts of a state. Military discipline was yet in its vigour in Media; and there were in the provinces many brave soldiers, who not being infected by the contagious air of Ecbatana, preserved in themselves all the virtues which flourished in the reigns of the former kings, Dejoces and Phraortes.

Mandana was thoroughly sensible of all the dangers to which she should expose young Cyrus, by carrying him to a court, the manners of which were so different from those of the Persians; but the will of Cambyses, and the orders of Astyages, obliged her, whether she would or not, to undertake the journey. She set out attended by a body of the young nobility of Persia under the command of Hystaspes, to whom the education of Cyrus had been committed: the young Prince was seated in a chariot with her, and it was the first time that he had seen himself distinguished from his companions. Mandana was a Princess of uncommon virtue, a well cultivated understanding, and a superior genius. She made it her business during the journey to inspire Cyrus with the love of virtue, by entertaining him with fables according to the Eastern manner. The minds of young persons are not touched by abstracted ideas, they have need of agreeable and familiar images; they cannot reason, they can only feel the charms of truth; and to make it lovely to them, it must be presented under sensible and beautiful forms.

From the Second Book: Cyrus and Zoroaster

T HE PRINCE OF PERSIA was so enamoured with Cassandana (the daughter of Croesus) and his thoughts were so entirely employed in furnishing amusements for her, that there were great reason to fear he would give himself up to an indolent life. He was daily inventing new shows and entertainments unknown before in Persia, and introduced all the diversions in vogue at the court of Ecbatana: he gave no attention to business, and even neglected military exercises: this kind of life exposed him

continually to be seduced by the discourses, of the young Satraps who were about him.

On the borders of the Persian Gulf there had been lately settled a famous school of Magi, whose doctrine was entirely opposite to those fatal errors. Cyrus had a taste and a genius which led him to the study of the sublimest science; and Hystaspes, without letting the Prince perceive his views, laid hold of this advantage to raise a desire in him of conversing with those sages: as they never left their solitude, shunning the courts of Princes, and had little intercourse with other men; Cyrus resolved to go see them in their retreat.

He undertook this journey with Cassandana, accompanied by Hystaspes, Araspes, and several of the Persian nobles. They crossed the plain of Passagarda, travelled through the country of the Mardi and arrived upon the banks of the Arosis. They entered by a narrow pass into a large valley encompassed with high mountains, the tops of which was covered with oaks, fir trees and lofty cedars; below were rich pastures, in which all sorts of cattle were feeding; the plain looked like a garden watered by many rivulets, which came from the rocks all around and emptied themselves into the Arosis. This river lost itself between two little hills, which, as they opened, presented to the view successive scenes of new objects, and discovered at distances fruitful fields, vast forests and the Persian Gulf, which bounded the horizon. Cyrus and Cassandana, as they advanced in the valley, were invited into a neighbouring grove by the found of harmonious music. There they beheld, by the side of a clear fountain, a great number of men of all ages, and over against them a company of women, who formed a concert. They understood that it was the school of the Magi, and were surprised to see, instead of austere, melancholy and thoughtful men, an agreeable and polite people.

These Philosophers looked upon music as something heavenly, and proper to calm the passions, for which reason they always began and finished the day by concerts. After they had given some little time in the morning to this exercise, they led their disciples through delightful walks to the sacred mountain, observing all the way a profound silence; there they offered their homage to the Gods, rather by the voice of the heart, than of the lips. Thus, by music, pleasant walks and prayer, they prepared themselves for the contemplation of truth, and put the soul into a serenity proper for meditation; the rest of the day was spent in study. Their only repast was a little before sun set, at which time they eat nothing but bread, fruits and some portion of what had been offered to the Gods concluding all with concerts of music. Other men begin not the education of their children till after they are born, but the Magi seemed to do it before. While their wives were with child, they took care to keep them always in tranquillity, and a perpetual cheerfulness, by sweet and innocent amusements, to the end that from the mother's womb the fruit might receive no impressions, but what were pleasing, peaceful and agreeable to order.

Each sage had his province in the empire of Philosophy; some studied the virtues of plants, others the metamorphoses of insects; some again the formation of animals, and others the course of the stars: but the aim of all their researches was to come to the knowledge of the Gods, and of themselves. They said, that the sciences were no father valuable than they served as steps to ascend to the great Oromazes, and from thence to descend to man. Though the love of truth was the only bond of society among these philosophers, yet they were not without a head; hey called him the Archimagus. He, who then possessed that honour, was named Zardust or Zoroaster; he surpassed the rest more in wisdom than in age, for he was scarce fifty years old; nevertheless, he was a consummate master in all the sciences of the Chaldeans and Egyptians, and had even some knowledge of the religion of the Jews, whom he had seen at Babylon. Having observed the corruption which had crept in among the Magi, he had applied himself to reform their manners and their doctrine.

When Cyrus and Cassandana entered the grove, the assembly rose up and worshipped them, bowing themselves to the earth, according to the custom of the East; and then retiring left them alone with Zoroaster. This philosopher led them to a bower of myrtle, in the midst of which was the statue of a woman, which he had carved with his own hands. They all three sat down in this place upon a seat of verdant turf, and Zoroaster entertained the Prince and Princess with a discourse of the life, manners and virtues of the Magi.

While he was speaking, he frequently cast a look upon the statue, and as he beheld it his eyes were bathed in tears. Cyrus and Cassandana observed his sorrow at first with a respectful silence, but afterwards the Princess could not forbear asking him the reason of it. That statue, answered he, is the statue of Selima, who heretofore loved me, as you now love Cyrus. It is here that I come to spend my sweetest and my bitterest moments. In spite of wisdom, which submits me to the will of the Gods; in spite of the pleasures I taste in philosophy; in spite of the insensibility I am in, with regard to all human grandeur, the remembrance of Selima often renews my regrets and my tears. True virtue, though it regulates the passions, does not extinguish tender sentiments. These words gave Cyrus and Cassandana a curiosity to know the history of Selima. The philosopher would have excused himself, but he had already betrayed his secret by the sensibility he had shown, and could not go back without failing in due respect, to persons of such high rank: having therefore wiped away his tears he thus began his narration. I am not afraid of letting you know my weakness; but I should avoid the recital I am going to make, if I did not foresee that you may reap some useful instructions from it. I was born a Prince; my father was sovereign of a little territory in the Indies, which is called the country of Sophites. Having lost my way one day when I was hunting, I chanced to see in the thick part of a wood a young maid, who was there reposing herself. Her surprising beauty immediately struck me; I became immoveable, and dared not advance; I imagined she was one of those aerial spirits, who descend sometimes from the throne of Oromazes, to conduct souls back to the Empyren Heaven. Seeing herself alone with a man, she fled, and took refuge in a temple that was near the forest. I dared not follow her; but I learned that her name was Selima, that she was daughter of an old Brachma, who dwelt in that temple, and that she was consecrated to the worship of the fire. The Estals may quit celibacy and marry: but while they continue priestesses of the fire, the laws are so severe among the Indians, that a father thinks it an act of religion to throw his daughter alive into the flames, should she ever fall from that purity of manners which she has sworn to preserve.

My father was yet living, and I was not in a condition to force Selima from that asylum; Princes have no right in that country to persons consecrated to religion. However, these difficulties did but increase my passion; and the violence of it quickened my ingenuity: I left my father's palace; I was young, a Prince, and I did not consult reason. I disguised myself in the habit of a girl, and went to the temple, where the old Brachman lived. I deceived him by a feigned story, and became one of the Estals, under the name of Amana. The King, my father, who was disconsolate for my sudden leaving him, ordered search to be made for me everywhere, but to no purpose. Selima not knowing my sex, conceived a particular liking and friendship for me. I never left her; we passed our lives together in working, reading, walking and serving at the altars. I often told her sables and affecting stories, in order to point forth the wonderful effects of friendship and of love. My design was to prepare her by degrees for the final discovery of my intentions. I sometimes forgot myself while I was speaking, and was so carried away by my vivacity, that she often interrupted me, and said, one would think, Amana, to hear you speak, that you feel in this moment all that you describe. I lived in this manner several months with her, and it was not possible for her to discover either my disguise or my passion. As my heart was not corrupted, I had no criminal view; I imagined, that if I could engage her to love me, she would forsake her state of life to share my crown with me: I was continually waiting for a favourable moment, to reveal to her my sentiments; but alas! that moment never came.

It was a custom among the Estals, to go several times in the year upon a high mountain, there to kindle the sacred fire, and to offer sacrifices: we all went up thither one day, accompanied only by the old Brachman. Scarce was the sacrifice begun, when we were surrounded by a body of men, armed with bows and arrows, who carried away Selima and her father. They were all on horseback; I followed them some time, but they entered into a wood, and I saw them no more. I did not return to the temple, but stole away from the Estals, changed my dress, took another disguise and forsook the Indies. I forgot my father, my country and all my obligations; I wandered over all Asia in search of Selima: what cannot love do in a young heart given up to its passion? One day, as I was crossing the country of the Lycians, I stopped in a great forest to shelter myself from the excessive heat. I presently saw a company of hunters pass by, and a little after several women, among whom I thought I discovered Selima: she was in a hunting dress, mounted upon a proud courser, and distinguished from all the rest by a coronet of flowers. She passed by me so swiftly, that I could not be sure whether my conjectures were well founded; but I went straight to the capital.

The Lycians were at that time governed by women, which form of government was established among them upon the following occasion. Some years ago the men became so effeminate during a long peace, that their thoughts where wholly taken up about their dress. They affected the discourse, manners, maxims and all the imperfections of women, without having either their sweetness or their delicacy; and while they gave themselves up to infamous laziness, the most abominable vices took the place of lovely passions; they despised the Lycian women, and treated them like slaves: a foreign war came upon them; the men being grown cowardly and effeminate were not able to defend their country, they fled and hid themselves in caves and caverns; the women being accustomed to fatigue, by the slavery they had undergone, took arms, drove away the enemy, became mistresses of the country and established themselves in authority by an immutable law. From that time the Lycians habituated themselves to this form of government, and found it the mildest and most convenient. Their Queens had a council of senators, who assisted them with their advice: the men proposed good laws, but the executive power was in the women. The sweetness and softness of the sex prevented all the mischiefs of tyranny; and the counsel of the wise senators qualified that inconstancy, with which women are reproached.

I understood that the mother of Selima having been dethroned by the ambition of a relation, her first minister had fled to the Indies with the young Princess; that he had lived there several years as a Brachman, and she as an Estal; that this old man having always maintained a correspondence with the friends of the royal family, the young Queen had been restored to the throne after the death of the usurper; that she governed with the wisdom of a person who had experienced misfortunes; and lastly, that she had always expressed an invincible dislike to marriage. This news gave me an inexpressible joy; I thanked the Gods for having conducted me by such wonderful ways near the object of my heart; I implored their help, and promised never to love but once, if they would favour my passion.

I then considered by what method I should introduce myself to the Queen; and finding that war was the most proper, I entered into the service. There I distinguished myself very soon; for I refused no fatigue, I avoided no danger, I sought the most hazardous enterprises. Upon a day of battle, on the success of which, the liberty of Lycia depended, the enemy put our troops into disorder; it was in a large plain, out of which there was but one narrow pass for the fugitives to escape. I gained this pass, and threatened to pierce with my javelin whoever should attempt to force it. In this manner I rallied our troops, and returned to charge the enemy; I routed them and obtained a complete victory. This action drew the attention of all the army upon me: nothing was spoken of but my courage; and all the soldiers called me the deliverer of their country.

I was conducted to the Queen's presence, who could not recollect me; for we had been separated six years, and grief and fatigue had altered my features. She asked me my name, my country, my family, and seemed to examine my face with a more than common curiosity. I thought I discovered by her eyes an inward emotion, which she endeavoured to hide. Strange capriciousness of love! Heretofore I had thought her an Estal of mean birth; yet I had resolved to share my crown with her. This moment I conceived a design of engaging her to love me as I loved her; I concealed my country and my birth, and told her I was born in a village of Bactria, of a very obscure family; upon this she suddenly withdrew without answering me.

Not long after, she gave me, by the advice of her senators, the command of her army; by which I had free access to her person. She used frequently to send for me, under the pretence of business, when she had nothing to say; she took a pleasure in discoursing with me. I often painted forth my own sentiments to her under borrowed names; the Greek and Egyptian mythology, which I had learned in my travels, furnished me with abundant arguments to prove that the Gods were heretofore enamoured with mortals, and that love makes all conditions equal. I remember, that one day while I was relating to her a story of this kind she left me in a great emotion; I discovered by that her hidden sentiments; and it gave me an inexpressible pleasure to find that she then loved me as I had loved her. I had frequent conversation with her, by which her confidence in me daily increased: I sometimes made her call to mind the misfortunes of her early youth; and she then gave me an account of her living among the Estals, her friendship for Amana, and their mutual affection. Scarce was I able to contain myself when I heard her speak; I was just ready to throw off my disguise; but my false delicacy required yet farther, that Selima should do for me what I would have done for her. I was quickly satisfied; an extraordinary event made me experience all the extent and power of her love.

By the laws of Lycia the person who governs is not permitted to marry a stranger. Selima sent for me one day, and said to me: My subjects desire that I would marry; go tell them from me, that I will consent, upon condition that they leave me free in my choice. She spoke these words with a majestic air, and almost without looking upon me. At first I trembled, then flattered myself, then fell into doubt; for I knew the Lycians to be strongly attached to their laws: I went nevertheless to execute the commands I had received. When the council was assembled I laid before them the Queen's pleasure, and after much dispute it was agreed, that she should be left free to choose herself a husband. I carried to Selima the result of their deliberation: she then directed me to assemble the troops in the same plain where I had obtained the victory over the Carians, and to hold myself ready to obey her further orders; she likewise commanded all the principal men of the nation to repair to the same place. A magnificent throne being there erected, the Queen appeared upon it encircled with her courtiers, and spoke to the assembly in the following manner:

'People of Lycia, ever since I began my reign I have strictly observed your laws; I have appeared at the head of your armies, and have obtained several victories; my only study has been to make you free and happy – Is it just that she who has been the preserver of your liberty should be herself a slave? Is it equitable that she who continually seeks your happiness should be herself miserable? There is no unhappiness equal to that of doing violence to one's own heart. When the heart is under a constraint, grandeur and royalty serve only to give us a quicker sense of our slavery: I demand therefore to be free in my choice.'

This discourse was applauded by the whole assembly, who immediately cried out: 'You are free, you are dispensed from the law.' The Queen sent me orders to advance at the head of the troops. As soon as I was come near the throne she rose up, and, pointing to me with her hand – 'There,' said she, 'is my husband; he is a stranger, but his services make him the father of the country; he is not a Prince, but his merit puts him on a level with Kings.' She then ordered me to come up to her; I prostrated myself at her feet, and took all the usual oaths; I promised to renounce my country forever, to look upon the Lycians as my children, and, above all, never to love any other than the Queen. After this she stepped down from the throne, and we were conducted back to the capital with pomp, amidst the acclamations of the people. As soon as we were alone: 'Ah Selima!' said I, 'have you then forgot Amana?' It is impossible to express the Queen's surprise or the transport of affection and joy which these words gave her. She knew me, and conjectured all the rest; I had no need to speak, and we were both a long time silent: I at length told her my family, my adventures and all the effects that love had produced in me. She very soon assembled her council, and acquainted them with my birth; ambassadors were sent to the Indies; I renounced my crown and country forever, and my brother was confirmed in the possession of my throne.

'This was an easy sacrifice; I was in possession of Selima, and my happiness was complete: but alas! this happiness was of short continuance. In giving myself up to my passion, I had renounced my country, I had forsaken my father whose only consolation I was, I had forgot all my duty: my love, which seemed so delicate, so generous and was the admiration of men, was not approved of by the Gods; accordingly they punished me for it by the greatest of all misfortunes; they took Selima from me, she died within a few days after our marriage. I gave myself up to the most excessive sorrow; but the Gods did not abandon me. I entered deeply into myself; wisdom descended into my heart, she opened the eyes of my understanding, and I then comprehended the admirable mystery of the conduct of Oromazes. Virtue is often unhappy, and this shocks the reason of short-sighted men; but they are ignorant that the transient sufferings of this life are designed by the Gods to expiate the secret faults of those who appear the most virtuous. These reflections determined me to consecrate the rest of my days to the study of wisdom. Selima was dead, my bonds were broken, I was no longer tied to anything in nature; the whole earth appeared to me a desert; I could not reign in Lycia after the death of Selima, and I would not remain in a country where everything continually renewed the remembrance of my loss. I returned to the Indies, and went to live among the Brachmans, where I formed a new plan for happiness. Being freed from that slavery which always accompanies grandeur, I established within myself an empire over my passions and desires, more glorious and satisfactory than the false lustre of royalty. But now notwithstanding my retreat and the distance I was at, my brother conceived a jealousy of me, as if I was ambitious of ascending the throne, and I was obliged once more to leave the Indies. My exile proved a new source of happiness to me; it depends upon ourselves to reap advantage from our misfortunes. I visited the wise men of Asia, and conversed with the philosophers of different countries: I learned their laws and their religion, and was charmed to find, that the great men of all times, and of all places, had the same ideas of the Divinity, and of morality. At last I came hither upon the banks of the Arosis, where the Magi have chosen me for their head.'

Here Zoroaster ended; Cyrus and Cassandana were too much affected to be able to speak. After some moments of silence, the philosopher discoursed to them of the happiness which faithful lovers enjoy in the heavens when they meet again there; he then concluded with these wishes: 'May you long feel the happiness of mutual and undivided love! may the Gods preserve you from that depravity of heart which makes pleasures lose their relish when once they become lawful! may you, after the transports of a lively and pure passion in your younger years, experience in a more advanced age, all the charms of that union which diminishes the pains of life, and augments its pleasures by sharing them! may a long and agreeable old age let you see your distant posterity multiplying the race of heroes upon earth! may at last one and the same day unite the ashes of both, to exempt you from the misfortune of bewailing like me the loss of what you love! my only comfort is the hope of seeing Selima again in the sphere of fire, the pure element of love. Souls make acquaintance only here below; it is above that their union is consummated. O Selima, Selima! we shall one day meet again, and our flames will be eternal: I know, that in those superior regions your happiness will not be complete till I shall share it with you; those who have loved each other purely will love so forever; true love is immortal.'

The history which Zoroaster had given of his own life made a strong impression upon the Prince and Princess; it confirmed them in their mutual tenderness, and in their love of virtue; they spent some time with the sage in his solitude before they returned to the court of Cambyses. It was during this retreat that Zoroaster initiated Cyrus into all the mysteries of the eastern wisdom. The Chaldeans, the Egyptians and the Gymnosophists had a wonderful knowledge of nature, but they wrapped it up in allegorical fables and this doubtless is the reason that venerable antiquity has been reproached with ignorance in natural philosophy. Zoroaster laid open before Cyrus the secrets of nature, not merely to gratify his curiosity, but to make him observe the marks of an infinite wisdom diffused throughout the universe, and thereby to guard his mind against irreligion.

One time he made him admire the structure of the human body, the springs of which it is composed, and the liquors that flow in it; the canals, the pumps and the bason which are formed by the mere interweaving of the fibres, in order to separate, purify, conduct and reconduct the liquids into all the extremities of the body; then the levers and the cords, formed by the bones and muscles.

At another time he explained to him the configuration of plants, and the transformation of insects. They had not our optic glasses to magnify objects and bring them near; but the penetrating spirit of Zoroaster saw farther than the eye can reach by their help; because he was acquainted not only with all the experiments of the ancients and their traditions, but also with the occult sciences revealed by the Genii to the first men. Each seed, said he, contains within it a plant of its own species, this plant another seed, and this seed another little plant, and so on without end. These organic moulds cannot be formed by the simple laws of motion: they are the production of the great Oromazes, who originally enclosed within each seed all the bodies to be derived from it. None but he alone could thus conceal innumerable wonders in a single imperceptible atom. The growth of vegetables is but the unfolding of the fibres, membranes and branches by the moisture of the earth, which in an admirable manner insinuates itself into them. One blade of grass presents more various and amazing objects to their view, than all the waterworks in the enchanted gardens of the King of Babylon. If poets were philosophers, the bare description of nature would furnish them with more agreeable pictures than all their allegorical paintings; the poor resource of a hoodwinked imagination, when reason does not lend it eyes to discern the beauty of the works of Oromazes. Heroes were in former times philosophers, and conquerors were fond of knowing themselves how to repair in part the mischiefs occasioned by their battles and victories.

At another time, the sage carried the thoughts of Cyrus up into the higher regions, to contemplate the various phenomena which happen in the air. He explained to him the wonderful qualities of the subtle and invisible fluid which encompasses the earth in order to compress all the parts of it, keep each of them in its proper place, and hinder them from disuniting; how necessary it is to the life of animals, the growth of plants, the flying of birds, the forming of sounds and numberless other useful and important effects. Then Zoroaster raised his thoughts to the stars, and explained to Cyrus how they all float in an active, uniform and infinitely subtle fluid, which fills and pervades all nature. This invisible matter, said he, does not act by the necessary law of a blind mechanism. It is, as it were the body of the great Oromazes, whose soul is truth. By the one he acts upon all bodies, and by the other he enlightens all spirits. His vivifying presence gives activity to this pure aether, which becomes thereby the primary mechanical spring of all the motions in the heavens and upon the earth: it causes the fixed stars to turn upon their axes while it makes the planets circle round those stars; it transmits with an incredible velocity the light of those heavenly bodies, as the air does sounds; and its vibrations as they are more or less quick, produce the agreeable variety of colours, as those of the air do the melodious notes of music.

We are struck with surprise continued the Philosopher, to see all the wonders of nature, which discover themselves to our short and feeble sight; but how great would be our amazement, if we could transport ourselves into those aethereal spaces; and pass through them with a rapid flight? Each star would appear an atom in comparison of the immensity with which it is surrounded: what would our wonder be, if descending afterwards upon earth, we could accommodate our eyes to the minuteness of objects, and pursue the smallest grain of sand through its infinite divisibility? Each atom would appear a world, in which we should doubtless discover new beauties. There is nothing great, nothing little in itself; both the GREAT and the LITTLE disappear by turns to present everywhere an image of infinity through all the works of Oromazes. What a folly is it then to go about to explain the original of things by the mere laws of matter and motion? The universe is the work of the great Oromazes: he preserves and governs it by general laws, but these laws are free, arbitrary, and even diversified in the different regions of immensity, according to the effects he would there produce, and the various relations he would establish between bodies and spirits. It is from him that everything slows; it is in him that everything exists; it is by him that everything lives; and to him alone should all things be referred. Without him all nature is an inexplicable aenigma; with him the mind conceives everything possible, even at the same time that it is sensible of its own ignorance and narrow limits.

Cyrus was charmed with this instruction; not worlds seemed to be unveiled before him; where have I lived, said he, till now? The simplest objects contain wonders which escape my sight: everything bears the mark of an infinite wisdom and power. The great Oromazes ever present to his work, give to all bodies their forms and their motions, to all spirits their reason and their virtues; he beholds them all in his immensity; he governs them, not by any necessary laws of mechanism; he makes and he changes the laws by which he rules them, as it best suits with the designs of his justice and goodness.

While Cyrus was thus entertained with the conversation of Zoroaster, Cassandana assisted, with the wives of the Magi, in celebrating the festival of the Goddess Mythra. The ancient Persians adored but one sole supreme Deity, but they considered the God Mythras and the Goddess Mythra, sometimes as two emanations from his substance, and at other times at the first productions of his power. Every day was sacred to the great Oromazes, because he was never to be forgotten: but the festival of the Goddess Mythra was observed only towards the end of the spring, and that of Mythras about the beginning of autumn. During the first, which lasted ten days, the women performed all the priestly functions, and the men did not assist at it: as on the other hand the women were not admitted to the celebration of the last. This separation of the two sexes was thought necessary, in order to preserve the soul from all imaginations which might profane its joys in these solemn festivals.

The ancient Persians had neither temples nor altars; they sacrificed upon high mountains and eminencies; nor did they use libations, music or hallowed bread. Zoroaster had made no change in the old rites, except by the introduction of music into divine worship. At break of day all the wives of the Magi being crowned with myrtle and clothed in long white robes, walked two and two with a slow grave pace to the mount of Mythra; they were followed by their daughters clad in fine linen and leading the victims adorned with wreaths of all colours. The summit of the hill was a plain covered with a sacred wood; several vistas were cut through it, and all centred in a great circus, which had been turned into a delightful garden. In the middle of this garden there sprang a fountain, whose compliant waters took all the forms which art was pleased to give them. After many windings and turnings these crystal streams crept on to the declivity of the hill, and there falling down in a rapid torrent from rock to rock frothed and foamed, and at length lost themselves in a deep river which ran at the foot of the sacred mount.

When the procession arrived at the place of sacrifice, two sheep white as snow were led to the brink of the fountain; and while the priestess offered the victims, the choir of women struck their lyres, and the young virgins joined their voices singing this sacred hymn,

Oromazes is the first of incorruptible natures, eternal, unbegotten, self-sufficient, of all that's excellent most excellent, the wisest of all intelligences; he beheld himself in the mirror of his own substance, and by that view produced the Goddess Mythra; Mythra the living image of his beauty, the original mother and the immortal virgin; she presented him the ideas of all things, and he gave them to the God Mythras to form a world resembling those ideas. Let us celebrate the wisdom of Mythra, let us do her homage by our purity and our virtues, rather than by our songs and praises.

During this act of adoration, three times the music paused, to denote by a profound silence that the divine nature transcends whatever our words can express. The hymn being ended, the priestess lighted by the rays of the sun a fire of odoriferous wood, and while she there consumed the hearts of the sheep, sung alone with a loud voice,

Mythra desires only the soul of the victim.

Then the remainder of the sacrifice was dressed for a public feast, of which they all eat sitting on the brink of the sacred fountain, where they quenched their thirst. During the repast twelve young virgins sung the sweets of friendship; the charms of virtue, the peace, innocence and simplicity of a rural life.

After this regale, the mothers and daughters all assembled upon a large green plot encompassed with lofty trees, whose shady tops and leafy branches were a defence against the scorching heat of the sun and the blasts of the north wind: here they diverted themselves with dancing, running and concerts of music. Then they represented the exploits of heroes, the virtues of heroines and the pure pleasures of the primaeval state before Arimanius invaded the empire of Oromazes, and inspired mortals with deceitful hopes, false joys, perfidious disgusts, credulous suspicions and the inhuman extravagancies of profane love. These sports being over, they dispersed themselves about the garden, and by way of refreshment bathed themselves in the waters. Towards sunset they descended the hill and joined the Magi, who led them to the mountain of Oromazes, there to perform the evening sacrifice; the victims which were offered served every family for supper, (for they had two repasts on festival days, and they cheerfully passed the time till sleepiness called them to rest).

It was in this manner that Cassandana amused herself, while Zoroaster was discovering to Cyrus all the beauties of the universe, and thereby preparing his mind for matters of a more exalted nature, the doctrines of religion. The philosopher at length conducted the Prince with Hystaspes and Araspes into a gloomy and solitary forest, where perpetual silence reigned, and where the attention could not be diverted by any sensible object; and then said; It is not to enjoy the pleasures of solitude that we thus forsake the society of men; to retire from the world in that view would be only to gratify a trifling indolence, unworthy of the character of wisdom: but the aim of the Magi in this retreat is to disengage themselves from matter, rise to the contemplation of celestial things, and commence an intercourse with the pure spirits, who discover to them all the secrets of nature. When mortals have gained a complete victory over all the passions, they are thus favoured by the great Oromazes: it is however but a very small number of the most purified sages who have enjoyed this privilege. Impose silence upon your senses, raise your mind above all visible objects and listen to what the Gymnosophists have learned by their commerce with the Genii. Here he was silent for some time, seemed to collect himself inwardly, and then continued.

In the spaces of the Empyreum, the highest level of heaven, a pure and divine fire expands itself; by the means of which, not only bodies but spirits become visible. In the midst of this immensity is the great Oromazes, first principle of all things. He diffuses himself everywhere; but it is there that he is manifested after a more glorious manner. Near him is seated the God Mythras, or the second Spirit, and under him Psyche, or the Goddess Mythra: around their throne in the first rank are the Jynges, the most sublime intelligences; in the lower spheres are an endless number of Genii of all the different orders.

Arimanius chief of the Jynges aspired to an equality with the God Mythras, and by his eloquence persuaded all the spirits of his order to disturb the universal harmony, and the peace of the heavenly monarchy. How exalted soever the Genii are, they are always finite, and consequently may be dazzled and deceived. Now the love of one's own excellence is the most delicate and most imperceptible kind of delusion. To prevent the Genii from falling into the like crime, and to punish those audacious spirits, Oromazes only withdrew his rays, and immediately the sphere of Arimanius became a chaos and a perpetual night, in which discord, hatred, confusion, anarchy and force alone prevail. Those aethereal substances would have eternally tormented themselves, if Oromazes had not mitigated their miseries; he is never cruel in his punishments, nor acts from a motive of revenge, for it is unworthy of his nature; he had compassion on their condition, and lent Mythras his power to dissipate the chaos. Immediately the mingled and jarring atoms were separated, the elements disentangled and ranged in order. In the midst of the abyss was amassed together an ocean of fire, which we now call the sun; its brightness is but obscurity, when compared with that pure aether which illuminates the Empyreum. Seven globes of an opaque substance roll about this flaming centre, to borrow its light. The seven Genii, who were the chief ministers and companions of Arimanius, together with all the inferior spirits of his order, became the inhabitants of these new worlds, which the Greeks call Saturn, Jupiter, Mars, Venus, Mercury, the Moon and the Earth. The slothful, gloomy and malicious Genii, who love solitude and darkness, retired into Saturn. From hence flow all black and mischievous projects, perfidious treasons and murderous devices. In Jupiter dwell the impious and learned Genii, who broach monstrous errors, and endeavour to persuade men that the universe is not governed by an eternal Wisdom; that the great Oromazes is not a luminous principal, but a blind nature, which by a continual agitation within itself produces an eternal revolution of forms. In Mars are the Genii who are enemies of peace, and blow up everywhere the fire of discord inhuman vengeance, implacable anger, distracted ambition, false heroism, insatiable of conquering what it cannot govern, furious dispute which seeks dominion over the understanding, would oppress where it cannot convince, and is more cruel in its transports than all the other vices. Venus is inhabited by the impure Genii, whose affected graces and unbridled appetites are without taste, friendship, noble or tender sentiments or any other view than the enjoyment of pleasures which engender the most fatal calamities. In Mercury are the weak minds ever in uncertainty, who believe without thinking and doubt without reason; the enthusiasts and the freethinkers, whose credulity and incredulity proceed equally from a disordered imagination; it dazzles the sight of some, so that they see that which is not; and it blinds others in such a manner, that they see not that which is. In the Moon dwell the humoursome, fantastic and capricious Genii, who will and will not, who hate at one time what they loved excessively at another; and who by a false delicacy of self-love are ever distrustful of themselves and of their best friends.

All these Genii regulate the influence of the stars. They are subject to the Magi, whose call they obey, and discover to them all the secrets of nature. These spirits had all been voluntary accomplices of Arimanius's crime. There yet remained a number of all the several kinds who had been carried through weakness, inadvertency, levity and (if I may venture so to speak) friendship for their companions. Of all the Genii these were of the most limited capacities, and consequently the least criminal. Oromazes had compassion on them, and made them descend into mortal bodies; they retain no remembrance of their former state, or of their ancient happiness; it is from this number of Genii that the earth is peopled, and it is hence that we see here minds of all characters. The God Mythras is incessantly employed to cure, purify and exalt them, that they may be capable of their first felicity. Those who follow virtue fly away after death unto the Empyreum, where they are re-united to their origin. Those who debase themselves by vice, sink deeper and deeper into matter, fall successively into the bodies of the meanest animals, and run through a perpetual circle of new forms, till they are purged of their crimes by the pains which they undergo. The evil principle will confound everything for nine thousand years; but at length there will come a time, fixed by destiny, when Arimanius will be totally destroyed and exterminated; the Earth will change its form, universal harmony will be restored, and men will live happy without any bodily want. Until that time Oromazes reposes himself, and Mythras combats; this interval seems long to mortals, but, to a God, it is only as a moment of sleep.

Cyrus was seized with astonishment at the hearing of these sublime things, and turning to Araspes said to him: what we have been taught hitherto of Oromazes, Mythras and Arimanius, of the contention between the good and the evil principle, of the revolutions which have happened in the higher spheres, and of souls precipitated into mortal bodies, was mixed with so many absurd fictions, and wrapped up in such impenetrable obscurity, that we looked upon those doctrines as vulgar and contemptible notions unworthy of the eternal Being. I see now that we confounded the abuses of those principles with the principles themselves, and that a contempt for religion can proceed only from ignorance. All flows out from the Deity and all must be absorbed in him again. I am then a ray of light emitted from its principle, and I am to return to it. O Zoroaster, you put within me a new and inexhaustible source of pleasures; adversities may hereafter distress me, but they will never overwhelm me; all the misfortunes of life will appear to me as transient dreams; all human grandeur vanishes; I see nothing great but to imitate the immortals, that I may enter after death into their society. O my father, tell me by what way it is that heroes re-ascend to the Empyreum. How joyful am I, replied Zoroaster, to see you relish these truths; you will one day have need of them. Princes are oftentimes surrounded by impious and profane men, who reject everything that would be a restraint upon their passions: they will endeavour to make you doubt of eternal Providence, from the miseries and disorders which happen here below; they know not that the whole earth is but a single wheel of the great machine; their view is confined to a small circle of objects, and they see nothing beyond it, yet they will dispute and pronounce upon everything; they judge of nature and of its author like a man born in a deep cavern who has never seen the beauties of the universe, nor even the objects that are about him, but by the faint light of a dim taper. Yes, Cyrus, the harmony of the universe will be one day restored, and you are destined to that sublime state of immortality; but you can rise to it only by virtue; and the great virtue for a Prince is to make other men happy.

These discourses of Zoroaster made a strong impression on the heart of Cyrus; he would have staid much longer with the Magi in their solitude, if his duty had not called him back to his father's court. Scarce was he returned thither when everybody perceived a wonderful change in his discourse and behaviour. His conversation with the Archimagus had stifled his rising prejudices against religion. He gradually removed from about him all the young Satraps who were fond of the principles of impiety. Upon looking nearly into their characters he discovered not only that their hearts were corrupt, void of all noble and generous sentiments and incapable of friendship; but that they were men of very superficial understandings, full of levity and little qualified for business. He then applied himself chiefly to the study of the laws and of politics; the other sciences were but little cultivated in Persia. A sad misfortune obliged him at length to leave his country and travel: Cassandana died, though in the flower of her age, after she had brought him two sons and two daughters.

None but those who have experienced the force of true love, founded upon virtue, can imagine the disconsolate condition of Cyrus. In losing Cassandana, he lost all. Taste, reason, pleasure and duty, had all united to augment his passion for her: in loving her he had experienced all the charms of love, without knowing either its pains or the disgusts with which it is often attended: he felt the greatness of his loss, and refused all consolation. It is not the sudden revolutions in states, nor the heaviest strokes of adverse fortune, which oppress the minds of heroes; noble and generous souls are little moved by any misfortunes but what concern the objects of their softer passions. Cyrus first gave himself wholly up to grief, not to be alleviated by weeping or complaining; this silent sorrow was at length succeeded by a torrent of tears. Mandana and Araspes, who never left him, endeavoured to comfort him no other way than by weeping with him.

Reasoning and persuasion furnish no cure for grief; nor can friendship yield relief in affliction but by sharing it. After he had long continued in this dejection, he returned to see Zoroaster, who had formerly suffered a misfortune of the same kind. The conversation of that great man contributed much to mollify the anguish of his mind; but it was only by degrees that he recovered himself, and not till he had travelled for some years.

From the Fourth Book: Cyrus visits Sparta

AFTER SOME DAYS SAILING the vessel entered the Saonic gulf, and soon arrived at Epidaurus, from whence the prince made haste to get to Sparta, the principal city of the Lacedaemonians. This famous city was of a circular form, and resembled a camp. It was situated in a wild and barren valley through which the Eurotas flows, an impetuous river which often lays waste the whole country by its inundations. This valley is hemmed in on one side by inaccessible mountains, and on the other side by little hills, which scarcely produced what was necessary to supply the real wants of nature. The situation of the country had contributed very much to the warlike and savage genius of its inhabitants.

As Cyrus entered this city, he beheld only plain and uniform buildings, very different from the stately palaces he had seen in Egypt; everything still spoke the primitive simplicity of the Spartans: but their manners were upon the point of being corrupted under the reign of Ariston and Anaxandridas, if Chilon one of the seven sages of Greece had not prevented it. These two Kings of the ancient race of the Heracles, shared the sovereign power between them; one governed the state, the other commanded the troops. They received Cyrus with more politeness than was usual for the Spartans to show to strangers. They seemed to have very little curiosity about the manners, sciences and customs of other nations; their great concern was to make the Prince of Persia admire the wisdom of their lawgiver, and the excellence of his laws. To this end they presented Chilon to him. This philosopher had by his talents acquired great credit with the Kings, the senate and the people, and was looked upon as a second Lycurgus; nothing was done at Lacedaemon without him. The Spartan sage, in order to give Cyrus a lively notion of their laws, manners and form of government, first led him to the council of the Gerontes, instituted by Lycurgus. This council, where the two Kings presided, was held in a hall hung with mat, that the magnificence of the place might not divert the senators' attention. It consisted of about forty persons, and was not liable to that tumult and confusion which frequently reigned in the debates of the people at Athens.

Till Lycurgus's time the Kings of Sparta had been absolute: but Eurytion, one of those Kings, having yielded some part of his prerogatives to please the people, a republican party was thereupon formed, which became audacious and turbulent. The Kings would have resumed their ancient authority, but the people would not suffer it; and this continual struggle between opposite powers rent the state to pieces. To establish an equal balance of the regal and popular power, which leaned alternately to tyranny and anarchy, Lycurgus, in imitation of Minos, instituted a council of twenty-eight old men, whose authority keeping a mean betwixt the two extremes, delivered Sparta from its domestic dissentions. An hundred and thirty years after him, Theopompus having observed, that what had been resolved by the Kings and their council, was not always agreeable to the multitude, established certain annual magistrates called Ephori, who were chosen by the people, and consented in their name to whatever was determined by the King and Senate; each private man looked upon these unanimous resolutions as made by himself; and in this union of the head with the members consisted the life of the body politic at Sparta.

After Lycurgus had regulated the form of government, he gave the Spartans such laws as were proper to prevent the disorders occasioned by avarice, ambition and love. In order to expel luxury and envy from Sparta, he resolved to banish forever both riches and poverty. He persuaded his countrymen to make an equal distribution of all their wealth and of all their lands, decried the use of gold and silver and ordained that they should have only iron money, which was not current in foreign countries. He chose rather to deprive the Spartans of the advantages of commerce with their neighbours, than to expose them to the misfortune of bringing home from other nations those instruments of luxury which might corrupt them.

The more firmly to establish an equality among the citizens, they eat together in public halls; each company had liberty to choose its own guests, and no one was admitted there but with the consent of the whole, to the end that peace might not be disturbed by a difference of humours; a necessary precaution for men naturally fierce and warlike. Cyrus went into these public halls, where the men were seated without any distinction but that of their age; they were surrounded by children who waited on them: their temperance and austerity of life was so great, that other nations used to say, it was better to die, than to live like the Spartans. During the repast they discoursed together on grave and serious matters, the interests of their country, the lives of great men, the difference between a good and bad citizen, and of whatever might form youth to the taste of military virtues. Their discourses contained much sense in few words, for which reason the Laconic style has been admired in all nations; by imitating the rapidity of thoughts, it said all in a moment, and gave the hearer the pleasure of discovering a profound meaning which was unexpressed; the graceful, fine and delicate turns of the Athenians were unknown at Lacedaemon; the Spartans were for strength in the mind as well as in the body.

Upon a solemn festival, Cyrus and Araspes were present at the assemblies of the young Lacedaemonians, which were held within a large enclosure, surrounded with diverse seats of turf raised one above another, in form of an amphitheatre. Young girls almost naked contended with boys in running, wrestling, dancing, and all sorts of laborious exercises, the young men were not permitted to marry any but such as they had vanquished at these games. Cyrus was shocked to see the liberty which reigned in these public assemblies, between persons of different sexes and could not forbear representing it to Chilon. 'There seems,' said he, 'to be a great inconsistency in the laws of Lycurgus; his aim was to establish a republic which should consist only of warriors, inured to all sorts of labours, and at the same time he made no scruple to expose them to sensuality, the most effectual means to sink their courage.'

'The design of Lycurgus in instituting these festivals,' replied Chilon, 'was to preserve and perpetuate military virtue in his republic. That great lawgiver was well acquainted with human nature; he knew what influence the inclinations and dispositions of mothers have upon their children; his intention was to make the Spartan women heroines, that they might bring the republic none but heroes. Besides, continued Chilon, gross sensuality and delicate love are equally unknown at Lacedaemon; it is only in these public festivals that the familiarity which so much offends you is allowed. Lycurgus thought it possible to deaden the fire of voluptuous desires, by accustoming the eye sometimes to those objects which excite them. At all other times the women are very reserved; nay by our laws new married persons are permitted to see one another but rarely, and that in private; and thus our youth are formed to temperance and moderation, even in the most lawful pleasures. By this means also are prevented those disgusts which frequently arise from the permission of an unbounded liberty in the marriage state. The constraint, which the Spartans are under, keeps up the ardour of their first flame; so that marriage does not make them cease to be lovers. On the other hand, stolen amours and jealousy are banished from Sparta; husbands who are sick, or advanced in years, lend their wives to others, and afterwards take them again without scruple. Wives look upon themselves as belonging to the state more than to their husbands. The children are educated in common, and often without knowing any other mother than the republic, or any other father than the senators.'

Here Cyrus, struck with a lively remembrance of Cassandana and of the pure pleasures of their mutual love, sighed within himself, and felt an abhorrence of these odious maxims. He despised effeminacy, but he could not relish the savage fierceness of the Spartans, which carried them to sacrifice the sweetest charms of society to ambition, and to think that military virtues were inconsistent with tender passions; however, as he was sensible that Chilon would little understand what he meant by these delicate sentiments, he contented himself with saying; Paternal love seems to me a source of great advantages to a state: fathers are careful of the education of their children, and this education obliges children to gratitude; these are the original bands of society. Our country is nothing else but many families united; if family-love be weakened, what will become of the love of one's country, which depends upon it? Ought we not to be afraid of such establishments as destroy nature, under pretence of improving it? The Spartans, answered Chilon, all constitute but one family. Lycurgus had experienced, that fathers are often unworthy, and children, ungrateful; that both are wanting to their reciprocal duties, and he therefore trusted the education of the children, to a number of old men, who considering themselves as the common fathers, have an equal care of all.

In reality, children were nowhere better educated than at Sparta: they were chiefly taught to obey, to undergo labour, to conquer in combats and to face pain and death with courage. They went with their heads and feet naked, lay upon rushes and eat very little; and this little they were obliged to procure by dexterity in the public banqueting rooms. Not that the Spartans authorised thefts and robberies, for as all was in common in that republic, those vices could have no place there; but the design was to accustom children who were destined for war, to surprise the vigilance of those who watched over them and to expose themselves courageously to the severest punishments, in case they failed of that dexterity which was exacted of them.

Lycurgus had remarked, that subtle speculations, and all the refinements of science, served often only to spoil the understanding and corrupt the heart; and he therefore made little account of them. Nothing however was neglected to awaken in children the taste of pure reason, and to give them a strength of judgment; but all kinds of studies, which were not serviceable to good manners, were looked upon as useless and dangerous occupations. The Spartans were of opinion, that in the present state of human nature, man is rather formed for action than knowledge, and better qualified for society than contemplation.

Cyrus went afterwards to the Gymnasia, where the youth performed their exercises; Lycurgus had renewed the Olympic games instituted by Hercules, and had dictated to Iphitus the statutes and ceremonies observed in them. Religion, warlike genius and policy, all contributed to perpetuate the custom of solemnizing these games; they served not only to do honour to the Gods, to celebrate the virtues of heroes, to prepare the body for the fatigues of a military life, but also to draw together from time to time in the same place, and unite by common sacrifices, diverse nations whose strength was in their union. The Spartans employed themselves in no sort of labour but the exercises necessary to qualify them to dispute the prizes in the Olympic games. The Helots, who were their slaves, manured their lands, and were the only mechanics among them; for they esteemed every employment as mean and ignoble, which regarded only a provision for the body.

Cyrus, having learned this maxim of the Lacedaemonians, said to Chilon: 'Agriculture and the mechanic arts appear to me absolutely necessary to preserve the people from idleness, which begets discord, effeminacy and all the evils destructive of society: Lycurgus seems to depart a little too much from nature in all his laws.'

'The tranquillity and sweet leisure of a rural life,' replied Chilon, 'were thought by Lycurgus to be contrary to a warlike genius; besides the Spartans are never idle; they are continually employed in all those exercises that are images of war, in marching, encamping, ranging armies in order of battle, defending, attacking, building and destroying fortresses. By this means a noble emulation is kept up in their minds without enmity, and the desire of conquest preserved without shedding blood: everyone disputes the prize with ardour, and the vanquished take a pride in crowning the victors; the pleasures which accompany these exercises make them forget the fatigue, and this fatigue prevents their courage from suffering any prejudice in times of peace.'

This discourse raised in Cyrus a curiosity to know the military discipline of the Spartans, and he soon found an opportunity to inform himself in it. The Tegeans, who inhabited a part of Peloponnesus, having entered into a league with several cities of Greece had raised troops, and were coming to attack the Spartans upon their frontiers. The latter prepared to repulse the enemy, and Cyrus resolved to signalize his courage on this occasion, but he would first know the reasons of the war, and Chilon explained them to him in the following manner.

'The Spartans,' said he, "being arrived to a flourishing condition by a strict observance of the laws of Lycurgus, laid a scheme first to make themselves masters of Peloponnesus, and then of all Greece Courage and success begot in them a thirst of dominion, contrary to the original design of our great lawgiver: his intention of forming a republic of warriors, was not to disturb the peace of other cities, but to preserve his own in union, independence and liberty. That we might never entertain the unjust, ambition of making conquests, he forbad us the use of money, commerce and fleets, three helps absolutely requisite for those who set up for conquerors. The Lacedaemonians therefore departed from the spirit of Lycurgus, when they resolved to attack their neighbours; their first design was to fall upon the Arcadians, but having consulted the oracle of Delphos, the Pythian priestess advised them to turn their arms against the Tegeans. The Spartans, depending on a deceitful oracle, marched out of their city, and carried chains with them in full assurance of reducing their enemies to slavery. Several battles were fought without victory's declaring for either side. At length, in the beginning of the present reign, our army was put to flight; our prisoners loaded with the same chains which we had prepared for the Tegeans, were yoked like beasts, and condemned to draw the plough. The bad conduct of our Princes was the source of these calamities: I should be far from discovering to you their faults if they had not had the courage to correct them.

'Ariston, who governed the state, was naturally of a sweet disposition, affable and beneficent; he put an equal confidence in all those who were about him; Anaxandridas who commanded the troops was of a quite contrary character, dark, suspicious and distrustful. Prytanis the favourite of Ariston had been educated at Athens, and had given himself up to pleasure; having a great deal of fine wit, he had the secret of making even his faults agreeable; he knew how to suit himself to all tastes, and to all characters; he was sober with the Spartans, polite with the Athenians, and learned with the Egyptians; he put on all shapes by turns, not to deceive (for he was not ill-natured) but to gratify his prevailing passion, which was the desire of pleasing, and of being the idol of men; in a word, he was a compound of whatever is most agreeable and irregular. Ariston loved him, and was entirely governed by him. This favourite led his master into all sorts of voluptuousness; the Spartans began to grow effeminate; the King bestowed his favours without distinction or discernment.

'Anaxandridas observed a quite different conduct, but equally ruinous to the state: as he knew not how to distinguish sincere and honest hearts, he believed all men false, and that those who had the appearance of probity were only greater hypocrites than the rest. He entertained suspicions of the best officers of his army, and especially of Leonidas, the principal and most able of his generals, a man of strict honour and distinguished bravery. Leonidas loved virtue sincerely, but had not enough of it to bear with the faults of other men; he despised them too much, and was regardless both of their praises and favours: he humoured neither princes nor their flatterers; his hatred of vice was such, that it rendered his manners fierce and rugged, like those of the first Spartans; he looked for perfection in every body and as he never found it, he had no intimate friendship with any person; nobody loved him, but all esteemed and feared him; for he had all those virtue which make men most respected and most avoided. Anaxandridas grew weary of him and banished him; thus did this Prince weaken the strength of Sparta, while Ariston corrupted her manners.

'Our enemies drew advantage every day from these divisions and disorders. Perceiving the misfortune which threatened our country, I went to the young

Princes, and spoke to them in the following mannner: My age, my long services and the care I have taken of your education, give me a right to tell you freely, that you both ruin yourselves by contrary faults; Ariston exposes himself to be often deceived by flattering favourites, and you, Anaxandridas, expose yourself to the misfortune of never having a true friend. To treat men always with the utmost rigor they deserve, is brutality and not justice; but, on the other hand to have so general a goodness, and such an easiness of temper as not to be able to punish crimes with firmness, or to reward merit with distinction, is not a virtue but a weakness, and is frequently attended with as bad consequences as severity and ill-nature itself. As for you, Anaxandridas, your distrust does more hurt to the state than the too easy goodness of Ariston. Why do you entertain a diffidence of men upon bare surmises, when their talents and capacities have rendered them necessary to you? When a Prince has once honoured a minister with his confidence, for good reasons, he ought never to withdraw it without manifest proofs of perfidiousness. It is impossible for him to do everything himself, and he must therefore have the courage hazard sometimes the being deceived, rather than miss the opportunities of acting; he should know how to make a wise use of men, without blindly yielding himself up to them like Ariston; there is a medium between an excessive diffidence, and a blind confidence; without this medium no government can long subsist. Reflection and experience rectified by degrees the faults of Ariston, and he dismissed Prytanis; but the morose temper of Anaxandridas could be corrected only by misfortunes; he was often defeated in his wars with the Tegeans, and at length found the necessity of recalling Leonidas. Our troops since that time have been more successful; we have recovered our prisoners and obtained several victories; but these advantages have made the Tegeans more jealous of us, and we are become the object not only of their hatred, but of that of all the Greeks.'

Cyrus listened with attention to this account given him by Chilon, and then said to him, looking upon Araspes: 'The history of your Kings will be an eternal lesson to me to avoid two faults very common with Princes. As for the rest, I observe that the republic of Sparta is like a camp always subsisting, an assembly of warriors always under arms; how great a respect soever I have for Lycurgus, I cannot admire this form of government. You assure me that your law giver in constituting such a republic had no other design but to preserve it in union and liberty; but would a legislator who has only these pacific views banish from a state all other professions except that of war? Would he enjoin that no member of it should be bred to any other exercise, study or occupation, but that of making himself dextrous in destroying other men? Lycurgus has indeed prohibited the use of money, commerce and fleets, but are these necessary to the conquest of Greece? I rather believe, that he made these prohibitions only out of policy, in order to conceal from the neighbouring cities his ambitious designs, hinder the Spartans from becoming soft and luxurious, and deprive them of the means of dividing their forces by foreign and distant wars. Your lawgiver has again departed both from nature and justice; when he accustomed each private citizen to frugality, he should have taught the whole nation to confine her ambition. An able politician ought to provide not only for the liberty of his own state, but for the safety of all the neighbouring ones. To set ourselves loose from the rest of mankind, to look upon ourselves as made to conquer them, is to arm all nations against us. Why do not you reform these unjust maxims? Why don't you put an end to the war? Why have you not recourse to the supreme council of the Amphictions to terminate your differences with the Tegeans!'

'The reason,' replied Chilon, 'is the obstinacy of the Tegeans; they are so enraged against us, that they refuse to submit to the arbitration of that council; they breathe nothing but our destruction; they have engaged several cities of Peloponnesus in a league against us. The notion which is entertained of our designing to conquer all Greece, has excited the hatred and distrust of our neighbours. Such is the present state of Sparta.'

Not many days after this, the Lacedaemonians, having advice that the Tegeans were advancing towards their frontiers, marched out of Sparta to give them battle. Anaxandridas appeared at their head in his military habit, his casque was adorned with three birds, of which that in the middle was the crest, upon this cuirass he bore the head of Medusa, all the insignia of the God Mars were represented upon his shield, which was a hexagon; and he held in his hand a staff of command. Cyrus marched by his side; his buckler resembled that of Achilles; upon his casque was an eagle, whose plume and tail overspread his shoulders; upon his cuirass was engraved in bas relief the Goddess, Pallas Athena wise and warlike, to express the inclinations of the Prince. Araspes and Leonidas less magnificently accoutred accompanied the two Princes, who thus left the city followed by the Lacedaemonian troops. The whole army formed into a square battalion, a double rank of cavalry enclosed a third rank of archers, which encompassed three inner ranks of pikemen and slingers, and left an empty space in the centre for the provisions, ammunition and baggage. All the soldiers marched to the sound of flutes, and singing the hymn of Castor. The Spartan general, Leonidas, knowing how fond the Prince of Persia was of information, entertained him in the way after the following manner.

'Greece is divided into several republics, each of which maintains an army in proportion to its extent. We do not affect to bring prodigious armies into the field like the Asians, but to have well-disciplined troops; numerous bodies are difficult to manage, and are too expensive to a state; our invariable rule is to encamp so, that we may never be obliged to fight against our will; a small army well practiced in war may, by entrenching itself advantageously, oblige a very numerous one to disperse its troops, which would otherwise soon be destroyed for want of provisions. When the common cause of Greece is to be defended, all these separate bodies unite, and then no state dare attack us. At Lacedaemon all the citizens are soldiers; in other republics the dregs of the people are not admitted into the soldiery, but the best men are chosen out for the army, such as are bold, robust, in the flower of their age, and inured to laborious occupations; the qualities required in their leaders are birth, intrepidity, temperance and experience; they are obliged to pass through the most rigid trials, before they can be raised to a command; they must have given signal proofs of all the different sorts of courage, by greatly enterprising, executing with vigour, and above all by showing themselves superior to the most adverse fortune. By this means each republic has always a regular militia, able officers, soldiers well-disciplined and inured to fatigues. The Spartans in time of war abate somewhat of the severity of their exercises and austerity of life; we are the only people in the world to whom war is a kind of repose; we then enjoy all those pleasures which are forbidden us in time of peace. Upon a day of battle we dispose our troops in such a manner, that they do not all fight at once like the Egyptians, but succeed and support one another without confusion. We never draw up our men in the same manner as the enemy, and we always place our bravest soldiers in the wings, that they may extend themselves, and enclose the opposite army. When the enemy is routed, Lycurgus has required us to exercise all acts of clemency towards the vanquished, not only out of humanity but policy; for hereby we render our enemies less fierce. The hope of being well treated, if they surrender their arms, prevents their giving way to that desperate fury which often proves fatal to the victorious.'

While Leonidas was speaking, they arrived in the plain of Mantinea, where they discovered the camp of the Tegeans, which was covered on the one side by a forest, and on all the other by a terrasse, with parapets, palisades and towers at certain distances. Anaxandridas encamped on the banks of the river Eurotas: Leonidas gave orders, and immediately the soldiers hung their casques on their pikes struck in the ground, and fell to work without putting of their cuirasses. The river made the camp inaccessible on one side, the other three were surrounded by lines of circumvallation; the waters of the Eurotas quickly filled the ditches; portable houses were erected, the different quarters of the officers regularly disposed, the cavalry put under shelter, a moveable city was raised with four gates, several large streets crossed one another and had likewise a communication by others that were less.

The river Eurotas ran between the two camps, and was a security against any surprise: Leonidas took this opportunity to show Cyrus the military exercise in use among the Greeks, and made his troops often pass in review before the Prince: they were divided into divers bodies of horse and foot; at their head were the Pelemarchi, and the commanders of the several corps. The soldiers were clothed in red, that in the heat of action the sight of their blood might not terrify either the wounded or their companions. Upon the least signal of their commanders, the different cohorts separated, reunited, extended themselves, doubled, opened, closed their ranks and ranged themselves by various evolutions and windings into perfect squares, oblong squares, lozenges and triangular figures.

The Spartans waited several days in their camp to take advantage of the enemy's motions. In the meantime, divisions arose among the allies; the wisest of them desired peace but the greater number were eagerly bent on war. Cyrus understanding their dispositions, offered to go in person to the camp of the Tegeans, and speak with their leaders. The King consented, and the young Prince passed the Eurota, and advanced to the confederates; their chief officers assembled about him and he addressed them in the following manner.

'People of Greece, I am a stranger, the desire of knowing your laws, sciences and military discipline has engaged me to travel among you. Your wit is everywhere extolled, but I cannot admire your wisdom. The Spartans would be much in the wrong to make any attempt upon your liberties, but neither is it just in you to endeavour their destruction. They are not afraid of war, they love fatigues and dangers, and are prepared for all events; but they do not refuse to grant you peace upon honourable conditions. I understand that you have in Greece a wise council, whose business it is to terminate the differences that arise between your cities. Why have you not recourse to this council! The mutual war you make upon each other, and your domestic jealousies, will weaken you by degrees, and you will fail a pray to some conqueror emboldened by your divisions.'

All the old men looked upon one another while he was speaking, and seemed to approve of what he said; their General, on the contrary, fearing lest the Prince's advice should be followed, murmured within himself; he was a young impetuous hero, a martial fire sparkled in his eyes, he had a sprightly, a masculine and captivating eloquence, capable of inspiring courage into the most timorous. When Cyrus had done speaking he raised his voice and answered him thus. 'Whoever you are, O stranger, you are unacquainted with the boundless ambition of the Spartans; their fundamental constitution tends to destroy all the neighbouring states. Lycurgus their lawgiver laid the foundations in Lacedaemon of a universal monarchy, and inspired his countrymen with a desire of domination, under pretence that Greece cannot maintain her freedom and independency while divided into so many petty republics. Ever since that time the avaricious Spartans are greedy of what they have not, while they refuse themselves the enjoyment of what they have; when they are weakened and brought low, they moderate their ambitious desires; but they have no sooner recovered their strength, they return to their old maxims; we can have no security but in their total destruction. Scarce had he pronounced these words, when a confused murmur rose among the soldiers, the fire of discord was kindled anew in their breasts, and they all cried out: 'War! War! Let the Spartans be destroyed.'

Cyrus perceiving the fury which animated them, and that they would no longer hearken to him, returned to the camp of the Lacedaemonians. They immediately called a council of war, and it was resolved to attack the enemy in their entrenchments. Cyrus offered to pass the river at the head of a chosen body of cavalry, and this being agreed to, he waited for night to put his design in execution; he passed without any opposition; and at break of day the infantry followed him on rafts and buckskin boats. The Tegeans taking the alarm left their camp and drew up in battalia. The two armies advanced with their pikes ported, each phalanx in the closest order, buckler struck to buckler, helmet to helmet, man to man; the battle began; the left wing of the Lacedaemonians commanded by Cyrus quickly broke the right wing of the Tegeans; Araspes pursued the fugitives warmly, and put them out of a condition to rally; they fled to a neighbouring fortress. Cyrus returned with his troops to sustain the centre of the Spartan army which began to give way; but while he was putting the enemy into disorder, the right wing of the Spartans fled before the left of the allies; Leonidas who commanded it gained an eminence, from which he could discover all that passed; when he saw the happy success of Cyrus's skill and bravery he encouraged his men, called them and returned to charge the enemy. The Tegeans, finding themselves, attacked both in front and rear, dispersed and fled, and where almost all cut in pieces taken prisoners: the few that escaped in the night took refuge in the same fortress with the others.

The battering engines and other machines, which have since been used in attacking of towns, were not then known to the Greeks; on these occasions they disposed their men in a certain form which they called a Tortoise. The next day Leonidas gave the word of command, the Spartans drew up and marched to the fortress; the foremost ranks covered themselves with their square bucklers, the rest raised them over their heads, pressed them against one another and then gradually bending formed a kind of sloping roof impenetrable to arrows. A triple stage of this sort raised the assailants to the height of the walls. The besieged rained down a shower of stone and darts; but in the end the besiegers made themselves masters of the fortress. Four thousand Tegeans were slain in the two actions, and three thousand taken prisoners.

After the battle a new council of war was called Leonidas by the King's orders made encomiums upon Cyrus in presence of all the commanders, and ascribed the victory to his conduct and courage. All the soldiers sent up shouts of joy, and looked upon the Prince of Persia as a divine man sent by the Gods to save Sparta in her weak and tottering condition. It was afterwards proposed in the council to carry the Tegean prisoners to Lacedaemon, and to treat them like slaves, as they had done the Spartans. Cyrus then rose up in the midst of the assembly, a divine fire darted from his eyes, wisdom descended into his heart, and he said: 'You are going, in my opinion to violate one of the principal and wisest laws of Lycurgus; he has enjoined you to treat the vanquished with clemency; the right of conquest even in a lawful war is the least of all rights, and is never just but when it is made use of to render the conquered happy. A conqueror who seeks only to domineer, ought to be deemed a usurper upon the rights of nations, and an enemy of mankind who sports with their miseries only to gratify his brutal and unnatural passions. It is by reason alone that man should subdue man; no one deserves to be a King but he who engages in the toils of empire, and subjects himself to the slavery of governing purely out of compassion to men incapable of governing themselves. If therefore you desire to become masters of Greece, let it be only by showing yourselves more humane, and more moderate than all the other cities. The rest of the Grecian states, when they see your wisdom, your courage and your excellent laws, will be eager to put themselves under your protection, and with emulation sue to be received as members of your republic. It is by this means that you will sweeten all minds, and captivate all hearts.' Anaxandridas influenced by this discourse granted peace, on condition that the Tegeans should for the future be tributary to Lacedaemon. He detained the chief men among them as hostages, and carried them to Lacedaemon, where he granted them all the privileges of citizens.

Cyrus at his return to Sparta revolved in his mind all that he had seen and heard, and formed great ideas relating to the art of war, which he resolved to improve one day in Persia. After he had thoroughly studied the laws, manners and military discipline of the Spartans, he left Lacedaemon to visit the other republics of Greece. Chilon and Leonidas conducted him to the frontiers of their country. He swore an eternal friendship to them, and promised to be always a faithful ally of their republic; and he was true to his word for the Persians had never any war with the Greeks in that conqueror's time.

Cyrus resolved before he left Peloponnesus, to visit all its principal cities.

The Cyropædia; or, The Institution of Cyrus

MAURICE ASHLEY-COOPER (1675–1726) was the younger brother of the philosopher Anthony Ashley-Cooper, the Third Earl of Shaftesbury. While the philosopher stands as one of the most celebrated names in the history of English thought, Maurice has remained somewhat overshadowed. The two brothers were in passionate conflict for much of their adult lives, but the ideas of the philosopher are evident throughout Maurice's work.

He enjoyed a respectable career in the House of Commons, managing the not inconsiderable feat of winning two different seats during the same parliamentary election. However, his greatest achievement was his translation of Xenophon's *Cyropaedia*, which remained the standard English version for over a century. Maurice believed the life of Cyrus, as told by Xenophon, carried crucial contemporary relevance, which he highlighted in his philosophical preface to the translation: The character, morality and political principles of the Persian king were the very qualities needed for the ruling elite of his own time.

Maurice's text has been considered a 'classic of *deism*,' the strain of Enlightenment thought which challenged the power of the Church, but did not deny the presence, or possibility, of a divine power in the universe. Outspoken rejection of Christian faith remained a capital offence, with the last execution for blasphemy occurring as recently at 1698. Thus, Maurice's references to 'real religion' and 'real Christianity' are carefully coded allusions to a philosophy that was potentially radical. Whether *deism* constituted a religious belief in its own right, or a philosophical attack on the established Church, can never be fully answered – the term embraced a range of ideas that ranged from moderate reform to virtual atheism – but it was nevertheless deeply subversive. Precisely what Maurice means by 'God' is deliberately ambiguous: to a Christian reader it may suggest the deity familiar from the Bible; but to the libertines and freethinkers who were challenging the social and moral order of Early Modern England, it could represent anything from contemplative philosophy to nature itself. In using the life of Cyrus to express these views Maurice was bringing the legacy of the Persian king into the most pressing of current concerns.

Preface

A MAN WHO IS INDEBTED to the public for leisure, and for freedom from servile employment, is under obligation to acquire knowledge, and principally in religion, policy and the art of war. You will, in probability, think, that morals ought to be added to the number; but as religion may be divided into two sorts, real and political, and that real religion can, by no means, be disjoined from morals, it does not seem proper to mention them as a distinct head. The objects of the mind, in real religion, are the greatest in the world, the divinity and all divine things. When the mind has imbibed a full knowledge of these to its utmost capacity, it may be said to be religious: it then sees the divinity in all things; it sees it in human nature, and in all the laws of affection and duty in its several relations; it sees it in the whole world, and in every part of it, from the highest to the lowest productions, both animate and inanimate.

False opinions, and an over valuation of riches, honours and all the other meaner concerns of life, whence all vice arises, cannot be entertained where this knowledge is. Our duty may, indeed, be divided into three parts, as settled by our three principal relations; to God, to other men and to ourselves; and they may be differently termed, but they are but the main branches of the one moral science.

If morals be disjoined from their relation to what is divine, and confined to a certain system of manners, contrived for the regulation of our own personal concerns of body and mind, and to guide us in our conduct amongst men, they then become something entirely different from what is before meant, and they dwindle into an Epicurean moral, an art of settling certain rules of behaviour upon a principle of interest, convenience or pleasure. The case of religion is alike ill when so disjoined from human concerns; for then is the Divine Being, like Epicurus's divinities, confined to the highest heavens, and unconcerned in the administration of the lower world. And this, in the Epicureans, was but excluding Providence from the world with a sort of compliment, that seems to have been intended as a screen from the reproach of atheism, rather than to have arisen from any real opinion of such beings: but real religion is the summit and completion of all knowledge; runs through all, and arises from collecting what is divine in all things. This is Christianity, or the doctrine of our Saviour, is real religion, and is not to be found but in the mind of the wise and good, and of the few who enter in at the strait gate.

But when religion comes to be spoken of as a national establishment, it is no longer the real, but makes part of the state; it has its lawful forms and ceremonies under the administration of its ministers, who are regulated by the state, and paid for their service. One may very justly think that he has but little knowledge of Christianity and real religion, who does not see the evident difference: great zealots they certainly were for the political religion, but in the real they had no knowledge, and had nothing to do with it.

The different turns that have been given to established religions, as governments have differed from each other, or changed within themselves, will serve to illustrate this distinction of religion into real and political. The Greek religion differed remarkably in cities and people that differed in their genius and policy. The best and bravest of the Greeks applied their principal worship to the noblest and most chaste of their deities, as to Hera or Pallas Athena: others of them, that were more tyrannical in their form of civil government, and more loose in their manners, addressed their principal worship to an Aphrodite or a Dionysus. The same deities had a chaste and decent worship paid them in one place, and, in another, a more pompous one, and more loose. This partiality of particular cities and people to particular deities, as their different forms of government and genius lead them, is intimated in Homer by the great partiality he expresses in particular deities to particular cities and people. This divine partiality reached even to private men, and differed according to their characters: one deity favoured Achilles; another Odysseus; another Paris. As amongst states, which are political persons, and different in characters, one deity favoured Athens, another Argos and another Paphos. The Roman religion, by the account of their historians, was more plain and decent in their earlier and better times; but, in the time of Julius Caesar, it was become full of lewdness and extravagance. Not very long after Julius, Christianity arose; it was the real and true religion in the breasts of its few true professors, long before its name was embraced by multitudes, armies and emperors, and so became the public religion. After this its establishment, what has been the variety of forms it has appeared in? Through many changes, it at last appeared in the complete papal form, which long prevailed almost over all Christendom. And, in this form, how many mean turns has it served? How has it been made subservient to the interest of princes and priests that were its votaries? About two hundred years ago, established Christianity took another turn, and appears now, in several nations, in different forms. But in England particularly, and since the change made at the reformation, how have some of our priests used it in different turns of government? Many have made it a support of the tyranny of princes, and destructive of the civil rights of men. Real Christianity, meanwhile, is none of all these changeable establishments and human institutions, nor ever can be, but stands upon its own foot; and whether it be the religion of the multitude, and national or not national or whatever be the forms of it in national establishments, is one and the same in itself, firm and unalterable, and will undoubtedly remain to the end of the world, whether owned or not owned by any public establishment indifferently.

If it can still be objected, that real religion and Christianity are now become the established and political religion; and that, of consequence, they are the same, and not to be distinguished, I must, in answer, repeat, that real religion is the science of the Divinity, and of all things divine, and is to be learned from the great volume of nature, as well as from scripture; as geometry from Euclid, and other sciences from like means. And every man is so far knowing in a science as he has applied his own faculties to the laws of it; for no man is master of any science by another's understanding. This, therefore, stands entirely upon private judgment, and must ever do so. Established religion is a form of public worship, chosen by the public; and its rules are prescribed by the political power, with certain persons appointed to administer in it according to those settled rules.

It is, undoubtedly, proper that every nation should have their artists in religious concerns, as the Persians had; but if these men assert, that they are the last resort in affairs of religion, let the priesthood consist of those who, of all the proprietors of the territory, are most venerable for nobility of birth, for wisdom, for years passed with untainted integrity; these will be better directors than the necessitous, the mean of birth, the unwise and the young; but can be no more than proposers and helps to men in their choice; the last resort remains still with the choosers.

When the public, therefore, has chosen its religion, which must be done, both that it may discharge its own duty, and to prevent the multitude's being left undirected, and at the mercy of superstition and every private guide, it may then be asked, whether this religious establishment ought to be imposed upon all private men? That it may be imposed by power is certain; for the magistrates and multitude, or the absolute monarch and his army, after having made their own choice, may act in this as they please.

For, as Cyrus says, 'God has so established things, that they who will not impose upon themselves the task of labour for their own advantage, shall have other taskmasters given them.' Supposing, then, that the ecclesiastics have reduced the rest of men to their obedience, as every the meanest priest is entitled to rise to the highest dignities; and, when admitted to his freedom in the hierarchy, is not debarred from knowledge and letters, as those of the laity are; as their monarch and grandees are elective, and not hereditary; and the absolute sovereignty is not lodged in the single person, but their general councils claim a share with him in it; the body of them then ought to take care that their own chiefs do not affect a tyranny over them, and serve them as Caesar did Rome.

As religion is divided into two heads of science, so may virtue be divided into several; as, for instance, into real, political and military, as well as others. The real falls into the head of morals and real religion, and is one and the same thing under several names. But temperance, with respect to eating and drinking, to be able to deny one's self one's usual rest, ability to undergo toil and labour, to sleep in open air, contempt of danger and death; these are military virtues, that may arise from custom and institution, or from necessity, or from ambition, and may be the virtues of robbers and pirates. The hero in the following papers will give you cause to think of this distinction, particularly in his speech when he is grown a man, and is setting out upon his Median expedition, as well as upon many other occasions.

What is here sent you, to take up some hours of your leisure, relates to religion, as well as to politics and war, though this last seems to be the chief subject of it.

As to politics, the account given of the Medes and Assyrians, the luxury and effeminacy of the Median court, the absolute dependence of all upon the prince's will, the effeminacy and meanness of the people, the poorness of their military discipline, the manner of protecting the territory by fortresses and garrisons, the waste of lands upon the borders inhabited only by wild beasts, show the nature of arbitrary governments. The nobler orders established amongst the Persians, the education of the ingenious amongst them, the rights of sovereignty lodged in a public council, and laws of public weal established as guides both to prince and people, bravery in the people, and wisdom in their military discipline, show the virtue and power of free governments. There seems indeed to be something in the story that suggests this defect to be in the Persian frame; that the free, the ingenious, the gentlemen, the noble, (call them by which name you please,) are reduced to too little a number; and too small a number of great ones commonly implies their riches to be too great with respect to the rest of the people: or, if the riches and power of the gentlemen be but inconsiderable, and that the people have them not, then the prince remains too weighty in the scale, and the rest are but dependents and servants. Now, in either of these cases, the ambition of great families, or that of a single one, always prevents the division of the riches and estates amongst greater numbers, and presses on to further increase, till the few become yet fewer, or the single one yet greater; and, at last, either the prince, or one of the overgrown few, by riches and numerous dependents, assumes the tyranny; then to him all become servants, his will is then the only law: he must hold his power by an army; and to complete all, must hold his own head at the will of that army. This shows the folly of the abettors of arbitrary sway, who pronounce it to be so vile a thing, for the prince to be said to hold his power at the will of the multitude. Whereas the prince must of necessity hold at the will of a multitude; for, supposing him to have destroyed the interest of the honest multitude, who were in possession of the lands and commerce of a country, and to have subjected their power by means of an army, he must then of necessity hold his own power at the will of that multitude of mercenaries. Whoever knows anything of the story of the Roman and Turkish armies and emperors, and considers the nature of things, must see that an absolute prince is a creature and servant of a military multitude, and ever comes uppermost when the mercenary crew have destroyed the civil power. So that in politics the voice of the people is the voice of God, and multitude must and will be the last resort here.

There is a natural gratitude in the people to the descendants of those that have been benefactors to men, or are thought to have been so; and a natural deference to superior and divine powers; and erectors of tyranny, who have had neither knowledge of God, nor regard to him themselves, nor love to man, always act the impostors, and abuse and play upon the understandings and passions of the multitude. The claim of divine right is the modern art; and princes would undoubtedly have still more divinity and sanctity bestowed upon them, as they had in old days, if the ecclesiastics were not competitors with them in it, and could spare it from themselves. But even these frauds can never be of any effect, if they fail of their intended influence upon the people. Caesar, therefore, trusted to other means: he never talked so idly of sovereignty, protection, and obedience, as some modern dealers in politics, who confound themselves and others with these words. Caesar's empire, and that of Cyrus, mentioned in the following papers, were not built upon such foundations. Absolute sovereignty is never applicable to a prince, whether at the head of a legal government or of a tyranny; for, in a legal government, the prince has law for his rule as well as the people: his property and rights are limited by that rule; and so are those of the people.

But how such sovereignty differs from tyranny, how such protection differs from power to oppress, and how such obedience and subjection differs from servitude, can never be made out. And, as tyrannies rise thus in a particular state, so great empires, that are but extended tyrannies, make their way through the world by the vice and impotence of neighbouring states. Whereas, by order within themselves, friendship and good faith with each other, little states repel the impotent attacks of great empires, that are powerful only by the vice and weakness of their neighbours. Such hints in the course of the story, and the observations that may be made upon them, seem to me to let one more into political knowledge than most of the books and pamphlets that are now written upon that subject.

The advices given, with respect to the art of war, are obvious; and, with all their plainness, are more than most of our present military men now think of. And the few instructions, with respect to the established religion and the priests of those days, are not inapplicable to our present times. Nor can it be said but that the spirit of piety and deference to superior powers, which runs through the whole, though blended with the established rites, does in some measure relate to real religion, and must needs be pleasing to those who have a sense of it.

The following papers contain a plain translation of the *Cyropaedia*, or *Institution of Cyrus*, written by Xenophon, who lived about four hundred years before the birth of our Saviour, in an age productive of great men; though it was the age in which expired those noble forms of government, to which all future ages are indebted for literature, and all noble knowledge. He saw the republics of Greece, after their brave defence against the Persian power in the age before, by wars amongst themselves, nursing up a brood of mercenaries to be their own destruction, which was completed by Philip of Macedon, at the battle of Chaeronea. He was a friend and disciple of Socrates, that great man, who was a remarkable instance of what is before observed with respect to the consequences of broken governments; for he fell a sacrifice to faction; and one of his accusations was, a disregard to the established religion, he who had evidently the utmost regard to real religion, had as much knowledge of it as was possible, and was ever strictly observant of the established forms: his disciple, Xenophon, felt likewise the displeasure of his countrymen the Athenians, for his partiality to the interests of Sparta, and, of consequence, for not favouring the turbulent ambitious measures that his own city approved. Xenophon was extremely beautiful in his person, and had great modesty and goodness of temper. He was a man of great knowledge and learning, but it was of an ingenious, noble, gentleman-like sort; not sedentary, not pedantic and not servile, as all learning may justly be called that is acquired to get money or maintenance by; he was a great master of political and military skill; he was extremely religious, and very knowing in all the established rites and ceremonies, of which he was a strict observer upon all occasions. The precept he puts into the mouth of Cambyses, father of Cyrus, never to engage in any action without consulting the gods, makes a remarkable passage in his book to this purpose. He puts several cases wherein men had sadly miscarried by means of neglect in this kind, and, though he does not name persons, yet it seems evident that he had his eye to particular men, well known to himself and to his countrymen in those days.

This treatise of the institution of Cyrus is undoubtedly fabulous. The *Iliad* and *Odyssey* of Homer are fables likewise, though of another kind. And there is certainly no more pretence to truth of fact, in this of Xenophon, than those of Homer: yet the whole of it is so true to nature, that it may be said to be almost as natural as if it were really fact; and, of consequence, is instructive, and, perhaps, more instructive, than what is called real history; there being very little of that which is not abundantly more false to fact than these ancient fables are to nature. There is, indeed, a plainness and simplicity in this piece of Xenophon, that may seem childish and contemptible to some judgments: but what our Saviour said to his disciples, when he placed a child in the midst of them, 'Unless you become us little children, you shall not enter into the kingdom of heaven;' and what he says in another place, 'When the eye is single, the whole body is full of light,' may be applied to the disposition of the mind, with respect to all other good knowledge, as well as with respect to religion. Your disposition of mind is thus chaste and single, and you therefore will perhaps not be displeased with this.

There have been some who have imagined that the establishments made by Xenophon's Cyrus are a model of perfect government: others, however, will reckon that Cyrus is no more proposed as a model to be followed, than Achilles is in the *Iliad* of Homer. The wrathful great man, and the effects of his wrath, are plainly seen in the *Iliad* and the ambitious great man, and the effects of his ambition, are as plainly to be seen in the *Cyreid*. The arts that Cyrus used with private men, and with whole nations, in order to gain them to his purpose, were certainly right; but this does not prove that that purpose of his was honest. In like manner, all his regulations, with respect to the establishment of his scheme of tyranny, were as certainly rightly contrived to serve that end; but yet this is no proof that such tyranny is not a most unjust, unequal and barbarous establishment. And, when the foundation and rise of the empire of Cyrus is directly ascribed to a free government; when his own education under such a government appears to be the foundation of all the virtue that he has; and when the effects of this empire erected are declared to be a general defection from all virtue in the people, and the misery of the prince's own family; then, let any one Judge whether the moral of this fable of Xenophon's does decide in favour of tyranny.

I know the affectionate concern you have for the liberty of your country; which you value, that the integrity and simplicity of human minds may be protected, and not overborne by tyrannical impositions, or debauched by imposture; that they say be kept as the chaste spouse of divine truth; and that innocence and virtue may not be violated by the ungoverned passions of the mighty. I know the joy you ever expressed for your country's successes in a just war. You will therefore allow this to be my excuse, for thinking these subjects not improper to entertain you with. I cannot but believe that even the statesman, the soldier, the divine and the learned in the law, of our present age, would readily excuse the addressing these matters to a lady, when they should consider that this is but the translation (and indeed pretends to be no very good one) of a book where these subjects are treated in a childish, romantic way, and not so suitable to their understandings. They will be little concerned that such an author should recommend the sciences and arts of war and government, of justice and religion, to the study of the gentleman: for, by means of ignorance in these things, the gentleman is rendered incapable of judging whether the mercenary in these professions do their duty for their money. The noblest arts are thus left to the mercenary alone, and they become the guides and governors of the world.

'The Reigns of Kay Kavus and Kay Khosrow' from *The Rawżat aṣ-ṣafā*'

MUHAMMAD IBN KHVANDSHAH IBN MAHMUD (*c.* 1433–98), also called Mirkhvand, was an Iranian writer, generally regarded as one of the greatest historians of the Persian language. His *Rawżat aṣ-ṣafā*' (*c.* 1490), literally 'The Garden of Purity,' is a universal history of the world from an Islamic perspective. It includes accounts of the legendary kings of Iran from the pre-Islamic era, figures who had become central characters in Iranian literature and folklore. Mirkhvand drew on a wide range of texts and legends that had been told and retold for centuries, creating a comprehensive summary of Iranian mythic and historical traditions.

The legend of Kay Khosrow displays remarkable parallels with the figure of Cyrus in the Greek tradition especially. The character of Afrasiab, an archenemy of Iran echoes the Median Astyages: he was the king of Turan, which becomes conflated with Turkmenistan in later Iranian tradition, and is therefore often referred to as 'Turkish;' while the figure of Piran Viseh, a senior general in Afrasiab's service, plays the role of Harpagus, saving the infant prince from the evil intentions of his own grandfather.

The extracts below, translated by David Shea in *The History of the Early Kings of Persia* (1832), include the reign of Kay Kavus, grandfather and the predecessor of Khosrow, which include the stories of Khosrow's parentage and youth; and of Khosrow himself. These stories show how loosely remembered historical figures become embroidered in new cultural settings, becoming an integral part of that culture's memory and identity.

The Reign of Kay Kavus

THIS PRINCE, who is said by some historians to have been the son of Kobad, and by others his grandson, was beautiful of aspect, graceful in manner, athletic in frame; and so large in person, that few horses could carry his weight: –

> When he mounted his swift dapple-grey steed,
> Through awe of him trembling fell on the mountains:
> When he gave full reins to his charger's speed,
> He raised clouds of dust from earth-bearing Piscis to the skies.

He exhibited the greatest energy in the diffusion of benefits and the performance of generous acts, the protection and assistance of the distressed. With all this, there was great capriciousness in his disposition; for, although he occasionally exhibited unwearied attention and perseverance in matters of detail, he too frequently, in cases of great importance, deserted the path of prudence, in which the truly wise invariably tread. It is related, that when the Governor of Mazenderan, abandoning the path of fidelity and gratitude, had interposed the shield of hostility before the face of concord, and, notwithstanding frequent admonitions by letters and remonstrances replete with prudent counsels and sundry exhortations, was not prevented from persevering in such conduct; on the return of the envoy sent from the foot of the imperial throne to conciliate him, and his laying before the king the state of affairs, the flame of indignation and vengeance blazed with violence in the breast of Kay Kavus, the marks of resentment became visible in his features, and he instantly issued orders for assembling his forces and providing equipment and arms. There was speedily marshalled, under the shadow of his victorious banners, from the regions of Arabia and Ajem, a host so mighty and a force so immense, that the conceptions of calculators and the imaginations of accountants were unable to comprehend their power or number. At the head of these troops, habituated to victory and vengeance, he set out to dispel the blast of presumption from the head of his foe by the well-tempered sabre. The ruler of Mazenderan, on learning this, knew well, that if the red-headed sparrow should meet the falcon in battle, he exposes himself to inevitable destruction and ruin: consequently, to preserve his reputation, he withdrew from the course of the flood; and retired into a fortress, rivalling in strength the rampart of Iskander, and elevating its lofty summit to the empyreal skies. Kay Kavus encamped at the foot of this fortress, and persevered a long time in the blockade of it; directing against it many a battering ram and towering catapult: the champions also carried on the assault in every direction; but, notwithstanding their greatest exertions, the standards of victory and the banners of triumph appeared in no quarter. On this, the chiefs of the troops, and the principal commanders of Kay Kavus, began to despond, seeing themselves unable to subdue this fortress and triumph over their foes: they were long perplexed how to decide this matter; but, finally, the king's reflection, and that of the whole army, determined on this measure: – 'Whereas the superiority of our troops, the multitude of people and the greatness of our train, are of no avail, we may however encompass our object by ingenious stratagems and refined artifices, and by means of deceit and fraud precipitate our enemy into the abyss of woe.' In pursuance of this, they published reports of their retreat, tore up their tent ropes; and departing from the environs of the fortress, halted some marches in the rear of it; from whence they despatched a company dressed as traders, who, in the guise of merchants, introduced into the castle many commodities and abundance of merchandize, which they bartered for wheat, barley and other grain: these one night set fire to the granaries; and then represented, 'This event has occurred without our knowledge and wishes.' When, by this stratagem, no magazines were left in the fortress, the army of Kay Kavus returned unexpectedly; and having taken the place by storm, so laid about them on that day with the ruthless sword, that the fortress of Mazenderan became a desert, and its plain a *Jihun* (of blood); and the wealth of the country was confiscated to the royal government. Some historians relate, that Kay Kavus was made prisoner in Mazenderan: on learning which, the hero Rustam, singly, proceeded to that country by way of Haftkhan, and, having put to death the rulers of the kingdom, liberated Kay Kavus; who returned to his capital in safety, enriched with great spoils.

Kay Kavus next marched to Hindustan: after the conquest of which, on his return by way of Mekran, he remained some time in Sistan; where Rustam received him with the rights of hospitality, and every mark of distinction, to the utmost of his power. The monarch of the world having spent some days at Nimrooz in the enjoyment of pleasure and delights continued from night to morning and from morning to night, returned to his splendid capital. When some time had elapsed, he set out against Zu al-Asghar, the king of Yemen. Although dissuaded by his Ministers from engaging in that enterprise, their remonstrances were of no avail; and after long and toilsome marches, he drew near that country. Zu al-Asghar, with his blood-shedding troops, advancing to encounter him in battle, an engagement ensued, in which the Arab prince was defeated, and fled somewhere. At this moment he conveyed to Kay Kavus this intelligence: – 'The king of Yemen possesses, within the sanctuary of chastity, a virgin, such, that from her the sun himself solicits light.' Kavus, who had never beheld her, gave his heart away, and proposed peace, stipulating for the marriage of the king's daughter; and the ruler of Yemen, being forced to comply, delivered up his daughter, whom the Persians call Soodabeh. On this event, the sovereign of Iran reared the pavilion of delight to the sphere of the sun and moon: but, in the meantime, Zu al-Asghar, taking advantage of a favourable opportunity, seized and imprisoned Kavus in one of his forts, along with Tus, Gustahem, Bizhen and the other champions of Iran. Immediately on hearing this dreadful intelligence, Rustam Dastan set out for Yemen with a thousand chosen heroes: but no sooner had he approached that country than Zu al-Asghar made advances towards a reconciliation and set at liberty Kavus and the other captives. He also dismissed in the king's train his daughter Soodabeh, with abundance of valuable presents, and a thousand damsels beautiful as Perees.

In those days, Afrasiab, the Turkish king of Turan and the great enemy of the Iranians, took advantage of the conjuncture to lead an army into Iran, where he reduced many cities under the bonds of conquest, committing the most unrestrained and indiscriminate slaughter and pillage; but on learning the liberation of Kai Kavus, he retreated to Turkestan with great booty. Kai Kavus, on arriving in his own realms, wrote a royal diploma to Rustam, to the following purport: 'Whereas we have promoted Rustam from the state of vassalage to the rank of sovereignty, we hereby bestow on him the dominion of Sistan and Kabulistan, conferring on him also the titles of Champion of the World, and Tahamtun (irresistible in might): we place on his brows the cap of gold brocade, set with gems, such as is generally worn by the sovereigns of Ajem; and we also permit him to be seated on a throne of gold or silver.'

Rustam thus, with augmented pomp and power, returned to his native soil; and the regions of Nimrooz and Kabul were embellished and gladdened by the auspicious justice and equity of the mighty champion. When Kai Kavus once more enjoyed the undisturbed possession of the throne, the sovereigns of the world and the haughty rulers of distant lands hastened to offer their submission and congratulation; whilst every class of his subjects passed their life in the enjoyment of abundance, and uninterrupted security and tranquillity.

At this period the kingdom of Turan was in an exceedingly flourishing and prosperous state, through the splendid fortune of the Turkish prince: the military and the cultivators, freed from every anxiety, passed their time in music and feasting. However, in the course of these events, the portals of discord and woe were again thrown open, and the paths of security and peace once more blocked up: the abstract of all which is as follows: – Kai Kavus had, by one of his wives (not Soodabeh), a son, endued with the perfection of reason and intelligence, joined to consummate beauty and grace: this prince, whose name was Siyawesh, was educated at the court of Rustam Dastan, where he became so exceedingly accomplished in all that related to social intercourse and war, that the report of his perfections was spread over the most distant parts of the earth: the tidings of his virtues and noble qualities also reached the ears of Kai Kavus so that on his return from Yemen, and was a second time firmly re-seated on the throne of sovereignty he issued forth commands to Sistan, requiring the presence of his intelligent son: on which, Rustam sent the young prince, with all possible honours, to his father's court. Kavus, being struck with astonishment at his noble carriage, beheld him with the eyes of respect and parental affection: and when the account of the manly proportions of Siyawesh's figure was reported to Soodahah, a vehement longing for his intimacy and society so overpowered her soul, that the fire of love and the flames of desire blazed forth with inextinguishable violence. She therefore addressed this request to Kai Kavus: 'Permit the prince to enter the Harem, that I may exhibit towards him a mother's affection, and enjoy for a short time the delight of contemplating your admired son's glorious aspect.' The simple-hearted king, on this, said to his son, 'The recluse matrons who dwell in the chambers of chastity request to be indulged with your conversation and society: it is therefore necessary that you go to the harem, and illuminate the king's apartments with the light of your countenance.' Although Siyawesh regarded this proposal with horror, he saw that obedience to the royal mandate was his only resource; and therefore, though much against his inclination, entered the private palace. When Soodabeh heard of his approach, she hastened to meet him with hurried steps: at the first meeting, she was bereft of strength and peace of mind: her manner and gestures soon made Siyawesh perceive the passion which agitated her breast, and he consequently arose immediately, to leave the palace. Soodabeh in vain entreated him to delay, even a moment longer; but Siyawesh answered, 'This is the first time of my entering the king's apartments, and modesty forbids me from ever presuming again to come into your society.' Having said thus, he departed, leaving Soodabeh to pine in the flame of separation. Soodabeh however again, under pretence of affiancing the prince to a maiden of royal blood, sent for him, by the order and permission of Kai Kavus. The queen, having now a manifest reason for an interview, chose a place for a private audience, where she openly laid before him the secret purpose of her soul. Siyawesh, from a sense of filial duty and of the paternal dignity, was struck with horror and aversion at the declaration: and though Soodabeh had recourse to the most pressing solicitations, her efforts were altogether unavailing and fruitless. As no hope of his compliance now remained, she accused him to his father of an attempt to dishonour the Harem. Although Siyawesh strenuously endeavoured, by convincing proofs, to clear himself from the imputation, Kavus remained dissatisfied. It was then at last resolved, that a great fire should be made, through which these two silver-bodied models of beauty were to pass; and whichever went through the crucible of trial with undiminished standard, the coin of that person's existence was to be declared free from impurity and alloy. The fire now blazing forth, the flames mounted to the *pharos* of the sun; and Soodabeh, conscious of her guilt, would not set foot in the destructive element: but Siyawesh, like a salamander, thought not about the flames, but entered the consuming fire at one side, and came out at the opposite extremity without receiving the smallest injury. After such a proof, Kai Kavus lavished on him the greatest kindness, and proposed to punish Soodabeh for her crimes; but through the intercession of Siyawesh, the treacherous woman was rescued from the fangs of death.

In the course of these events, the king's spies reported to him, that Afrasiab had crossed the Jihun with an army of intrepid warriors, and had encamped in the district of Balkh, prepared for war and battle. In order to avert this evil,

Kai Kavus at first proposed to march in person, and shake to its foundation the palace of his vile enemy's existence: but Siyawesh, whose mind was broken down with affliction by Soodabeh's accusation, requested that the expedition might be entrusted to him so that by a short absence from court he should banish from his soul the remembrance of the dreadful circumstance which had occurred. Kai Kavus granted his virtuous son's request, and said, 'Whatever is requisite, in point of money and troops, is all ready.' Siyawesh on this, having selected twelve thousand cavalry, with as many infantry, made this representation to the king: – 'The assistance of Rustam Dastan, the asylum and stay of the king and the army, is indispensably necessary in this crisis.' The king having assented to this proposal, thus ordered: 'Let the prince first proceed to Nimrooz, in order that Rustam may on that day gird his loins in the prince's society.' Siyawesh having thus completed all his arrangements, departed from the capital, and directed his course to Sistan. As soon as the report of his arrival was published in that region, Rustam hastened to meet him with due ceremony; and returning in the prince's train, conducted him to a suitable halting place.

When forty days had passed in feasting and enjoyment, they both set out towards the regions of the East. Afrasiab also, at the head of the brave warriors of Turan, marched forward, to give them battle. Both armies now drew near each other; but when they were only two marches apart, the Turkish Prince who during three successive nights had seen terrible visions, became quite melancholy. He communicated to his Ministers and confidants the nature of the occurrence; on which they all answered: 'It is our interest to enter by the door of accommodation with our enemies, and make our goods and chattels the means of preserving our lives and honour.' Afrasiab having listened with attention to the unanimous counsel of his Ministers, sent his brother Gurshiwaz with presents, precious gifts, and letters, in which Rustam was mentioned with the greatest respect. Gurshiwaz having obtained the good fortune of an audience, proposed an accommodation. The reflection of the prince, enlightened as the sun, in concert with the elephant bodied champion, the overthrower of armies, returned this answer: 'This object will be attained as soon as Afrasiab shall make restitution of whatever has been procured by plunder in Iran, and when every dwelling, which has been destroyed by the passage of a foreign army, shall be restored to its former habitable state: lastly, one hundred persons, selected from the relatives and nobles of Afrasiab, shall be sent as a pledge to the imperial presence, to form part of the train of the victorious and fortunate sovereign.' Gurshiwaz, on returning to the royal presence, explained the result of the conference; and Afrasiab immediately complied with all the demands made by the Prince and Rustam and sent them a hundred persons by way of hostages. The edifice of peace being thus built on a sure foundation the conditions were ratified on both sides by solemn oaths; after which Siyawesh sent ambassadors to his father to acquaint him that peace was made. Kai Kavus on receiving this intelligence, was mortified and astounded; so that he appointed Tus, the son of Nauzer, as his envoy, to convey this message: – 'At last, the wiles and artifices of Afrasiab have made an impression on you, so that you were deceived by receiving a hundred obscure individuals, who are not, collectively, worth a barber-surgeon's fee: but whenever the aged entrust matters of importance to boys, such is always the result.'

The sum of the instructions of Kai Kavus to Siyawesh was as follows: 'Send in chains to me the hundred hostages delivered by Afrasiab: return his presents: lead your army into Turan, and quit not that country until further orders: but if you are unable to acquit yourself of this important charge, transfer to Tus, the son of Nauzer, the banner of Gavah, the treasure, and the army, and return to me.' When Siyawesh and Rustam had learned the king's displeasure and wrath, Rustam was so offended, that he immediately returned to Zabulistan: and Siyawesh said: 'I do not esteem it lawful to violate my oath or break my promise: in my sight, the commands of God are superior in authority to the orders of princes.' Siyawesh having sent back the hundred hostages to Afrasiab with every demonstration of honour and respect, then delivered the command of the army to Tus, the son of Nauzer; and, accompanied by his own train, went into Tunin along with Piran Viseh, one of the most distinguished nobles of Afrasiab: he then proceeded to kiss that monarch's hands, and was received by him in due ceremony. He commanded two thrones to be placed on the court of audience; on one of which he himself was seated, and the young prince of Iran on the other; and making a great feast, he assigned to him both revenues and lands. The dignity of Siyawesh increased every day; so that at last, from the rank of the king's guest, he attained the honour of being his son-in-law, and received from the Turkish prince his daughter Ferangiz in marriage. After this, the rank of Siyawesh was so greatly advanced, that the brothers and relations of Afrasiab envied him greatly, and continued with one accord to plot his ruin, until the fatal period, when, by the calumny of Gurshiwaz, they were enabled to lay the axe to the foot of the gracefully waving cypress of the streams of majesty, and lop the head from the stem.

It is related in the *Tarikh* of Hafiz Abru, on the authority of other writers, that the residence of Siyawesh was at some distance from that of Afrasiab; and that this place had been enlarged by him into a great city in which were erected many princely mansions. Gurshiwaz and the other slanderers took occasion from this to slander him so to Afrasiab, that he at last sent Gurshiwaz to see Siyawesh, saying to him: 'If things be as reported by these persons, let Siyawesh be put to death,'

> *The Turkish monarch listened to the slanderer's words.*
> *May shame await him, for unjustly shedding Siyawesh's blood!*

The night preceding the arrival of Gurshiwaz, Siyawesh saw a vision, which he interpreted as announcing the approaching termination of his life: he therefore thus spoke to his queen, who was at that time pregnant: 'Thy father has formed a design against my life, and I every moment expect the arrival of someone to put me to death: take thou, therefore, good care of the son whom thou now bearest; for as soon as he reaches maturity, they will come from Iran to seek him, and carry him thither: perhaps God will give him grace to recompense the oppression to which I fall a victim, and to avenge his father's blood.' Whilst he was yet speaking, Gurshiwaz arrived with a great multitude; and having summoned Siyawesh to appear before him, began to enumerate his imaginary crimes; and under this pretext they cut off his head on a golden vase. When Rustam was informed of this dreadful event with burning heart and streaming eyes he hurried to the court of Kai Kavus, the flames of wrath ascending from the furnace of his bosom to the highest heavens, and streams of blood-tinged tears gushing from the fountains of his eyes. Before entering into conversation with Kavus, he dragged Sodabeh out of the Harem, and put her to death. The account of Siyawesh's death being thus made public, the men clothed themselves in sackcloth, the women went with dishevelled hair, and Kai Kavus, with all his nobility, on this calamitous event, clothed themselves in black; which custom was long continued. When Afrasiab had fixed on putting

Siyawesh to death, it so happened that Piran Viseh, his wise advisor and general, was then absent; but Piran Viseh no sooner learned the news, than, giving himself up to lamentation and regret, he came into the presence of the Turkish monarch, and loaded him with reproaches and invectives: but as the event had taken place, it was now impossible to remedy it.

> *Watch carefully the proper season of everything; for of no avail*
> *Is the healing draught given to Suhrab after his death*

After this, the enemies of Siyawesh summoned Ferangiz, then pregnant with Kay Khosrow, to appear before them; and endeavoured to contrive some way of separating the foetus from the mother; but Piran Viseh resolutely opposed the project, and turned them from this dreadful purpose. He then took Ferangiz under the asylum of his own dwelling; where, when her time was completed, she was delivered of a son of exquisite beauty and charms, to whom they gave the name of Kay Khosrow, and whom Piran Viseh brought up with the greatest attention: but, according to some writers, no sooner was the young prince born, than Piran Viseh committed him to the care of some shepherds, who kept him in the wilderness, until Geev the son of Gudarz took him to Iran. It is said, that, after this, Kai Kavus held a general mourning; and having given Rustam whatever troops and arms he demanded, he then despatched the elephant-bodied champion, with the banner of Gavah, accompanied by an immense force, towards Turkestan. When Rustam crossed the Jihun, Afrasiab fled; but Gurshiwaz, being taken prisoner, was put to death, by way of retaliation: some writers however say that the death of Gurshiwaz did not occur until long after this period: others maintain, that when Rustam directed his march towards the regions of the East, Afrasiab sent Shidah, his son, with a hundred thousand horsemen to give him battle: as soon as the armies encountered, there ensued a dreadful combat and immense slaughter: in the course of the engagement, Fariburz, the son of Kavus, coming up to Shidah, hurled him from the saddle, and threw him on the plain, with such force as to break his neck: –

> *Such is the custom of this harsh and cruel world;*
> *A person is at one time mounted; at another, grovelling in the dust.*

Ferdowsi relates, in the *Shahnameh*, (a Persian epic poem of the tenth century), that Shidah fell in Kharezm, by the hand of Kay Khosrow: on the whole, it must be observed that historians differ widely on this point; their accounts being so various, that if they were all enumerated, this work would become so long-winded as to augment the fatigue and ennui of the reader: consequently, the pen of description following the middle path, thus continues: – Rustam having subdued the metropolis of Afrasiab, all the public treasures and concealed hoards of that prince fell into his hands: and although the conqueror, after this event, despatched spies and scouts in every direction, he could learn no intelligence respecting Kay Khosrow and Ferangiz, who had been sent away by Afrasiab into the most remote parts of Turkestan. Rustam, after this great and decided success returned to Iran where Kai Kavus received him with every demonstration of honour and respect seated him in his presence on a throne of gold and conferred on him every mark of favour and munificence; after which he permitted him to depart to his own kingdom of Nimrooz.

It is recorded by many historians that the sovereign of Iran, in consequence of a vision, sent Geev, the son of Gudurz of Isfahan, by himself into Turkestan, to find out Kay Khosrow: during seven years, notwithstanding his unceasing exertions, Geev was unable to attain this object: at last he observed Kay Khosrow in a meadow, engaged in the sports of the chase, and recognised the prince by intuition; and he, who was well worthy of the Iranian throne, being inspired by Heaven, showed due respect to the heroic Geev: they both went to Ferangiz; and adopted this resolution, that having borrowed the rapidity of the lightning and winds, they should instantly set out to attain their object. It is said that Siyawesh had a steed which disappeared on the day of his death, and had never since submitted to any one's power or control; but when Kay Khosrow and Geev went out to look for horses, they observed this one in the herd: when Kay Khosrow approached, the horse stood quietly, until he had bridled, saddled, and mounted him; at which instant the rider vanished from the sight of Geev. The champion of the world was lost in astonishment; and said to himself: 'During seven years I have undergone innumerable toils and difficulties; but the moment I was permitted to behold the auspicious features of Kay Khosrow alas! some evil spirit has torn him away.' At that moment this inestimable pearl of royalty became suddenly visible on the summit of a mountain. – Geev having devoutly returned thanks to the Almighty, went along with the prince to Feranglz; and, accompanied by her, they hastened with the greatest expedition towards Iran. At this juncture it was reported to Piran Viseh, by his spies, that someone who had come from Iran to find out Kay Khosrow had taken both him and his mother to that country. Piran, being greatly troubled at the intelligence, immediately despatched three hundred warriors of repute to pursue the fugitives, and bring them back, wheresoever they found them: this detachment overtook them at midnight, whilst Kay Khosrow and Ferangiz were asleep; but Geev, who kept watch, so unfurled the banner of slaughter and contest in that fight, that most of the assailants fell beneath his avenging sword: those who survived the carnage fled with rapid flight, to implore the help of Piran, to whom they related all that had befallen them. Piran replied, 'Tell not this circumstance to anyone; as it would be the height of disgrace for three hundred famed warriors to be defeated by a single knight.' Then Piran himself, with whatever force he had ready, set out in pursuit of Geev and Kay Khosrow; neither did he desist, night or day, until he came to the foot of a mountain, the summit of which Khosrow and Ferangiz had attained, in order to descend the opposite side; and Geev, about midway up the mountain, was slowly holding on his course. Piran, on recognising the friends, pushed towards them with all haste.

Ferangiz and Khosrow, with the wings of speed, urged on their way to the plains; and as Geev went sometimes rapidly, sometimes slowly along the road, Piran was induced to think that he might possibly take him prisoner: he had now got some distance from his men; and drew near Geev, who suddenly throwing the lasso, dragged him from his horse, and brought him to Kay Khosrow. The prince, on beholding Piran in this state, burst into tears, and addressed him with profound respect: as Geev was preparing to put him to death, the prince interceded so powerfully, that finally Geev was satisfied with fastening Piran's hands together under his dress: he was then placed on his steed; being first obliged to swear, that, until he reached his own abode, he would neither order nor permit any one to untie his hands. When the fugitives arrived at the River Jihun, they could nowhere discover the vestige of a boat or boatman: on which, Ferangiz gave way to alarm and lamentation; but Kay Khosrow observed: 'If God be our protection, what need of boat or boatman!' On this, committing himself to the cable of eternal mercy, he plunged with his swift courser into the Jihun: Ferangiz and Geev following his example, they in a short time crossed over from the gulf of destruction to the shore of safety, and were thus delivered from the terror and power of Afrasiab.

When Kay Khosrow had in this manner passed the Jihun, the intelligence of his approach was soon conveyed, by couriers, to Rustam and Kavus. At whatever city the young prince arrived, he was met in due ceremony by all the inhabitants; who, from his auspicious looks, drew anticipations of joy, and fancied: 'Surely this is Siyawesh restored to life!'

When the pearl of the casket of royalty appeared before Kavus, this sovereign beheld the signs of excellence and the characters of magnanimity evidently impressed on his brow: he therefore placed his grandson on a throne near himself, and transferred to him the cares of administration and the management of the military. He also exalted the dignity of Geev by various acts of royal favour – the gift of the golden crown, the diamond-studded zone, and splendid robes of honour. It is related, that when first Kai Kavus entrusted the reins of indulgence and restraint along with the concerns of the human race, to the vigorous intellect and talents of Kay Khosrow, Tous the son of Nauzer (a cousin of Kai Kavus), from loyalty to Prince Fariburz, the legitimate son of Kavus, began to dispute the succession; and matters at last came to such extremities between him and Geev, that the dispute nearly terminated in deadly strife. It was at last agreed, that whichever of the rival princes subdued Behmen Diz in Ardebil (the battlement of which, for many years, had never been seized in the noose of subjection to any prince however powerful) should be seated without dispute on the imperial throne. Fariburz and Tous first set out to besiege this fortress; but although they displayed the greatest energy, and adopted every means for succeeding, their efforts were unattended with any useful results, and they were consequently obliged to return with blasted hopes. But no sooner was the radiant glory of the mighty prince, the favourite of Fortune, reflected on the fortress and its defences, the props of which were as firm and immoveable as the Pyramids of Egypt, than they seemed to crumble to pieces. Kay Khosrow having returned crowned with success, Kavus adorned by his auspicious presence the royal throne, and confirmed Geev in the post of Vizir and General of the armies of Iran. Shortly after this, Kavus, preferring a life of seclusion and abstraction from worldly affairs, employed himself wholly in supplicating mercy and pardon, after a reign which is said to have lasted one hundred and fifty years. This monarch's title, in the Mufatih-al-ulum (Keys to the Sciences), is said to have been Nimrod, which is interpreted, *iam Yamut*, or 'Immortal.'

Among the prophets who entered on their mission during his reign are reckoned Daood and Sulaimdn, on whom be the peace of God!

Among the culpable actions ascribed to Kavus, is his attempt to ascend to heaven (his supposed 'flying throne,' as related in the *Shāhnāmeh*): but this tradition is exceedingly improbable, as he was a sovereign of profound sagacity; and had besides in his service a number of learned men, all of whom knew, to a certainty, that without the intervention of Jabreel and the assistance of Borak it is impossible to set foot in the emerald canopy of the skies. It was one of his maxims, that: *The best of things, is counsel; the most excellent, health: the most complete, security; the most delicious, wealth; the most precious, religion; and the purest, justice. He also says, Actions are the fruits of thought; which they resemble, just as the fruits of trees assimilate to the parent seeds: that is; if the workings of intention and the operations of reflection be applied to the attainment of perfection in our pursuits, and to the correction of evil propensities, all our actions will necessarily terminate in the path of righteousness and the causes of prosperity. He has also said: purity repels misfortune; and events are pledged to their seasons.*

The author of the *Tarikh Maajem,* in concluding the History of Kavus, speaks thus:

> *Although in splendour he reared his throne to the sides*
> *He finally bore his splendour to the cavern of the tomb.*
> *Fate had now disposed of the mansion of his body,*
> *And hurled him down from the throne to the bier, –*
> *The world has done many deeds of this kind;*
> *Fortune has not thus acted for the first time:*
> *On the head of one she places the golden crown,*
> *And lays another prostrate in the gloomy dust:*
> *On one she bounteously confers pomp and power,*
> *And consigns another to foul disgrace.*
> *No one has power to utter a word against her laws;*
> *Nor must anyone be astonished at this circumstance.*
> *'We must deliver over our concerns to the Creator's care;*
> *"For all the Creator's acts are done in wisdom.'*

The Reign of Kay Khosrow

T HIS PRINCE was the precious pearl of the necklace of fortunate
sovereigns, the most excellent production of the seven heavens
and the four elements: such was his might, that he could cope
with the empyreal heaven and the revolving skies: the irresistible
force of his mandates appeared as a type of Destiny and an example
of Fate. No sooner had the sound of the imperial kettledrum reached
the hearing of the human race, than the kings of remote regions and
the rulers of every realm assembled under the shadow of the standard
distinguished by victory; and Kay Khosrow, both by hereditary right
and superior talent, assumed the reins of empire, and regulated the
arrangement of public affairs.

He rescued from violence and oppression the cultivators who had been buffeted
by adversity and trampled under-foot by tyranny: he always regarded as an
imperative duty the conferring of grace and honour, benefits and notice, on all
men, in proportion to their state and suitably to their rank. In all the statutes and
ordinances of government, he closely imitated the precedents of his ancestors:
without exaggeration, whatever be the hyperbole or force of expression
employed in the chapters which record the virtues and glorious attributes of
this distinguished prince, even to this very day the fingers of description confess
their weakness and inability to enumerate them in a suitable manner.

The urgent concerns of the State being now settled, and the affairs of the
military and cultivators being definitively arranged, the desire of avenging the
blood of Siyawesh broke out in the king's breast: and as to this were added the
excitement of Kavus and the exhortations of Rustam, he therefore assembled the
nobles of his realm and the Ministers of the presence, whom he thus addressed:
– 'Our principal and most suitable concern is, to regard with attention the state
of the cultivators, in order that all ranks of my subjects may have the necessaries
of life prepared for them: in the next place, the property of this class should be
so secured against oppression, that they may cheerfully devote themselves to
the service of the Great and Glorious God; and, also, execute on every occasion

our commands, which are in every way conformable to the pleasure of the Almighty: and, lastly, that they should be enabled to pray continually for the perpetuity of our daily-increasing prosperity: –

> *Let this form the main object of all your desire,*
> *To be ever vigilant in promoting the cultivator's happiness.*

'You all well know the cruel oppression exercised by the tyrannical Afrasiab towards Siyawesh, my sire. At present, resolution and honour equally render it my sacred duty to require my lamented father's blood at his hands. Now say. What determination does your wisdom form on this head?'

On this, one of the assembled chiefs, distinguished for consummate prudence and intelligence, returned this answer: –

> *We are all the king's devoted bondsmen,*
> *Geev, Gudarz, and all here present:*
> *On whatever the king may finally resolve,*
> *'We unanimously gird our loins in obedience to his behest.'*

All the leaders and chiefs with one voice represented: 'Our only desire in this world is, to unsheathe the avenging sword: through the Divine favour, and the splendour of the royal fortune,

> *We shall make the world too narrow for the wicked,*
> *And bring destruction on the prosperity of Afrasiab:*

as the sovereign of the world, splendid as Feridoon and glorious as Jemsheed,

> *Through the falsehood of the iniquitous Gurshiwaz*
> *Had the features of his prosperity overcast with gloom.'*

When Kay Khosrow heard the chiefs express themselves in this manner, he issued his mandate to Fariburz the son of Kavus, and Tous the son of Nauzer, with thirty thousand horsemen, the lions of the forest of battle and the crocodiles of the sea of contest, to direct their march on Turan, and exert all might and main to ravage its cities and bind their opponents in chains. When Siyawesh, from alienation towards his father, took shelter under the powerful protection of Afrasiab, he is said to have loved a distinguished maiden, related to Piran Viseh; by whom he had a son, on whose beauteous form, had he been now in existence. Reason herself would have burst out into panegyric, and have recited the evil-averting charms on the fair proportions of his limbs. Siyawesh gave him the name of Ferood; but when the alliance with Ferangiz, the daughter of Afrasiab, took place, in order to remove all grounds of dispute, by the advice of Piran Viseh both mother and child were sent to her father's house. Kay Khosrow, knowing that his brother Ferood then governed one of the fortresses of Turan, when bidding adieu to Tous, at the moment the expedition was setting out, thus addressed him: 'You must take heed, in the advance of the army, to adopt such a route, as not to have my brother's castle in the line of march: but supposing the route of the troops to be in that direction, tread in the path of mildness and humility: for as soon as he learns the object of our expedition, and becomes acquainted with the reasons which induce the men of Iran to pass through those regions, he will espouse my cause, and, from the ties of consanguinity, use all his energy to obtain retaliation for the blood of Siyawesh.'

When he had thus given full instructions, Fariburz the son of Kavus, and Tous the son of Nauzer, set out. It so happened, that the army took the road which led to the vicinity of Ferood's castle; and the youthful prince had no sooner heard of their approach, than, with the rashness and impetuosity natural to youth, he came out of his castle at the head of a numerous body of intrepid warriors, for the purpose of giving battle. The determination of Tous to observe forbearance towards the young prince became changed, so that he grew incensed at the violent disposition of Ferood and his provocations to battle: however, his unshaken prudence and powerful reason curbed the reins of passion from giving way to feelings of wrath: he therefore showed no eagerness to accept the battle but sent ambassadors with this message: – 'The prince is a scion from the garden of the Kaianians, and a shoot transplanted from the orchard of royalty: a brother is like the blossom in the garden of joy, and the bestower of delight on the days of life: it therefore behoves the prince to quit the attitude of hostility towards us. But if he act not in concert with us, at least let him reflect on the propriety of avoiding violence: for even if the dust raised by me were to settle on the skirts of his reputation, it would alienate the royal mind, and bring distraction into the king's soul.

When we were setting-out for this region,
The justice-practising monarch bound me by oath:
'Walk thou only in the paths of Truth,
And deviate not from her words and deeds.'

Ferood, however, from the presumption of youth, making light of the counsel of the experienced sage, persevered in determined hostility: he disregarded as base this wholesome counsel and advice and rashly stood in the foremost ranks in the centre of the fight: but this tender rose was soon hurled down into the dust of ruin by the boisterous blasts of calamity. As soon as the tidings of this dreadful event reached Kay Khosrow, he gave himself up to anguish and woe to lamentation and mourning; and he immediately wrote to his uncle Fariburz a letter to this purport: 'On you is hereby conferred authority over the army, with full powers, unchecked and undivided by the interference of any other. Send to me Tous the son of Nauzer in chains, under the care of a numerous body of vigilant guards: after which, at the head of the troops committed to your zeal, you are to advance into Turkestan; and not be under any apprehension about Afrasiab, as I shall very shortly, with a well-appointed force, direct my steps towards that region.' Fariburz, in obedience to his sovereign's mandate, having loaded Tous with chains, sent him to the imperial court. On his arrival there, Kay Khosrow ordered Tous to a place where he could in person address him in the language of reproach:

Thy descent from Minucheher and thy grey hairs
Give thee the glad assurance of life;
Otherwise I would have ordered that instantly
The executioner should sever thy head from thy shoulders.

In the meantime, Fariburz, at the head of the army, entered the territories of Afrasiab, accompanied by the chiefs of Fars, among whom was Gudarz the son of Kishwad: on learning which, the monarch of the East despatched Piran Viseh, with a multitude of experienced warriors, to meet the invaders. The armies soon encountered, and mutually planted in each other's bodies the sword and dagger; the Angel of Death was unceasingly employed, from the dawn of morning until the approach of night. At last, the Turkish army obtained the victory: Fariburz was obliged to fly; and seventy persons of the family and household of Gudarz were plunged into destruction: this hero, after a thousand wiles, was scarcely able to extricate himself, with a few of his sons, from the scene of slaughter: he, however, at last re-joined Fariburz; and they hastened, with the remainder of their force, wounded and dispirited, towards the king –

> *Their bodies perforated like sieves, from arrow-wounds,*
> *And every cheek tinged with jaundiced hues;*
> *One smitten on the head by the ponderous mace,*
> *Others crushed by the wielder of the club;*
> *The faces of some still covered with clotted gore,*
> *And others still smarting from the well-tempered sword.*

Kay Khosrow, on beholding their condition, was exceedingly afflicted, and lost in amazement: he gave full loose to the reproach of his uncle, and addressed him with bitter taunts: – 'The cause of this catastrophe, and the source of this dreadful misfortune, proceeded from disobedience of my orders and neglect of my instructions. You leagued yourself with Tous, and therefore did not adhere to my advice. It has been observed by the sage, that whenever subjects oppose the sovereign's rules, and deviate from his commands, the constitution of the world is thereby corrupted; the interests of mankind go to ruin, military discipline is subverted, and the concerns of the cultivator neglected.'

The complaints made by Gudarz, of the want of firmness on the part of Fariburz during the action, caused additional blame to be cast on him: the world-protecting sovereign, however, distinguished Gudarz by his royal favours; to which he added liberal promises, and ordered him, at the head of the rank-breaking heroes, once more to return to Turan, and avenge himself on Afrasiab. At this time, also, Tous, having found intercessors, was set at liberty; and an imperial edict was issued, enjoining him to accompany Gudarz on the expedition. As soon as a mighty army was again assembled, the chiefs of Iran once more turned to the regions of the East; and Afrasiab, on learning the intelligence, appointed Piran with a force of valiant champions, who regarded the day of battle as the night of revelry, to encounter Gudarz. When the armies drew nigh each other, they became agitated, and put into movement, like the heavens: with death-dealing weapons they mutually displayed scenes of heroism and intrepidity: but at last, the soldiers of Iran were again put to rout, and obliged to fortify themselves in Mount Hamavun, which is also called Nartu; and the men of Turan, having come to the foot of the mountain, exerted themselves in making prisoners, slaughtering, and harassing them. In the course of these events, the Khakan of China, and Shaukal Prince of Hindustan, with mighty armies more numerous than the sands of the sea, came to assist Piran Viseh: on which, the soldiers of Iran began to despair of safety. After this despondence, by the mandate of the king, whose munificence is boundless as the ocean, Rustam Dastan joined the soldiers of Iran; and having again elevated the standard of slaughter and contest, he seized, in the lasso of captivity, Kamus, who had assisted the invaders. The flames of carnage and battle raged with increased violence during many days, until the Khakan himself was taken prisoner: on this, the remainder of the invaders, crying out 'Whoever saves his head has acquired great gain,' turned away from the field of battle. The rose-bowers of Khorasan being thus delivered from the vile thorns of traitors and rebels, Rustam and Giidarz, crowned with triumphant success, hastened to kiss the feet of the monarch of the human race.

Sometime after this event, Kay Khosrow, again reflecting with himself on the iniquitous proceedings of the Turkish prince, issued forth an order to four Generals, each accompanied by several thousand horse, to advance, in four opposite directions, on the capital of Afrasiab: among these, Gudarz with the banner of Gavah, which the kings of Iran never lost sight of, was detached towards Balkh; it being the king's intention to set out immediately after him, in the same direction. When Afrasiab heard of the arrival of Gudarz, he sent Plran Wisah and his brothers with a mighty host, numerous as the stars of heaven, powerful as the ocean-billows, to give the invaders battle; heedless of this truth, that when prosperity is to be succeeded by reverses, and happiness exchanged for calamity, no advantage can then accrue from abundant preparation, extent of power, greatness of wealth or the number of troops; – according to the saying of the sage:

When the period is expired, no resource is of any avail.

When the two armies met, and the hostile ranks on both sides encountered, the lion-like champions, and the heroes of the lists of war, shot, like the sun's rays, over the field of battle: with four-bearded arrows, heart-rending daggers and head-crushing maces, they made the expanse of the field of battle like the red willow. The dreadful slaughter continued three days, with such unceasing fury, that the wide plain was turned into mountain and hill from the heaps of the slain and wounded: –

> *If with the eye of reflection you contemplate this earth,*
> *You will discover thousands of heads under your feet.*
> *How could you discover congealed blood in the heart of the stone,*
> *If a thorn from heaven had not pierced the bosom of the mountain?*
> *The rosebud imprints a scar on the breast of the ocean;*
> *Or if not, from what cause proceeds its parched lips and humid eyes?*
> *Pass with the rapidity of wind over the tulip beds,*
> *That you may behold the crowned heads in the dust,*
> > *drowned in blood.*

In this battle, Piran Viseh fell by the hand of Gudarz; Yazdah, a Turanian chief, was slain by Yazdah of Iran; and Gurshiwaz, brother to Afrasiab, met with the recompense due to his deeds: on the whole, nearly two hundred thousand men fell on the side of Afrasiab, and the rest fled in dismay. At the moment of gaining this memorable victory, the Pisciform royal banner of Kay Khosrow became visible in the horizon of the field of battle: on which Gudarz commanded every bannered chieftain to raise his standard and place around their respective ensigns their prisoners and slain: after giving these orders he hastened in due ceremony to meet the royal train and laid the position of affairs before the king. Kay Khosrow casting a glance on each ensign, knew by this how each chieftain had conducted himself. When he came to that of Gudarz, and beheld the body of Piran Wisah, he burst into tears, and, alighting from his horse, laid his blessed face for some time on that of Piran: he then gave orders for the body to be well washed; after which it was wrapped up in pure garments of great value, and interred in a suitable place. At the foot of Geev's banner he beheld Gurslilwaz lying prostrate; on which he again dismounted, and severed the traitor's head from the vehicle of his body. He next held a public assembly, in which he rendered the chiefs of the army delighted and encouraged by royal distinctions and munificent donations. To Fariburz he gave the provinces of Kerman, Ky, and Mekrán: to Gudarz, the revenues of Isfahan, Jirjan, and Kuhistan: the other chiefs were also rewarded in the same proportion, so as to satisfy their desires, and secure their attachment. When the account of Piran Viseh's death reached Afrasiab, he sent his son Shidah, with a great and powerful army, to give Kay Khosrow battle. The hostile armies encountered each other in the plains of Kharazm; and a dreadful combat ensued, in which Shidah having fallen by the hand of Kay Khosrow, that prince said, *'Kh'ar razmi bud,'* i.e. 'This was an easy victory,' or *Khar razmi* from which expression the country was called Khorazmia.

The victorious monarch then directed his march to Kunk, the imperial residence of Afrasiab, in the fort of which he besieged him; and that prince, at last despairing of succour, fled from the castle through a mine, which he had prepared against an emergency of this nature. On this, Kay Khosrow having won the castle, all the relations and veiled beauties of Afrasiab fell into his hands; but they found so secure an asylum in the shelter of the victor's generosity and attention, that no kind of violence was offered them. Afasiab long wandered about, as a fugitive, in different parts of the world; but was at last made prisoner in Azarbaijan, and brought before Kay Khosrow. Some writers say, that at the expiration of three days he was put to death, by the command of the sovereign of the world; whilst others assert, that the king, on beholding him, felt emotions of compassion to such a degree, that Gudarz, alarmed lest Afrasiab should obtain a guarantee for life, without the king's permission delivered the captive's body from the incumbrance of his presumptuous head. Kay Khosrow being thus delivered from the hostility and alarm of Afrasiab, removed from Azarbaijan to Balkh. Whilst in that country, he one day having assembled the chiefs of the military, the Ministers, and the chief cultivators, thus addressed them: – 'The deductions of reason, and the evidence of History, uniformly prove, that whatever proceeds from nonentity to the high road of existence is impressed with the calamitous traces of death; and also, that whatever assumes the garments of creation and permanence in the regions of existence, falls under the dread necessity of perishing. What reliance can therefore be placed on an accident which comes to an end? or on a power pregnant with the seeds of dissolution and destruction? My direct road and sure path is to dissever, with the shears of divine grace, all connection and attachment to worldly concerns; so that perhaps, through the attraction of God's inspiration, joined to holy illumination and desires,' I may finally be associated with the inhabitants of the angelic spheres, and become the companion of those who dwell in the mansions of holiness.

As long as Thy love has not entirely divested me of egotism
I cannot sit with Thee according to my wishes, freed from self:
I am the thorn of my own way. Release me from myself,
That distinctions of persons may be effaced, and Thou and
I blended into one

[It is unnecessary to observe, that these four lines allude to the Sufi doctrines of absorption or identification with the Deity].

When he had concluded this harangue, he appointed Lohorasp his successor; at the same time earnestly exhorting and entreating all people to pay due deference to his commands and prohibitions. Having urged them on this head with anxious earnestness and impressive eloquence, at the expiration of the same day he bade adieu to his former officers of State, and the veiled matrons of unspotted honour –

At the moment when the peacocks of the stars
Expanded over the skies their pinions and tails;
When they enveloped the face of Nature in pitchy darkness,
And filled with smoke the space from earth-bearing Piscis to the moon.

He then departed from among the people, and no one ever after found a trace of him. It is recorded in some *Tarikhs*, that Sulaimdn (on whom be peace!) having made preparations for seizing Kay Khosrow, that prince fled from Istakhar towards Balkh, where he perished. Ferdowsi also relates his disappearance in such moving strains, that tears stream from the reader's eyes whilst sympathy burns up his heart. Whoever desires more knowledge on this subject, must read some of that writer's works. The generality of historians assign to Kay Khosrow a reign of sixty years; but the author of the *Tarikh Maajem* says thus: –

When during a hundred years this celebrated prince
Succeeded in accomplishing whatever he desired,
He was, like the truly sage, at last convinced
That this world is but a mirage, and we the thirsty travellers:
The more the parched wanderer urges on his speed,
The more he increases his consuming thirst.

He conferred the imperial diadem on Lohorasp,
And declared him heir to the Kaianian throne and crown.

Hafiz Abru thus records in his *Tarikh*: 'Historians inform us that Kay Khosrow made for himself a shrine with a pulpit; which accompanied him in every expedition and every place of residence: in this, like the Prophets of old, he offered up prayers, worshipping God in unity, and exhorting mankind to adore the High and Almighty Lord.'

Some of the people of Faraistan state him to have been a prophet: they also say that he made restitution of whatever had come to him from former kings, which had been extorted from the cultivators by unjust means: also, if one cultivator oppressed another, he took back from the oppressor the property of the injured person, and restored it to him who had been wronged: he also granted an alleviation of imposts, and maintained the military from the treasury. He summonsed none but the military to his service: the Rayas were masters of their own conduct; and in whatever aid he demanded of them, he adopted no vexatious proceedings. This prince deliberated carefully on every affair he undertook. The very first day on which he ascended the throne of sovereignty, he exhibited due attention to the commanders of the military, the nobility, the learned, the Ministers of the State (that is, the masters of the sword and pen, who moved in the circle of his majestic train), the chieftains, feudal barons and all his subjects in general; thus conciliating and rejoicing their hearts, and encouraging them by his promise of justice and equity. The Kazee Baizawee relates, in the *Nizam-ut-tuwarikh*, that among the illustrious sages contemporary with Khusrau were Pythagoras and Lokman the Sage: this, however, contradicts the tradition which ascribes to the former, in the time of Jemsheed, the discovery of the science of Music, as has been before stated in these pages.

It is one of his sayings, *'Know that the stability of the king and the cultivators is founded on wealth, which the Almighty has constituted the means of putting in order the concerns of this world and the next: cultivation is the source of wealth, nay, its mine:'* That is, the stability of the king and his people depends on wealth, which God has appointed the means for both worlds: cultivation and improvements are its fountain and its mine; that is, the concerns of the world, and the advantages of the children of Adam, are set in order by means of wealth: in the season of undertaking and engaging in important concerns, it is impossible to enter into or commence them without the possession of riches, which therefore constitute the most precious happiness and the most valued present conferred by the nine heavens or the four elements: regard them, therefore, as being of high importance, and expend them on the proper occasion; for the source of wealth, nay, its mine, arises from the diffusion of justice, the increase of liberality, alleviation of imposts to the cultivators, and the increase of population: it therefore behoves every prince, who is desirous of treading with firm and unshaken step the sanctuary of dominion, or of remaining free and secure from the capricious revolutions of Fortune, to attend carefully to these maxims, and never swerve from these principles. Kay Khosrow's title was, Mubarak, or Blessed; and, by the blessing of God, his story is now completed.

Note from: *The History of Persia* (1815) by John Malcolm

The history of Kay Khosrow corresponds, in several particulars, with the history of Cyrus, as given by Herodotus. Siawush was the son of Kai Kavus, but educated by Rustam. He was compelled, by court intrigues, to fly to Afrasiab, the king of Turan, whose daughter he married, and by whom he was afterwards slain. He left a son called Kay Khosrow; whom Afrasiab resolved to put to death, lest he should revenge his father's death: but this cruel intention was defeated by the humanity of his Minister, Piran Viseh, who preserved the child, committed him to the care of a shepherd and had him educated in a manner suitable to his rank. The young prince afterwards effected his escape to the court of his paternal grandfather, Kai Kavus, and was placed on the throne of Persia during the lifetime of that monarch. The first act of his reign was to make war upon his maternal grandfather, Afrasiab, whose armies were commanded by Piran Viseh. This humane Minister was defeated and slain, Afrasiab met with the same fate, and his territories fell into the possession of his victorious grandson. Kay Khosrow, after this conquest, and many other achievements, determined to spend the remainder of his days in religious retirement: he proceeded to the spot he had selected, where, we are told, he disappeared; and his train, among whom were some of the most renowned warriors of Persia, perished in a dreadful tempest. – This tradition seems to allude to the slaughter of Cyrus, and of his whole army, by the Scythians under Tomyris.'